I0831963

I'll Make You Cry

ALL NAMES, CHARACTERS AND EVENTS ARE FICTIONAL.

ANY RESEMBLENCE TO THE REAL WORLD IS PURELY

COINCIDENTAL.

THE NEARS ON THE OTHER HAND, WELL YOU BE THE JUDGE.

Order this book online at www.trafford.com
or email orders@trafford.com

Most Trafford titles are also available at major online book retailers.

Artwork by 'EM'

Note for Librarians: A cataloguing record for this book is available from Library and Archives Canada at www.collectionscanada.ca/amicus/index-e.html

Printed in Victoria, BC, Canada.

ISBN: 978-1-4251-1495-4 (sc)
ISBN: 978-1-4269-2669-3 (dj)

Our mission is to efficiently provide the world's finest, most comprehensive book publishing service, enabling every author to experience success. To find out how to publish your book, your way, and have it available worldwide, visit us online at www.trafford.com

Trafford rev. 5/27/2010

www.trafford.com

North America & international
toll-free: 1 888 232 4444 (USA & Canada)
phone: 250 383 6864 • fax: 812 355 4082

THE NEARS OF AFAR

Written by

OWEN WAGG

ACKNOWLEGDEMENTS

I WOULD LIKE TO THANK the one who helped me through the long journey of this tale. To write for the public is a personal journey as well, as the story is told.

It has been an honor for me to know those who supported me when I needed it the most.

Steve who knows how to navigate his way through the words.

EM and her artwork.

I am forever thankful.

O

NEAR PREFACE

Dear Reader,

Long have I wished to express what has been deep inside me that wanted to come out over the long span of my life. Bubbling up now and then, an image here, a few words there, fleeting then gone. The events in my life though vast in number, transpired in the twinkling of an eye.

I come from a long line of storytellers whose task it was to keep the imagination kindled, by relating original oddities never written, until now. These stories held the attention of eager faces, dimly seen in the quasi-light of the coal oil lantern on the kitchen table, long ago when I was young. So strange was the content and often so deep the meaning behind the words, it forced you to ponder your days away. The entertainment woven in such stories allowed a person to think about something other than the tedious hard life, lived in the beautiful wilderness of Muskoka.

I am such a storyteller, forged from a medley of raw stories, molded together one strange tale upon another, until sufficiently tempered, the words now flow out bringing your imagination to life, as you read this book.

This book, 'The Nears Of Afar' is one such creation, formed lying in bed thinking, when the room was too cold to want to get up; evolving, materializing from the world of silence from whence all thought comes.

When you see trouble visiting another, it seems so far away. That is, until it comes to you, then it's as close as your heartbeat, as near as your thoughts. Your quiet, contented life changes in an instant for the worse. What brings this to you, seemingly out of your control, this terrible tragedy, this tearful horrible surprise? Something so bad it causes your life to change direction without you wanting it to.

This is the story of the Nears, who's task it is to bring the misery of tears to Man at the command of their master, Lord Misanthropy, whose name means 'hater of all mankind'. No this isn't 'Satan' that everyone relates to, rather Lord Misanthropy has a different agenda, and should you read this book, you will find out why. Each Near has the unique ability to bring trouble their own way and with specific forte. Eager to have you shed tears, they would prefer you actually bawl your eyes out, if they had their true way of things. They have to do this not because they don't have anything else to do, rather it is a necessity.

You see, they live on our tears, consuming and feasting with a voracious appetite that cannot be satisfied, so gluttonous are they.

This unusual story is the attempt of three people to thwart the cruel influence the Nears hold sway over us, by performing an act of bravery that even I would shrink back from, if the task were assigned to me. Luckily, my only role in this tale is to relate what happens when so noble a cause is thrust against such vile power.

This is a tale of a pure work of fiction, but as such you may find it surprising, to see an aspect of your own life reflected somewhere in the story.

It is my true hope you will enjoy reading this book. However, always remember one thing; when it comes to fiction, there is always an element of truth hidden deep somewhere within, if you have eyes brave enough to see.

Thank you
O

NEAR NAME DICTIONARY

THIS IS A LIST OF the Nears who make an appearance in this book, however, there are many more, which I can't mention here to avoid confusion. Those names will come in the later books.

Nears usually work alone at their important jobs, at other times they will work together as a team to accomplish their one goal, to make you cry at any cost.

NEAR ABUS

This Near is responsible for giving people the thoughts and impulses to abuse themselves and the world around them.

NEAR ACIDANT

This Near is one who delights in causing accidents of any kind, in every possible way it can think of.

NEAR ACOLYTE

This Near is a spiritual student learning the fine art of causing tears in humans, so one day it will be able to assume the reins of ruination.

NEAR ADIKTIV

This Near has the important job of influencing humans to think they are addicted to all manner of substances or behaviors.

NEAR AFLIK

This Near is responsible for having humans think and believe they have nothing but trouble in their life.

NEAR BAET'L

This Near is responsible for all the wars and battles fought by mankind for any reason, real or imagined, thinking they have an enemy.

NEAR BANE

This Near has the revered job of bringing mischief to a person until they think they are going insane.

NEAR CRAV

This Near causes the thoughts of lust for anything that goes beyond a desire, the person becomes blind to the truth, lusting after whatever it is until it ruins their life.

NEAR CREDO

This Near has the enviable task of making man think excessive thoughts of zeal for a religion until they become violent against others to prove they and their religion are the only truth.

NEAR DISSEVER

This Near hates all living vegetation causing man to destroy as much as possible until the Earth is barren like the Land of Afar.

NEAR ENVY

This Near causes humans to think such concentrated thoughts on something, they become totally attached to it especially when they can't have it.

NEAR HEBEJEBE

This Near has the important responsibility of placing thoughts of fear in every form that results in humans not moving ahead, where they should be in order to have the experiences they need to grow.

NEAR HUBRIS

This Near causes vanity, which is excessive pride, to dominate a person's thoughts resulting in their ultimate destruction.

NEAR IMMOLATION

This Near has the enviable job of making humans think of sacrificing themselves or others in any way will bring about better conditions.

NEAR IRATE

This Near has the important task of getting humans to think thoughts of anger usually through stimulating their ego.

NEAR JINGOST

This Near makes man think aggressive thoughts about nationalist policies influencing other nations into believing their policies are truth for all, even if violence is required.

NEAR NATURAS VANDALIC

This Near has the pleasurable task of causing and influencing all natural disasters and unusual weather phenomenon to harm humans and their world around them.

NEAR PIQUE

This Near brings the important thoughts of resentment to humans against others who have what they believe they don't have.

NEAR PROTEKTOR

This Near has the important job of protecting their master and other Nears when there is a need for it.

NEAR QUIETUS

This Near has the job envied by all other Nears, to be present at the death of all humans, collecting their souls for safe keeping.

NEAR SCORER

This Near had the venerated task of keeper of all parchments and books of the history of the Land of Afar.

NEAR SERVITOR

This Near has the unenviable job of serving other Nears their meals.

NEAR THRALL

This Near has the unenviable job of being a servant for their Lord and other Nears, making sure everything runs smoothly in the Land of Afar.

NEAR VENAL

This Near brings the thoughts for needing money at any cost to the humans.

INTRODUCTION

My boyhood summers spent on the farm were an adventure. There was always something different every day.

One Sunday I awoke to my grandfather calling me, wanting to know if I was going fishing or if he was going alone.

Poppa did the chores as I collected a sufficient quantity of grasshoppers in a mason jar for our outing to the river. Talking while you walk anywhere seems to make the journey go much faster. Before I realized it, we were sitting on the riverbank, fishing poles in hand watching the bait in the water.

It was very peaceful until a few minutes later Poppa turned, looked at me and asked. "Have you ever been to the Land of Afar?"

I shook my head no.

"I didn't think you had. I should explain what I know of it to you, so you will get a better understanding of what I am talking about. It is a land that has been around for as long as we've been here. It is a land that is mystical by nature when you are away from it, but can be as real as you and I when you are there. Worse, should one or more of its residents come for a visit to see you; your life is never the same.

Should you ever be really bored and want some high adventure, I will tell you how to get there. Start off on the sunny trail through the woods, until you reach the fields of wild flowers at the base of the mountains. Follow the stony trail as it climbs and winds its way up, further and further, until you start to feel tired. You will suddenly realize nothing green is growing there, not even moss or lichen among the rocks. You will see cool foggy wisps hanging out in the empty space between you and the next mountain slope off in the distance. There is a strange silence you hadn't noticed before. Even the gentle breeze that was with you is long since gone.

The trail is winding and you can't see what's up ahead, but you decide to go a little further. Since you've come this far it would be a shame to turn back now.

The fog has gotten thicker and it is harder to breath. You start to slow down as feelings you don't like become stronger. Breathing hard, you look around and through the relentless fog you can just make out a bridge up ahead. It's just a ghost of an outline barely discernable through the haze. You're interested enough and you decide a quick look is worth a few steps. You can always hurry back home in time for supper once you've inspected it.

Walking up to the bridge you can see it has been there a long time and there is no evidence of dust and debris on the bridge. It is obvious it has been used extensively in the past. The thing that catches your attention is the sign posted out front beside the bridge. You hadn't noticed it there before. It must have missed your attention focusing on the bridge. The lettering is quite faded so you move over to take a closer look but you have to step onto the wooden planks of the bridge to read the sign. Suddenly it is now on the far side of the bridge even though you could have sworn it was out at the front when you first saw it. Curiosity gets the better of you and knowing you must read it, you move closer.

Suddenly afraid knowing you are alone, a heaviness comes over your heart area. You unconsciously reach up and touch it with your hand. You realize it is a useless gesture and put your hand back down, breathing deeply. You hold back the tears that want to spill out uncontrollably.

You don't know whether it's the faded sign or the tears welling up in your eyes. The sign seems out of focus so you wipe your eyes with your hands and are able to read;

SEE BEYOND
THE LAND OF AFAR
ENTER AT ONCE
SICK OF HEART YOU ARE
YOU WHO LIVE IN FEAR
PLEASE ENTER HERE
SHED YOUR TEARS
AND YOU WILL BE FREE
TO HELP US NEAR

No matter how you try, you can't turn around and go back. You turn your head to look for the way home. However, the fog is so thick you see nothing past the far end of the bridge from where you just came. The sunny warm home you left a short time ago, is now just a fond faded memory. The sign looked encouraging when you read it, perhaps there is someone that can help. You take the last steps along the planks to the end of the bridge looking for some guidance out of there and back home. You are heart sick and full of despair; your breath comes in short shallow gasps. You are trembling, sweat covers your brow, your stomach is upset but food is the furthest thing from your mind.

You take one last look back at the bridge that was once there, but is now totally shrouded in fog, only a sign catches your attention, identifying the bridge you just crossed, it reads.

BRIDGE OF DESOLATION

You turn looking at the road ahead knowing you can't go back the way you came, because the fog is so thick. You peer down at the road and then a sign embedded in the road catches your attention. You bend over to have a good look, hoping maybe it will tell you directions to get out of there, but you read:

ROAD OF ANGUISH
MADE FROM THE BLOOD
BUILT BY THE SWEAT
PAVED WITH THE TEARS

Gazing down at the sign not quite believing what you are reading, a single tear falls silently from the corner of your eye. Splashing on the road there is a flash of light. Rolling thunder slowly comes out of nowhere. It surrounds you in an uncontrollable wave of sound embedded within the thunder. It is the sound of quiet persistent sobbing of many souls who had the misfortune of coming to this place before you did. A sound registry of nameless voices caught in a world of woe. You cry out in your anguished helplessness.

Your sobbing cries mix in harmony with those you hear. You are now one of the many lost in the Land of Afar.

Looking around wide-eyed in disbelief, you gaze down the road to see the tear illuminating the road. There is a brilliant wave of light, moving along the glistening road. You follow, not knowing where else to go.

You run to escape the haunting wailing echoes reverberating in your ears. Running for what seems like forever, crying in your world of hurt, anguish and despair. Finally when you think you can't go on, you see through your teary haze the TOWER OF TEARS, a golden tear-shaped edifice. Home of the Nears.

Going up to the magnificent structure you notice the sign at the door:

WE ARE THE NEAR
AND IT IS CLEAR
YOU HAVE COME HERE
TO SHED YOUR TEARS
SO HAVE NO FEAR
AND ENTER HERE

The door is very short so you must enter head bent down. Once in through the door you realize it is a trap and you are stuck in this position. The Nears come, introducing themselves in your mind. They are as near to your soul as anything could possibly get, showing you their names. The names are every possible hurt, tragedy, or offence that could happen to you in your life. The things of life, that give you the most pain. All things, that would cause your tears to fall. There in front of you is a tear cup with your name on it. You fill it with your own tears until the Nears are satisfied they have done their job and you are allowed to go. You don't even remember getting back to the bridge, but you run for your very life to cross it, hoping to get home.

Never look back.

If you look back they will take you with them to the Land of Afar forever."

Lord Misanthropy stood gazing out over its domain, the Land of Afar; its forever. There was no beauty to the barren land. Everything was a shade of dull brown, seemingly lifeless without the infusion of color from living plants. All was rock and sand, forming shapes and sizes, to break up an otherwise bleak panorama.

The only contrast was low mountains off to the west, continuing until they faded from view. To the east, low hills swept to the south in an arc, stopping at a plain.

Looking to the north, the golden spire of the Tower of Tears dimly glistened in the light.

From the tower could be seen a thin ribbon of liquid slowly moving down hill, until it reached a ledge of rock called the Falls of Affliction, before entering the lake.

Lake Lamentation was a repository, for all the tears that poured out from unfortunate souls, who had the privilege to visit the Tower of Tears. The lake glistened not from the light that would normally be reflected from any body of water. Instead the sparkling energy came from the woeful infliction caused by the Nears in the Tower of Tears.

The lake was calm, except when there was a rare stiff breeze causing waves. On those days coming from the waves, the low sound of sobbing and crying could be faintly heard. The heartache energy had a means to register its woeful grievance to an unheeding Land of Afar. This land cared not. It was heartless.

The land was shrouded in twilight from the constant cloud cover that existed. It never allowed the nurturing healing sun through to brighten the land. Now and then thunder could be heard in the vicinity of the mountains. What rains that did accompany the storms, never reached this area. At the darkest times, the lightening illuminated the barren landscape in a ghostly manner that would frighten any mere mortal.

This made Lord Misanthropy's sneer more defiant.

This land was its and its alone, since time here began. It wished to be nowhere else. Its only true desire was that the lake was larger; it needed it to be much larger. It loved watching the flow of the stream increase. Especially, when mankind went through some calamity and had to come to the Tower of Tears.

Its sneering grimace became intense, thinking about it. Thinking how only mankind could be so foolish as to believe in happiness.

A cart rattling over the stony trail pulled by two Nears interrupted its thoughts. A third walked behind, giving curses and berating the others. They headed down to the lake to fill it with more tears.

"Hurry you sorry excuse for Nears! You're late again for the daily draw of tears. You know they don't taste the same drawn from the lake this late. Now get a move on or I shall be forced to rip a strip off each of you and hang them in the Great Hall. They will serve as a reminder to the others of what happens to Nears when they are late for anything!"

The Nears all looked up, seeing the cold, white-teary, piercing eyes following their every movement. It made them pull even harder. The one in the rear pushed for all it was worth. Lord Misanthropy sneered loving its power over these pathetic creatures.

It raised its gnarled, ancient hand over its eyes, having a good look when it spoke. Squinting, the tears that were forever in its eyes acted like binoculars. They allowed it to see the smallest details at great distances. It scanned the horizon slowly.

It suddenly stopped and peered closely, a fearsome sneer crossed over its face, screaming.

"I don't believe this! Get me Near Dissever at once! There is something that needs attending to."

One of the Near Acolytes that was standing inside the door hurried off to summon the Near without hesitation.

The Near Acolyte without hesitation, moved through the maze of corridors of the basement. It came to a door adorned with an ancient dried miniature tree, roots, branches, and leaves. Quietly opening the door, the tree gave a quiet rustling noise, announcing intrusions into the room from outside.

Near Dissever sat behind its desk sleeping. It dreamt about vast areas of forests being destroyed by fire, floods, pestilence and the hand of man. It reveled at the scale of the destruction. It showed an unbelievably disgusting sneer, witnessing the death of nature from so many different causes.

Breathing, a green mist would escape from its nostrils, floating up to a green vapor cloud in the room. From the vapor a noise like the wind in the trees could be heard rising and falling in harmony with its breathing.

Near Acolyte stood for a few moments watching, knowing the vapor was the life essence energy from all living plants that the Near had destroyed. The sound was like the wind of a thousand forests, all sighing at the same time with different sounds, blending together in a harmoniously sad, floral lament.

The Near Acolyte gently cleared its throat, causing Near Dissever to awaken. Suddenly the green vapor became a vortex, howling like a hurricane back into its nostrils. Near Dissever sneezed from the rush of energy. Little puffs of green vapor promptly disappeared into the air.

"What is the meaning of this disruption to my quiet natural solitude?" Queried Near Dissever without any formal greetings.

"The Lord requests your presence immediately, Near Dissever."

"Good! I assume this is a mission. It has been too long since the last one," replied the Near rubbing its green stained hands together.

Its hands were green from the grinding up and destroying countless plants over the eons of time. Its tunic was adorned with the dried decorations of a variety of souvenir extinct plants. Its beard had numerous dried flowers sticking out as a form of garniture.

Turning, it spoke sternly. "Mother, be sure to keep nature under control until my return!" Sneering hideously, knowing there was nothing she could do.

"You may watch your sceno-viewer, to keep you amused."

A small statue of a beautiful fairy-like figure that Near Acolyte hadn't noticed before, whispered back. "As you wish."

Mother Nature sat on a dried out toadstool that served as a bookend, reverently but sadly acknowledging the Near's authority. Her appearance would be easily mistaken as a fairy, slight of build but exuding raw natural beauty. A true beauty, so great and wondrous, that even now the most beautiful place on earth was a mere imitation of Mother Nature's real beauty.

A picture frame sat on the table in front of the toadstool showing a scene of great natural beauty. The picture would change every few seconds into another scene of raw, natural beauty. These pictures were her memories of what the Earth once looked like when she could be who she once was.

The earth once looked beautiful when she truly ruled, before being captured by Near Dissever and made its pet. Her memories of how the earth's beauty shone were faded staying in this room, perhaps a prisoner forever. The earth lost its beauty as her energy faded, affecting climate and nature in horrible ways. She curtsied long and low in servitude.

Once it left she started a slow, lamenting dance in front of the picture frame, watching her once wondrous works of beauty.

Near Dissever spoke, "I and near Naturas Vandalic share her as the need dictates."

Hissing through its sneer. "I slipped in a picture of what one the humans did to one panoramic vista, after they put up a five star resort and wall to wall condos, complete with two golf courses and amusement park. That should really keep her amused."

Suddenly, back in the room a quiet, desperate sobbing and anguished crying could be heard.

Near Dissever gestured to Near Acolyte to proceed reaching the balcony where it's Lord stood waiting, bowing in deep respect for its Lord.

"Yes my Lord! What is your bidding?"

"Near Dissever, a plant of some kind has dared to enter my realm. See to it immediately!" It pointed its gnarled hand in the plant's general direction. Near Dissever made note of the direction.

Backing up bowing, it reached the door turning to go inside. In its office it grabbed a bag containing some of its instruments of destruction and an empty bottle. It paid no attention to anyone it encountered except to give them a nod and a sneer.

Any Near who saw it knew it was on an important mission for its master, leaving it alone. Outside it walked briskly towards the lake wanting to fill its bottle since it would miss supper, considering the distance it would have to travel. Close to the lake it noticed the Nears filling the wagon tanker for supper's meal. Approaching it spoke. "Make sure it's the freshest tears tonight; the Lord's in a mood. It would be good for you to get the best."

Both near Thralls bowed in respect, grateful for the hint of warning that could save them from regret later, tossing the bucket further out. Near Dissever filled its bottle from the tap on the tank for its journey. Saying nothing else, it sneered leaving. The Nears bowed thanking it, wishing it speed on its journey. They didn't ask where it was going. In the Land of Afar sometimes it was better not to know.

Near Dissever left content, knowing it was doing its part to keep the Land of Afar in its pristine condition with no plants. Its true wish was it could get the whole earth looking like its home did; devoid of any living plants.

It hated plants and nature, despising them beyond words. It received great comfort when it could influence some human's thoughts to destroy or remove vegetation. It relished it when they replaced vegetation with concrete or asphalt. Replace nature with any non-living thing, tricking them into thinking it was beautiful and natural.

It loved it when it made man poison plants, eliminating them at all costs. Man's mind was so easy to manipulate. All it took was the whisper into the ear of ignorance and greed to convince them of the rightness of their cause of self destruction. It was able to influence man like all the Nears and bent them to their wills, living in their illusion of their relationship with the earth and Mother Nature. When it got Near Venal involved, it was all so easy destroying the forests for profits. The humans were blind, ruining their lifeline for living and breathing.

Its grimacing sneer was at its best when it located the plant in a patch of soil between two rocks. The seed of the plant's intention was good but it made the mistake of floating into the wrong place, the Land of Afar.

It stared at the small plant with hatred, studying the plant with two small blue flowers that had somehow rooted here in such an inhospitable place, before speaking,

"PRETTY PLANT
GROWING SO FAIR
ASK ME IF I CARE
AS I SHRED YOU BARE
RIP AND TEAR
UNTIL NOTHING'S THERE
A LIVING PLANT
IS NOW GROUND MADE BARE"

Reaching down it grabbed the plant, and with one quick twist ripped it out of the soil, roots and all. It held it up to ensure it hadn't missed any parts of the plant.

Once satisfied, it placed its hand over the flowers and gave a mighty squeeze, crushing the once beautiful blue posies. It put them near its gnarled nose, breathing deeply as if enjoying a sweet smelling rose.

Instead of an odor, out floated a bluish green wisp, once the life essence of the flower. Without hesitation it breathed the wisp in. It weaved slightly like it was in a trance for a few moments.

Opening its eyes a horrible sneer came across its face, tossing the plant to the ground. The instant the plant hit the ground, it shattered into a puff of brown, grey ash scattering into the slight breeze that blew, disappearing, forever gone.

It howled with delicious contentment, knowing there was one less green plant alive. It reached down, pulling out its flask. What was needed now was to celebrate with a good chug of tears to slack its thirst from such paradisiacal work.

After resting for a while, it put the flask away. It grabbed its bag and left without looking back, anxious to tell its master the good news. Everything was as it should be.

Lord Misanthropy watched it go to do its duty, satisfied everything was as it should be. It lowered its hand allowing the sleeve to cover it. The sleeve and its entire black robe were adorned with golden teardrop shaped patterns, hemmed by a continuous bordering of gold made from the tears of ancient kings and queens.

A teardrop shaped golden colored hat covered its pitch-black straight hair hanging to its shoulders, accenting its white eyes. Its face, beardless and wizened made its permanent sneer even more insidious.

If you ever met it in the dark, it would scare more than the life right out of you.

Content, it decided a nap was in order before they served dinner. Grabbing its staff, it turned and walked towards the doorway and its throne.

It never went anywhere without its staff. This was its true power made from dried tears, retrieved from the beginning of time. The end was adorned with a tear crystal filled with liquid tears, stolen from what we would call Gods that once inhabited the earth before weakling men came to be. The only sound was the quiet squishing of its slippers, made from tears that never dried. They sounded like wearing water soaked boots, leaving marks on the floor.

Giving one last glance around, a look came over its face, sensing something wasn't quite right but it couldn't tell what it was. It turned going in the door. Time would tell.

Lord Misanthropy entered the Great Hall, its robe dragging on the black colored stone floor. White streaks coursed throughout the square slabs. The streaks formed a definite teardrop motif, as did the entire castle. From the outside, the castle looked like one big golden teardrop, with several smaller ones off to the sides that made up adjoining areas.

It was said that the entire structure of the castle was made from the hardened human tears of those lost in life, missed by those so dear. The gold came from the coins once thrown in the wishing wells throughout the world of crying souls, who wished their lost dear ones would someday come back to them.

Looking around surveying the Great Hall, it took in the scene. The Great Hall was used for special occasions and feasts. There was a dining area for all the Nears to gather, sup and converse about the latest gossip or storytelling. There were long tables with chairs made from hardened tears on both sides for them to seat themselves. The throne sat higher for the Lord to sit on and be observed while paid homage to by the Nears.

The table and throne had ornate tear designs and the legs were figures of humans who appeared to be crying. Their two hands raised in supplication to their God asking to remove their misery, served as supports for the table and throne.

The walls had teardrop-shaped designed ornate sculptures everywhere. From some of the structures that stood out, small waterfalls streaked down the walls to small catch basins in the floor. It wasn't water coming out from the structure: instead it was tears. The tears of countless hearts ripped apart, a constant flow of never ceasing misery that never dried up.

You see, there was an endless supply. Man, without knowing it, made sure of its never ending existence. If you looked closely, the structures on the wall were in the shape of an eye, with tears flowing out of the corner of the eye.

Coming out from the walls was the quiet murmur of sobs and wailing emanating from the cascade of tears making its presence known to this world.

In the middle of the Great Hall, a large golden teardrop shaped stone fountain had a continuous flow of baby's tears. In an endless babbling cascade, the echo of all the innocent tears of all the young humans in the world, too young to understand the harm or neglect inflicted upon them, reverberated.

The sound coming from the fountain was different from the sound being emitted from the walls. The sound from the walls was from those who knew and understood the reasons for their tears. The sounds coming from the fountain were the sounds of the unknowing wailing of children too young to understand. They had no idea of why there was such an uncaring and hurtful world out there.

Standing in the Great Hall listening, the sounds blended into one unremitting chorus of lamentation that would drive any of us insane with grief. It took several steps, turned and bellowed to no one in particular. "I go for a rest and will not be disturbed. Is that clear?"

All of the Near Thralls going about their duties heard it froze or hid behind whatever cover they were closest to. None wanted to be singled out for any special treatment by their master. Two Near Acolytes who always accompanied it, hid behind the throne for safety. It strode through the doorway, encountering shadow-changed colors, reflected faintly from the window made from hardened tears. The window had colored tears flowing down it causing it to refract the light like a rainbow. As a result any shadow always had the appearance of dark coloration. The Near Acolytes took up sentry duty outside the room, one on each side of the door. They made low sobbing noises and closed their eyes.

With a grand gesture it pulled its robe around itself, lying down on the fabric embroidered with golden teardrops on a black background. It closed its cold white eyes, dripping tears from the corners. Its mouth was slightly opened as low sobbing escaped its grey lips.

If you looked at it, you would believe it was asleep, but it wasn't. It never slept. It visited in its mind's eye all the tragic events that had occurred to bring so many tears, thanks to it and the Nears. Its hideous mouth drew up into a sneering grin, relishing in its quiet slumber. It dreamt the countless dreams of man's baneful calamities and their tears.

THE CASTLE BECAME QUIET. No Near dared make a sound, even the falling tears in the Great Hall quieted it's never ending melody of man's baneful calamities and tears. The Near Thralls all went far away to do their duties, for none would dare want to disturb the Lord's quiet slumber or some baneful calamity would result in their own tears. Beneath the castle, the odd Near went back and forth through the many rooms and passages of the basement quietly.

In one such room sat Near Immolation, sleeping comfortably in a chair. There hadn't been much call for its expertise lately. Humans had generally given up the practice of sacrificing each other in rituals, which meant it had been assigned to listening to the Risibility Machine.

It sat there with its head nestled against the stone back, one leg sprawled over one arm of the chair, and its hairy body nestled into the rest. All Nears were black hairy creatures, with muscular build and black beards or goatees in all shapes and designs. Some had hair on their heads, others did not. They all wore their Near tunic of distinction, although they each had a preference as to what design it was made up of.

Near Immolation's waxed goatee were long curves, almost touching its large, dimpled snoring nose, emitting a rather violent wind with every breath. If it weren't for its goatee being firmly attached, it would surely be sucked right in, choking it to death.

The goatee moved rhythmically, except when it could chortle or make a noise, enjoying a dream about some hapless human screaming and crying. Such were the last moments of humans being sacrificed on an offering slab, somewhere in the distant past by a secular hierarch. From a civilization that believed the sacrifice would somehow enrich the well being of their society.

Slumbering, it watched the scene of a massive stone outdoor temple. Humans dressed in ornate costumed, feathered headdresses, sang ancient songs to some imaginary god as a knife rose and plunged into the writhing helpless sacrifice.

Suddenly, there was another noise that interrupted the expected screams, a sound that shouldn't be there. It annoyingly woke from its well-deserved sleep. It wasn't sure of what was going on, but then it heard it again, faintly but distinct.

Turning its head in every direction to see if it was another Near causing the noise, all was silent. Closing its eyes, it yawned and settled back down to its pleasant dream. Suddenly it heard it again, the unmistakable sound.

It opened both eyes with a startled sneer on its blood stained face. The blood was a permanent marking that never wore off. It was the testimonial of the human blood spilled by humans, sacrificing other humans for so long. It was just in time to see the metal rod suspended inside the Risibility Machine vibrating.

It couldn't believe it until it saw the rod move stronger to the sound of laughter. The Risibility Machine, since the beginning of time, listened for the distinct true sound of laughter. So complete was man's life of misery in the world, that no Near around had ever heard it.

The Near stared at it in total bewilderment. History unfolded in front of it, making it scream. "No!!"

It realized the implications of what this meant, slamming its hand over its mouth knowing it must alert someone.

The foreign noise got louder, giving it great pain. It covered its ears hoping to drown out the uncomfortable noise. It stared at the machine wishing this were just a nightmare.

Finally the noise stopped. Cautiously uncovering its ears, it kept its hands at the ready in case this stridence returned. It relaxed hearing nothing new coming from the machine, but was sweating tears and shaking, talking to itself.

"Oh my, what's a Near to do? This is something new. How am I going to tell you-know-who!"

The noise came faintly again, causing it to put its forefinger up to its lips saying.

"Shh! Shh!" It had its other hand out erect, hoping perhaps the machine would see its attempt to make it be quiet and comply.

Whoever was making the laughter wasn't seeing its efforts to stop a crisis that was unfolding. As the noise continued, it paced around the room holding onto its goatee, wringing it for all it was worth.

At wits end, it was time to get a second opinion. It was time to see the head Near, Near Quietus.

Out the door it waved its hand in the air as if this would cause the machine to respect its demands. It mumbled about how it wasn't going to be sacrificed on the Lord Misanthropy's Alter of Inversion, by being turned inside out.

Traveling through the winding labyrinth, ignoring any Near it encountered, it came to a door. A real skull and cross bones attached indicated this was the Office of Death. The bones displayed on the door were from Near

Quietus's first victim. A hapless human declared the first human evolving from the apes after the Great Metamorphoses.

Near Immolation quietly opened the door, peering into the dark room to see if Near Quietus was there.

The room was immense with shelves on all sides to the high ceiling. On the shelves flickered countless small iridescent lights as far back as could be seen. The small tear window casting an ever-changing faint rainbow of colors was the only other source of light.

The lights were souls of all who had been claimed by death over the eons of time, locked away forever. They were the trophy collection of Near Quietus.

Near Quietus was slouched over in its large chair. Its black frame contrasted with the sparkling lights behind it. It gave out two loud snores then a third. The last loud breath rattled quietly with a sighing noise, and then no movement occurred for a few moments. It was like it had just died.

At that moment, the black Shadow of Death blocked out all view of the lights behind it. It rose up from its shoulders above its head, hanging there until the loud breaths continued again. Then the shadow would lower down, disappearing in it until it would rise again as if on command from the loud breaths.

Its long beard was decorated with a pattern of cross bones made from bones of infants dead early in their lives. A miniature skull hung from its neck, attached to a gold chain resting on its chest. The lower jawbone of the skull opened and closed like it was breathing in rhythm to Near Quietus's chest as it snored. Near Immolation quietly slipped into the room fascinated at the sleeping apparition. However, unnoticed by it, the door had a natural tendency to close by itself. The latch made an audible click, waking Near Quietus.

Its bright white eyes sprang open at the intrusion. The black shadow of death plunged back inside the Near with such speed it gave an audible snap like a burst of static electricity. It stared intensely at Near Immolation for a moment trying to understand what had just happened. Realizing who was there, it spoke, "What is the manner of this uninvited intrusion Near Immolation? Shouldn't you be monitoring the machine?"

Embarrassed at not knocking first before entering, Near Immolation stammered out, "I'm afraid the machine has spoken!"

Near Quietus stared incredulously. "Nonsense, this hasn't happened for as long as I know. You must have dreamt it."

"There was no mistake, it spoke several times. Please come, listen!"

"First, come see my collection. I have stored the finest selection!"

Going to the far end of a room, Near Immolation followed. Looking at the shelves of souls, it noticed that each shelf showed countless souls.

Stacked in rows as far as the eye could see, they had been collected by Near Quietus. Each shelf had one thing in common. Every soul had died the same or similar way. It was obvious from the number of shelves visible that there were countless ways to die.

Near Immolation was mesmerized, its mouth partly opened, stroking its beard with both hands.

"You find this interesting, my friend?" Spoke near Quietus.

Near Immolation nodded its head answering, "Your job is much more interesting than mine was. Once you've seen one sacrifice you've seen them all."

Near Quietus chuckled sneering, "Death is the same no matter what the cause, it also gets boring after a while, I'm afraid. As man develops his technologies they get a little more creative at how they dispose of each other so it keeps my interest up."

Reaching for a brightly sparkling vase, it said, "Take for example, this group of 138 here. This one is part of the group still in their excited state," handing it to Near Immolation, placing it in its hand.

Near Immolation closed its eyes seeing the history of the last moments of some young woman aboard the same aircraft as the rest. It watched the woman looking out at the engine ignite in flames as the ground whizzed by, taking the wing off meter by meter during the crash. It felt the same emotions she did, hearing the same sounds of shouts and screams including hers when they died in the fiery crash, including her terror and fear.

Near Quietus, at this point, took away the vase causing Near Immolation to come out of its trance, sweating tears, gasping for breath, visibly shaking.

Near Quietus put the vase back on the shelf saying, "The interesting thing about all this is no matter how they die, there is always the same expression on their face when I come and they see me for the first and final time." Slapping its friend on the shoulder sneering, "None escape when I come calling, all must come to me in the end, no exceptions." Near Immolation sneered viciously.

"As far as laughter is concerned no human has known true laughter since the beginning when they lived in caves. I have some in the back if you would like to hold one to see," sweeping its hand to the back of the room which appeared to be at least a day's walk away.

"No thanks. I have to get back to the machine."

"I think this is still a figment of your bored mind. Nothing more."

"I tell you it is true! Please come down and see for yourself. I'm not making this up out of boredom."

Near Quietus sighed, "Well after the snooze I realized I slept like the dead, so a stroll might liven me up," ushering Near Immolation out the door. It gave out a loud moaning sigh and the Shadow of Death appeared out of nowhere sitting in the chair.

"Someone has to be in charge while I'm gone. What if some human dies and there is no one to take care of them?" It sneered hideously.

They passed several Near Thralls but no one stopped to chit chat, seeing the two of them together. They were sure they were on the master's duties.

Reaching the room, they went right in standing before the now silent machine until near Quietus finally said, "Well?"

"I assure you it spoke. We must just be patient and it will speak," replied Near Immolation.

Suddenly a faint noise came from the machine. Near Quietus listened to the sounds of two young humans laughing before throwing its hands up to its ears to lessen the effects. They left the room running until they were out of range of the inharmonious sound.

"We must tell our Lord immediately! This abomination cannot and will not be allowed to continue. How dare any human, never mind two, be happy enough to register on the machine? The machine hasn't spoken for millennia. Our Lord must be notified and you, being the listener of the machine must tell it. I will be your backup and hope it doesn't do anything rash to you."

Near Immolation paled thinking about bringing this bad news to its master. It had seen others reprimanded for less. Sneering a scowl, it nodded its head in agreement, resigning itself to its fate. Coming out of the basement they could hear the soft moaning, sobbing wails coming from the tears flowing down the walls of the Great Hall.

"I never tire of hearing that sweet music. It gives me shudders every time I hear it," commented Near Quietus.

Near Immolation wasn't in the mood for music right now, glancing over at the entrance to its master's slumber chamber. The two Near Acolytes usually guarding the door were absent. It seemed like an eternity crossing the room to the door. Entering through the door, Near Immolation hoped it wouldn't be shedding tears like the window it saw in the dimly lit room when its Lord heard the news.

They observed their master asleep in front of them on an alter bed. A loud chorus of sobbing and wailing could be heard coming from two black swirling clouds hovering above it. Suddenly, two ghostly faces appeared from the clouds staring at the unwanted guests. The Near Acolytes appeared out of the cloud, standing in front of their master who was now waking up. It opened its white eyes sitting up on the bed, staring at the intrusion standing before it. Both Nears bowed deeply. It spoke in a commanding voice. "What is the meaning of waking me from my slumber!"

"My Lord! Near Immolation has something to say of utmost importance." Pointing to its stunned, quivering friend.

Near Immolation wanted to run away, anywhere, right now but it couldn't.

"Millennia ago you told me to listen to the Risibility Machine for signs of human laughter and it has happened."

Lord Misanthropy's eyes opened wider, "What has happened?"

"It has spoken my Lord. Laughter has been heard finally." Closing its eyes, it waited for its master's wraith; however none came prompting it to open its eyes to see its Lord staring at Near Quietus.

"I have heard it as well my Lord!" It announced. "I'm afraid it true, laughter has indeed risen after all this time."

Lord Misanthropy turned to Near Immolation. "If you had come to me with this news by yourself I would have had you turned inside out and hung on a post at the border of the Land of Afar, as an example. Since you were wise enough to consult Near Quietus whom I trust the most, I will come to hear for myself!"

Grabbing its staff it brushed past the Nears silently except for the quiet squish of its slippers. Both Nears followed quickly, with the Near Acolytes scampering down the stairs trying to keep up with their Lord. Reaching the room with the machine, it entered immediately. The two Near Acolytes stood guard at the door. It stared intently at the machine maintaining a very serious sneer. Time passed and when it seemed like luck wasn't on their side, out of the machine came a loud laugh and giggle.

Their Lord's arms flew up in the air to shield it from the noise, dropping the staff. Near Immolation grabbed it before running out of the room with everyone else.

Finally away, Lord Misanthropy snarled. "This is an abomination! I won't have it! I will destroy these insolent humans where ever they are! No one laughs while I exist! Do you hear me!"

This was usually the part where somebody got turned inside out. Instead it stared at them.

"Fetch me the Sneakeeze!"

For the Sneakeeze, it wasn't much for living quarters but it was home. Once they were roaming the mountains far to the south until Near Dissever captured them. Now freedom was a foggy distant memory for them.

Lurky still blames Slinks for not hearing the Near come up to them when they were sleeping. No matter the blame, they languished in their two room cell. It was spacious for them, being slightly bigger than a dog, including their hairy body and red eyes that glowed in the dark. They walked like we do, but their arms were longer and the really peculiar thing was their large ears. They were the size of a soccer ball that could stretch out listening for sounds. This was their special talent: being able to hear sounds we would call impossible over great distances, which was the reason for the heated discussions over how they got caught.

Their cell was one large room about four meters by four meters. A barred front was enclosed by solid tear walls, floor and ceiling. A smaller room had a hole in the floor for a waste drain. A small barred window allowed in the light and relieved the smells.

If they piled their two chairs side by side on the small table they could hold onto each other, standing together looking out at the freedom they once had. This is when they would wrap their ears around each other's head for mutual support and affection. Sighing out loud together, they would relate stories of the good days and talk about what they would do if free again.

The window also provided the occasional entertainment and food, in the form of a bug or flying insect that made the error of coming in. Catching them, they had races with them if they crawled or if they flew they would release the bug, allowing it to fly. If it was getting away they would bat it down with their long arms until it got hurt or exhausted at which point it was decided to eat it.

This was when the wrestling matches started, to decide who got the prize. Squaring off in opposite corners, they wailed, hissed and yelled insults. They would fling themselves at each other, rolling around on the floor. Once one was pinned, the match was over and the winner declared, doing it until they were exhausted.

The winner got the half with the head still attached while the loser had to be content with the rest. It seemed a little crunchy delicacy of an insects head was a big deal to them when their only food was tear soup every day. Being fair about the whole thing, they took turns eating the head even though the wrestling match decided the outcome of the meal. It helped pass the time and gave them exercise.

Today no such match occurred since no insect wanted to come in and play. Lurky sat on a chair keeping watch out the window, waiting for the daily ration of tear soup.

Slinks stood at the barred door, holding it like a lifer in a prison. He stared out at the always empty hallway, empty except for the spider making a web high up in a corner past their cage. Not taking his eyes off the spider he said, "Come little spidey! Come plays with Lurky and me's. We's have greats fun playin' spin the spidy webs with you's."

"He's a smarts spidey, that's one. We's not even see's him come in. Is no ways he's be stupid's and plays with you's Slinks," spoke Lurky nonchalantly.

"Well if I's don't ask, you's never knows maybe's he's come's play," replied Slinks not taking his eyes off the spider.

A centipede crawled out of the sewage hole over in the corner. Lurky cast a quick glance to see if Slinks noticed, but he was too busy trying to coax the spider to come down. Lurky pretended to relieve himself, grabbing the centipede. Popping it into his mouth he headed back to his chair without eating it.

Banging the chair by accident caused Slinks to turn around. Lurky pretended to be adjusting his chair looking innocently. He was smiling, from the tickling as the bug desperately tried to get out of his mouth. Any chewing motion or noise would alert Slinks to the fact he was eating, so he just sat there putting up with the aggravation.

Just when he thought he couldn't put up with it anymore, he heard a distant noise coming down the hall. Both ears rotated trying to figure out what was going on. Slinks heard it as well. The spider coaxing was forgotten. Turning to Lurky he said, "Is not teary soup time yet. Lurky, what's goin' on?"

Lurky didn't say a word. The centipede would crawl out of his mouth if he opened it the tiniest bit. In a few moments a Near came along, the same one who always brought the tear soup. This time he wasn't carrying the two bowls. Instead he held a set of keys.

Coming straight to the door he announced in an official sounding voice: "The Lord wants to have a word with you two right now!"

He opened the screechy door, both Sneakeeze stood dumb founded, not knowing what to do, until he said flatly. "Well?'

It was suddenly every Sneakeeze for himself trying to get through the door at the same time.

Slinks shouted. "I's was here's first! Lurky gets out of my's ways!"

Lurky allowed him out, not saying anything for fear of letting the centipede ruin the moment. Slinks started doing a dance in the hallway. Lurky joined right not wanting to look suspicious.

Slinks chanted over and over: "We's Sneakeeze and we's free! Free Sneakeeze is we!!" The Near just shook its head at being forced to be around lower life forms like the Sneakeeze. But it was doing the Lord's bidding.

Starting down the hallway, it said. "Follow me."

It tried to keep a distance between itself and the dancing fools behind. Both Sneakeeze were so happy they could hardly contain themselves. From time to time Slinks would give a questioning look at Lurky. He seemed unusually quiet, even though he was dancing with his usual grin on his face.

They found themselves in the Great Hall where they had never been before.

At one time when they were first brought to the castle, they were allowed the run of the basement. That was until Lurky got them into trouble snooping around in Near Quietus office. They met the Shadow of Death sitting in its master's chair, dreaming of how it might someday become Death itself, not just a mere shadow.

Being a Sneakeeze, it was simple to sneak by the Shadow of Death into the back where all the bright lights flickered. That in itself wasn't wrong. But when they accidentally knock over a tray of fresh souls waiting to be sorted according to their death, they caused a deadly nightmare. The long and short of it was they were never allowed out of their cell again.

Their chatter and dancing stopped. They now followed closely, afraid of getting separated from their guide.

They almost ran into the Near when it stopped in front of the Lord, who was staring at the big eared creatures.

Both Sneakeeze jumped back a step, seeing the figure of malevolence seated before them. It sneered with a disapproving grimace on its face, flanked by both Near Acolytes.

There was dead silence for a moment until. "I have summoned you two for an important mission." It stopped, staring at Lurky, pointing and screeched, "What is that?"

Lurky, in his state of awe and fear had opened his mouth slightly. It was enough, to allow the tail of the centipede to wiggle out of the corner of his lips, trying to escape its oral prison. Lurky's eyes opened wide when he realized he had forgotten about the food in his mouth. He looked down at an angle trying to see how much of the insect was visible. Slinks looked over to see what the Lord was pointing at. Seeing the insect hanging out, he forgot about Lord Misanthropy, hitting Lurky over the head with his fist, shouting. "Lurky no share buggie! Now Lurky gets sluggy!"

Lurky bit off the tail of the helpless centipede. It fell to the floor, writhing like it had a life of its own. Lurky swallowed what was still inside his mouth. He decided Slinks had no right to hit him and a wrestling match began on the floor. Pounding each other, their legs were wrapped around each other, shouting insults at the top of their lungs.

The Near stood back, its mouth open, at this display of total disrespect for their Lord. Lord Misanthropy stared at them as they rolled around on the floor, shaking its head slowly in disgust at the lunacy in front of it.

The Near looked at its Lord, deciding enough was enough. Pulling them apart, it flung Slinks several meters across the room. The fight ended, when both Sneakeeze realized they were one command away from being imprisoned again, possibly forever. Deciding that perhaps they should be on their best behavior, they crawled over on all fours in front of the throne. They groveled and held each other for mutual support.

Lord Misanthropy sat in silence for what seemed an eternity, cleared its throat and began. "As I was saying before I was rudely interrupted, I in my most gracious mood, have decided I have a mission for you two. If you can stop fighting long enough! I require you to search the lands outside of Afar for any signs of laughter from humans. We have detected laughter from our machine but can't locate the source. This is where we need your help with your ears.

Find this offending source; report the location back to me at once and you will be freed. If you have any thoughts of escaping, I will send my Nears after you and drag you back here to face a fate even worse than being turned inside out. Do you understand?"

Looking at it incredulously, the words started to sink in.

Slinks glanced at Lurky, then up at the Lord who had the worst sneering glare he had ever seen, causing him to stammer. "Yes Lordie Misphtpht we's understands and will do's as you's asks."

Lurky could only softly whisper. "Yes Lordie Misphtpht we's understand and we's do as you's asks."

The Lord waved to have them removed from its sight, before it changed its mind or regretted its decision about letting them free to accomplish its mission.

The Near turned to the Sneakeeze, pointing to a side door in the corner of the Great Hall where they were to go. Passing the fountain they could hear soft wailing coming from the tears flowing from it. Looking around to see who was making the lamenting sounds he saw no one as they continued. The Near led them to a room that was a storage room with a door at the far end.

The Near gave them both a bag with a strap. "You will find enough bottled tear soup to keep you both for your journey until you return. A word of advice: I wouldn't dally on the way. The Lord has no patience, expecting your swift return with news. Don't disappoint the Lord! You've been given the words to come back across the great bridge. Don't forget them!"

At the door, it pulled it open, revealing their long awaited freedom. Both Sneakeeze mouths dropped open, not quite believing their newfound good luck. They ran for the door, making it there at the same time, shoving and squeezing, trying to get through the door. Falling outside in a heap from tripping over each other, they lay tangled together on the ground. The Near slammed the door shut, glad to be rid of the nuisances, shaking its head in disgust at such stupid creatures as Sneakeeze.

Both Sneakeeze lay, not quite comprehending they were finally outside, after so long being in the basement. Once the shock subsided, they picked themselves up and decided to get going before somebody changed their mind.

Half running, half scampering, they moved down to the main trail heading toward the Towers of Tears. At the main trail they stopped, looking back to make sure no one was following them. Seeing the coast was clear, they put their arms around each other, walking and skipping towards the Tower of Tears, they sang at the top of their lungs.

"WE'RE THE SNEAKEEZE
WE LOVE'S OUR BIG EARS
WHEN THERE'S LAUGHTER IN THE WORLD
WE'S BOUND TO HEAR
SO IF YOU'S LAUGHING
BE QUIET AND LIVE'S IN FEAR
BECAUSE WE'S THE SNEAKEEZE
AND WE'S WILL TELL'S THE NEARS"

Their singing didn't go unnoticed as Lord Misanthropy stood watching the two make their way towards the tower. Its white teary cold eyes focused intently on the figures dancing their way to the edge of Afar. Muttering quietly to itself, it looked at the crystal on the top of the staff.

"I SEE, I SEE, I SEE
YOU WILL NOT HIDE FROM ME
NOWHERE WILL YOU FLEE
THAT I WILL NOT SEE
THOUGH SNEAKEEZE YOU MAY BE
MY EYES WILL STILL SEE THEE"

The crystal glowed a bright white, briefly. Lurky suddenly felt a cold shiver on his neck, causing him to stop.

"Slinks, its sees us. Can't you feels?"

Slinks just nodded his head in agreement, dragging Lurky to get as far away, as soon as possible.

They passed the golden Tower of Tears without seeing any Nears, but just past the tower they saw a figure coming towards them.

Rushing off the road they hid behind a large boulder.

They were astonished to see a man, his clothes in shreds and blood-stained. Half running, half staggering with a wild look on his face, tears flowed down his cheeks.

"My wife! My children dead! Gone! What is to become of me!"

When he entered the Tower of Tears, they left their hiding places and ran fast.

Lurky asked Slinks. "Whys does the humans keep comin's?"

"As long as the Lord Misphpht has powers over them and they allows the Nears to come for a visits to thems, theys will keeps coming. Maybes, one days theys wills learn how's not to lets the Nears hurts thems.

By the time they were done talking, they had reached the bridge. Scampering across to the other side, they were glad to be out of the Land of Afar. Through the thick fog they could see three roads coming together at the bridge. They chose the road to the left. No sooner had they started down the road, they could hear people, some moaning, others shouting, and wailing children coming toward the bridge from the other roads.

Lurky looked at Slinks.

"The Nears are busy. It must be Near Baet'l causing humans wars again."

Lurky was silent. Nothing they could say or do could help any other life forms that were the helpless victims of the power of the Nears or Lord Misanthropy.

What was clear as water was, they had to get as far away from Afar as fast as they could.

The bobber floated in the clear water of the small creek. A hapless victim of a worm squirmed, trying to get away any way it could. But it had to resign itself to being bait, bait for a hungry trout. Dave held the fishing rod barely moving, not wanting to scare any fish. Dianne crouched beside him, watching excitedly.

"When it bites I'll snag it and it's all yours to reel in Dotty since I caught the last one."

Dianne stared, hardly able to contain herself watching her brother. Leaning over she whispered. "Thanks for putting the worm on for me. I can't stand their squirming. I hope the fish kills it faster than robins do." After watching a robin pull a worm out of the ground and ripping it to shreds, she never forgot how nature took its course.

"Look Dotty. There's one checking it out. See the bobber moving?"

She felt the excitement rise in her. The bobber took several serious dips into the water, going under. Dave jerked back on the rod, setting the hook.

Confident he had the fish hooked; he gave his sister the rod. She almost dropped it in her state of exhilaration. She slowly reeled the trout towards them. Putting on a serious face, she focused on bringing the fish in.

"He's a real scrapper!" She explained.

"You're doing fine! Keep it coming and I'll grab it at the bank." She pulled the fish over towards her brother. He tossed it up onto the grass. There was no chance of it getting unhooked.

Dianne pounced on the flopping trout grabbing it with both hands.

She handed it to Dave, who took the hook out of the fish's mouth, breaking its neck so it didn't suffer. He didn't let anything suffer if he could help it.

He was taught to respect creatures that gave up their lives as food for him and to never let them suffer.

"That's a nice fish for your first, Dotty! You should be proud!" Dave said

She looked at him saying seriously. "I saw this before, even the exact words you spoke Dave. This is really important."

Her brother was used to her experiencing these things. There were times when she saw things that came true later on. He took things seriously whenever she said anything like this. He knew she wasn't making it up.

"It's probably because it's your first one, Dotty. Let's see if you can get one more so we can have one each for dinner tonight. OK?"

He reached his hand over on her shoulder, trying not to get any fish slime on her shirt with his fingers.

She looked at her brother with a smile, saying. "Yes lets! Mom will be so pleased. Let's try again. This time you catch it. I wouldn't want to risk losing it."

Dave tossed the worm out into the flowing stream. It desperately tried to wiggle its way out of the hook's cruel sting. Suddenly the bobber went under with one swift motion.

"Look! Something big has it!

"This is a whopper Dotty! He's really fighting!" The fish broke the surface jumping, trying to get away from the hook. They both gave out a collective, "Oh!" at the awesome size of the fish.

"Don't lose it!" Dianne was jumping, shaking her hands at her sides, the excitement getting the better of her. Dave paid all his attention to the fish. Swimming hard, it almost got to some sunken logs. Dave pulled hard enough to guide it away in time.

After a few moments, he reeled it to shore and took care of it the way he did the others. He laid it down with the other two. It dwarfed the other two fish.

Dianne exclaimed. "He's a monster! Look at the size of him compared to the others, Dave!"

"I dreamt this Dotty! I forgot about the dream, constantly dreaming about many things. The only drawback about night dreaming is, you can't always remember them and this was one."

"Won't mom be surprised when we get home with these fish and our stories?" Exclaimed Dianne excitedly.

"This is most unusual Dotty, that we both had this happen at the same time. Yes, mom will be surprised." They packed up for the walk back to the house. He strung a stick through the fish's gills to carry back. Kicking a hollow in the ground, he dumped the remaining worms in and covered it over.

Turning to his sister, who already had the fishing pole in her hand, he said. "Ready?"

His sister just nodded, heading back by the path they had come. Dianne was in the lead, doing a walking dance singing:

"FISHY FISHIN'
FISHIN'S A FUN WAY
FISHY FISHIN'
TO SPEND A DAY
FISHY FISHIN'
FISH CAUGHT TODAY
FISHY FISHIN'
TASTE GOOD I SAY"

Dave smiled as Dianne did her victory dance and song. He was happy she caught her first one. She was his best and only friend. He was happy when she was. He followed along content to hear her made up tune, while the fish dangled flopping in time on the end of the stick.

The house, a modest white storey and a half old farmstead had been there for as long as anyone could remember. It had originally been a pioneer's dream of a new life. The stone rows marking the edge of the grown over fields showed the work and determination that had gone into establishing that dream.

It had been bought by the children's parents years ago as a hobby farm. It was a dream to have children grow up in a natural wholesome setting away from the hustle and bustle of big city living. Something they too had experienced themselves as children.

The dream lived, until one day a drunken driver killed their dad on a highway, coming back from the city. The dream was now only a shadow of its former self, as their mother continued on living there with them.

The children walked through the path from the creek near the house. The smell of hay waft through the warm air. Dave breathed deeply the fresh pleasant smells, never tiring of the aromas. Even from the smell of the birds and the two goats, Nan and Nelly in the small barn.

The goats saw the children, knowing they were familiar figures, giving several "Naahhs." This call was different from when a stranger came into the yard. The sounds were louder, more of a warning than a greeting.

Dave called back to the goats, "Goaties! Goaties!"

He learned a long time ago birds and animals would talk to you in their own way. He had learned things living out in the middle of nowhere, things you wouldn't learn in a different setting, such as the city. He found any of the kids he met from the city had to have noise. They couldn't seem to just relax and be quiet inside, like he had learned to be. Different environments result in different effects. They were always bored and had to continuously be doing something to keep busy, otherwise they wanted to go back to the city.

Being out there with no friends didn't seem to really bother him. He preferred the quiet living. A huge forest surrounded their home. Their driveway at the end of a very quiet gravel road, wound for kilometers out of the bush before the first paved road. The nearest neighbor was an elderly couple several kilometers away. His only real friend was his sister Dianne, making them constant companions.

The old white painted house was surrounded by overgrown remnants of flower and vegetable gardens, cared for with love in happier days. A row of tall pine trees on the side of the house shaded it in the heat of the summer and broke the wind in the winter. A large willow faced the bedrooms of the house. It served as a nesting spot for robins year after year.

Reaching the screened in porch, the barn was one hundred meters away. Dianne got to the door first. Opening it with gusto, it squeaked out a complaint at the rough treatment.

She opened the kitchen door yelling, "Mom! Mom! You're never going to believe this!"

Seeing her mother in the kitchen baking goodies, she bounced up and down, squeezing her hands then letting go and shaking them in excitement, waiting for Dave. Her mother smiled.

The smile lines took over from the sorrow that had developed since her husband was killed. She brushed back her slightly graying lock of hair that had fallen over her one eye.

"What's got you so excited Dotty? I haven't seen you this happy since you brought in your first garter snake to show me."

Dave proudly held the fish up.

"My! Look at the size of the fish. That's a good day's catch for anybody," exclaimed Susan.

"You both did well, so we'll have them for supper. I'll pan fry them. How's that?"

Dave spoke up. "Dotty caught her first fish by herself without any help," making Dianne glance at the floor embarrassed.

Her mother placed her hand on her shoulder. "I'm glad you had fun fishing. This is indeed a blessing for us. Since this is your first fish, eating them tonight will bring continued good luck, every time you go fishing. I'll look after getting the fish ready if you two want to go out and feed the critters."

Dianne was out the door shouting for Dave when his mother said. "There's something I want to talk to you two about at supper." This brought an over-powering silence from him as he moved away, thinking.

Heavy dense cool fog brought an over powering silence that enveloped the land. The dense fog made talking futile, so stifling was the effect.

Two figures slowly emerged moving cautiously and silently. Lurky and Slinks tread along the path, saying nothing. They took turns watching the unfamiliar trail winding down the mountains. Even the sun couldn't penetrate the fog. The foggy blanket held this part of the land in its grasp.

Stopping to catch their breath, they listened for any sound. Nothing could be heard. It was difficult even for a Sneakeeze to pick up noise in this fog. The only sound was the occasional clatter of stones, as they hastened to remove themselves from the Land of Afar.

They continued, afraid they would be returned to the dreadful cell. They were anxious to go somewhere, anywhere new and wonderful compared to the barren wasteland of Afar.

Down the mountains, the fog lost its tight grip on the land. The Sneakeeze saw where they were going with more clarity. Vegetation grew scattered amongst the rocks. Finally small trees enveloped them on all sides.

Seeing growing things lifted their spirits. Stopping at the same time, they turned around to the receding trail, ears at the ready listening. There was only silence from where they had come. They both let out a collective sigh of relief.

Lurky said, "Slinks I's don't knows abouts you's, but I's glads we's out'a of theres."

"You's righty right abouts that Lurky. I's thought we's would nevers gets away from them and their teary soup."

He tossed the tear water containers they had been given to the ground kicking them, cautiously looking around.

Lurky kicked them in agreement, saying. "I's hears waters running over theres. Let's go."

In the direction Lurky had pointed to, they came to a clear stream off the mountain. They headed for the water quickly, jostling to be the first one to drink. There was plenty of room, lying down beside each other, sucking in the cool refreshing mountain water. Their ears instinctively flopped back and forth into the water as if taking a drink of their own. Finally, they both lifted their heads, their ears dripping water.

"Ah!" They both said, voicing their contentment at finally having something truly good to drink. Staring at each other laughing, they put their hand over their mouths to silence the noise.

Lurky spoke quietly, "We's better nots laugh too louds or Lordy Misphpht's machine wills hears us Slinks."

"Yes, but that's means it woulds sends us outs looking for us cause we's laughs. So it woulds takes a longs time for us to finds ourselves. Maybes nevers!"

Lurky stared at his companion as it sunk in. A broad grin turned into laughing out loud, louder and louder. Slinks joined in until uncontrollable laughter echoed around them. Tears of joy so long hidden flowed from them in streams like the brook beside them.

The water from the stream had washed away all the built up negativity from drinking tear water all this time. Genuine joy, peace and long forgotten happiness swept through them for the first time in so long. Laughing until they couldn't possibly laugh any more caused their heart to ache in that feel good kind of way.

Out of breath, they lay down, slipping off into a contented deep sleep, the kind they hadn't had since they were captured by the Nears long ago.

They dreamt Sneakeeze dreams, dreams of high adventure, exploring life's many wonders, and having fun. Not the kind of tear water dreams, dreams dark and unsettling, the kind that make you toss and turn while you cry out in a fitful sleep.

Lurky and Slinks dreamt the good things in their lives, now that the power of the negative tear energy had been washed away.

Snoring, their ears gently fanned in rhythm, until a fly buzzing by was interested in the ear movement and landed on Lurky's ear. A fun thing to do, in an otherwise boring fly day!

Walking about on this new smell it had discovered, it tickled his ear, causing it to twitch uncontrollably to this irritant.

Poor Lurky's ear twitched so bad it smacked him full across the face, causing a startled 'snorpht', waking him up. Almost jumping into the stream, he realized they had fallen into a sound sleep without knowing it. He gave a nervous look around, since this was how Near Dissever had caught them in the first place.

This time no Near was around, but a fly buzzing around made him realize what had woke him up. With lightening reflexes, he snatched the fly out of mid air. The fly finding itself trapped, emitted high-pitched shrieking buzzing noises.

He held his hand up to his ear.

"Yous luckys I's hates flies since yous don'ts makes good flies pies. So flies little fly, flies for the sky." Opening his hand without harming the insect, he let it go. Lurky had learned long ago that they weren't the best tasting things on the insect menu. Besides it was also a matter of where had they been and what they did.

It immediately realized its good fortune and flew fast, bobbing and weaving as far away as possible from the strange creature.

The fly reminded Lurky they hadn't eaten anything good. Besides the fact his stomach was making audible gurgling sounds.

Grabbing a handful of pebbles, Lurky decided it was time Slinks stopped snoring and was up too. With careful aim, he dropped them one by one on Slinks' ear. Each time one landed Slinks jerked until finally after the fifth stone, he snorted awake.

Lurky quietly reached behind himself, unceremoniously dropping the remaining pebbles so Slinks wouldn't notice. Slinks jumped to his feet looking around confused.

Lurky said nonchalantly. "Looks at olds, sleepy heads Slinks, wasting his days, whiles I's keep the nastys old Nears aways."

Slinks stared suspiciously, rubbing his ear not knowing what was wrong with it.

He retorted, "The onlys ways yous could keeps the Nears aways is ifs you's runs aways, Lurky."

"I don'ts knows abouts yous but I'ms hungry." Both looked around for food. It didn't take long when the menu is anything within easy reach.

It was every Sneakeeze for himself and every bug fleeing for their lives. They scampered and jumped, after anything resembling an arthropod that crawled, skittered, or flew.

They kept themselves busy doing their best to fill their stomachs. After all, it wasn't polite to speak with your mouth full, even for a Sneakeeze. There was quiet until they had their fill. There was also relief for the arthropod survivors, who had to watch their closest neighbors or relatives disappear in a flurry of deglutition. The survivor insects busied themselves, crawling under anything they could find or flying for dear life.

Slinks and Lurky stopped in their scrounging foray, taking a breather, still chewing on some hapless victim.

Slinks spoke, after picking out a still twitching leg from between his teeth: "That's hits the spotty, eh Lurky?"

Lurky stopped chewing and replied: "Muchs betters thans the ones in our cells Slinks." A wing from a victim flew out of his mouth floating and tumbling to the ground. This was the only evidence that the creature once existed. They washed down pieces of food stuck in their throat, before sitting back to look around at their surroundings.

"I's guess we's has to do's what old Lordy Misphtpht wants," Slinks said. "If we don't do's the masters biddings, it will locks us aways forevers and forevers. So let's goes do this, maybes Lord Misphtpht wills frees us as a rewardys."

"What abouts the teary soup?" queried Lurky, pointing at the flasks beside a rock.

"We's leaves them's here's until's we get's backs," replied Slinks nonchalantly.

"Let's goes. There's no ends of waters to drinks. I'd rather drinks old muds puddles than that's." Lurky spat in the general direction of the flasks, before turning his back on them. He flicked dirt with his feet as a true signal of contempt. Slinks did also, in agreement.

Heading down the trail, doing a little two-step now and then, showed they were quite content in their present circumstances. The birds chirping in the trees made Lurky chirp along mimicking their cheerful sounds.

Slinks didn't pay attention to Lurky. After moving for several hours, he interrupted Lurky's expanding birdcall repertoire, pointing to a rise of land off in the distance.

"That's where we's goes. Theres our's listening's place."

Lurky had almost forgotten why they were there. He was daydreaming that he was flying like a bird. He so envied birds, wishing he could fly. Fly away up into the wide-open sky, free. That would be the perfect life, flapping his big ears and soaring.

His ears were going back and forth as he daydreamed. When Slinks spoke, his fantasy and birdcalls came to a halt, much to the relief of the birds.

Lurky sighed, remembering why they were there, climbing up the rocky hill with a panoramic view of the surrounding hills. Secretly, he wished he and Slinks could be free.

HALF WAY TO THE BARN, Dianne stared at the panoramic view of the surrounding hills. Her thoughts were interrupted as Dave came out, trying to get free of the door. "Get away from there, Dotty!"

Dianne loved doing the chores with her brother. It was one of the few times they really talked. It was their time together, something special. She cared for her critters as she called them. She had grown up with them, looking forward to chores after home school. Now summer vacation was here, it seemed to make it even more enjoyable.

Her brother gained on her, making her increase her speed to the door. The object was whoever touched the door first got to open it. She managed to get there just ahead of him hesitating for a second, before tapping the old door.

"Getting slow are we brother?" she teased.

"Only because I talked to mom and tried to put my rubber boot on," he said, giving her a shove. "Not like your face plant!"

"Whatever!" She retorted. There was an element of truth to what he had said.

One day he had slipped out and hadn't been noticed. He was dancing around teasing her, as she struggled to put her rubber boots on. She didn't quite get one rubber on properly. Leaping off the porch, the boot almost came off, causing her to trip and land face down in the mud.

Laughing, the memories of that day swirled through their minds. She opened the door, creaking in protest, showing its age.

The noises outside the barn, made the critters aware of their presence. They all voiced their happiness at being fed. Nan and Nelly stood in their pen making quiet 'Naa, Naa' noises, recognizing the children.

Dianne went right over. "Naa! N. and N. How are my goaties doing today?"

Standing, waiting to be scratched, Dianne obliged, scratching their favorite itchy spots.

Without looking at her brother, Dianne said. "I'm concerned about something. I feel a change is coming but I can't quite get a sense of what it is, but it makes me feel uneasy deep inside." Suddenly a chill ran through her.

"I know. I've been having disturbing dreams; just bits and pieces and they don't make me feel good either."

Dave grabbed the pail with the goat's grain, trying to shake off the horrible feeling of the dreams. He poured the food for the goats, who decided food was more important than affection from Dianne. They grabbed a mouthful of the crunchy goodness, grinding it in their mouth.

"I've had dreams about a man as well and I'm not sure who he is, but he seems alright. We sit and talk a lot."

"About what?"

"That part I can't remember. That's the part I hate about dreams."

"For me, I don't always see things. It's more like a hunch that turns out right or a nagging feeling that I sense something. But I can't quite get a grasp on it, until it happens later."

"Yes, it's like trying to remember something you learned in school but can only sort of remember the general part, not the details. That's how my dreams are quite often."

"Well, there's one thing for sure; we are both in this together."

"You got that right sis. Now let's go feed the birds before they pluck their feathers out waiting."

"Yes, we wouldn't want them to waste away into a pile of feathers. We would have to stuff a pillow with them, and embroider it, 'Here lays a pillow made from birds of a feather that wasted away together '."

"Ya, whatever. Let's go."

Dave sprinkled the feed around, dumping the rest into a dish for them to eat later.

"I've also been having dreams of flying over mountains and a place that I can't quite describe. I don't know what it means and I don't feel good about it." His sister looked at him wishing she had dreams about flying. It sounded so neat.

Pointing at old Fred the rooster, Dave said. "Are you sure you would want to make a pillow of old Fred here?" pointing to the dust-coated bird.

"Well, maybe not old Fred. A pillow does have some limits." Dianne laughed.

Mischievously, he reached down grabbing some ends of grass."Let me introduce you to my new friend Mr. Spider."

Dianne jumped back. A fear of spiders caused her to scream. Not knowing he had reached down for the grass, she saw the ends sticking out from his hands. She turned and ran. Securing the eggs in the pail, he ran after her, pretending he had the spider.

"I'm going to put him in your hair, Dotty!"

She shrieked, running to the house. "Don't you dare!"

He opened his hand showing nothing was there, saying, "Got ya!" Laughing he changed his shoes ready to go into the house. "Maybe what mom wants to talk to us about has something to do with this."

Dianne looked at him surprised, since she hadn't heard the conversation. "What did mom say?" Dave said nothing, going inside. She followed, interested but suddenly concerned, catching her breath.

CATCHING THEIR BREATH, THEY SAW the land stretching out, unconcerned about the rolling hills interfering with what they did.

"Who's turns is it Lurky?"

It had been so long, Lurky couldn't remember either. Reaching down he grabbed a stone with a flat side and round side.

"Flat's I's listens, rounds you's listens."

Flipping the stone into the air, it bounced and came up flat.

"Well that's answers that's!" Slinks remarked. Kneeling down, Lurky climbed up on his shoulders, standing up on his feet. Slinks, in one swift move, stood up.

Lurky spread his ears out in a large fan shape, getting the maximum effect for listening. Without a word, he pushed down on Slink's shoulders with his heels. Slinks started turning around slowly. Lurky's ears were picking up amplified noises that would be impossible for humans to hear. A cricket several kilometers away, birds across a lake, so many noises so far off he wasn't sure what they were. Around and around they silently went, but they didn't interfere with his listening.

Lurky, his eyes closed, maintaining unbroken concentration, listened and filtered out unwanted sounds. His listening range increased further and further out. Finally, he heard two sounds of laughter, far off in the distance. Saying nothing, he raised his hand in the direction he heard the sounds. Slinks stopped moving around. He listened to make sure; since a wind will affect the precise spot sound comes from. Satisfied he had a true fix, he put his hand back down. Suddenly, they spoke together in unison.

"THERE'S NO SOUND
WHEN SNEAKEEZE TURN
THAT CAN'T BE'S FOUND
TOGETHER WE'S BOUND
TURNING, TURNING
TO HEAR THE SOUND
LISTENING FOR LAUGHTER
LAUGHTER'S SOUND THAT'S BEEN FOUND"

Slinks reached up grabbing Lurky's feet, tossing him backwards off his shoulders, saying. "Well, let's goes."

Lurky was taken totally by surprise at being tossed backwards. Arms flailing the air, he came down hard on his back. His ears hit the ground with a loud swoosh causing debris to fly in all directions. Without a word, he gathered himself up, shaking off the dust and the shock of the sudden fall.

Slinks moved down the hill in the direction the sound had come from. Lurky dug his heels in, jumping onto Slink's back. His ears flailed Slinks head and ears, biting into the back of his neck.

Lurky's momentum knocked them tumbling down the hill flailing and biting. Slinks tried to get Lurky off. Lurky did his best to do as much punishment as he could.

Shouting and yelling insults at each other, they made it down to the bottom of the hill. Pummeling each other for all they were worth, a cloud of dust obscured who was who. They rolled around until they let each other go, panting out of breath. Slinks said, "Readys to goes?"

"Okays."

Dusting themselves off, they made sure nothing was too damaged. Their ears and heads were red from the abuse, but they had come through the ordeal relatively unharmed.

Lurky took the lead, after seeing the farthest landmark from his vantage point on top. He left the path moving towards the sound. It was always the rule. The listener got to take the other towards the next listening place. Lurky's painful bruises reminded him with quiet assurance; it was going to be Slinks turn to be the next listener standing on his shoulders. A slight grin came across his face.

HUGH HAD A SLIGHT GRIN across his face watching the hawk soar above him while taking a break; this was a good omen. He had walked seven days from his home heading for his brother's place, skirting the vast range of mountains. He stretched, feeling the effects of too much strain on his many old wounds from the violent encounters with life.

Seated on a rock he watched the hawk until it floated down behind trees looking for prey. That reminded him he was hungry. Grabbing an energy bar, he bit into it greedily causing a crumb to choke him. Coughing, he grabbed his water bottle taking a long gulp. Suddenly he realized, he had just drunk all his water. "Great! Now what do I do for water. I still have a ways to go." Looking down the slope he noticed a sparkle that he hadn't seen among the rocks.

"Awesome! Spirit always provides." He said, starting down the hill until he reached a tiny stream. Checking it out, he was pleased to see it was clean and drinkable.

Removing his pack, he reached down for a taste. He took a slurp and then refilled his water bottle. His problem was now solved, but the water made him need to relieve his bladder. Stopping at a rock, he suddenly noticed something protruding behind it. If he hadn't looked directly at it, he probably would have missed it.

Interested now, he walked over picking up what were two flasks made from what seemed a hardened substance. He had no idea what they were. Giving them a shake, he heard a liquid. He opened the plug of one flask for his nose to smell. It smelled like seawater. Since there was no ocean anywhere near, this caught his attention. Looking down, he noticed the liquid caused the grass to sizzle and turn into ash. The liquid itself had turned into a black gel like substance. He put the stopper back on the neck of the flask, before turning the flask around. He noticed the flask had an embossed image of a tear, and now realized the liquid was in fact, tears.

Throwing the flask on the ground, he whispered, "No!" He knew these flasks belonged to the Nears from that night he first met them. They never went anywhere without them and didn't stash them behind rocks for safekeeping. He scanned everywhere for any sign of a Near, but saw nothing. Washing his mouth, he rid himself of the teardrop he had just tasted.

He headed straight down the path as fast as he could. Maintaining a constant vigil for any Near, which to his relief, never happened. A stern look came across his face. Concern slowly crept into his usually peaceful consciousness. His mind drifted back to when he had the misfortune to meet Nears. It wasn't actually a meeting; it was actually seeing them for the first time.

His brother Pat had picked him up to spend the week at his new hobby farm, he and his wife Susan had bought. He was to help them renovate it.

He and his brother were closer after their parents died when they were younger. They both read a lot and engaged in many discussions on world events and life. They weren't opposed on many issues. They always enjoyed the other's point of view.

Driving to the farm, they were discussing the finer points about politics. They came around a corner glancing at each other making their arguments. They didn't notice the other car had drifted over the centre line, caused by the effects of impaired driving, until it was too late. Pat didn't have time to brake as Hugh shouted a warning. There was a terrible bang and a shower of countless brilliant sparks of cars tearing each other apart.

Hugh awoke lying on the road looking up at the stars. It caught his attention for a moment until he realized where he was. The car lights were somehow still on. He could see, although things would blur at times.

He shouted for his brother. A low moaning made him turn his head toward the noise. Pat was lying on his back, sprawled across the car seat, not moving. Hugh desperately tried to move over to his brother. He wasn't going anywhere. He had many broken bones including both arms and legs. All he could do was lay there watching.

He looked to see the other driver slumped over the steering wheel of his car, moaning and talking incoherently, unaware of what had happened. Hugh shouted for help but all he heard was silence that seemed to suddenly get intense.

That's when he noticed three black figures sitting on the roof of the other car staring at him. His attention was on their cold, white, shining eyes.

One turned to the others and in a cackling voice spoke. "How is it this human sees when all others are blind? He is unusual for a member of mankind."

"What do I care, it is neither here nor there if this one sees, when all the others are blind to seeing the truth about life anyway. We've much work to do before we are through this night."

Hugh screamed, "Who are you!" Fear and panic overwhelmed him.

"We are the Nears. We have come to do our masters bidding." Replied the one, as the others snickered and climbed down off the car roof.

One went over to the driver of the other car talking quietly to him. "I am Near Adiktiv and I made you drink the poison of soul and made your mind shout More! More! Until all common sense was gone. Lost in the fog of your intoxication, now pain and anguish is your reward for what you have done. Regret will be the hangover that you will never get over."

It pulled out a flask pouring some liquid into the driver's mouth causing him to almost choke. Tears flowed down his cheeks blending with the blood covering his face. Hugh could distinctly hear the tears hitting the floor of the car one bloodied splat at a time.

He looked over at the other Near approaching his brother, who still wasn't moving.

"Don't you touch him!" Hugh screamed trying to get his body to work but helpless. But all he could do was stare.

The Near spoke, "I am Near Quietus and this one has reached the end of his time and now he's mine. None escape me no matter how they beg and plead even down on bended knee." It reached out a similar flask, pouring some liquid on his lips. Pat took three deep breaths and then he died.

Hugh watched a small bright light in the shape of a body come out of his brother. The Near waved its hand in the air. The light whirled until it was just a point of intense multi-colored light before the Near snatched it from the air, putting Pat's soul in its pocket.

Hugh stared at his brother's lifeless body. Lifeless, except for tears slowly streaming down his face. The tears staining the car seat became a memento mori of his brother who once was.

"I am Near Acidant and you will not share the same fate as these two, but you will suffer for being here by accident. Therefore feel the aches and pains of being in this accident the rest of your days."

Pulling out its flask it grabbed Hugh's hair with its black fist, trickling some tears into his mouth, causing him to gag. His tears began, as he sobbed uncontrollably out loud. He couldn't look at the hideous face with the white eyes any longer. Turning his head to the side, everything went black.

Walking along now remembering, gave him shudders. The mind will convince you over time it had all been a bad dream. Now he was convinced that the sooner he got to where he was headed, the better off he would be. Ever since the accident, his bones gave him no end of discomfort, especially with weather changes. They constantly ached, a continuous reminder of that night. He had found some relief in walking. It seemed to help with the unremitting low pain. Today, after finding the flasks, the pain seemed to intensify. He tried to keep his thoughts under control.

Entering the kitchen, the children inhaled, hardly able to control their thoughts about food, after smelling the appetizing odors. Fresh baked buns gave off even more desirable smells, luring them over to the table. A freshly baked berry pie caught Dave's attention. He bent down inhaling all the delicious aromas coming from the mixture of berries.

"Get out of that pie young man or we will have it and you'll only get the crumbs," Susan laughingly joked, entering the room.

"Oh maybe we'll leave one small piece smeared with berries on it for him Mom. We wouldn't want him to starve." Dianne said, taunting him.

"Very funny, Dot! You'll be lucky if your pie doesn't disappear in my fork fang-dangling magic act. Dave said, waving his fork in the air like a sword.

They laughed at the lack of swordsmanship.

"More like you won't be waving anything, with a cast on your arm after Dotty gets through, if she catches it in her piece of pie. Now go wash up before we sit."

He put the fork back, going over to his sister at the sink. They tried to jokingly shove and squeeze each other out of position in front of the tap. She finished first and grabbed the towel to dry her hands. Dave decided to flick water off his fingertips at her face to aggravate her.

"Mother, could we see if we can trade him in for a different brother model? One that just sits there and does what you say without bugging a person all day long," Dianne quipped, flinging the towel at him.

"I tried that already dear; they make the same disgusting creature for brothers everywhere. Apparently, only different features give any variety to the same model, I'm afraid. Now come let's eat before it all cools. I am starved."

"Hey, if it wasn't for me you two would have nothing to complain about, so just appreciate the fact I'm here to bug you! Now stay out of my way or you'll suffer fork wounds," Dave retorted laughingly, flicking Dianne with his finger.

"Mother, see what I have to put with!" Dianne said. Smoothing back her hair with her hand, she gave her brother looks that would kill. Apparently you are treading on dangerous ground when you mess up a girl's hair, even if it is your sister's. Seeing he crossed that unspoken line, he quietly sat down.

Their mother dished the food up, giving both children larger portions of the trout. The children were happy to see their reward sitting there in front of them, steaming. The smells made their stomachs yearn for the food. Their mother, satisfied that everything was ready, picked up her glass of water and said, "Raise your glass as we give thanks to spirit for this bountiful harvest of food. We give thanks to the fish that gave up their lives so we could eat. We give thanks to the vegetables that gathered up the nourishment from the soil, the sun and rain that nourish our bodies as they give of theirs."

The children raised their glasses in response, clinking them together in a symbolic gesture. Taking a sip symbolized drinking of the waters of life. They were taught it came in many forms, whether from food, the sun, the very air they breathed or love shared at a table full of food.

They greedily began to taste the repast in front of them. Dianne carefully picked apart the fillet of fish looking for unwanted bones. Dave just scooped a forkful into his mouth, munching and crunching bones and all.

"This fish is delicious right out of the creek, not like the stale frozen fish from the store we usually get. That one was so big it gave us more than enough for a good meal. There's still more on the stove if you want it," Susan said.

Both children nodded, their mouths full of food, not wanting to be impolite by talking.

"I had déjà vu when we caught the fish Mom and Dave had a dream about it too. What does that mean? Is it something important? We thought it was, since we both had these experiences at the same time." Dianne said.

"This is indeed a sign; the larger one is of particular importance. The fact that you caught three fish and the largest one last means an event that is larger than all of us is coming. The three fish means it involves all of us at this table. Perhaps it has something to do with what has happened to me, being the largest fish."

Dianne wondered what her mother was talking about. She looked back at her mother, listening patiently without questions.

The children listened intently because after their father died so long ago, their mother had gone through spiritual transformation. Being so young at the time, they had no comprehension what that was.

Before the accident, she use to go to church regularly and they would accompany her sitting in the pews. Their father rarely went, showing up only on special occasions like Christmas or Easter. Being young, they were fascinated with the appearance of the church, its ornamented works of art and the well dressed people sitting with them, all singing verses from various books used during the service.

It was all quite splendid, since they were doing this for someone called God, who apparently lived somewhere that they couldn't see. In fact, no one they knew had ever seen or talked to God, but everyone was sure that at the end of each service he would be happy they had done the singing and speaking verses. Apparently it didn't take a whole lot to keep the old fellow happy on his celestial throne in a place called Heaven.

That was until their father died, then their mother changed. Shortly after his death she went into a deep depression, and even though the minister would come for visits to the house, it didn't do any good. When she asked why this happened, all he would say is God works in mysterious ways. Their mother said one day, she would do what she could to understand, so she began reading and reading. She would bring home so many books from different libraries and she bought many books on all different spiritual religions and teachings, that eventually she had her own personal library.

She started to change, seeing life and spirituality in a different way compared to her church days. Once the children got older and could understand what she taught, she showed them things.

Dave couldn't wait any longer, blurting out. "What has happened that has caused this?"

Their mother took a deep breath before beginning, "You know I've been taking this long distance course for several years now. Well, they want me to go to the school for an advanced training program, which means staying in the city for three months. They say computers are the way of the future, so I have a good chance at a career now. Perhaps one day we will be able to communicate with the world by computer. We don't even get good television reception out here, so that would be wonderful."

"Oh boy! When do we pack?" Dave replied enthusiastically. A trip to the city was just what was needed right now to finish off the summer vacation. It would be entirely different, until home school started back in the fall. Dianne's face lit up, thinking of the exciting possibilities ahead.'

Their mother looked at both of them with a look they didn't like. "That's the problem, I have to live on campus and there isn't enough room. I have to go alone."

Dianne looked down at her plate and asked, "How long did you say you would be away?"

"It will take three months sweetie; no longer, then I will graduate and it will be over."

She reached out with both hands placing one on Dianne and the other on Dave's shoulder.

"You know how important this is for all of us. The insurance benefits will run out and I have to support us somehow."

That wasn't the problem. The real problem was, they were close and ever since the accident they hadn't been apart for any length of time. This news was coming as a shock.

Dianne stared at her mother, "Mom that's not what worries me. Are we going to look after ourselves while you are gone? What about groceries and feed for the animals? What do we do if something bad happens?"

"I've arranged all of this, the grocery and feed store have a delivery service so that's not an issue. You just have to phone when you need anything and it will be taken care of, and I've also arranged for someone to stay with you."

Both children's eyes opened wide, exchanging glances, before they both asked at the same time. "Who?"

"Your Uncle Hugh." The children had met their uncle after the accident when they went to the hospital to see him. Neither of the children could really remember what he looked like because he was covered in bruises and casts. All they remember was the feeling of wanting out of there. It wasn't a pleasant sight. They were much younger; it all seemed like a nightmare. Their mother and uncle had kept up with each other on the phone. He had never visited, since the accident, because he didn't drive after that. Living where he did, it was too long for a day trip. They only talked to him rarely, when he called their mother.

This was all quite an unexpected shock as their mother kept going over the details. They were unnerved by this sudden turn of events; there was something else behind all this that they couldn't get a grasp of; something hidden but important.

They pretended they were happy for their mother who was excited talking about what all this meant for them. As they listened, part of them wasn't happy with it all. It was going to mean a secure future, but it caused them to ponder what the unknown future might really be, given the dreams, déjà vu and spiritual messages they had seen today.

They each gathered up their dirty dishes. This was usually left to their mother except on the days when they earned their allowance. Tonight was different. They wanted to stay with their mother, partly for security reasons and partly to gather more answers.

"When is he coming?" Dianne asked.

"Well, I'm not sure, in the next couple of days."

"Why don't you know?"

"Because he's walking cross country through the nature reserves to get here, so when he shows up that's when he gets here."

Both children stared at each other in disbelief. Dave silently mouthed the word 'walk' then shook his head.

"Mom, that's got to be close to two hundred kilometers in a straight line, never mind the hills and mountains."

"Yes I know. But he said he was going to skirt the mountains and stay along the hill country. It can get dangerous this time of the year with slippery rocks from the night fogs higher up, so he thought it wouldn't take as long, and it wouldn't aggravate his arthritis."

"He has arthritis?'

"Yes, ever since the accident he has suffered from arthritis, because of all the broken bones."

Both Dianne and Dave stopped what they were doing and asked.

"What did happen?"

Their mother looked at them with a hurtful expression slowly creeping across her face. She wiped her hands dry and sat down at the table with them.

"Your father picked up your uncle Hugh to bring him here for the weekend to help finish the barn. Your father hadn't planned to do this, but when your uncle called by chance, he insisted on coming to help. Your father picked him up, but on the way back there was a drunk driver. He struck their car, your father was killed, while our uncle suffered terrible injuries, but the drunk driver got off with just a few minor wounds. Your uncle became a changed man after the accident, becoming very quiet and wouldn't talk for the longest time. The ambulance attendants said he kept screaming something ridiculous like, "The Nears are here!" or something like that. Who knows when you are in so much pain? He claimed he watched your father die. I don't want to talk about this anymore, not when so much positive is about to happen."

The children could see from the expression on her face that it was better to drop the topic for now. They decided to change the subject by relating the story of the fishing trip, telling the details of the unforgettable event. The look on her face slowly faded, along with the memories receding into that area of the mind, where resides the past.

The Sneakeeze walked slowly in no hurry to go back to the Land of Afar. Putting all their memories away for now of the past, they were going to make the most of this. Wandering along, they touched flowers and plants absentmindedly, almost toying with them, feeling the different shapes and textures. They learned this when they were quite young. Just by the feel of the plant, they knew which ones tasted good. Lurky picked a golden colored plant, before handing Slinks a piece for him to try.

"This is a good's one Slinks, tries it." Slinks gave it a sniff and stuffed it into his mouth before shaking his head in agreement.

"Lurkys always knows a goods plant when he's tastes it," replied Slinks.

Lurky accepted the compliment, vigorously waving his ears. He scraped his foot across the ground embarrassed by his friend.

"Well I's practices alots," answered Lurky, matter of fact.

"Slinks does yous thinks we could finds plants like this goldy rod that would's makes us invisibles to old Lordy Misphtpht?"

"I's don'ts knows Lurkys. It's already puts the look-sees on us when we's leaves Afars, so mosts likely not." Disappointment came across Lurky's face as the reality set in.

"I's was justs hopings. That's all's."

"Me's toos, buts you's nevers knows. I's never gives up hopes." Slinks said giving Lurky a sincere look. Lurky's ear turned down stroking his hand in affection.

"Come, let's goes does what we's was freeds ups to do's before a Nears shows up heres." Lurky looked around cautiously, nodding his head in agreement.

Traveling on through the day, they finally entered a small grove of trees, picking and eating plants and flowers. Lurky reached down without looking, grabbing a flower top with a bee collecting nectar on it. It stung him on the hand. He tossed the flower to the ground howling, causing Slinks to jump back startled. This allowed the bee to fly up into a tree. Slinks realized what was there, seeing the bees swarm around a large hive, hanging several meters above their heads. Lurky licked his hand trying to reduce the pain from the sting, as Slinks pointed up at the tree saying, "Looks Lurky's, there's honeys on the Sneakeeze menu todays!"

Lurky's ears almost pointed straight up at the word 'honey'. This was Sneakeeze's favorite food above all else.

Walking a short distance away so not to disturb the bees, allowed them to quiet down and go back into the hive. Lurky had forgotten his sore hand, rubbing them together bouncing up and down with anticipation at the thought of having honey. This time Slinks lost the toss, so he approached the tree with a long stick. Lurky concealed himself crouched down behind some bushes.

Summoning up his courage, Slinks went underneath the hive, took a deep breath. He gave the hive a hard smack, knocking it off the branch. The hive hit the ground, coming to a rest with the hole sticking up, allowing every bee with a stinger left, the opportunity to come out. Slinks stood over the nest, giving it several flaps with his ears to make sure he got every bees attention.

His ears did the job, as every bee focused on the two large round targets, stinging without mercy. Slinks straightened up with his ears covered with bees. He ran away with his swarming stinging entourage, yelling, "Ouch! Ow! Oh! Ouch!"

Lurky waited until he was satisfied the bees were gone with Slinks, and grabbed the honey cones from the destroyed hive. He ran off, hiding from any bees that might decide to come back. He listened to Slink's complaints about the bee attack growing fainter. Licking at the honey that had gotten on his hands, he waited. He saw Slinks coming through the bushes, running as fast as he could without the bees. Slinks had taken the bees far away before making a mad dash to get rid of them.

Lurky observed Slinks ears, almost wincing at the appearance. "Is yous alrights Slinks? They's was a lots of bees in this hive."

Slinks stared at his friend proudly, "It's takes more's than some nasty's old bees to keeps Slinks away from some honeys! Let's have some's!" He said rubbing his hands together.

Lurky brought out two piles of honeycomb covered in liquid honey. Slicks started licking his lips in anticipation.

Lurky gave Slinks the largest comb, since he did all the work taking the abuse from the bees. He licked at the gooey dripping ambrosia, making audible awing and moaning noises showing his satisfaction at having this special meal.

Suddenly a bee came buzzing up to them. Slinks snatched the bee, flinging it down onto the log, where it bounced buzzing furiously. Slinks barely looked as he reached down and gave it a well-aimed finger flick, which sent the upset bee hurtling though the air into some bushes. After several minutes it regained its awareness, shakily flying off. Lurky watched as Slinks gave a audible 'Huh", basically saying one bee was nothing. They were quiet until they had licked every last morsel of the honey off their hands.

Lurky walked off, while Slinks just watched, thinking he had to go to the bathroom. He came back with a handful of mud and various pieces of ground up plants mixed with it. Sitting down he dabbed the mixture on Slink's ear welts, telling Slinks how brave he was to get them a treat and how he appreciated it. Slinks closed his eyes make "Ahs" and "Ohs' at each application of healing mud, grateful his friend cared enough to help him in his time of discomfort.

Once done, making sure he got all the stings, Lurky sat down beside Slinks. Their ears wrapped around each other's shoulders to settle in for the night as darkness started to descend upon them. Lurky was careful not to wrap his ears too tightly on Slink's sore ears. They closed their eyes for some well-deserved sleep as nightfall enveloped them. The bird's chorus of low chirping lulled them into a deep dream about mounds of honey.

HUGH WALKED FAST, FOLLOWING THE game trail, listening to the bird's chorus of low chirping. He used the easiest path possible, except for the odd windblown deadfall tree across the trail. His thoughts were deep in a daydream he didn't particularly like. After a while, his body warmed from the exertion and he started to enjoy the walk. He loved being out in nature, smelling the unique smells and subtle odors of decaying vegetation. He enjoyed listening to and watching the wildlife. He tried his best to walk quietly; he got to see more wildlife that way. There was a large forest reserve near where he lived. The city had put walking trails through it and he thoroughly enjoyed going for strolls, taking pleasure in all that nature offered.

Other times he would stay off the trails heading cross-country, but when he told people this, they said he was crazy and would end up lost. He knew he would always come out somewhere, so that made it fun.

Moving along, his thoughts couldn't stay away from the past and the fear. It was like having a constant loud dialogue with someone else, while he tried to maintain emotional control.

He was preoccupied with his thinking and didn't hear it coming, but he was lucky enough to see the deer loping towards him on the trail. He was standing still beside a hemlock bush. The deer didn't notice him, running by with its eyes bulging with fear. It was putting distance between itself and whatever was up ahead on the trail.

After allowing it to run out of sight he looked ahead, but there was nothing to see. He took a deep breath, keeping vigil of any sign of movement. He had gone about one hundred meters when he heard a faint noise off to the right. He ducked behind an upturned root.

To his surprise, a creature a little larger than a dog came bursting out from behind some bushes. It waved its arms in the air around an enormous pair of ears. There was a small swarm of bees chasing it. Obviously it had gotten into a hive and was reaping the benefit of the angry bees. He could hear the creature yelling as the bees made their anger known, before running back off through the thicket, out of sight. He had no idea what it was. It certainly didn't look like a Near he had seen that night. He instinctively knew it had something to do with finding the flasks.

He waited until he was sure it was gone, proceeding with the utmost caution. He scanned all around, not sure what to expect. After going several hundred meters he quickened his pace, doing the best he could to get away. He wasn't sure of what he had just seen or what this creature was capable of, if he confronted it.

Making sure nothing was following him; he noticed it was getting darker. Normally he would break out his gear to camp for the night, but this was not going to be one of those times. Taking a deep breath, he continued down the trail. Glancing behind every now and then, he reassured his mind nothing was following, waiting to pounce on him. Darkness enveloped him. Finally he came to a logging road, stopping he got out his compass to be sure of which direction to take. Satisfied, he headed down the road. The moon came up shining a ghostly bright grey, giving enough light to allow him to see ahead, without tripping on any debris. He made excellent progress in what would have been a troublesome endeavor without the moonlight.

He walked the entire night. He was happy he had bought a good quality packsack, moving like he was. The hours went by as the moon did its silent glide across the night sky on its preordained path. He was glad he was used to walking through bush, since it could get quite spooky at night when you couldn't see much.

On occasions, he would startle animals that would flee noisily into the overgrowth, causing him to jump. Finally the moon reached the horizon, as he came to a small valley with a large creek splashing down over some rocks. He stopped before going towards the sound, electing to stay up higher. He didn't realize how tired he was until he stopped. Pulling off his pack, he grabbed the flashlight to scan for a dry place to rest. Finally in his sleeping bag, he was glad to be able to rest. He retrieved his hunting knife and laid it down on the ground beside him, just in case.

Nervous from his encounter earlier, his mind still shouted thoughts. He tried desperately to get some rest. He closed his eyes, not wanting to think any more about what had gone on. He deliberately made his mind bring up good scenarios from his life to get it off the track it was on.

He focused on breathing, so that his mind would settle down. Eventually, he sank into a light sleep where he was dreaming, but also aware of noises around him. However, his dreams were disturbing in their fanciful content of a barren land shrouded in fog.

In the fog, the semblance of a black face slowly emerged. Ghostly, white, shining eyes stared intently at him. He realized the eyes were aware of him watching. Out of the fog he could see other black shapes moving about as a voice cackled, "I'll make you cry!"

He bolted upright gasping, holding his knife, not aware that he had even grabbed it, quickly scanning around for any sign of a threat. His wide-open eyes showed the terror he felt inside. Seeing he was in no danger, he laid back down, wondering what to think of the dream.

In the daylight the birds were in full chorus of greeting the world. He inhaled deeply, relieved to find he was there listening to nature, instead of facing whatever was in the dream. He decided a cup of herbal tea would help, so he removed the small propane cooking unit and a small pot from the pack, placed the pot on it and lit it. He pulled out an energy bar and started eating. He knew this part of the country well. He had hunted most of it over the years with his father and brother. This was why he was able to reach the road in the night. The road went for a hundred kilometers through the wild land, as a logging road and firebreak. It was always said that if you were lost and you reached the road, you were home.

After being out here for years, he learned certain signposts, like a large pinkish colored boulder, or a large pine on a hill or certain contours of the land. People not looking at maps before venturing in, occasionally got lost. Some came into the wilderness, leaving suddenly without taking their belongings; some leaving in the middle of the night. The long gouged-out tire marks on the gravel roads attested to the terror they had experienced by whatever it was that visited them. It was an unwritten rule of the locals, not to talk about it in civilized conversations. The word 'haunted' can cover many different things to different people. Sometimes these things were better left unspoken.

Hugh sat staring thinking about these things. After witnessing what he had yesterday, he realized why people fled leaving behind their tents and belongings. He was sure if he told anyone what he had seen, they would never believe him. He decided silence was his best friend. This area was familiar ground, and he regretted it had been such a long time since he had come back. He listened to the water flowing down below, and reminisced about hunting trips he had with his brother before the accident. Thinking about the past, especially the good things can make the present go fast. He realized it was time to leave, so he packed his things and began the journey. Feeling his body, reminded him of yesterday's exertion.

Laughingly he said out loud, "Don't worry bones, there's plenty of time to moan when I get to where I'm going."

He headed down towards the creek watching he didn't slip. At the bottom he followed the flow of the water. He followed the game trail along the edge, allowing him to miss brambles and brushy spots that flourished near the water.

It was a beautiful day, the sun warmed the air, and this made him feel good. Finally he came to the top of a small hill, with the valley spreading out before him. In the distance was the farm that was his brother's dream. It had been there as long as he could remember. His family knew Mr.

Wilson who had lived there alone all his life, and who eventually moved to a facility for the elderly and sold the place to his brother.

He took a deep breath and started down the slope. Eventually, he noticed two fresh sets of children's footprints in the soft soil, indicating they had been down to the creek recently. Standing at the edge of the field gazing out at the white house, he saw the run-down appearance of everything. The place needed fixing, since it was obvious no one had done anything for awhile.

He now realized there was more than one reason he had ended up there. He rested for a moment a little apprehensively, feeling the sun's warming strength and yet knew he would be glad to see the children, and Susan, the real reason he had come.

THE FLY HAD BEEN RESTING apprehensively on the tree as the sun's warming strength increased, seeing a spider nearby. It buzzed any dew off its wings, lifting off weaving and bobbing, flying through the early morning stillness. It started to tire, deciding to rest on a warm large soft object.

Quietly landing, it realized this smelled much different than the usual rotting heaps of animal dung or organic matter. It started crawling around for a good inspection.

Slinks lay snoring on his side, his ear rose up and down with his breathing. He dreamed about mountains of delicious honey, oblivious to the real world around him.

The fly buzzed its wings, tasting new flavors from Slinks ear, tickling it, causing it to jerk around from reflexes. The jerking caused the fly to really start buzzing, tumbling over the sensitive surface of the ear. This made the ear even more active.

Now, in Slinks dreamland of honey, things were changing as the sound of the fly's incessant buzzing registered. The sound appeared in the dream like millions of angry bees, appearing out of a mound of honey that had no bees a moment before. They swarmed him, causing his legs to jerk and his arms to flail around, whimpering 'Ouches and Ows'.

His flailing hit Lurky sleeping beside him, waking him up. The fly decided it was time to get away and fly to Lurky's ear. In its haste, it flew right down into Lurky's sensitive ear, making an extremely loud buzzing sound. It sounded like bees. Lurky's eyes flew open and he screeched, "Slinks! Bees is back!"

He rolled around on the ground, swinging out at the imaginary bees swarming him. The fly did its best buzzing, trying to get back out into the daylight. Slinks jumped backwards, stumbling and swinging his ears for all he was worth, hitting them that aggravated the old stings.

He thought he was being assaulted again, screaming for all he was worth, "Ouch! Ow!"

Lurky managed to get to his feet allowing the angry fly to get out of his ear. The buzzing in his ear stopped. Lurky stopped screeching, realizing he wasn't bitten and there were no bees, just a fly that flew incessantly in front of him.

He grabbed the fly out of the air with his hand, holding it by the wings, making sure it wasn't a bee or a distant cousin of a bee.

Satisfied it was no threat, he held it up for Slinks to see, who was still swinging, thinking he was under attack.

"Look Slinks, its onlys a flys! Nots a bees!" Slinks stopped flailing around hearing Lurky's reassuring voice. He looked around to make sure Lurky was right. Satisfied there was no danger from the bees, he rubbed his tender ears gently with his hands and went to inspect the fly.

"Sees Slinks, justs a buzzys old flys."

Slinks didn't laugh, popping the fly in his mouth chewing savagely, before spitting the pieces out all over the ground. Lurky got a serious look on his face feeling sorry for the poor fly.

"Wells it was just a flys Slinks! The creeks overs theres, since yous mights wants to wash your mouths outs." He made a grimacing gesture at the thought of eating a fly. They weren't on the menu, especially after seeing what a fly's favorite foods were.

He preferred bugs, the big fat juicy ones that crunched when you ate them. In reality he would eat just about anything, even a nice squirmy dew worm fresh out of the ground. All this thinking about food made him hungry. There were some tasty flowers in front of him, so he contented himself with having them for a first snack

Slinks returned to find Lurky happily munching away.

"What's yous eating theres Lurks?"

Lurky grabbed a handful of flowers, pulling them off the plant and thrusting them in front of Slink's face, "Flowies. Wan' sombes?"

Speaking with his mouth full, caused one petal to fly out of his mouth floating in the air right to Slinks nose. He went cross-eyed, attempting to see what it was. Lurky burst out laughing seeing the look on his friend's face. Laughing so hard, he stepped backwards and fell over a log, flinging the flower petals in the air all over Slinks. Slinks didn't particularly get the humor of the situation. He watched Lurky roll around on the ground, waiting patiently until the laughing subsided somewhat.

"Is yous dones? We's gots a longs ways to does, don't ya knows."

Lurky got up off the ground, still snickering as Slinks said, "Let's goes. Yous the listener," pointing in the general direction they had to go in.

Lurky spread his ears and slightly rotated side-to-side getting a fix.

"Noises echoes says that'a way!" pointing in a direction that almost paralleled the creek. Off he went, saying nothing, while Slinks followed. Sneakeeze had the unique ability to pick up an echo of a sound up to several days after it was made. It kept them on track, depending on the type of noise made and how far away it was.

They walked in silence enjoying the morning freshness of the air. The sun evaporated the dew off everything, as little wisps of fog rose into the air above the plants and ground. They enjoyed listening to the birds talking and singing. It made them feel like they weren't in the quiet of nowhere. Their spirits were lifted by the melodies, making Lurky sort of chirp along, although he wasn't very good at it. Finally he turned to Slinks, "Birdies makes me happys Slinks. Likes everythings okays evens if it seems nots."

Lurky had a point. Slinks never heard a bird sing an angry song or an unhappy song, even when the weather was at its worst. Usually if anything, they would quiet down during inclement weather, but even during the worst nature could produce, their songs had a hopeful 'soon it would be over' note to their singing.

"Yous righty right Lurky old buddys. They's seems happys todays." Realizing he was feeling much better inside. However, every now and then, it seemed like they were being watched by something dark, something not happy. This feeling of being watched would bring out the worst dark thoughts about what could happen to them, if they failed in their mission for Lord Misanthropy.

For now he chose not to think about this, instead he chose to enjoy listening to Lurky do his worst imitation of what otherwise would be a good bird song. They picked at flower tops and any edible bugs that had the misfortune of crawling or flying within their reach. There is a Sneakeeze saying, 'bugs and flowers does a meal makes'.

Slinks stopped to pick a flower, while Lurky kept walking ahead. Enjoying the flower, Slinks watched Lurky jump off to the side into some bushes. A quiet squeaking and squawking noise came from the spot. Several birds flew out, intent on flying away as fast as they could. He moved to where he last saw Lurky. Suddenly Lurky came out of the bushes munching on something.

Slinks gasped as he saw a large portion of a bird's wing sticking out of the corner of Lurky's mouth. He was happily chewing on the rest of the bird. Slinks couldn't believe that Lurky hadn't shared, especially a bird.

"Lurkys! You's didn't saves me a pieces of birdies! Hows coulds yous!" exclaimed Slinks, not understanding his friend's greed. Lurky shook his head no, maintaining a silly grin, munching merrily away. Slinks became furious. His ears flapped back and forth indicating a fight was about to take place. Lurky saw he was pushing Slinks, so pulling out his hand he from behind his back, he revealed another limp bird.

Smiling he said, "That's causes I's gots ones for you's toos!" Several bird feathers shot out of his mouth as he spoke. Slinks didn't notice these. His full attention was on the breakfast that Lurky was holding in his hand. His ears stopped flapping, and a smile replaced the look of scorn as he graciously accepted Lurky's gift.

Lurky laughed at the joke he had just played. His laughing, dislodged some more feathers from the wing still in the corner of his mouth, making their way down his windpipe. His laughing immediately turned into a coughing fit, making feathers fly from his mouth in all directions.

It was worse than a pillow fight on Friday night, until he managed to cough out all the stuck feathers. He stood there for a few moments, breathing heavily, before bending down to pick up the wing he had coughed out. He stood there for a few moments, breathing heavily trying to resume some control.

"The wings is the bests parts."

Slinks just shook his head in disgust as he tore off the wings of his bird and handed them to Lurky.

"Heres, haves mines toos thens." He popped the rest in his mouth, grateful to have it and his friend. Lurkys eyes widened with surprise at the gift he just received. Grinning he knew he had done the right thing by getting the birds.

Lurky said nothing more as he continued onwards, making little crunching and chewing noises.

Every now and then, a feather would quietly float in the air, a mute testimony of a bird that once made a happy sound. Forever silent, they slowly landed, lying still on the cool damp ground.

INSTEAD OF A SLEEP THAT was silent, Dave stirred, hearing noises and he knew why. The birds were making happy sounds. Their songs brought him peace and contentment, especially when he was troubled. Remembering his dreams from last night, a dark feeling came over him.

He tried to recall the details, but all he could get was flying over the same barren land he saw in other dreams. This time, hideous creatures followed on the ground, trying to grab him to pull him down.

They were running along shouting, "Have no fear, when we Nears are here!" He was terrified of them and knew if they grabbed him, his life would be changed forever, for the worst.

In the dream, the more he paid attention to them, the more he sank down towards them. They increased their verbal beckoning for him to join them. He was flying several meters above them and they were trying to grab him.

Feeling a pain in his heart, he looked down at this chest area. A flash of golden light made him jolt awake. With his hand on his chest, his heart racing, he lay there trying to calm himself down. Now he realized that's what woke him, not the birds.

The trouble with dreams was they were confusing and weren't always logical. Sometimes, he didn't remember his dreams until days later. Right now, he wasn't in the best of moods and would rather forget the whole thing. He then heard several dishes rattling, meaning his mom was up and making breakfast. Suddenly, he had intense hunger pains, prompting him to get up and get dressed.

Dianne stirred in the next bedroom and dropped something. Dave heard it, and wanted to beat her downstairs before she grabbed the favorite chair. He threw on his shirt without adjusting it, pulled on his jeans, and fought to get his socks on right. Listening for noises from his sister's bedroom, everything was quiet. He flung the door open, thinking she had already beaten him downstairs. Entering the hallway, he took three steps and was suddenly pushed backwards by his sister, who was waiting to ambush him.

It caught him by surprise as he shouted, "Hey that's not fair! I was ahead of you!"

"Not so loser! My door's closer to the kitchen. Besides, losers always complain how unfair it is to be behind the winner!" She headed down the stairs as fast as she could, squealing and laughing. He tried to grab her from behind, but she slipped away. He ran behind her, giving a hideous monster-type laugh, which made her squeal louder.

"Mom he's after me! Save me from this horrible fiend!"

"I see now, why he didn't even brush his hair before coming down."

Dianne agreed with her mother, and was standing behind the favorite chair.

"Besides he smells too, even though he wears deodorant, besides all monsters smell. Right mom?"

"What would you know?' Dave said, slipping into the favorite chair in front of her.

"Mom, that's not fair, I was here first!" Dianne said, smacking Dave in the head.

"Losers talk about being first. Winners sit down! Besides you know the rules. First one sitting gets the chair; everyone else is left standing there." Dave teased. Dianne stuck her tongue out at him in defiance.

"Next time buster." She whispered in his ear with malicious intent.

Their mother brought over the steaming oatmeal pot, placed it down on the table. Dave breathed deeply savoring the delicious smell.

"There's nothing like a good bowl of oats in the morning. After all what's good for the goats to eat, has got to be good for this critter," rubbing his hands in anticipation. His sister gave him a contemptuous look. He greedily helped himself to the cereal, heaping the bowl until there was little room for milk.

Dianne retrieved one large ladle full, plunking it in the middle of her bowl leaving ample room for milk. Talking to no one in particular she said, "I suppose it is better to be a goat than a pig."

"Naaaht that it matters, but once a goat always a goat." He replied flickering his eyelids, sprinkling cinnamon over his cereal.

"You two stop bickering. I need you on your best behavior today, when Hugh hopefully arrives." Both children immediately forgot what they were talking about.

"When is he coming mom?" Dianne asked, realizing she had forgotten her mother was leaving and a strange person was going to be looking after them.

"Any time now, dear. I want the two of you not to give him a hard time. This will be difficult enough for him. He has no children of his own. Is that understood?"

They both looked down in silent agreement, before verbally agreeing to cooperate.

"He's not weird is he?" Dave asked seriously.

"No, in fact he's a wonderful man. That's the reason he's the only one I trust with you two. "

She suddenly got this dreamy, happy look for a brief moment. It was like she had just let out a thought from her private side. The side the children were never allowed into.

"It will be good to be around someone else besides me, even though it will be new for the both of you. I have a good feeling about all this.' She said smiling at the children who were trying to assimilate what was being said. Fears and concerns about the unknown, were beginning to invade their consciousness.

Their mother placed an arm around their shoulders, giving them both a hug and kiss.

"I am so lucky I have the two of you in my life. I know you will do your best to help Hugh out. Besides I will call when I can, so you see that everything will be okay. If it's not, you will let me know. Agreed?"

"Yes mom." They both spoke in unison understanding her phone calls were their safety valve.

"Now can you two do the chores when you are done breakfast? I have some last minute packing to do, so when he comes I can leave right away."

She started humming some unrecognizable song. The children sat watching her go.

"She only hums when she's really happy," whispered Dianne.

"I know. It's almost like she's glad he's coming."

Finishing their oatmeal, Dianne used her spoon politely, scooping out the remnants. Being a boy, Dave saw no need for that unless you were with company. He simply picked up the bowl, placed it to his lips, and with deliberate slurping, emptied what was left, giving out a loud, "Ahhhh!"

"I knew your mouth was rather large, but that's the first time I ever saw it fit right around the bowl. Be careful, if you accidently swallow it, I am sure you will go cross-eyed when it comes out the other end."

Dave just ignored her, placing the bowl and spoon in the sink, "Well, I won't end up being a Naaanny when I'm older."

Seeing Dave heading for the door, was the signal for her to beat him to the barn. She rose, tossing her dishes into the water in the sink with a splash.

"Not so fast buster! Just watch this goat girl out run the piggy any old day!" He was running off the porch without touching the stairs, but he stumbled, rolling over onto the dirt. Dianne saw the advantage she had been given, gave out a shriek and ran down the steps and across the yard shouting, "Is that where a piggy starts their day? A good morning kiss to the dirt! Ha!"

"This piggy eats girly goats for breakfast every day!" He yelled, chasing after her.

They made it to the barn with her slightly ahead of him. This wasn't usually the case, so she rubbed it in.

"The galloping goat girl made it ahead of the wiggly piggy boy. The crowd goes wild! Yah!" Doing a little dance, and raising her arms in the air like a winning athlete would.

"That wasn't fair! I slipped!"

"Cry me a river piggy boy. I need to go for a boat ride!" Dianne said, lifting the latch on the barn door. The latch had seen better days, and suddenly broke off in her hands.

"Well, that's the last one in the barn that latched, so now none of them work."

Looking around, it suddenly became painfully clear, the state of disrepair. Now all the doors had binder twine latches. There were boards that had been just nailed back on haphazardly. Broken tools leaned against the walls where they were last left. Debris had accumulated over time and dust-coated spider webs hung from virtually every post, beam and corner. They both gave out a loud sign, as the reality of their life came back in harsh focus.

"I'll go get some more binder twine. After all it's the farmer's best friend when a repair is needed." Dave said, trying to make light of what otherwise would turn into a depressing examination of their world. It never seemed to change, one melancholic day into the next.

As Dave looked over at his sister's clothes and his, he was very aware of them being second hand from the local charity store, where his mother had to go to supplement their food. He looked at the rundown house. Everything about their home showed a state of disrepair. He was a boy, with no idea how to fix these things, so this was their life. He made the best of it, unknowingly using humor as a salve for the soul.

"You go get some food for the goats, I'll fix this. Once the hinges fall off the doors, the critters will be able to go in and out as they please. We'll just leave the grain bag out in the middle of the yard so they can help themselves."

His sister gave him looks like he was short a kernel of corn in the grain bin. "Whatever! Just remember what happened to Nanny when she helped herself to the grain all night?"

Dianne looked at the two goats lying in the corner. Both goats gave out a quiet Naaah, knowing it was feeding time. They put their heads up waiting for a scratch and pet from the girl.

"How's my goaties today? Did you have a good sleep?" She said, giving

Nelly a scratch under the chin, while Nanny gave her an affectionate lick on her hand.

"I had an unusual dream again about that place I fly over, but this time there were these hideous creatures trying to capture me. It was so awful, I woke up." Dave said.

"I know I keep getting weird, scary premonitions but I can't sense where they are coming from. I did get just a flash of a horrible dark face with cold, white eyes that seemed to look right through me. I don't like it." Dianne said giving a shudder.

"I wonder if any of this has to do with Uncle Hugh coming. I hope this is a good thing, him staying here. I haven't had any bad dreams about him."

"I haven't felt anything bad about him. In fact, strange as it seems, I feel all right about him coming," replied Dianne.

She waited, while Dave strung the binder twine to make a latch. Stepping out into the bright light, they squinted when she looked over at the far field. A figure was coming their way.

"Look, someone's coming! I think it's him!" She grabbed Dave by the arm.

LURKY GRABBED SLINKS BY THE arm. A feather was lodged in his throat making him gag. Finally, he ended up in a real coughing fit, trying to dislodge the stubborn thing. Squinting across a field, he pointed to the creek nearby, indicating he required a drink to wash it down.

"That's will teach you to eats bird's wings Lurky. It's probably's the birdies revenge." Lurky just stuck his tongue out at Slinks, as a response. Bird's wings tasted pretty good once you acquired a taste for them, or so he thought.

Going over to the water, he took a mouth full, gargled with his head bent back, almost singing. Slinks stood there shaking his head, with hands on his hips, waiting patiently.

Lurky spit the water out. Satisfied he had gotten rid of the ticklish piece, he sprayed water several meters away. Lurky realized this was fun. Bending down, and getting another mouthful of water, he pretended he still had a feather problem. He sprayed the far bank trying to knock a caterpillar off a branch. After three tries, Slinks knew he wasn't having any real troubles.

"Don't makes me come over there's and drowns you Lurky!"

Lurky knew the play time was over, pretending to clear his throat. He took one last good swallow water, stood up and went back to Slinks,.

Lurky started quietly singing, plucking flowers, flinging them at Slinks. Slinks said nothing, until a whole plant including roots, landed with a slight thud behind him.

"You's be's carefuls or you's be eating plants, roots and alls."

Lurky grabbed a whole handful of flowers, shoving them in his mouth all at once, mumbling, "Hows can I's whens my mouths fulls!" He said laughing, dancing, twirling. He grabbed a large bouquet of flowers and stuck them between his nose and upper lip.

"Looks Slinks! I 's gots a rosey posie on my nosie."

He heard a familiar noise in the flower, noticing a bee. He looked cross-eyed knowing what it was. Shrieking, he ran backwards trying to get away without dropping the bouquet. Slinks just laughed.

Suddenly, Lurky really screeched, dropping out of sight. Slinks heard a loud splash. He hurried to see if Lurky was alright. Arriving at the edge of the lake they hadn't seen, he saw Lurky sitting waist deep in water sputtering and spitting.

"Yous tolds me yous coulds smells a lake a longs ways aways Lurky." Slinks laughed.

"I cans hears better then smells Slinks! Besides I's founds it, didn't I's?" looking at the lake.

"The sounds stills comes from theres, but its gettings fainters."

The lake was large and it would take a walk to find the far end. "Let's takes a breaks and you's dries. We's goes to the fars end and I's listens then."

Sitting in the sunlight, he had his ears extended like umbrellas soaking up the heat. "Let's fills up our's teary flasks with waters before we's goes backs to the Lands of Afars. I's don'ts wants to drinks their teary soups untils I's has to," spoke Lurky.

"That's suits me's fine buddys. I's hates their teary soups," replied Slinks spitting on the ground in disrespect. He picked up a rock, throwing it at a tree to emphasize the point.

Lurky realized spitting was a good way to disrespect Nears, but not being a veteran of this despicable practice, his aim was off. His spit hung off the corner of his arm, slowly dripping off in a long string. He pretended it hadn't happened, since Slinks hadn't seen his poor aim. He put his arm down, brushing it off with leaves, without looking obvious. He decided, sometime he would have to practice more, but for now that was enough.

Deciding to pass the time like Slinks, he picked up a rock to toss, but apparently aiming is an issue in several areas of his life. The rock glanced off several trees landing in some bushes, making an unusual clunking noise before coming to rest. Looking at each other with surprise they went over to see the source of the sound. Hidden in the bushes was an overturned hunter's boat.

They both knew what a boat was. They came across humans camping by a river once. They were having a drink of water, when they heard noises upstream as people in a canoe floated by. The Sneakeeze had hidden behind brush, watching the canoeists having a great time.

It seemed like humans were happy gentle creatures, so they followed them. Lurky and Slinks decided that night to introduce themselves, hoping to get some of the great smelling food. It seems humans don't take kindly to company late at night. When they said hello, the campers said goodbye, or at least the screams and shrieks indicated that's what they were saying. The humans left all the great smelling food and almost everything else behind.

Whoever drove the vehicle sure knew how to make it move. It was no time before all was quiet and the humans were gone. They had a good feast, finishing off all the food that was left behind. There was no sense in wasting any of it, especially human food. They decided they wouldn't be so friendly to humans after that, since they seemed so unpredictable. Happy one minute, screaming the other.

Today, looking at the boat they had just found, they decided it would be a lot easier to float to the other side of the lake. They picked the overturned boat up and put it in. The overturned boat immediately sank.

"Slinks we's doing somethin's wrongs" Lurky said, looking inquisitively at the boat.

"Let's lifts it outs and turns it over." Sure enough when they did this, the boat floated like it should. Lurky was so happy they figured it out that he jumped right in almost capsizing the boat. He sat on the seat before almost falling in. Once the boat settled, he motioned for Slinks to climb in and without knowing what else to do Slinks gave it a little shove sending the boat further out into the lake.

They drifted there for a few minutes. It was such an unusual sensation to be out on the water, instead of in the water getting wet.

"Whats does we's do nows Slinks?" queried Lurky not having a clue what to do. Slinks remembered the humans held long sticks when they used a boat. Looking back at the shore, he noticed in their excitement, they had forgotten to get the sticks that came with the boat. It was too far away now, since the wind had picked up, propelling them farther out into the lake.

To jump in now would mean certain death. Neither of them knew how to swim. Slinks gave out a big sigh. He hated it when things didn't go as planned. This was one of them, stuck in a boat on a lake, without a paddle.

They drifted as the wind picked up, dark clouds were appearing over the mountains. He could faintly smell rain. Looking down at the rippling water, he watched a leaf with an upturned end getting pushed by the wind. He noticed Lurky's ears flapping in the breeze. He suddenly had an idea.

"Holds your's ears outs as much's as you's can Lurky." Lurky did and he felt the boat surge forward.

He stood behind Lurky stretching out his ears too. The boat picked up noticeable speed. Lurky noticed it as well, exclaiming, "Well that's whys I's hangs outs with yous Slinks causes I's gives you goods ideas!"

"Ya that's whys I's hangs outs with yous Lurkys, cause yous bigs ears is goods for something."

"Hey!" Replied Lurky, not sure if that was a complaint or not. Slinks kept looking at the darkening sky behind them. He noticed where they wanted to get to was much closer. The lake was choppy but before long they made landfall very close to where they wanted to go. Much to their relief but disappointment, the adventure was over. They could hear the sound of thunder, rolling behind them. It was strange standing on firm ground, after getting use to the movement of the boat.

Lurky stuck his ears up for a moment. "I's lost the hearing. Slinks it's your's turns."

They saw a hill off in the distance and decided it was a good spot to try to pick up the noise. They knew the storm was approaching fast. Once at the top of the hill Slinks climbed up onto Lurky's shoulders, while Lurky rotated around and around. Slinks kept his eyes closed, focusing his concentration, filtering out any noises other than the one he wanted. Hearing the two noises, he raised his hand pointing the way. They had to be sure. Confident he had the right bearing they spoke together.

"THERE'S NO SOUND
WHEN SNEAKEEZE TURN
THAT CAN'T BE FOUND
TOGETHER WE'S BOUND
TURNING, TURNING
TO HEAR THE SOUND
GOING AROUND, AROUND
LISTENING FOR LAUGHTER
LAUGHTER'S THE SOUND
THE SOUND THAT'S BEEN FOUND"

Slinks looked down at Lurky saying.

"Wells that's was easys. Lets gets goings." Expecting, Lurky to let him down.

Apparently Sneakeeze and elephants don't forget. Without speaking a word, he held onto Slink's feet falling backwards. Slinks got the full impact of the fall slamming onto his back, knocking the wind out of him.

The fall had shaken his body hard. Lurky just got up, wiping his hands off in an up and down motion saying, "Yup Slinks olds buddy that's that!" He started down the hill like there was nothing wrong.

He took four steps when Slinks caught up to him flying through the air snarling. Grabbing Lurky from behind, they tumbled down the hill entangled, arms and feet kicking. There was an animated discussion on who slammed who the hardest. They pummeled, screamed, and growled at each other all the way down to the bottom of the hill. The fight started to get serious. To their surprise, a bolt of lightning exploded from a tree nearby, causing such a thunderclap that they immediately let go of each other.

They had forgotten about the approaching storm, and now the rain started coming down. Looking around for shelter, they were fortunate enough to see an outcropping of rock that would shelter the two of them, if they snuggled together. Getting in against the rock, they were all right except for their fronts and legs, which were getting wet. They raised their ears out like umbrellas to make a protective barrier as the rain started to pour.

"This is a really's bad storms from the mountains of Afars Lurky," whispered Slinks shivering slightly from getting damp.

"Maybes the Lordie Misphphts is mads at's us. Once the rains stops maybes we's should gets goings." Replied Lurky, looking out at the weather. Slinks shook his head in agreement, snuggling to keep warm.

The storm the Lord had made did it's best to make the whole world miserable.

Lord Misanthropy sneered, knowing it was doing its best to make the whole world miserable. Deep in thought, it stared out at the barren landscape, listening to the tears splashing over the falls. Pure music to its ears was the occasional crying out, moaning, or sobbing as some newer tears went over the fall's edge. It never tired of the sweet music only it could hear, as humanity registered its helpless chorus of despair.

A gust of wind caused it to rewrap the loose corner of its robe to where it should be. Over the mountains, the clouds dark and ominous in their appearance signified a storm approaching. It sneered, realizing the black clouds suited the wonderful mood it was in. Suddenly, a brilliant flash of lightning from one of the clouds, gave it a sinister sneer.

"Ah!" as it inhaled deeply.

"Just what I need, change in the weather."

It extended its hand out towards the clouds over the distant mountains.

"Thank you for that flash of inspiration, even if it did come from me." A flash of lightning lit up all the clouds in one brilliant flashing, flickering display of power.

"I want to see Near Naturas Vandalic at once!" A Near Acolyte appeared at the door, bowing deeply.

"At once my Lord!" hurrying off across the Great Hall to fulfill its duty.

The Near wound its way downstairs, finally coming to a door that when you looked at it, you would just see a swirling mass of dark colored clouds. There was nowhere to knock. The Near grabbed the gold colored handle in the shape of lightning bolt. When it did the door cloud lit up in many jagged flashes of lightning. There was no shock from the bolts of lightning that flashed back and forth within the clouds, accompanied by the low rumble of thunder.

From behind the door a voice sounded like the sound of a ferocious windstorm.

"Enter!" Was all it said. The Near pushed on the thin cloud door and it opened inwardly.

There, at its desk sat Near Naturas Vandelic, dressed in a black raincoat. About a meter above its head, a dark ominous cloud poured rain like a monsoon all around it, and yet it wasn't wet. Its skin and hair were completely dry. However, the raincoat showed rain pouring down it. The floor and desk were dry as well.

On the wall behind it, a large mural of the worst hurricane you could imagine showed the wind ripping trees apart. Humans were in their disintegrating buildings, crying and begging for help. The storm surge flooded the building several meters deep. Suddenly, several screaming people were flung by a gust of wind, tossed into the foaming waters. They disappeared from sight, along with their last agonizing cries.

A film of dark clouds covered up the scene as all went quiet. The clouds dissipated, to reveal a huge tornado slowly creeping across farmland, tearing everything apart in its path. Farm buildings were reduced to matchsticks by the violent winds.

The swirling, massive, debris cloud in the sky surrounded the vortex of the tornado. Near Acolyte watched a bawling cow floating, tumbling and rolling in the violent swirl. It was followed by a squawking chicken, its feathers being ripped from its body, swirling around the cloud's debris edge.

Right behind them floated a man, woman and a child tumbling over and over at the whim of the wind. They had been sucked out of a house because there was no other shelter. The child screamed for its parents. Near Acolyte watched the look of horror on its face as it sped around the tornado, then out of sight, but not before the tears were virtually ripped off its young cheeks by the sheer force of the winds. The parents did not answer the pleading cries, they were already dead. They moved like two puppets animated by invisible strings of the merciless wind, before they too were gone from view.

Near Acolyte stopped watching the scenes of natural destruction. Its gaze focused on the Near seated in front of it. Now, there was no cloud above its head or sign of rain dripping down the raincoat.

"My Lord would like to see you out on the balcony. If you are not too busy working?"

"I assure you this is by no means work my friend," casting a hand at the mural which now had gone completely blank. The Near was amazed to see nothing but a wall where there had been scenes of destruction a few moments ago. It turned to walk out through the doorway, glancing at the door. It now was a solid door with a normal rounded faded brass handle, not the doors of clouds it had seen earlier. It was like it had imagined what it had just seen. It didn't look to see if Near Naturus Vandelic was following. It had other duties to do, so left the Near to go see the Lord by itself.

Near Naturus Vandelic wondered, why it was being summoned. It had kept up with its quota of violent storms as instructed long ago, sure to bring tears to any human who had lost their home, or loved ones from nature's fury.

It managed to do this by borrowing Mother Nature from Near Dissever. Once it had her, it would tease her, before throwing her into a small clear colored tear case. Shaking her violently, cursing and berating her with insults, it would manage to rouse her anger. Her anger would erupt as small flashes of lightning, which were transferred to the mural when she was placed on a stand in front of it.

It went out to the Great Hall without encountering anyone. It could hear the anguished cries from the tears cascading down the walls and the babies tear fountain lamenting choking wails. It knew, it might have had some small hand to play in making such exquisite sounding tears. A sneer crossed over its face at the thought of it all.

Going to the outside door, it was greeted by the Near Acolyte standing guard, who seeing Near Naturus Vandelic bowed sweeping its hand out towards the balcony, indicating the Lord would see it.

Near Naturus Vandelic walked up to its Lord who was staring out at the scenery. The voice of Near Naturus Vandelic even outside its office, sounded like a voice calling out in a wind.

"How may I be of service my Lord?"

Lord Misanthropy stared out over the lake. "Does the lake look like it could use more tears? It looks low." The Near stared at the brim full lake. The crying and sobbing coming from the Falls of Affliction seemed normal.

"How is the weather these days?" asked its master still gazing at the lake.

"It goes as planned. I must contend with the seasons thanks to Mother Nature's meddling before her capture, they interfere with the severity and duration of the storms." Answered the Near.

"Have the humans sufficiently ruined their environment to allow for more extreme weather?" it queried.

"I've seen a subtle change that could sway things to our advantage and wreak more havoc on them. This gives me the opportunity to play with seasons and global natural cycles. If they continue in their destructive ways, they will be easy to manipulate to do more.

"Good. See what you can do my friend. I believe it is time for a change in the weather."

Saying these words caused the clouds off to the south to light up with lightning. Thunder quietly rumbled until gone, across the bleak landscape.

Near Naturas Vandelic straightened up realizing it was not in trouble. Hearing the thunder made it realize even though it controlled the weather, its master controlled more than it.

"As you wish my Lord," replied the Near.

"I know you will, I have complete trust in you," placing its cold hand on its shoulder. This was a rare gesture of confidence not bestowed to just any Near. Near Naturas Vandelic sneered viciously.

"Thank you my Lord. I will begin," leaving with a bow.

Hurrying down the stairs it rubbed its hands together at the thought of conjuring up more storms. This time it was going to do what it could to make the human's lives miserable so that not only rain would fall but tears as well.

It raced to retrieve Mother Nature from Near Dissever's office. Making it back to its office the door opened automatically at its approach. The clouds on the door followed it, swirling around it. The door closed on its own and clouded back over.

Moving over to a shelf, it stared intently at four vases. One was a white snowflake, another light green grass shoots, and one had colored flowers, the last one had colored leaves all in ornate designs. Pulling the four seasons off the shelf, it sneered, "Nothing like shaking the weather up a bit."

Pouring some of the liquid from each vase into the clear case, over Mother Nature's head, it then gave it a severe shaking. There was a violent reaction, as the energy of the four seasons collided in the lightning she gave off. This was a total violation of nature. Mother Nature was powerless against this misuse, once these vases had been taken from her during her capture.

Near Naturas Vandelic sat at its desk, closing its eyes, saying,

"NEVER HAS THERE BEEN
SUCH AWFUL WEATHER
WITH WINDS AND RAIN
SNOWS, ICE SO TERRIBLE
HURRICANES, TORNADOS

SNOWSTORMS UNBELIEVABLE
DROUGHTS, FLOODS
FROSTS MOST FEARFUL
THAT I NEAR NATURAS VANDELIC
MAKE UNBEARABLE"

The room became quiet as clouds of the blackest color rose from the case. Lightening and rumbles of thunder could be heard in the clouds. Its chanting moved the clouds into a vortex, becoming a violent storm. The storm grew with an increase in the light and noise until it was deafening, making the whole castle shake. In a few seconds, the whole room was one gigantic storm. The Near was no longer there, it was now the storm and the storm was at its command. Suddenly the room went black as the Near went out to do its master's bidding, determined to see the current conditions change. The wind slowly died down from a roar to a whisper, and then was gone.

Walking up to the house, he was even more determined to help see the current conditions change. There were many things to be addressed. Going up to the front door, the curtain moved ever so slightly, meaning he was being scrutinized. He had seen the children running to the house. It was no surprise, when the door opened immediately after he gave it a hard knock, revealing Dave with Dianne standing behind him.

"Good morning Squire Dave and Lady Dianne. I am your uncle Hugh and I have walked field and forest to get to your humble abode. Every day is an excellent day but some more excellent than others and this is one. Is it possible I might enter and rest my weary body and refresh my lagging energy?" He requested bowing.

Both children's mouths fell open. This was not what they had expected, definitely not this. Dianne and Dave moved against the wall to allow their uncle to enter.

All Dave could say was, "Please come in."

Closing the door, he did notice birds were singing way more than they usually did. They were normally not singing at this time of day.

Dianne went upstairs looking for her mother, "Mom! He's here downstairs!"

Her mother appeared flustered, straightening her clothes, checking her appearance in the mirror. Dianne was surprised, since she hadn't seen her this way before. Dianne waited for her mother, not wanting to be alone with her uncle right away.

Going downstairs, they found Dave had taken him to the kitchen table. When they entered he stood up.

"Thank you for having me Sue. It has been such a nice change, going for a walk. I didn't realize how much I needed some fresh air and to stretch my legs. Being around new surroundings was just what I required."

"I'm the one who should be thanking you Hugh, for helping us out. I had no one else I could depend on and trust with the kids." She went over and gave him a hug. Both children gave each other a quick glance. This was not their usual mother. She was acting totally out of character with Hugh here. This was not the time to say anything.

"How was your walk over here? It is such a long ways to come. I hope everything was all right?" Hugh didn't hesitate. He wasn't about to tell them anything about what he had seen.

"Oh it was lovely! I communed with nature and thrilled at her many complexities and interactions of life. It was very entertaining and educational. There is nothing like forgetting the events we call life and becoming one with nature. It helps you realize and reconstruct your relationship with your world and life around you."

Both children snickered because of the way he spoke, rather than what he said. They, without realizing it, liked him. Totally at ease with him, neither could have said why. Their mother gave them a stern look without chastising them. It was enough to make them behave.

However Hugh saw it, saying. "Have fun with life, even the way you talk about it. Humor is the salve of healing for the soul. Especially, if life isn't the way you wish it to be. Life can be mundane, or it can be an adventure. It's all in how you choose. Take nature for example, how many people go outside first thing in the morning and just stand there listening and watching the world around them?

Would they notice nature is going about its business without worrying about their day, whether it will be good or bad. The birds sing their little hearts out greeting each other and sending out the beauty of their songs for the world to hear. Many humans on the other hand don't even notice nature. Instead their egos have them enslaved, either worrying about the future or regretting about yesterday's past. Ask them if they are having fun at whatever it is they are doing and the answer is usually NO!"

The children just sat there, dumbfounded, trying to understand what had just been said. It was true they didn't really notice nature around them especially when they were preoccupied with problems.

Hugh said nothing more and then looked at Susan. "I hope you are close to packed. There's a storm brewing over the mountains, so it wouldn't hurt to leave early."

Dave looked out the window. He hadn't noticed clouds in the sky, never mind a storm. His attention was brought back to his uncle.

"Perhaps you two could give me a grand tour of the premises, while your mother is finishing packing. I especially would love to see your livestock. You know I will enjoy the invitation to shown around," They were eager to show him everything. They headed for the door, babbling about the names of the animals and birds and what they do to take care of them. Hugh looked at Susan with a smile, "Well I'm in for it now."

"I'm sure you'll do fine." She turned to finish packing, giving him a silent verbal, "Thank you."

The children were motioning him to follow them, excited that he was actually interested in the place. They were determined to be the ultimate tour guides.

They started by taking him to the barn, telling him the history of how they got the goats and birds and their names, and how they enjoyed having them. Their uncle seemed preoccupied, scanning everything, noting every detail. He was making mental notes of what had to be replaced or repaired. Entering the barn, he saw the makeshift door latch.

"Who was the creative person that made up this twine door latch?"

Dave stared at the fix-it job he had just done, staring down at the ground.

"I did sir. I know it wasn't very good. I didn't know what else to do." Dave said embarrassed at his lack of skill. "Well, I don't know if you've noticed but I've had a lot of practice around here."

"First, don't call me sir. Call me Hugh. I want you to think of me as a friend. You did a remarkable job with what you had, Dave. You have learned to make the best of a situation. That is an admirable quality to have in a predicament. It means you can use your creative abilities when needed the most."

"I helped with the goat pen gate when the latch broke too, Hugh. Come and see." Dianne said, grabbing his sleeve to show her handy work.

"My! You both are intelligent and creative; you have done well with what you had to work with." Both children beamed with pride. Both goats came right over to Hugh when he stuck his hand over the top of the boards. They immediately started licking his hand, like they had known him for years.

Dianne was taken by surprise saying, "The goaties never do this with a stranger. They always hid over in the corner saying nothing. They really like you."

"I told you I like nature and in turn nature likes me." He spoke quietly to the goats, telling them how pretty they were. From there, he was given the grand tour of the chicken coup. He watched the birds scratching the last remnants of the grain thrown down earlier.

Hugh started saying. "Whawk, Whawk," out loud to them and they started talking back. The children stood there, not believing he could talk to birds and they would answer him.

"Well, shall we venture back to the house to see how your mom is getting along?" They said nothing but were in awe of this stranger who had shown up and was now showing them so much. Going across the yard, Dave heard a low noise off in the distance. Dark clouds of a thunderstorm filled the horizon.

"Look Hugh, you were right, there is a storm coming."

Hugh didn't even look, saying, "It's going to be a hum dinger. I wouldn't want to be caught in it. Now come on let's see how your mother is doing."

Entering the kitchen, Hugh kept observing everything. Reaching the porch, he turned gazing at the ominous clouds. He knew something wasn't right. There was high-pressure weather over their area. A storm of this size shouldn't be developing like it was.

He saw the children looking at several suitcases, by the door in the living room. Sensing the situation with their mother leaving was now sinking in, he spoke. "Why don't you two see how your mom is doing upstairs?"

They took his advice and quietly went upstairs. He retrieved a notepad and pen from his pack and started writing in it. Reaching the top of the stairs, they heard their mother in her bedroom humming a song as she completed her packing. They said nothing watching her. She didn't hum unless she was really happy which wasn't very often. They knew this was something very important to her.

Without looking at them, she stopped before speaking. "I'm going to miss you two more than you know." Turning around, there was a tear forming in the corner of her eye. Dianne went over throwing her arms around her, crying.

"I'll miss you mom. I know you have to do this. It's just we haven't been apart like this before since…"

"I know dear. This is going to be difficult for me too. I will think about you all the time I'm away. You will be in my thoughts and heart, and it is only for a short while. When I'm back I will be able to work here using the Internet. Just think, we will finally have a computer and you two can explore the worldwide internet. Won't that be exciting? Are you two comfortable with your uncle being here?"

Dianne spoke up, "Oh yes! He's a wonderful person. I get good feelings from him. Even my goaties liked him right away."

"Well, that says it all when Nanny and Nelly like him!" She said, laughing and wiping the tears off her cheeks.

"Are you alright son?" Dave wasn't one to cry in public; however a lump was gathering in his throat that he was desperately trying to control.

"Yes, I will make sure things go okay while you're gone."

"I knew I could count on you. I am so proud of you." Sue said, giving her son a long hug which he accepted, putting his arms around her.

"In fact, I'm so proud of both of you. I will miss you terribly, but I will call when I can, hopefully every day." She barely had enough money to do what had to be done.

"Help me with my bags. I'm ready and if we stand here doing this anymore, I won't go."

Dave grabbed her suitcase as the women went down the stairs together.

Suddenly, he had déjà vu about carrying the bags and the conversation the women were having. But he said nothing. He got downstairs where Hugh was waiting.

Hugh said, "Susan can I see you a moment alone please?"

Susan, wondered what was up, as he went into the living room, while she followed.

"Here's an envelope with $5000 dollars for you to use as you need and my calling card so you don't have to pay for the phone calls to the children."

"I can't accept that!"

"Yes you can and you will or I won't let you go. Got it!" He said smiling.

She didn't know what to say, she was so surprised. Instead she kissed him full on the mouth and hugged him whispering. "Thank you."

Hugh was taken by surprise by the thank you gesture, stammering.

"You're more than welcome!" The children were in total shock, but said absolutely nothing at the events that were taking place. Hugh didn't know what else to say, so he grabbed her suitcases.

"I'll take these out to the car."

"Mom, you are such a tart, even at your age!" exclaimed Dianne, making her mother blush.

"I was just saying thank you," replied Susan.

"Sure you were mom," interrupted Dave. "When we get the Internet, I'm going to look up older people's mating rituals for sure."

"Stop it you two. You're embarrassing me to no end." She hoped the conversation would change. "I must go before it gets dark. I'll call you the first chance I get. Please be good with Uncle Hugh. He didn't have to do this."

"We know mom. Don't worry we'll treat him like he's one of our own, especially since you kissed. It means you have to get married. That's the rural code."

"Stop that!" Sue said laughing, "Now give me a hug and I'll be on my way."

They shared a quiet moment together as only a family can, embracing each other. Tender kisses were exchanged bringing tears to their eyes. They followed her out to the car then stood with Hugh, saying nothing more. Instead, they waved as she pulled out of the driveway, watching her go until she could no longer be seen. What Dave did see, was the clouds. They appeared to be following her, but he said nothing. He didn't want to make the present moment any worse than it already was.

Lord Misanthropy stayed out on the balcony after dismissing Near Naturas Vandalic, watching the clouds moving away. It knew, it was going to make someone's present moment worse than it already was. For the humans, it was so easy making life miserable in many ways.

Nothing made the tear river flow better than that of the history of man's religions. It had an idea and it sneered in a most delicious way, pondering all this. Its eyes squinted as tears slowly flowed down its black cheeks, which it caught with its hands. Licking the salty sweet tasting liquid, it started moaning out loud at the ecstasy of tears energy, flowing from its own being.

The noise that came out of its mouth was the wailing crescendo of man's tormented misery. Bottled up for too long, it now needed to be expressed in its truest form. The sound echoed loudly back from the distant hills, rolling in intensity like thousands of civilizations heartsick. It was the sound of desolation expressed all at once, causing the castle to tremble with the vibrations. Nears came running to the door of the balcony to see if their master needed help, the Near Acolytes shooed them away, who were standing on guard at the door.

Finally Lord Misanthropy wheeled around to the door, causing several tears to fly off its cheeks landing on the stone floor, hitting with a loud bang. Small pieces of tear stone flew into the air. Small puffs of the black smoke drifted for a few moments, and then disappeared.

"Fetch me Near Credo at once!" This sent one of the Near Acolytes running for the hallway leading downstairs. Sometimes it skipped a stair, often colliding into the walls, and went around some corners too fast, to do its master's bidding.

Rushing down a long hallway, it finally came to do a door covered with various objects religions had used as icons or symbols to signify their distinct religion.

The Near didn't hesitate to use the knocker situated in the middle of the door. It slammed the hinged bronze symbol of a long forgotten religion against the door. A chanting sound, like thousands of people saying the invented name of their deity, echoed throughout the hallway.

After a few moments the chanting stopped, as a loud singing voice inside announced, "Enter these hallowed halls!"

Opening the door revealed Near Credo sitting at a table made of the finest gold, bordered with the most exquisite gemstones. It was also covered with the symbols of many different types of religions that man had followed throughout history. Its head was down, staring at empty pages of a large thick book made from the finest leather, bordered in gold leaf. Mumbling like it was doing some kind of incantation at the opened book; a stream of golden light flowed from its eyes to the blank pages acting like a pen, inscribing words on the pages.

Without looking up, it motioned for the Near to come in until it was finished. Raising its head, its golden eyes shone brightly at the Near Acolyte, sparkling with countless truths like continuous flashes of golden lightning. The Near Acolyte had to look away as each flash assaulted it with a deafening roar of words that made the basis for some future religion. The Near Credo laughed out loud in a chanting voice.

"The truth is always too much for anyone, when you're not ready for it! This will be my new religion when the time is right," pointing to the book.

The Near looked around the room which was actually a many faceted walled room with doorways leading to other halls. Each had their own symbol above the doorway, indicating what religion it was.

Near Acolyte noticed its long bright colored bejeweled robe, and the tall jewel adorned hat that was squarely placed on its head, as Near Credo rose from its chair. Around its neck hanging down to its chest, were thick golden chains with symbols of the dominate religions of the humans.

Grabbing its golden staff topped with a large clear colored gemstone, inscribed with many words that Near Acolyte didn't recognize, it spoke, "Come see my collections."

Pointing to the nearest hall and lifting its staff, it touched the religious symbol with the clear crystal causing a spark to jump to the symbol. The symbol lit up in a bright golden light, as the hall suddenly became like a television screen, showing scenes of the discovery and evolution of that particular religion.

The pomp and pageantry, colorfully dressed keepers and way showers of the secrets of that particular truth could be seen, all the massive statues and architectural wonders built to glorify their deity. The chanting, singing and rituals could be heard embodied within that religion, in their attempt to tell the world of their discovered truth.

"You see my friend man, throughout history has relied on the truth coming to him from a source from outside himself, which is always made into a religion. Not understanding that he was soul and truth, the knowledge of what God was, was in fact there inside him all along. My master has made sure that man stays in his ignorance of this fact by having control over his mind, thereby blocking the truth.

Certain humans were allowed to receive certain elements of truth, according to the area of the earth where they came from, and at a certain time in their history. These truths were always written down in a book considered sacred by men, who believed what was being taught and a religion was formed. The problem was, truth quite often was hidden behind the written words as a result. The books were often taken too literally, usually resulting in diluted versions of the original truth of the religion. If man isn't united, he is in conflict, when it comes to the meaning of love and truth.

Religions had always been important in the evolution of mankind in whatever way is necessary, but I've put in enough doubt that man has on occasion had a conflict with each other over the concept of truth, making sure the tears flow. Unfortunately I am exceedingly good at making man resort to violence to try to change another's doubts instead of through love."

Near Credo made sure man searched for religions throughout time. The chanting stopped and Near Acolyte stopped swaying, something it didn't realize it was doing. "Here endth the lesson. Take me to my master now!" When Near Credo closed the outside door, voices called out, "All glory and honor and praises go to thee!" accompanied by religious music.

Almost running down the hall, its neck symbols clanged and jingled together. Near Credo heard the louder noise coming from the fountain, making it sneer sanctimonious, believing it was the only one responsible for them.

Reaching the balcony it saw its master holding the railing, trembling.

"My Lord! All praise be unto you! How may I serve you?" bowing in deep respect.

Without looking at him it pointed to the lake, "Doesn't it seem a little low my faithful servant?" Near Credo glanced at the lake saying," Whatever you say is truth my Lord!"

"How are the religions these days? Is it possible to have them fight amongst themselves, even more than in the past?"

"Yes my Lord. They are always eager to try to dominate another's point of view. It is relatively easy to silence the peace makers when the din of religious fervor achieves a loud enough volume."

"Good! Then do it my friend. I have always trusted you to do your best. Start now!"

Near Credo bowed deeply, "It will be done!" Turning to leave without seeing the face of its master didn't matter, knowing its Lord being pleased was enough. Its sanctimonious sneer showed every Near who met it all was well.

Entering its room it went immediately over to each of the religious symbols, pressing them all with the crystal staff. Each entrance lit up and the religious sounds became louder and louder as each religion tried to outdo the others. Bolts of lightning arched across from one symbol to another.

Near Credo listened to the sounds of religious fervor. Chanting over and over, its voice joined in with the rest. Rising from its chair, it slowly made its rounds of each religion, swaying or dancing according to that religion's music. Its eyes shone a golden and white light that seemed to light the entire room. The book on its desk turned page by page, whenever it moved to a different religion, while the chanting went on and on,

"MY RELIGION
IS THE BEST I KNOW
ALL MY SACRED BOOKS
TELL ME SO
WHAT YOU REAP
IS WHAT YOU SOW
AS SECTARIAN VIOLENCE
BEGINS TO GROW

SCRIPTURES HELD HIGH
CURSES EVER SO BOLD
LOVE'S ASSURED PROBITY
TRAMPLED UNDER SO COLD
TRUTH VEILED OVER
COMMANDS NEAR CREDO
MAKE PIOUS TEARS
INTO RIVERS THAT GROW"

It kept chanting louder and louder until there was one tumultuous racket of screams, curses and shouts of revenge as the lunacy of all out sectarian religious war broke out. Then there was silence.

Hugh broke the silence.

"Well who's ready to start a new life? There should be frozen pizzas in the freezer. Let's have some supper and talk about it."

"What new life?" Dianne asked, "We never had pizza, we couldn't afford it. What new life?"

Hugh removed the pizzas from the freezer.

"Would one of you set the table and the other get out the juice from wherever your mother would hide such things? I told her to keep this a secret and for dessert we have pie heated up with ice cream."

Dave went to the dry goods cupboards. On the shelves were numerous containers of different natural juices. Dave saw all kinds of things to eat that normally weren't there. This was going to be better for his stomach than he first thought.

The pizza was beginning to smell good. They sat down at the table.

"Hugh you mentioned a new life. What did you mean?"

"Ah, this is as good a time as any to tell you. When I had my accident, everything changed for me. Without realizing it at the time, I began a new life, starting when I woke up in the hospital bed. I was completely immobilized with many broken bones, with such pain that drugs barely helped. At first, I was told they weren't sure I was going to survive. I wouldn't accept what they said, drifting in and out of consciousness. I had one thought that became like a mantra and that was I was going to survive."

Once they realized I was going to make it, they told me I would be lucky if I ever would have proper use of my body. Knowing that I had willed myself to live, I could certainly will my body to heal through thought. It took complete focus and continuous positive thinking to begin to move every part of my body. The pain was intense, but I was able to overcome it by focusing away from the pain. I thought of recovery, one moment at a time. I found that if one allowed the mind to focus on the pain, it only intensified."

Hesitating for a moment, he said, "Say, that pizza smells like it's done."

The pizza aroma made the children breathe in deeply. "That does smell good!" exclaimed Dianne. Hugh placed the steaming pizza in the center of the table.

"Please go on Hugh, your story sounds fascinating. The pain must have been awful." Dianne said, while Dave couldn't take his eyes off the pizza.

"Over time, I was able to get my body mobile and as the various casts came off, I started rehab and started progressing quickly. The problem most people have, is when they are laying in a bed, they allow the body to relax beyond the point where it can quickly come back to full strength. The result is, it ends up being a long hard struggle to become whole again, and some people never recover. The doctors were amazed at my recovery. It was my continuous use of positive thought every day that did it and hard work. Had I listened to my negative thoughts, eventually I would have believed them and may have never recovered. Once thoughts become a belief, the person will make that belief a reality."

"What is a belief?" asked Dave.

"Well, it's being convinced something is true, either because we see it, are told it is so. Sometimes, we have thought the same thoughts over and over again and we believe they become true for us and becomes part of our world/life. Once we believe something to be true, we act in accordance, even if we haven't taken the time to look at all aspects or facts that may suggest our truth is able to change as life changes around us. An incredible thing happens with wars, people are told to hate other people in another country by those who are in power. Yet if you asked them, had they ever met a person from that country they hated enough to kill, they would say no. However, they will stick to a belief that they should take up arms and slaughter those people, because they have been told to hate them."

Both children continued munching, listening intently. The pieces dwindled in number; however there was more than enough. Hugh was enjoying watching the looks of contentment on their faces.

"You told us about a new life. What did you mean by that?" Dianne asked.

"It will take some explaining, which we won't be able to cover in one night, but I will give you some of the basics. It's not complicated and once I tell you, you will wonder why you didn't know about it sooner. Probably, because no one told you."

Seeing they had eaten all the pizza, he said, "Let's take our dessert outside onto the porch. I do enjoy the evenings with the crickets chirping and everything getting ready for the dark and sleep. I'll clean this up if you two would get the bowls, ice cream and spoons out. "

Outside, there was a gentle warm rain falling. With bowls in hand full of ice cream, they sat in lounge chairs on the porch.

"Smell that rain, what a nice smell." Both children looked at each other. Nowhere in their home schoolbooks did it mention you could smell the rain. They said nothing since there had to be something to it, the way their uncle talked.

Hugh spoke at the same time between mouthfuls.

"I will tell you how to have a better life, but first I want to ask you a question. Is life the way you want it to be?" Both children shook their heads no.

"Do you remember what I said about how belief will make your world what it is, if you believe it is true?" What makes your world is what you think over and over. The thoughts act like grooves on a record, especially negative thoughts."

"I had money stolen from my bag once in a mall and I told the security guard, but all he told me was, that it wasn't nice. Because I had left it near the hallway, he said they were long gone, so I'd never get it back. Now I always keep it close because I am afraid it will get stolen again." Dianne said.

"Exactly, your mind probably went over it a lot, making you very cautious and not trusting others like you once did. Am I right?" Dianne nodded her head in agreement.

Dave told his story about going to play at a boy's house and was bit by his dog, which caused him to be frightened of all dogs.

"Does your mind go over the same thoughts when you think of or see a dog?" Dave agreed, saying he got the same feelings and thoughts every time he thought about dogs and definitely a sharp emotional jolt of fear when he encountered any dog.

"This same thing happens all your life in little ways and unfortunately larger ways. Quite often you don't even realize the mind plays this trick on you. The problem is this fear, discouragement or whatever other negative feeling you get, tends to stop you from actually having experiences later in your life that would be positive and uplifting for you in some way."

"For example Dianne, it could stop you from trusting people with your money in all ways, from investing your money. You may be afraid of lending people money when they genuinely need help or giving to a charity or to a cause where your money could make a positive change. You could develop a deep distrust of people that could affect your relationships with anyone all your life."

Dave could develop a phobia about dogs or even all small animals and miss out later on the opportunity to have a pet, especially a dog. He could miss out on an opportunity that could teach him how to love and give support to animals that need it. Like working at an animal shelter as a volunteer or give to charities that support abused animals. The effects of these incidences have a negative influence on us far beyond the actual experience, and unfortunately make up a lot of how people see and judge the world around them. Do you understand?"

Both children nodded in agreement.

Hugh swiped his finger around in his empty bowl, scouring the remnants of the ice cream.

"Now what I want you to understand is, this is false thinking by the mind. You see, the mind is only a living computer. The computer only responds to what it considers to be important to us, and any negative emotional reaction we have, it will make a file of it. So when we see dogs or lunch money, the mind automatically downloads the negative file and we start reacting like we did to the incident in the past, with all the emotions. So we start thinking about it again and this reinforces more negative thoughts about the subject, and the mind files it away again. Eventually this file is so large and powerful, we just start acting according to it. So how do you change it? You catch the mind when it's downloading the thoughts, and change them. Introduce new thoughts, and over time the negative will be wiped out and the positive stored in the file. Is that enough for today?"

Both children agreed it was, they were beginning to feel tired.

"Think about it when you get the chance and you will see what I mean."

He paused staring out at the rain gently falling down. "Have you ever listened to the rain? There's actually music in the raindrops if you listen close enough."

"There isn't music in rain Hugh." Retorted Dianne skeptically.

"Sure there is, would you like to hear it?"

"All you have to do is get comfortable, look out at the rain for a few minutes, not thinking about it but just watch it. Then, close your eyes, pretending you still see the rain falling and still listen. Don't try to hear the music, just listen and see the rain falling down in your mind's eye. That blank screen is where you see things in your mind when you imagine them. We'll do this until I talk again all right? However, we won't talk about what you hear now, we will do that later."

Eternity can be forever or a flash, depending on your reference, so when Hugh spoke quietly for the children to open their eyes, it seemed like it had been only a few moments. They both gasped, when they saw it was getting dark and they had been there for almost an hour. The children said nothing, when he told them it was time to go to bed since tomorrow was a new day, and there would be lots to do.

They felt they were floating on the raindrops they listened to and so complied going to their bedrooms. Each climbed into their beds, still caught up in the rapturous melody they had experienced. Sleep came, accompanied by the distant rolling of thunder, drawing them into the dream state.

As they did, there came from their uncle's bedroom, a repetitive noise unlike anything they had ever heard before. The lure of sleep's pull overcame the distant storm sounds, so they drifted off into the silence.

The Sneakeeze couldn't have any silence, as the storm sounds lasted all night. The odd bolt of lightning seemed to be focused at the Sneakeeze. They jumped in fright, whenever one struck close by. The thunder reverberated with violence, causing them to huddle closer together, shivering in fear. Sleep seemed impossible. There were dreams of Lord Misanthropy towering over them, snarling and cackling.

The storm finally abated to shower clouds, drifting away from them as the daylight started to show itself.

Slinks lay flat out on the ground with his head in close proximity to Lurky's bum. Breathing deeply, snorting and snoring, he lay in a deep sleep. Lurky was still sleeping, sitting up with his head nestled in his ears, stretched over himself like an umbrella.

Poor Lurky was still in the dreadful dreams of Lord Misanthropy, jerking and moaning, subjected to the horrors that only the Lord could produce.

Now it seems that certain birds when eaten by Lurky could produce copious quantities of noxious gas. It seems yesterday's bird just happened to be one of them.

One extremely vile part of the dream caused Lurky to tense, allowing a little gaseous fluffy to escape into the otherwise fresh air with an audible 'pht'. The gas cloud had nothing better to do than spread its odoriferous cheer out. Slink's unknowing nose inhaled a generous portion of the scent. His body twitched several times making him cough the odor out.

Apparently, once some brave gas was allowed to escape from Lurky's bowelled domain, the gas that was left behind got to vote on whether they should join their escaped friends out to the world of clean fresh air.

The vote was unanimous that they should all join their friend in one long quiet 'phht'. If anyone had of been there, they could have said with confidence, the air was probably blue as the mephitic cloud tried to find Slink's nose. Slink's nose had no idea what was coming until it was too late, inhaling more than should be allowed by law. It only took his nose a millisecond to realize it was about to die, making him cough, sneeze and retch all at once.

His brain was alerted to the environmental disaster unfolding, waking him from a sound sleep. His eyes flew open when the smell registered.

He let out an indignant howl, quickly rolling away, scrambling to get as far away as he could from the smell.

Still retching, he yelled, "Lurky's yous ate a smellies birds yesterdays!"

Lurky, blissfully unaware of what had just transpired was completely taken by surprise by Slink's shouting. He jumped up colliding with an overhanging branch. The only thing that remotely reminded him of head pain was the bees, flailing for all he was worth. Slapping himself on the top of his ears made him temporarily blind to his surroundings. He stumbled backwards, tripping on a log going end over end until he came to a stop.

He was a collapsed heap of jumbled ears, feet and hands that were still doing their best to swat at imaginary bees. He could see now, looking around wide-eyed searching for the elusive stinging bees, but none were to be found. He rubbed his head, finding a piece of bark embedded in his hair.

Looking around, he exclaimed. "Whats yous wakes me from a goods sleeps Slinks!"

Slinks was still gasping for fresh air. Chokingly he yelled, "Yous ates a smellies birds Lurky!"

"Theys alls looks the sames to me's. Hows does I's knows?"

What Lurky had noticed, was that the ones with the feathers that got stuck in his throat were generally the ones that smelled the worst. He wasn't about to let Slinks in on this secret, at least not right now. He looked down, noticing a centipede crawling around after being disturbed by the log. Snatching it up, he popped it into his mouth out of habit.

Trying to appease his friend he said, "Theres centipedes heres Slinks. Wants one?" Tearing apart the rotten log, he looked for more centipede family members to become breakfast. He held a squirming specimen up for Slinks to see. Slinks just shook his head no, unable to even think of food. Lurky shrugged a 'suit yourself' motion, proceeding to invite three other centipede family members into this mouth for breakfast.

"Lord Misphtpht sures was means last night withs that stormy its mades." Lurky said, trying to change the subject as Slinks still tried to get his breath.

"Yes it's mads at us, so we's betters gets goings," brushing himself off as well. He lifted his ears, taking the lead, happy to be in front of Lurky, not facing his behind. The 'smelly birds' had a tendency to announce their presence all day. They hadn't gone far when he heard the unmistakable sound of 'pht' coming gently from behind him. More gas voted to leave Lurky's bowels. Lurky on the other hand knew how to deal with secessionist gas. He fanned the air behind him with his hand to help dilute the obnoxious, just so no more environmental incidents occurred.

They ate all the plants they could that they knew were good and nutritious to help quiet the hunger. Slinks pointed out the ones to Lurky he knew were good for eliminating gassy conditions, even though Lurky didn't like the taste of them. Their movement would scare up various beetles and flying insects which made for an instant snack, supplementing the vegetation they ate.

Coming to the edge of a small clearing, Lurky spotted a large green grasshopper, one of his favorites. It flew beside Slinks unnoticed, as he looked out over the clearing. Lurky crept up for a real Sneakeeze pounce, wiggling his bum in anticipation like a cat. He launched himself right onto the grasshopper that was perched on a blade of tall grass, without making a sound. He grabbed the grasshopper with both hands, cupping it to show Slinks what he had missed. However, when his feet landed on the grass a loud squeak unlike any he had ever heard arose.

Shrieking in surprise, he jumped out of the grass, leaping into Slink's arms, who had just turned around to see what the sound was. With his arms around Slink's neck, he stared wide-eyed for the source of the noise. Lurky's sudden weight caused Slinks to topple backwards, landing on the ground with a thud. Slinks pushed Lurky off.

Lurky whispered to Slinks, "Whats was that's?"

Slinks shook his head indicating he had no idea, before asking, "Does you's see anythings?" Lurky got brave enough for a fast look around before bending back down to see if he could see anything, but he didn't. Together, they noticed a small red white and blue colored object nestled in the grass. It was obviously from the humans, which could be good or bad depending on what it was.

Like the time the humans were good enough to leave behind their stuff when the Sneakeeze decided to say hello that one night. After the humans so rudely departed, they explored through the various metal and plastic containers eating whatever tasted good. Trouble came, when Lurky found a metal container and pushed on the end of it. White, awful tasting foam blinded him when it sprayed out. Slinks had to throw him in the river to wash the stuff out of his eyes since he was unable to see. After that, Lurky didn't trust anything human in brightly colored objects.

He gave the round object a good once over, sniffing the air for danger. None came from the object. Lurky found a long stick, gently prodded it. It gave out a quieter version of the squeak that it had earlier. This caused Lurky to almost tumble backwards. Slinks tried to get out of the way this time. Lurky had the stick up in the air in a defensive posture, ready to defend himself, if need be.

Nothing happened, so he went back, smacking it with the stick. It gave out the same noise each time. Realizing it wasn't going to attack him, he summoned up his courage, gently picking up the ball, rolling around in his hands. However, it made no noise. He showed it to Slinks who still wasn't sure about this newfound thing.

He preferred Lurky was the one to get bitten by it, if this occurred. He gave it a squeeze producing a long low squeak causing him to almost drop it, but it didn't bite him. Squeezing it harder and harder, each time it gave a corresponding squeaking noise, making him smile, realizing he had a new play toy.

Slinks, wasn't sure this was a good idea to keep this human object, in case a human heard it and wanted it back. There was no persuading Lurky to leave it behind. He relented, continuing on as Lurky walked behind, curiously squeaking the ball.

Soon Lurky started squeaking the ball in rhythm to his footsteps. Slinks shook his head in disgust but let it go on for a while. As time went on, it started grating on Slink's nerves. Finally, Lurky put the ball in his mouth, swinging his arms like he was in a marching band, squeezing the ball to his footsteps. Slobber drooled down his chin, from his partly opened mouth.

Slinks, being more afraid of a human hearing than anything else, spun around without missing a step. He slapped Lurky on the top of his head with his open hand, saying, "Drops it! Drops it! Drops it!!" each time he hit him.

The ball gave out a loud squeak each time a blow came as Lurky kept mumbling, "Nos! Nos! Nos!"

Finally the pain became too much, dropping the ball. Slinks grabbed it out of the air, putting his hand over Lurky's eyes so he couldn't see, and tossed the ball hard into the bushes. By the time Lurky got his hand off his eyes it was too late, the ball was gone.

He gave out an awful whine, "That's was my onlys toys Slinks. You's didn't haves to dos that's!"

"If a humans sees us and we's don'ts finds the laughters sound, Lordie Misphtpht will uses yous as a squeakys toy forevers. Now let's goes!"

Slinks moved ahead, while Lurky stood there sulking, looking in the direction he heard the ball fall, but knowing he wasn't going to get anywhere. The fact that Slinks was right, won finally. He would continue on without his toy, like it or not. It still wasn't right he couldn't have a bit of fun. Life didn't have to always be so serious or at least he thought so. He didn't have much of a choice right now. He took his frustration out on a half dead weed beside him, whacking it back and forth until it almost snapped off, swaying aimlessly in the breeze.

He started off anxious to catch up to Slinks, who hadn't stopped to see if he was coming. He felt a little fluffy trying to come out.

A loud 'phhht' could be heard, before quietly saying, "Lordie Misphtpht plays with that toys!"

He caught up with Slinks saying nothing more, knowing one day he would get another toy.

Entering a large field, Slinks suddenly jumped ahead, catching something with his hands. He startled Lurky daydreaming about his toy.

"Whats yous got Slinks?" queried Lurky interested. Slinks said nothing turning around, holding a fat green grasshopper for Lurky as a gift. Lurky was shocked and surprised but eagerly accepted the gift. Holding it by the wings the helpless insect protested its capture, kicking with its hind legs and clawing at the air with its other legs.

Holding it out towards Slinks he said, "I'll shares withs you's Slinks!" Glad things were back to normal with his friend. Slinks shook his head no, seeing many other grasshoppers flying away. Lurky popped the grasshopper into his mouth, crunching down hard, allowing the juices to fill his mouth all at once.

That was how he liked his 'hoppers' as he called them. The large hind leg of the grasshopper stuck out of his mouth. It twitched once, attesting to its quick death, before joining the rest of its minced body, with a lick of Lurky's stained tongue.

A large, black dragonfly flew by, and Lurky jumped out of pure instinct. His ears were extended to lift him off the ground. He swatted it down, pouncing on it. Bringing it over to Slinks, he offered it to him by the wings. Slinks accepted the choice morsel from Lurky. These were his favorite food. Slinks took the dragonfly, shoving it in his mouth except for the four large wings, which were all that were left after he crunched down on it.

Slinks looked at Lurky, who was happy after getting the gift. "I's don'ts knows abouts yous but this makes me hungerys! exclaimed Slinks.

Lurky said nothing. Instead, he scampered around in front of Slinks making funny noises and gestures like he was eating grasshoppers.

This was the first time Slinks let down his serious side since they started out. They scampered around the field, jumping at anything that flew. Laughing and eating insects, rolling and romping like they did in the days before Lordie Misphtpht.

For hours they played and ate, forgetting all about why they were there. They slapped each other in gestures of affection, complimenting each other about their capturing skills, especially if they got their ears spread out right. They could almost hover, swatting elusive prey. Lurky crouched, watching a large dragonfly flying in his general direction. His bum moved back and forth waiting in eager anticipation before he leapt.

His mouth was open with his hands extended, ready to capture yet another morsel. In mid air, the sound of loud laughter assaulted his ears.

Forgetting all about the morsel, the noise reverberated his sensitive hearing. He let out an unconscious howl at the pain, hitting the ground with a thud, desperately covering his ears with his hands. He looked over at Slinks rolling around on the ground, in obvious discomfort.

They had found what they had been listening for. Rather it had found them. Without realizing it, they came right up to the source of the laughter. Now there was only one thing to do, get as far away as they could. Tumbling and running back in the general direction they had come from, they tried to get away before any more laughter came.

Luckily there was no more. They kept running, sending a spray of winged insects in all directions. They ran until there was no more wind left in their lungs. Stopping for a rest, they sat breathing deeply for the longest time, looking around. Lurky motioned he needed some water, going to the creek. They both lapped up the water, quenching the thirst they had from breathing so hard. Finally they stopped both looking down at the water flowing by.

"I's guess this means we's gots to goes back to Afars and mean old Lordie Misphtpht." Remarked Lurky solemnly.

"Yes we's dones our jobs, so we's better tells it or its bounds to sends the old Nears afters us." replied Slinks. "Besides I's sures it's wills rewards us. Maybes it's lets us go. Wouldn't that's be nicey of its?"

"Does yous thinks it's wills be that's nicey?" Lurky queried, thinking of freedom.

"Theres onlys one ways to finds out." putting his hand on Lurky's shoulder for reassurance. Something good had to come out of all of this. They arose together, each taking a deep breath for courage and started back the way they had come.

Although hoping for the best, small dark thought clouds still floated through their minds, causing them to become silent, reflecting on fears and misgivings, real or imagined, heading towards the Land of Afar.

They both found the return journey always seemed to go faster than when they first come, passing landmarks and sign posts that should have taken longer to get to, sped by. Going out there was so much new to see, hear and touch, time seemed to slow, but coming back was familiar terrain and nothing new, so time seemed to speed up.

They both started slowing down using any excuse to stop or take long breaks, both becoming melancholy about the future they would have to face. Now an unknown future.

Reaching the lake, they realized the wind was too rough to cross, so walking the shore was the only option, leaving after resting. Finally reaching the far end they decided to take a break. Something caught Lurky's attention, coming back with a blue butterfly on the back of his hand. He had always admired how they could fly with the movements of their wings, watching the wings move up and down. Chuckling every time it unfurled its tongue to his skin, he studied its uniqueness, perhaps butterflies were no longer on the menu unless necessary.

He said quietly, "Littles buttyflies would yous go tells old Lordie Misphtpht wheres the kids is at, so's we's could's stays here happilies forevers mores.?"

He shook his hand letting the butterfly go, but instead of it going to the Land of Afar, it flew back to where it was. Lurky stared down at the ground feeling helpless.

Slinks put his hand on his shoulder saying, "I's swears Lurky we's wills do this togethers, you's and me's. Somehows we's wills live happilies evers mores."

Lurky looked deep into his friend's eyes. "I's really hopes so."

"Let's eats and in's the morning we's feels betters." They settled down curling up, as their ears enveloped their heads to shield them from a cruel world, for just one more night.

There were no fun dreams that night, none they could remember and morning came way too soon to suit them. Nibbling absentmindedly, they found themselves back to the stash of flasks before they knew it, deciding it was time for a rest.

Watching the water tumble over the rocks, Slinks had an idea, "Let's empty outs the flasks and fills them with watey, then we's won'ts have to's drink teary soup for a whiles." Lurky thought that a wonderful idea watching several minnows fighting the current. Pouring his tears out the water turned it black killing them.

Seeing their bodies swirling and twirling in their death swim, he shrieked, "Looks at that's! Looks they's died of sadness! We's can'ts goes back. We's will surely dies of sadness if we's drinks teary soup agains!" His eyes wide open, trembling.

Slinks grabbed him by the arm," We's didn'ts dies before and we's won'ts now! Rinses outs the flasks and let's gets going. I feels old Lordie Misphtpht's eyes ons us agains, we's must goes or its finds us." Slinks helped Lurky, calming him down walking up the trail. They took their last long drink from the stream, before moving up towards the fog that slowly enveloped them. They became tired from the energy emanating from the fog.

Finally they stopped, silently staring out into the fog. There was no turning back, so they began.

"IN THE FOG
HIDDEN FROM SIGHT
HEARTLESS LAND
BLACK AS NIGHT
SEE IT NOW
THE LAND THAT'S HERE
THAT SEEMS AFAR
YET SO NEAR"

Looking ahead, the ghostly outline of the bridge could be seen waiting for them to cross.

"I's afraid Slinks."

"Me's toos buts we's gots each others. We's haves courage togethers." He took Lurky's hand firmly, took a deep breath and stepped up on the bridge. They crossed silently into the Land of Afar, leaving their freedom behind.

The fog swirled in behind them to make sure any thoughts of freedom were lost in a blanket of grey hopelessness, like fleeting dreams turned into a forgotten memories you thought you might once have had.

Morning came out of nowhere intruding into their sound sleep, making their fleeting dreams turn into forgotten memories they thought they had. The bright light made them both squint and blink, trying to get used to it. They heard sounds of nature already awake. With that, they heard a repetitive noise, almost singing but not quite, coming from the porch.

Opening their bedroom doors almost at the same time, Dave whispered to Dianne, "What is that?" She shrugged her shoulders following the sound, they went down to the kitchen and out to the porch. Hugh sat with his eyes closed, making the noise they heard. They just watched until abruptly he stopped. The children backed away from the window so he wouldn't notice them, and hastily went about making breakfast.

He came in from the porch scratching an itch on his scalp saying, "Ah, you're up! Good! It's a beautiful day after the rain, and if you don't mind I'd like you to show me around the whole place today."

After a brief conversation about what they would see first, breakfast was done. Dianne turned to her uncle, "I was wondering what you were doing out there on the porch?"

Hugh smiled, not realizing the children had heard him.

"Because of the way we have been taught about life throughout history, we believe we have no control over how our life works. This isn't true at all."

"It isn't?" queried Dianne. "If my day doesn't start out right and I am late, I find things go wrong, and I have a bad hair day."

"Exactly!" replied Hugh.

"Our thoughts, believe it or not, make our life. The energy we create with our thoughts will help draw to us the events in our life, whether good or bad. In other words, the energy of your thinking manifests what you want, by getting you to organize the materials necessary, and tools you require. You use your logic, imagination and creativity to produce whatever it is. The mind works on many levels.

Remember you control the mind. All it does is follow your commands. The interesting thing is the mind works with an energy force, the force that works with all of life. This energy is neither negative nor positive, the mind interfaces with it and creates from it, good or bad. So you wake up grumpy, you lay in bed past the alarm, daydreaming or worrying about bad things that haven't even happened and probably won't, but now you are late.

Nobody is pinning you to the bed. You are actually choosing to be late. So now you rush around, your mind thinking negatively. You can't find your clothes, you spill the milk, it's too late for breakfast, and you are watching the clock. Time seems to speed up. The list of possible bad things that may happen is endless.

You, through your thinking have created your day. The morning is critical. In fact it will set your day up. The mind has been able to connect with this force as you sleep. It is extremely powerful when you do your first thinking of the day. I learned a long time ago to do an exercise every morning that helps me connect with the mind and this force, in order to have the day start out and go the way I want it to, as much as possible.

Let's go back to the computer image. It's like I am typing into the computer all the positive things I want to happen, and this force within the computer obeys without hesitation, by making a printed copy of whatever I have put in. If what I am putting in is a bad hair day, then that's what's going to happen. If the printed copy is a good positive attitude and thoughts, it will carry me through the day, even if things go askew. Do you understand what I am saying?"

Both children found this fascinating that you could actually have some control over your life, and not victims of whatever happened to you.

"Let's just put the dishes in the sink to soak for awhile." Hugh said picking up a pencil and pad of paper.

"We have to feed the animals and let them out." Dianne said.

"I know, but first let's go out to the road."

The children followed not quite sure why, but an adventure was an adventure. At the end of the driveway, he made them look away from the house with eyes shut.

"Now turn around and face the farm. When you open our eyes, tell me the first thing that comes to your mind about what you see."

The children did as they were told, giggling quietly at first playing this neat game. When they opened their eyes, they both let out a discernable, "Oh!" The sight of the unkempt and rundown farm greeted them, causing their shoulders to sag. A look of despair crossed over their faces.

"How do you feel with what you see?"

"Awful. Our place looks really poor."

"Exactly! How do you feel about your lives?"

They both admitted they felt really poor and had nothing.

"People don't realize how much the world and what they have around them affects them. If your surroundings look poor and rundown, that's how you feel. If there's clutter, you will feel confused and disorganized. Even colors will affect your thinking. Most of the time people don't even realize it.

The other important part of this is, when other people see the same things, they think negatively in the same way. They will think you are poor. Believe or not, you pick up these energy thoughts, without even knowing it and this just reinforces your bad feeling about yourself and your life.

As a family, everyone will talk the same language of not having enough, of lacking, of poverty, and this just keeps feeding the negative thinking and the manifesting of these things. It's a vicious circle."

"Yes, but what if we don't have money?" Dave asked.

"Good point! But you know it doesn't take a lot of money to change things. Take for example the entrance to your place. Let's find some rocks and make garden planters on each side of the driveway. We can use soil from the barnyard and find some colorful weeds and wildflowers and plant them in the planters.

I saw two wagon wheels on an old wagon in the field when I came in, which would make a great backdrop for the planters. We will just lean them against the posts that are there, giving the place a hobby farm appearance. I'll see if I can get the mower working so we can cut the grass. People will feel more welcome to drive into the yard if they come for a visit.

Now you see, so far it hasn't cost a cent. You watch, the next time you come home from being away, you will feel much better about living here."

The children thought this was a great idea. Hugh could see the change come over the children. They had already brightened up and were enthusiastic to get things done.

"This is definitely how to start my day with some real excitement. We're about to make some change in our lives for the better!" Hugh announced in a loud voice, acting very dramatically like he was an actor on a stage. Then he yelled, "Show me the rest, to make real changes!"

He started skipping down the driveway like a kid. The children stood in shock for a few seconds that a grown man would act like this. Letting out giggles they joined in, skipping and twirling, missing the mud puddles, not remembering when they had this much spontaneous fun. Hugh sang.

"WITH CHANGE, WITH CHANGE
OUT WITH THE OLD
IN WITH THE NEW
THAT'S THE GAME OF CHANGE

THE SAME, THE SAME
MOVE THIS
FIX THAT
IT WON'T REMAIN THE SAME

MY DAY, MY DAY
SO MUCH BRIGHTER
SO MUCH BETTER
WHEN THE SAME BEGINS TO CHANGE"

He kept singing the verses as the children followed along as best they could, everyone skipping to the house. Hugh stopped to survey the outside. He suddenly jumped in a puddle with both feet pretending it didn't matter, staring at the house. The children laughed and laughed at his antics. Some of the shingles had blown loose from past storms. There was a crack in one of the windows, one corner of the vinyl siding was pulled off, and the rain gutters were pulled apart in several places. Hugh wrote all this down.

"Why are you standing in the middle of a mud puddle?" Dianne asked.

"It's good to get your feet wet now and then so you appreciate them better when they're dry." They stared at each other before deciding to try it. Jumping right in, they stood for a moment before laughing at the silliness of it.

He then turned and walked to the back of the house, humming and making "Ah-Ha's" seeing things that needed tending.

Hugh then took a critical look at the barn, definitely showing signs of needing repairs, from door latches, to roof, to needing a good coat of paint.

"Show me your animals." He said smiling. Dianne rushed past him to be his tour guide.

"Goaties! Are you hungry?" She called. Hugh noticed in the goat pens, there was only left over weeds on the floor for bedding, except for dried manure in the corner. The floor was bare wood and some of the boards in the pen were chewed and in need of replacing.

"Over here we have the chickens, we've got six and they barely lay an egg a day. If something scares them, we don't get anything." Dave said, deciding he'd like to be a tour guide for a while too, pointing towards another room. Dianne was till petting her goats.

"Those are her goats. Don't mess with them if you want to stay on her good side."

Hugh pretended he understood. "Don't worry buddy, I got ya!" Making like he was going to keep this little secret between them.

Hugh watched Dianne fling hay into the goat's pen without caring where it landed and Dave fed the chickens by sprinkling it around on the manure-covered floor. They went back to the house to bring some drinking water, while he stayed.

He was overwhelmed, seeing his brother's dream that was never fulfilled. Now that dream was slowly wasting away, like the memories that he had of his brother.

His brother was all he had and the melancholy crept in, his heart ached at the cruel and harsh reality of life's injustices.

He didn't have long to dwell in this lonely place of his mind, when he heard the screen door of the house slam shut and children's excited voices. They carried overfilled pails of water for the animals, spilling water everywhere.

"You two look like a pair of drunken sailors lugging water to swab the deck." Hugh said forcing a smile as dark thoughts still lingered in his mind, before being pushed aside by the vision of happiness on the children's faces.

"These are heavy uncle!" replied Dianne wiping a bead of sweat from her forehead.

Dave stuck out his chest boasting, "I could have carried them by myself, but she wouldn't let me."

"Ya, like that time when you carried them and one foot didn't know the other foot was going ahead at the same time, so you and pails greeted the ground at the same time." Dianne laughed.

"Shut up!" retorted Dave taking a swipe at his sister's arm. Dianne scurried behind her uncle pretending she was afraid.

"I'm sure you can do whatever needs to be done when the time comes Master Dave, even if your feet do get in the way," chuckled Hugh.

Hugh laughed out loud grabbing a pail, pretending to run away towards the barn from Dave in case he tried anything saying, "May the best feet win!"

Dave grabbed his pail not wanting to be left behind, despite Dianne's taunting. Dave bumped into her on purpose.

"Sorry! Sorry! I didn't see you. You're the same dirty shade as the wall."

"Ya, whatever!" she replied.

Hugh laughed as he watched the two jostled with each other.

"Come on, let's water these poor critters before they dry up like prunes." After watering the animals Hugh said, "Show me the tools we got to do our changes." They took him to a small room that had an assortment of old, used tools. Covered with dust on a small bench, sat jars of assorted fasteners and tools he gave a once over. Looking at the shovels picks and forks standing in the corner, he realized they would be useful once broken handles were replaced. He noticed there was no wheelbarrow, saying.

"Alright we are going to need another one if we want to accomplish any change, but the first rule is work smart, not hard. Without a wheelbarrow, it'll be difficult to carry rocks or dirt and anything else. Also we will need several handles, tools and hinges for the doors.

I've written everything down, so let's go order what we need from the farm supply store and get started. I saw some posts and wire, so we can make an outside pasture for the animals to graze on. We will have a portable penned in pasture that we move as they graze off the area. That way they will eat good quality pasture and we'll save money on hay until the winter.

The chickens need to earn their keep by laying eggs. I'll buy a good quality feed and we will let them roam around for bugs and gravel. Free ranging chickens will give a more nutritious egg, plus it will save on feed. Even old Fred there will enjoy being out. Sound like a plan?"

"I'm so glad you're here to help us," replied Dianne. Dave nodded in agreement.

"Sometimes it takes a fresh perspective to see an easy solution to a problem that seems unsolvable. Hugh said, then turned and started running to the house yelling, "Last one does the dishes!"

Dianne and Dave ran after him getting to the porch at the same time, which meant they would all do the dishes together.

"Just look at the time, it's almost lunch hour. Where does time go when you're having fun?" Hugh asked.

Hugh went over to the phone book and leafed through for the feed store number. He dialed the number and placed the order. This was the beginning of more changes than any of them could even imagine or believe were possible.

Holding hands, the Sneakeeze knew their lives were changing in ways they couldn't imagine or believe possible. They tread silently along the Road of Anguish, feeling all the terrible thoughts that made this place real. The negative energy swept over them, invading every pore, every molecule in their body and mind. The road was damp and almost sticky to walk on from the multitude of freshly shed tears. Slinks gazed down seeing distinct trails of tears leading ahead to the Tower of Tears.

"I's feels awfuls Slinks, just likes we's used to's in our cells."

"I's feels it too's. Old Lordie Misphtpht's causing this. Tries not to lets it bothers you. Thinks of all the good things we's did outsides."

"I's wish I's had my squeaky's toy."

Slinks smiled, remembering how happy Lurky was marching along squeaking that stupid thing. For a brief moment a wave of euphoria rose up overpowering the negative blanket smothering them.

Suddenly there was a flash of lightning and the rolling of thunder. In the thunder, their ears picked up unmistakable sounds of sobbing and crying of countless voices. A flickering flash of light on the road flowed ahead of them on the road. They were startled by it, causing them to jump to the side. They heard sounds of something coming behind them. Hiding behind a boulder, they quickly concealed themselves.

A man staggering, cradling a screaming baby and holding a young girl by her hand, was sobbing. The child was crying for her mother. Their clothes were shredded, blackened from burns, their bodies showing streaks of blood.

The Sneakeeze couldn't tell whose blood it was and they didn't want to know. The man was begging for help in finding his wife and boys. He screamed about bombs falling and why would God allow this. He suddenly stopped, causing Lurky and Slinks to crouch even lower hoping the man hadn't seen them.

The man pointed to the Tower of Tears, shouting maybe there was someone there who could help. Rushing down the road, he forced the girl to trot behind him in his haste.

Lurky and Slinks waited for the humans to go into the tower. Peering around they couldn't see anyone else, so they ran up the road getting past the tower.

Lurky looked at Slinks asking,

"Why's does humans do that's to each others?

"Cause they lets old Lordie Misphtpht send the Nears to make them thinks bad things about each others that aren't true. They's does terrible things to each other's so he's gets their tears.'"

"You two are going to shed tears if you haven't done what my Lord requested of you. You know he has absolutely no patience," said a Near standing behind a large boulder, almost snarling. Both Sneakeeze screeched in alarm at being startled by the presence of the Near they hadn't seen. They held onto each other, realizing this was the beginning of what they were dreading. Slinks summoned the courage saying, "We's founds what your Lordie was lookin' for." Lurky nodded his head in agreement.

"Excellent you worms! My master will be pleased. Follow me and be quick about it or I'll have to make up some lie to make you shed some tears once my Lord gets through with you."

Following the Near to get back to tell its master, they sank into their own world of hopeless despair as they marched along, not knowing what lay ahead once they were in front of Lord Misanthropy.

The walk to the castle seemed to only take a few minutes. The door was opened by one of the Near Thralls. They knew they were about to enter the world of greatest fears.

Stepping inside, all hope and courage was abandoned, lost somewhere outside. The door slammed shut with a loud, hollow noise. They could hear shouts and noises as the Nears told each other of their arrival. The sobbing, wailing and crying coming from the tears streaming down the walls, really made their hearts sink.

Lurky whispered to Slinks, "I's scared Slinks," showing genuine fear.

"Me's too. Don't lets Lordie Misphtpht see it's. It be's okays," placing his hand on his shoulder. Lurky straightened up. If Slinks could do it, so could he, quietly singing.

"SQUEAKY TOY
SQUEAKY TOY
SQUEAK A TUNE
FOR LURKY BOY

SQUEAKY TOY
SQUEAKY TOY
YOU'S SQUEAKY TUNE
BRINGS LURKY JOY

SQUEAKY TOY
SQUEAKY TOY
HOW I'S LOVES
MY SQUEAKY TOY"

Suddenly a voice shattered his inner peace. "Silence you despicable worms! No one sings or speaks unless I order it!"

In front of them sat Lord Misanthropy with a look that could kill, even the Nears stared at the floor. One Near swatted Lurky across the back of the head. Lurky winced but stared at the floor, seeing Slinks was doing the same.

"You two had better have brought me good news! Did you find them! Tell me or I'll turn you into something other than that waste of skin you are!"

Slinks looked up at the terrible face, "We's done what's you's wanted. We's founds them. It's two youngs children."

"Yes! That makes sense. Sometimes in my haste to make adult humans cry, I may overlook the small ones. In the future I shall pay more attention. There will be no more laughter! All will cry before I am through!" Its sneer became hideous.

Slinks shrank back but somehow summoned the courage to ask. "Since we's dids what you's asked, cans we goes frees?"

Lord Misanthropy couldn't believe the insolence of being interrupted. Leaning forward, it stared Slinks in the eyes, "You wish to go free?" Slinks saw a small glimmer of hope nodding his head agreeing.

Lord Misanthropy lifted one forefinger. Suddenly, four Nears grabbed them each by the arms, holding tight. Lurky screamed out in fright as Slinks yelled, "Oh no!" They didn't try to struggle, there was no use, waiting in dread for the voice.

"You wish to be free? Here's how you're going to be free." Pointing to Lurky," You will be free to take my Nears to these children, while you," pointing to Slinks, "You will be free to stay in your cell until he's back or not. How's that for freedom?"

Cackling contemptuously, it closed its eyes signaling the discussion was over. The Nears wheeled them around heading for the basement. Both Sneakeeze were distraught at the treatment they just received but that was the Land of Afar way.

Roughly treated with slaps and boots, they were rushed back to their old cell, making Slinks sigh and Lurky quietly wail. When Lurky went to go in, they slammed the door shut leaving him outside and Slinks in. "You stay out here worm to do my master's bidding!" Making them all sneer.

Lurky just stared at Slinks through the bars weeping quietly. Seeing this by the Nears who imitated him, they rubbed their eyes and leaned against each other, like they were sobbing.

"Boo Hoo!" they shouted, loving to see something cry first hand, until finally a Near said.

" Come on boys! We could do this all day but we gotta go. Time to say goodbye!" They all waved mockingly at the Sneakeeze saying.

"WAIL AND CRY
WAIL AND CRY
THE WHOLE LIVELONG DAY

WAIL AND CRY
WAIL AND CRY
BECAUSE HERE YOU'LL STAY

WAIL AND CRY
WAIL AND CRY
AS ALL HOPE FADES

WAIL AND CRY
WAIL AND CRY
YOUR MISERABLE LIFE AWAY

WAIL AND CRY
WAIL AND CRY
IT'S THE LAND OF AFAR WAY

WAIL AND CRY
WAIL AND CRY
BYE BYE, BYE BYE"

Sneering mockingly, they left, back into the dark hall, similar to Lurky's mood right now. Slinks let him cry until he knew they were gone. He gently shook him out of his stupor, "Lurky looks at me. It's alrights. Somehows its be okay."

"Hows Slinks?"

"I's don'ts knows. You's must do's what old Lordie Misphtpht says. You's are ours only hopes now. If yous does this rights maybe we's be frees. Do's this for yous and me's."

Lurky stared at him for a moment saying. "I's do's this for us Slinks," suddenly getting the determination for whatever was ahead.

"That's it!" Leaning over he whispered, "If's we's has to, we's will breaks out and leaves together. Cheers up Lurkys, we's still gots each others.

Besides, this cell has lots of rooms for me to roams while you's is frees livin' the goods life."

He started dancing and skipping around pretending he was having a good time. Inside he was distraught but he couldn't let Lurky know. He needed his friend to be strong. It was their only hope of anything good ever coming out of this.

"Besides we's still gots our flasks," proudly showing his. Lurky stared down at his realizing the Nears had forgotten to take them. "Let's haves a toast!" holding his flask in the air.

"To the waters of life! Drinks a drinks and alls wills be rights!" He poured some into his mouth. He swished it around in his mouth, making animated faces, pretending it was the best thing he ever tasted. He gargled, chortling out musical notes until he almost choked. With one last grand gesture, he swallowed giving out a loud, "Ahhh!"

His antics made Lurky smile and the water did taste good. "I's do's what you's says Slinks, then we's gets out of here's. You's will be's alones here," said Lurky.

Suddenly remembering, he returned from going around the corner.

"Holds outs your hands." He deposited the frightened spider into Slinks hands. "He's cans be your buddy's while I's gones or you's cans eats him if you's wants."

Slinks was surprised at this gift saying, "I'll keeps him as a friends but my true's friends is you's Lurky old buddies," getting choked up. He took the spider over to the corner of the table, gently putting it down. It immediately scurried for cover.

Sadness overcame Slinks, realizing the predicament they were in. He was reduced to having a spider as a companion while Lurky was about to try to do something he wasn't sure he could do. He turned, putting on his best smile, coming back over to the bars. "You's haves the waters of lifes Slinks. I's can gets more outside laters whens I's gones." Slinks appreciated this, knowing the water would be better than the tear soup they would bring. He hid the flasks in the corner of the bathroom so the Nears wouldn't see them when they came down.

Sitting down on the floor, they nestled against each other as best as they could through the bars. Lurky put his hand on a bar, prompting Slinks to put his hand on his friend's for comfort. They talked about the adventures they just had while they waited for the future. A future controlled by forces beyond their influence, except for whatever actions they took, to change the future in their own small way.

"There I ordered us a used wheely barrow, just what we need to change the future in our own small way. This is the latest in modern technology, a single axial, twin handled, variable speed, arm strong steering, workaholic model. Plus we have various fasteners, restrainers, retainers and technological wonderments required to get the job done." Hugh talked in an animated way, using an altered voice making the kids laugh.

"Now who's up for some lunch? I don't know about you but changes make me hungry."

Once everything was ready, Dianne asked, "What were you doing this morning on the porch?" Hugh knew the cat was out of the bag, so to speak.

"I learned a long time ago, wishful thinking won't get you far, for having changes occur in your life. In fact, most people wish their lives away, not realizing, if they want true change they must unfortunately take steps towards their goal, sometimes many steps, sometimes not.

The important thing is that you must do the actions, and then the force of spirit, if you want to call it that, will provide whatever is required to have things happen, which most people call miracles, or coincidences. We have been trained to believe we only get good things in life if we deserve them. Many people don't have good things happen, believing they don't deserve it for whatever reason and don't take the steps necessary to manifest what they want. It is too bad because most of the world never realizes what can be done by them if they only tried.

Sometimes it comes easily, other times not, but you must persevere against whatever obstacles show up. Just thinking about what they want in life will get them only so far, even though this is necessary for understanding, formulating and planning for their wants, needs and desires.

Unfortunately, this kind of mental processing won't bring true manifestation in the right way for them. What usually happens is they receive a watered down version of what they wanted. Usually, their energy is scattered, instead of focusing on each detail needed to accomplish the goal. Not everyone is going to become a king or queen but whatever their destiny in all areas, it can be fulfilled to the highest level possible, if they do it right. Even when you take the steps necessary and believe it is going to happen, you must be prepared to wait allowing it to come in its own time and place.

We are made of atoms of pure energy, assembled from energy, run on energy from the food we eat, the air we breathe. Even though we are made of flesh and blood, we are beings made of energy. Everything about us revolves around energy. Our thinking is a form of energy and believe it or not, our thinking works with the universal energy around us. There are ways to contact and work with the energy, so you have the best life suited for you.

The Chinese discovered there are energy pathways running through the body bringing out the science of acupressure. There are other energy pathways to contact and use the energy of the mind, thought and spirit. These are the pathways I use to help me achieve whatever is necessary. In order for the energy to work, our wants, needs and desires must leave us, go out into the universe, and then what we have desired is drawn back to us by our energy. This is accomplished by using an energy center in the body. This center is where energy flows in and out of our body and is located between our eyebrows, commonly referred to as ' the third eye '. When this channel is open, you are sending out your desire for whatever you would like to manifest, and over time, it will in whatever form it takes.

We do this all the time, whether we know it or not. Some people's channel works better than others. Things, jobs, situations just show up when they need them the most. Others barely have this channel working and as a result they live a life where they do without and never fulfill who and what they are.

In order for this channel to function in the proper way, there must be a sound to accompany it, a proper vibration to help move the energy along to do its job. All sound has a vibration and a sound could have a positive effect, while other sounds have a negative effect. To help the energy do its job, we say a sound that has the right vibration for this purpose, and that sounds is "Awh."

What you heard this morning was me saying the sound, in a long drawn out manner as I visualized what I want in my life.

Tomorrow, I will teach you how to do it, so you can do it for yourselves. Just remember, it can take time for things to come as Spirit sees fit, just be persistent and keep focusing.

For now let's partake of some hot dogs and French Fries. I'm starved, as I am sure you two are." Both children agreed. As they were eating they heard a noise.

"Sounds to me like the delivery truck has arrived with our changes. Right on!" exclaimed Hugh, rising from the table. Both children beat him to the door, since a visitor was a rare occurrence.

The truck pulled up to the end of the house. The children reached it ahead of Hugh in eager anticipation. The driver had a look of distain on his face, waving the bill in the air saying. "It's C.O.D. or I don't drop nothin' off"

Dave and Dianne looked at the ground embarrassed. This wasn't the first time they endured this kind of treatment.

"Don't you worry about that," Hugh said, taking the bill from him, giving it the once over. He paid from a wad of cash big enough to make the driver's eyes bulge. Paying more than the bill was originally for, Hugh said, "Buy yourself a coffee. This probably won't be the last time you'll be out here."

"Ya, it's goin' take more than this to fix this old place up." Answered the driver unloading everything, giving the place a once over with the same look.

"Oh this is just the beginning." Hugh said, making sure everything was there he had ordered.

"Where's the ball caps I asked for?"

"Oh ya, good thing you mentioned something. Compliments of the owner."

"Thanks. We can handle this from here," replied Hugh.

The driver got in the truck and drove off. Hugh turned to the children and said.

"Did you see how his look showed his inner feelings and belief about what he saw? Even though he has no idea what has happened to make this place the way it is. His feelings showed in his face, thinking how poor and uncaring we must be to live like this. Even though, he doesn't know the situation. This had only been verified when your mom was unable to pay the bill several times. He probably heard gossip at the coffee shop and made up stories to form his opinion. The look of the place just reinforced it. Both of you also reacted subconsciously to his thoughts, because you looked down at the ground and I could see the embarrassment on your faces. However, that's changed already!"

Hugh turned and picked up the ball caps. He spoke in a loud official sounding voice, "I present to you Sir Dave the Brave and Lady Dianne the Dotty, your caps of true change. These are only to be worn when you are attempting true change in your lives. When you feel them on your head, or see them on each other, you will know and believe that your life is changing for the better, no matter what you see or face. You have become Changees!"

Both Dave and Dianne accepted the caps, happy to have a physical symbol that they could touch and feel, to show them that change was real and about to happen. Placing his cap squarely on his head, he said, "I dub myself Hugh the Happy! Are you ready to begin change? Now I am warning you, change can sometimes take work and perseverance. Are you ready?"

Both children placed their caps on their heads and excitedly yelled "Yes!"

"We begin by practicing with the wheely barrow to get used to balancing heavy loads, by moving all this." Hugh said, sweeping his hand over the delivered feed and supplies.

"Ladies first, since Dave and I are gentlemen. The wheely barrow driver must turn their caps backwards. That's the sign of recognition that they have this important task to do." Dianne without hesitation turned her cap, and after Hugh lightly filled the wheel-barrow, she grabbed the handles and started moving.

She was off, heading for the barn giggling and weaving at a fast pace. Hugh and Dave followed behind, giving her instruction and encouragement until she reached the barn. They helped move everything inside.

Hugh had bought four large plastic garbage pails with lids saying, "I got these to stop mice and other critters from eating the feed, which means it will last a lot longer. I got the extra two pails for this reason. When you draw out a scoop to feed the goats or birds, shake off one tenth of it into the reserve pail. This is called the One Tenth Rule, which means you are able to save one tenth of everything to make it last that much longer."

The animals won't notice the difference in the ration. they can't count and it will save you ten percent on your feed costs. As well, there are feed dishes for each goat and one for the birds, so they don't trample and refuse to eat the feed. We do the same with their hay ration, saving the same ten percent for the same reasons. Also, I bought in bulk and saved more, so in total on all the feed we saved twenty-five percent. Simple solutions to save money, you can apply it to almost anything you buy."

"Alright, let's go!" commanded Hugh, pretending he was a traffic controller, waving his arms in the go ahead symbols. Dave weaved around slightly until he got control of the wheelbarrow, receiving encouragement as he went to get another load. It didn't take long to move everything with both children taking turns. Finally they stopped for a rest.

"Now are you ready for the next phase of making changes, my Changees?" Hugh said, rubbing his hands together looking and pretending he was some evil being.

He picked up a round mouth shovel holding it upright, snuggling it into his neck, stroking it gently like it was a pet.

"Allow me to introduce you to the single wooden handle, two-hander, back breaking, grunt producing, excavation device, known as 'The Sweatus Profusely'. This device has been the first initiation for many a hard working laborer of the world.

It can be your best friend compared to digging with your hands, or worst enemy to your body when used over an extended period of time. I'm an expert who learned to become one with the shovel. For us it is going to be the first implement of change making, so let us go back to the front of the driveway. I will educate you in the ways of using this marvelous technological marvel."

He headed off with the children, complete with wheelbarrow, gloves, caps and limitless enthusiasm. He wielded the shovel like it was an awkward baton, pretending he was leading a parade down a street. Dave pushed the wheelbarrow trying to dance, Dianne skipping and hopping along beside him. Reaching the edge of the driveway, Hugh scribed out two shapes in the grass where the two planters were to go.

He proceeded to turn over the grassy soil saying, "Please notice I'm using the wider steel end compared to the small wooden end to dig with. Apparently, in the beginning of its use, someone discovered you could get more done using it this way." Dianne and David were staring at the shovel intensely, then seeing Hugh grinning, realized there was nothing more to it than what he was saying.

"There Sir Dave would you like to attempt the other, while Lady Dianne and myself go and accumulate some sturdy, purty looking stones for a nice little retaining wall?"

Dave said nothing, grabbing the shovel to begin digging, wanting to try this for himself. They left with the wheelbarrow, going over to a stone pile in the corner of the field.

Hugh grabbed whatever stones he could find for the walls, tossing them out for Dianne to place in the wheelbarrow. She managed to wheel them back where Dave was just finishing up, but sweating.

Hugh noticed right away saying, "Come on! I feel the change happening already. We'll get more rocks to do the other bed, then some soil, wildflowers and a couple of shiners to accent the wildflowers.

"What's a shiner Uncle Hugh?" queried Dianne.

"Oh, that's rocks that have some shine to them compared to dull brown of these rocks. I saw a couple that would do the job nicely. Come on I'll show you."

Going to the rock pile, he picked out stones that would finish off the second bed. They loaded them into the wheelbarrow, making a heavy load that had Dianne weaving. She fought to keep the load on an even keel. In a few minutes, they had the second bed complete, then were off to the barnyard, retrieving enough loads of manure dirt to fill the beds.

Once completed, Hugh searched for just the right wildflowers to make the beds colorful. Transferring them to the beds, they placed them strategically by shape and color. They stepped back when they were finished to view what they had done.

"That's the most simple and marvelous change I've seen in a long time. I'm so proud of us! Your mother will be shocked when she comes home." The children's faces lit up, realizing they weren't doing this just for themselves.

"High five, everybody!" They all slapped hands together saying how well they'd done.

"Now give yourself a hug and a pat on the back! He bent both arms around so he was stroking and slapping himself on the back saying in an altered voice, "Good Hughie, you make changes so easy. Good Hughie, good Hughie!"

Dave and Dianne laughed out loud at the antics, joining in, doing the same thing. Had anyone seen them, they would have thought they weren't quite all there.

"Alright, that's enough for now. I need a break and a drink of water. Besides by the look of the sun it's around four o'clock."

They had never heard of anyone telling the time of day by the sun, but after being told Dianne ran for the house to find out. After a few moments she came running back out.

"Yes, its five minutes past four Uncle!"

"Darn! I was five minutes out, I must be getting old."

"How can you tell the time by the sun?"

"Well its rather easy; you just take into account your relative position to true north, the time of the year, the length of daylight available at that time of year, and you use the terrain to establish the time interval check-points and combining these factors together, you can tell time within a relative good degree of accuracy."

"What about cloudy days?" Dave asked.

"Ya. What about rainy days?" Dianne pitched in.

"Oh that's real easy. On cloudy days you wear a watch of course!"

Both children stared at him incredulously, realizing what he had just said. Hugh burst out laughing.

"As if! Uncle, we thought you were serious." Dianne yelled.

"I am serious! What I said is true. Think about it, you'll see."

"Okay then, what about the rainy days?" Dianne asked again.

"Those are the most interesting. What you do is get a watch, stand in the rain, and the angle the raindrop's fall will tell you the time of day."

"Okay, now we know you are exaggerating! Blurted out Dianne, making Dave laugh.

"Come on let's go for supper, that's enough for today, all that changing makes me hungry and tired."

"Is it true about telling time from the sun?" Dave asked.

"What did they do before clocks were invented?"

Hugh chuckled, liking the way things were going over time here.

Lord Misanthropy sneered, liking the way things were going over time. The river of tears sounded louder, as it watched the white billowing foam cascading down over the Falls of Affliction. The Nears it had sent out, were doing their duties rather well much to its approval. Its iniquitous nature rose in black abominating waves, bringing it great delight.

It swooned from the increased tear energy, feeling greater hatred and knew it had to make man's life even more baneful. It started sweating, tears soaking its robe, running onto the floor as gooey slimy puddles. Sparks began to erupt from the top of its head like small bolts of lightning dancing across one side and back. Other sparks did the same from its slippers, dancing over the puddles.

It needed something to keep the momentum of tears going. What was required now, was a morale booster to make them double their efforts. The idea came in a great shower of sparks, making it howl in odious recognition. What was required was a party and so a party it would be! A Near Acolyte rushed over, watching the lightning still dancing around, knowing there would be an announcement.

"Get Near Spiritus Frumentus here at once!" was all the Near needed to hear to know what was going on. Passing the other Near Acolyte, they quietly did a high five.

This was going to be fun. It had been a long time since there was a celebration at the castle. It recalled it was when one of the Near Thrall's was turned inside out after being too slow at its duties. It wasn't going to dwell on such gruesome things and spoil the moment. It needed to focus on what to do, eagerly walking through the halls until odors brought it to a set of doors.

These weren't like normal doors, these started up at the knees ending up at chest height so you could see over them. One was almost broken off at the hinges. The room was dark but it could smell the powerful smells of alcoholic beverages wafting out from within. A sign posted by the doors caught its attention, warning everyone who came here, had to read this aloud before coming in.

THE INEBRIATED STATE
IS THE STATE YOU'LL BE
WHERE SANITY'S LOST

AND WRONG WORDS
ARE SPOKEN FREE

COME THROUGH THESE DOORS
GET PREPARED TO SEE
THE STATE OF SOBRIETY
SOMEHOW BECOME
A USED TO BE

Inhaling deeply, it steeled itself against the powerful energy emanating inside. The energy kept coming in subtle waves, beckoning like an invisible finger. Here was a quiet oasis from the cruel, unrelenting, driving world outside. Here you could sit, relax and forget all about how hard your world was, having a nice stress relieving drink and be amongst friends.

The only problem was, once you put the wondrous glass to your lips there was no turning back. The life you had outside the doors was now a faded memory. Remembered only as the life you would rather not face, shown ever so plainly through the colored lens of the glass, as you tilt it back. Instead, it is an amazing new insight through that colored glass, as you try your hardest to empty the glass, only to look down and find it full again, waiting to be drank as well.

Your view of the world becomes distorted, as the effects of the drinks take over, clouding right judgments, encouraging wrong thinking, telling dirty little secrets and lies. You slowly become someone you weren't. You, in your oblivion, become accustomed to this new altered state where time and you become lost.

The Near did its best shaking off the energy coming at it, pushing open the squeaky doors, stepping inside looking around. The noise of the doors made lights come on and a piano started clinking out a merry tune. A Near sat at the piano swaying to the beat, hammering away on the keyboard of an ancient, broken-down piano.

Several bartenders stood behind a wooden bar showing many signs of abuse. The bar stools and chairs were in a deplorable state, many patched together and still rickety. One lay in a broken heap in the corner.

"Come in! Come in good sir! Rest a while. What may I serve you? You look parched. We have a fine selection to choose from for a thirsty traveler such as yourself. What may I pour you?" Exclaimed the Near wiping a dirty old glass with a dirty old rag.

It swept its hand behind it to show off its wares, "My name is Near Rummy the head mixologist and if my products are not your liking I have Near Vintner with a fine selection of wines or Near Brewster and its many beers. Let me add that our beverages are made from only the purest tears found in the Falls of Affliction."

Near Vintner cradled a well used bottle, showing tatters of a label, showing it off. Near Brewster held out a freshly poured foamy beer. It slapped it down on the bar spilling some of it, which it immediately wiped off with a brown hardened wash cloth. Most of the spill splashed down onto the sawdust covered floor.

"To enjoy some ambience, we had Near Virtuoso at the piano that does requests if it knows them, which it doesn't!" Giving the Near at the piano a vicious sneer. Near Virtuoso ignored it thumping away on the piano, lost in its world of musicology, until it swiveled around waving hello, while the piano kept right on playing. It turned back around, catching back up with the keys like it hadn't missed a beat.

"Yes sir, welcome to Ye Old Groggery!" pointing to a faded sign above the bar. "What may I serve you?"

"I'm not here to drink. I don't drink."

Suddenly the piano stopped playing. Near Vintner dropped a wine glass, gasping with the rest, "Everybody drinks after a hard day! If you don't drink how are you going to relax? I've never heard such a stupid thing, you must drink! It's normal! Don't you want to be normal like everyone else?"

"I'm here on official business of our Lord. Near Spiritus Frumentus is to see it at once!" giving a determined sneer. Near Rummy sighed, signaling for it to follow. "It's in the back. Follow me." Going through a door Near Acolyte could hear the others talking.

"The nerve of it! Coming in here and spoiling the ambiance."

"It thinks it's so high and almighty not drinking with us. I'm glad no one else was imbibing, its energy would have made them leave."

Near Acolyte paid them no heed, it was on a mission and didn't have time for a good scrap right now. Near Rummy turned a corner ahead of it, and suddenly a voice bellowed out.

"Not drink! Tha's perposteroush. Hic! Everybody drinks who comesh in here! Drag it Hic! in here an' wesh poursh it down itsh throat!"

Coming around the corner, Near Acolyte saw who was making the loud talking. It was Near Spiritus Frumentus, a barrel of a Near dressed in its original brewing attire that had never seen a wash, except by spills from alcoholic beverages. It had on one slipper while the other hung off its toes like it had tried to put it on but gave up. It was in a total state of intoxication. If it were asked when it last had a sober thought, it would result in a blank stare of incredulous disbelief. Every cell in its body was saturated with alcohol. Every pore on its skin oozed the remains of countless bottles consumed. It was black under both eyes, liver and kidneys totally gone, and between its eyes was a huge, reddish, pock-marked, bulbous nose.

It was in the middle of drinking a large brown bottle of something, when it saw Near Acolyte coming. Pulling the bottle from its lips, some spilled out, sloshing all over its front. Wiping its cheek it exclaimed, "Oh Ish you!" It slurred all its speech, the language of all truly intoxicated beings. "Whaz can I dosh for yoush? Have a drink! Hic!"

"My Lord wishes to see you now!"

I ish at 'ish Lordshipsh command! But first lesh me sho'ho you around," waving its hand in no particular direction. "Come shee!" Rising up, it knocked its chair backwards and swiping at it with its foot, the Near almost fell over.

"Damn floorz keep movin' around here! Yoush sure you don' wantsh some whine?" swinging its hand across several bottles, knocking them all over.

It stared at them before saying, "Wasn't that good!" flicking one bottle off the table. Weaving its way down the hall, it looked like it could keel over any second but it made it to a door going in. "Thish ish where we make h'our finest products! Hic!"

In front of it, it saw Near Thralls moving carts of various beverages. Two Nears pulled on a rope pulley, bringing up a sheep drenched from being submerged in a liquid. It gave out a forlorn Baaa! letting the world know it regretted ever getting lost and wandering into the Land of Afar one day.

"Thish wool ball has given ush tha best sheep dip we've hever made!"

Fascinated, Near Acolyte watched two Nears kicking shovelfuls of excrement into a noxious smelling vat. It thought about where they might get the excrement from but didn't ask.

Near Acolyte was interrupted by Near Spiritus Frumentus saying, "This ish our famous Kick-A-Poo Juice! Bottled only on tha third Thursday of eash month, to make shur thars kick in tha poo by agin' properly." Near Acolyte gagged at the thought of it, making Near Spiritus Frumentus sneer, "Don' worry sonny! Wesh filter it first!"

Near Acolyte glanced over a vat where a Near lay face up, mouth open, catching a leak by drinking it as it dripped.

"Oh thash Near Souse, our drip controller technichin. It makes shur nothin' good gets wasted. Ishn't tha' right l'il buddy?" Near Souse kept its mouth open waving its hand drunkenly. "Alwaysh busy tha' one! Hic! Theresh always a drip somewhersh!"

Near Acolyte looked over at a vat, where a pig in a pen had a small fire underneath it. Two Nears were wiping the sweat off it like window cleaners using squeegees, depositing the slime into a vat. The poor pig was so dehydrated it looked like if one more drop of sweat was extracted it would turn into a piece of bacon. Near Acolyte glanced at it inquisitively.

"Well ish hard to get a descent pig thesh days!Hic! To makesh good Pig Sweat."

It pointed to another room. "Come shee thish. Yoush get akick out'a thish!" There was a beautiful giant bathtub on a marine ornate pedestal. Sitting in the tub was a naked Near pouring a ladle of something on itself, scrubbing all over with a brush.

"Thish ish where we getsh our famous Bathtub Gin from! Made by Near Dipso," pointing to the Near. The Near waved its brush in the air saying, "Itsh so nice to have a vishitor. Hic! Usually everybodysh too drunk to get thish far!"

Poking Near Acolyte in the arm, it motioned for it to follow, but putting its finger to its lips it said, "Yoush gonna like thish but you're gonna have to be quiet. Hesh really shy."

There, standing in a stall facing forwards, stood a donkey. One Near held a bucket catching its pee while another Near stood up at its head, whispering words of encouragement to it to urinate. The donkey appeared that its only concentration was peeing as much as possible. When the bucket was full, it was poured into a fermenting vat. Near Acolyte winced with disgust, glad it didn't drink.

Near Spiritus Frumentus tiptoed away beckoning it to come, "If wesh scares him he won't peesh for a week." He makes the best Donkey Peesh I've ever tashted."

Moving along it said, "Now thish is where wesh makes our beer," Near Acolyte saw a large vat, with a plump Near swishing its fat belly into the liquid. Standing up, it would pick various pieces of mold off its belly, throwing them into the vat as another stirred. It could see the Near's belly was covered with lichens and fungi, staring at Near spiritus Frumentus.

"Thash Near Swillbelly. Each beer ish different, by how many timesh it swishes."

Near Acolyte stroked beer off its list if it ever drank. "Come shee our taste testers."

Near Acolyte saw a long table covered with bottles. At the first table, it was introduced to Near Tosspot. It had a small tin pot that it filled with a beverage. It opened its mouth, tossing the beverage onto its face, causing it to gag. After getting some in its mouth, it swished it around for a taste test while the rest soaked its clothes, chair and floor.

Next, it was introduced to Near Swigger. Its head tilted back with a bottle it never took out of its mouth since the bottom had been cut out. Another Near poured liquids into its bottle which it chugged until all gone.

"Bottomsh up Swigger old buddy!" exclaimed Near Spiritus Frumentus. The Near gave a thumbs up without losing its position.

Near Juicehead chugging beer, would pour it into its nostrils causing it to snort, making foam come out its ears. Near Tiddly watched its antics tee-heeing without let up, between drinks of its beverage.

Near Grogus had a tall dish in front of it, filled with an alcoholic beverage and placed its face into the dish drinking. "If it doesn't drink it all, itsh gonna drown in its sorrows."

Near Acolyte heard crying noises, which made it turn to see Near Maudlin drinking and crying into its beer. "Itsh just worried Near Grogus is drinkin' like a fish."

The whole time Near Acolyte could hear 'almost music'. "Pleash say hello to Near Fuddle. Hesh drunk as a fiddler. Play ush a tune good fella!"

Near Fuddle launched off into a rendition of some made up tune that didn't quite make a song. Most of the strings on its fiddle had been broken and tied together. It did its best, despite dropping its bow several times.

They came to a large tree with a Near precariously perched on a limb having a drink from a cup. "Thishish Near Tipsi whosh drunk ash an owl."

The Near tipped its cup in a salute but tumbled off its perch onto a pile of straw after saying, "Who! Who ish this? pointing to Near Acolyte.

Near Spiritus sneered, "I love it when itsh does that! Itsh such a show off!"

Walking away they could hear a muffled voice saying, "Who! Who ish gonna' help me!"

What really caught its attention, was an awful smell coming from a Near sprawled across a table, making little snoring grunting sounds.

" Thish ish Near Malodorous. Itsh drunk ash a skunk after tryin' to get stinkin' drunk," speaking in a low voice, motioning to leave. If they woke Near Malodorous, it would take up a lot of time talking about nothing, resulting in their own clothes smelling for weeks.

Near Acolyte looked up seeing a Near floating on the end of a rope like it was flying, jerked back and forth dressed in sheets. It held a whistle in its mouth, drinking a beverage through it before blowing the whistle.

"Thash Near Jag. Itz got a jag on, and now itsh high ash a kite, getting' three sheets to the wind, while it wets its whistle." Near Spiritus Frumentus spoke like it was an everyday occurrence. Near Acolyte glanced over at the Near pulling on a rope, seeing it was drinking from a bottle that produced small white flashes of light, every time it put the bottle to its lips.

"Thas Near Likker, itz drinkin' moonshine or white lightnin' as some tend to call it."

As Near Spiritus Frumentus spoke, the Near broke out in song after throwing liquor in its eyes, pointing at the Near floating around.

"MOONSHINE IN MY EYES
MAKES ME YAPPY
MOONSHINE IN MY EYES
MAKES ME CRY
MOONSHINE IN MY EYES
MAKESME MORE THE HAPPY
YOU'RE FLYIN'S IN THE SKY"

They moved towards an area lit up by thousands of candles, where a low moaning chant could be heard. A Near dressed in a decorated robe, sat cross legged on a stone pedestal. It appeared to meditate, pouring a ladle of alcohol over its head, mumbling what sounded like some religious mantra.

"Thish is Near Bacchus, a true Bacchanalian. A descendant of the drinkin' Gods of old. It continues with th'a tradihtion to thish day. It bowed its head in reverence.

Near Acolyte being in the training that it was, understood respect for Lords and such. It could hear the words of the mantra coming from the Near, as it poured the alcohol over its head.

"WHENEVER I GET DRINKING
NECTAR OF THE GODS
IT SLOWS MY THINKING
SO MY MIND IS AT ODDS

WHETHER I SHOULD DRINK
JUST BECAUSE I'M BORED
OR DRINK THE WHOLE KITCHEN SINK
AND GET DRUNK AS A LORD"

After paying homage to this demi-God, they moved on to where another Near stood on a stool saying nothing, just quietly drinking, watching them as they came up to it. Near Spiritus Frumentus spoke, "Thish is Near Wassailer. The toaster at all funcshions we have."

The Near held its cup out in front of it. "Well?"

"Does you haf to?" queried Near Spiritus Frumentus.

"This is my job and it's been a long time. I got new material. Please?"

Near Spiritus Frumentus placed its hand on the bridge of its nose, shaking its head in disgust.

"Oh fine jush this once!"

The Near took a big swallow from the cup, cleared its throat and began,

"TO YOUR HEALTH!
TO A LONG LIFE!
CHEERS TO US!"

Taking a big chug from the cup, it then thrust it out in front of it, it spilled liquid all over the place, including the two Nears listening to it. This only gave it a chance to catch its breath, continuing on in its saluting oracle.

"DOWN THE HATCH!
BOTTOMS UP! HERE'S HOW!
HERE'S TO ABSENT FRIENDS!
HERE'S TO YOU!
HERE'S TO CONFUSION TO YOUR ENEMIES!
HERE'S TO MUD IN YOUR EYE!
HERE'S LOOKING AT YOU!"

"Lez go." Near Spiritus Frumentus said, raising its eyebrows upwards and shaking its head. It touched Near Acolyte on the shoulder, which by now was quite happy to leave. Just as they were getting to the front door, Near Acolyte noticed a body lying on the floor in the corner.

As they walked by, Spiritus Frumetus gave the still body a soft kick in the ribs, however there was no response.

"Oh thas just Near Inebrious. Itz passed out dead drunk and feelin' no pain. We checked, hez not dead yet! Wells thas my friend, ish the tour of our 'umble place of toil and labor. So's hows abouts leading the ways to Lord MisHic! anthorpyHic! Are you sure you wouldn't like a drink before you goes. One for the road, you know?"

Near Acolyte turned for the door out of the saloon, thinking next time it would be the other near Acolyte's turn and it would stay with the Lord. The barkeeps waved a friendly goodbye, shouting in unison.

"Please Get Drunk Responsibly! Remember Don't Get Drunk And Walk!" Near Virtuoso played out a happy little melody until it went out into the hall. Suddenly, everything went quiet and dark, as if it had never even been there.

Near Spiritus Frumentus gave friendly waves goodbye shouting, "Keep the booze a flowin'! Don't drinks everythin' while I'm gone!"

In the darkness, it misjudged the doorway, slamming its shoulder into the side of it, almost knocking the door off its hinges. That spun it, so it headed down the hallway in the wrong direction.

"Sir it's this way" Near Acolyte yelled, pointing the other way.

Near Spiritus Frumentus gave its head a shake, trying to get its thinking working properly, or at least shake out some of the foam bubbles that had obviously taken up space in its pickled brain.

"Fine Mr. Shmarty Pants. Lead on."

Near Acolyte made a mental note not to ever apply for the job of Head Brewer. Looking back it saw the Near Spiritus Frumentus staggering, putting its hand on the wall for support, tottering along. The last bottle it drank was obviously taking effect. Its free hand was waving in the air, like it was a conductor in an orchestra. It sang.

"I'VE BEEN WALKING
IN THE HALLWAY
ALL MY LIVELONG DAY

CAN'T YOU SEE THOSE
CORNERS SNEAKIN' UP
THEY ALWAYS GETS IN MY WAY

RIGHT TURN, LEFT TURN
SO MANY DARN TURNS
MY HEAD'S TURNIN' I SAY

I'M LOST AND CONFUSED
HALLWAYS ARE SO NARROW
THERE'S NO ROOM TO STRAY

BUT I'LL KEEP ON WALKING
WALKING, WALKING
UNITL I SEE THE LIGHT OF DAY

Near Acolyte watched Near Spiritus Frumentus slam into the wall, spinning it around again, so it was going the wrong way again.

"Sir, you're going the wrong way. It's this way." Pointing to where they should be going. Near Spiritus Frumentus looked back at the Near with a look of total surprise.

How, how did you get behind me boy? I'm goin' keep my heye on you, you slippery little begger. Theresh more going on here, Hic! than meez the h'eye." Lifting its finger, it poked itself in its eye, yelling, "Ow!"

Bending its head down, it opened and shut its eye, thinking it had something in it and perhaps by bending over looking at the floor, it might fall out. It noticed its slipper was askew, which it always was but it just happened to notice it now. Bending over to fix it, it fell over.

"Boyz that floor is a long way down. I thought I was never goin' get there." It pointed at its slipper.

"Oh, look it fixed itself! Your shuch a good slipper! Always was! Glad to have you come along for the ride." It started waving its hand in the air.

"Lez go! You shure do take your time goin' to get someone to see its Lordship."

It burst into another rendition of its song that could plainly be heard upstairs as they got closer. Reaching the flight of stairs, it got a serious look on its face, and looked down at its feet.

"Watch these steps feet. You know how trHic!ky they is. They's get movin' out of the way just when I put yoush down." Winking at its feet, like they were listening. It made it to the top one careful step at a time.

"Now shows me Lord Mis Hic! Anthropy Hic," it commanded, in a mocked authoritarian voice. It straightened out its clothes and ran a hand through its hair. It took one step and landed face down on the floor.

Near Acolyte helped it up. It made it to the door leading out onto the balcony. Looking at the Near Acolyte guarding the entrance, it said, "How are you doin' young fella. By tha whay, watch those steps. Thez mean!"

It tripped again and landed at the feet of its master with a thud. It stared at Lord Misanthropy's slippers, shaking its head, "Oh Hi Lord! Hic!Long time Hic! No shee!" Continuing to look at the slippers, Near Spiritus Frumentus lie there, until finally Lord Misanthropy cleared its voice and quietly said, "Up here my faithful servant."

Near Spiritus Frumentus gazed up seeing the Lord's face, and finally got to its feet, trying to keep its weaving to a minimum.

"I can see you have been doing your job with the same zeal and dedication as always. Let me ask, do you have sufficient stock for a celebration?"

"Why wez could keep everybodyz happy forever let me shay. We'z has some new products I think you'sh will really get a kick outa."

"Excellent my good servant, I knew you wouldn't let me down. Go make preparations, there is much to do." It placed its hand on Near Spiritus Frumentus's shoulder, giving it a benevolent gaze.

The Near looked like a dog that had received its first pet from its master. Emitting quiet whimpers of ecstasy, its eyes glazed over, feeling the power of its master's touch pulsing through its body.

"While I have you here, would you ask Near Bacchus to pray harder to the Gods of Bacchanalianism, so the humans drink even more? You know how human's drinking produces tears in so many different ways."

"At once my Lord!" was all it could get out. It turned, weaving its way back towards the door sniffing the air with its huge red nose, like it smelt something for the first time. Looking at the Near Acolyte at the door it queried, "Whaz that smell young fella?"

"That would be fresh air, Sir."

"Oh! Thaz what it smells like," replied Near Spiritus Frumentus.

The Near led it over to the top of the stairs, then letting it go, it watched as Near Spiritus Frumentus didn't even try to navigate the first step. Instead, it bent over, losing its balance to begin its tumble to the bottom. The Near walked away, wincing every time it heard audible complaints coming from Near Spiritus Frumentus collisions with the hallway, on its journey back to its world of intoxication fabrication.

They were all wincing making audible complaints from the work on their muscles. It was agreed to have a simple supper after a hard day's work electing on casserole which while cooking gave them time to talk.

"Hugh would you tell us more about changes?"

"Yes. The mind loves familiarity and even in the worst situations, it will somehow convince you, it is fine where you are, but you don't have to stay there. Your feelings are the best way to determine whether you are where you should be. If you stand back and look at your situation whatever it is and negative feelings overwhelm positive ones, you need to really have a look at it.

If you want to try a new direction in life, it sometimes seems impossible to achieve. The mind will give you every excuse why this won't work. There is only one solution to reach any goal. You must take the necessary steps to obtain it. One step at a time that will turn into many, you must persevere until the goal is reached. The mind doesn't like change, it has enough to do looking after familiarity and the constant problems encountered. Your feelings are the real barometer, take example today. Now the appearance has changed by doing a few simple things, don't you feel better about living here already?" They both agreed.

"Now won't it be interesting to see the driver's face next time he comes and your mother, what will she say? She'll be happier seeing it.

Now let me ask you an important question. Did your mind tell you it couldn't be done every step of the way?" They agreed again.

"So did mine." They both stared at him realizing they weren't unique having their mind react this way. "The difference was, I ignored what my mind was saying to me, I did my planning, organizing, and gathered what I needed. I then broke the large task down into smaller easily manageable tasks that I could complete. I started and finished each task before moving on to something else, even if I became bored, frustrated or seemed to come up against obstacles. So to accomplish my goal, all it took was time.

Now time is a funny thing, time can be your ally or your enemy. Time will move, regardless whether you use it to finish what you start or not. At the end of a day, you can say either you did what you set out to do or you've lost the time and haven't completed it. The choice is always yours. During our time accomplishing our goal, I also tried to have some fun, see some beauty in it and get satisfaction from seeing the changes occur, without thinking about the time.

Once you've completed your goal, give yourself a reward, this helps you compete tasks, knowing something good is going to be there at the end of any goal.

Any goals, circumstance or situations large or small can be done with persistence and determination to see it through to the end. The only difficult part is, the mind has to generally be dragged kicking and screaming the whole way. You must learn to ignore the mind or the change won't occur especially one that takes days, months or years to complete. The mind will usually try to persuade you the change isn't necessary.

Now, I believe what is necessary, is we eat! I'm famished."

It was a sight to behold, as they voraciously consumed the delicious food. The orgy of culinary feasting finally came to an undignified end, when to put it quite simply, there wasn't anything left or to quote Dave, "You pigs ate it all! I hardly got any!"

They burst out laughing looking down at their empty plates. Afterwards the three of them cleared the table and washed the dishes. Each of them doing their part and focusing on what had to be done.

When the last utensil was washed Hugh said, "Why don't you two tuck the animals in and I'll reward us with a bowel of ice cream"

"Ya. I feel an empty corner in my stomach, just big enough for a bowel of ice cream!" Dave replied.

"You forgot about your empty leg. We could put all the food in the house down there!"

"Shut up Dotty, or I'll chew your leg off, just for something to do!" Dave said, making menacing growls and noises. "Run little girl! The leg chewer's on the prowl tonight and he's hungry!"

Dianne laughed, running out the door and to the barn with Dave in hot pursuit.

Hugh watched thinking how fortunate he was to be helping Susan, after all that had gone on, and being able to be around the children. They brought something back to him that had been lost a long time ago. Maybe not so much lost, as faded away with time and age. Hidden somewhere deep inside the dim area of the mind, where he seldom went anymore. He knew forgotten memories still lived unbridled in his mind.

He listened to the children's laughter, realizing there was still an innocent music to it that hadn't been squashed by the harsh realities of the world, yet. They hadn't been taught to shun the music, by those who train the young of the world. His heart ached for a moment, remembering when he once had the music still inside. Unfortunately life drove it out of him, making it go deep inside for protection, hiding before it was extinguished, perhaps for all time.

He didn't have much time to dwell on it. Apparently, children who know there is a bowl of ice cream waiting for them, can do chores in record time. His daydreaming was interrupted by both children running across the yard to the house.

Taking the bowls with them out onto the porch, they each settled into their favorite chairs. They decided sitting on the back porch was the only proper place to eat ice cream. Quietly mouthing their treat, they glanced around at the scenery. This had been a different kind of day, a new day, one they would never forget. It was the real beginning of something new, a new life, one of change.

Little did they know this was the beginning of constant change. Change that would take them places they never dreamed of. The breeze blew a leaf, left over from last fall that still lay free on the grass.

"Change is like the wind, once you allow yourself to be moved once by it, there will always be the tendency to keep moving. Although like the leaf, it won't always be where you plan to go. At times change, like the wind, will have a will of its own and will take you where it decides best. Be flexible because, you might not know it at the time but, where you end up is where you are supposed to be."

"Have you ever really listened to the wind? There is a sound behind the wind. Would you like to hear it?"

Dianne and Dave eagerly nodded their heads, since they enjoyed the experience of listening to the rain.

"Watch the wind in the tree, as it makes the leaves and branches move back and forth in waves. See the rhythmic movements as it ebbs and flows, back and forth, back and forth. Now remember what you see and close your eyes, and see the same thing in your mind's eye.

Sit back comfortably with your hands on your lap and keep your eyes closed while you watch the tree. Listen with your ears to the sound of the wind blowing through the tree. I will do the same."

Dave imagined the tree as Hugh instructed. Listening, getting more and more relaxed, he fell into a slumber of sorts, even though he could hear everything. He wasn't sure, but he thought his body was swaying to the rhythm of the wind. Slowly, the wind became louder and louder and his swaying became like a vibration. Suddenly, he felt lighter and lighter until he was floating.

Without realizing it, he was flying, like he did many times in his dreams. The wind was louder now, but the speed and force of the wind remained the same. There was a musical noise with the wind, at times like an orchestra playing a gentle melody. It would change to a flute, producing long drawn out notes that seemed to sustain his flight. He would rise on the note, then lower as it finished, only be picked up by another, carrying him along. He clearly heard the wind mixed with other sounds. Out of the corner of his eye, he was startled to see his sister floating over to him. Neither said anything, content to listen to the wonderful sounds coming with the wind. Speech was unnecessary; as their thoughts were understood and known on a level he didn't understand.

Floating along they suddenly heard from out of the deepest depths of the wind.

LISTEN TO THE WIND
THE WIND OF CHANGE
AS YOU TRAVEL ALONG

GLIDING, FLOATING
EVER FORWARD
ON IT'S GENTLE SONG

LIFE'S PATH UNKNOWN
YOU'LL COME TO UNDERSTAND
IT'S NEVER WRONG

THE WIND OF CHANGE
EVER BLOWING GENTLY
THE WIND OF SONG

He had no idea how long they flew through what seemed like a fog, until finally far off in the distance, he saw his uncle standing, waving to them, quietly saying, "Wake. Wake. It's time to wake."

He opened his eyes and realized he was still sitting in his chair. Dianne woke to the sound as well. Both of them gasped as they saw that the wind was no longer blowing in the tree and it was almost dark.

Hugh said, "Come let's go to bed, there is more to do tomorrow. We need a good night's sleep."

The children said nothing, anxious to see what else was in store in a new world being revealed, that up until now had been hidden behind a veil. It was now being shown one step at a time in a new way by their inner eye.

Lord Misanthropy scanned the Land of Afar with its inner eye. Now content that part of the feast was well in hand, but there had to be something else in store, something new in their world. The only other part was the food. It motioned with its forefinger, for one of the Near Acolytes to come to it. This time it was a fresh new face required for a fresh new job.

"Please go down to the kitchen to tell them we are having a feast for everyone."

"At once my Lord!" replied the Near, hurrying down the stairs lit only by the periodic torch light. Its shadow danced eerily against the walls. Finally, after what seemed an eternity, it turned a corner coming to a dead end.

The end of the hallway had been widened into a small patio. One of the few tear windows placed in the outside wall, permitted natural light to stream down to illuminate the space.

Arranged in the patio, were several small tables with two chairs, similar to a small sidewalk coffee shop. On each table, was a tablecloth that had been used too many times without being changed, accompanied with an ornamented tear vase, containing a small bouquet of dried teardrop flowers.

What drew its attention was the small opening in the center of the wall, closed with a curtain. On an old faded sign above it, read, 'The Teardrop Café'. Unsure of what to do, it walked over to the curtain, and stood there. Clearing its throat, it just stared at the curtain.

Suddenly, the curtain parted in the middle as both halves flew aside. On the other side of the wall, was a scruffy looking Near with a dirty, old, soda fountain hat tilted on its head. A half burned out cigarette stuck out on an angle from its mouth. It had been there so long it was glued to its bottom lip. Near Acolyte jumped back in surprise, at the sudden appearance of the Near behind the curtain. It ignored Near Acolyte, sticking its head though the opening looking left, then right. Satisfied Near Acolyte was alone, it pulled its head back in saying. "Well?"

"Well what?" replied the Near, not knowing what to say. The Near behind the wall, rolled its eyes. "What's your order?"

It held up an order pad that had been used so many times it was practically ripped to shreds. The pencil was so dull that Near Acolyte was afraid if the Near used it, it would totally destroy the pad.

"I need to talk to Near Catearer, if it's possible?"

"That's not an order, I need an order."

"I need to talk to Near Catearer."

"I'm the order taker!" demanded the Near in a loud voice, showing a mean sneer on its face. Its patience was long gone. "I need you to order!"

"I order you to get Near Catearer, for me to speak to,"replied Near Acolyte, not knowing how else to put it.

"That's better! Its brain does work!" replied the Near. The curtain slammed back into its original place. A plume of dust escaped from the curtain. It could hear voices from behind it, talking. It parted again, to show a large Near with a chef's hat sitting on its head on an angle. A long wooden spoon tucked between its hat and ear on one side, and a long handled fork doing the same on the other, seemed to balance the hat. It had a beard, coated with dried remnants of food that had dripped down onto the chef's apron, as well.

Near Catearer pushed its head through the opening, looking around like the order taker did.

"See, there's no one with it and it doesn't know how to place an order either!"

Placing its beet red hands on the sill of the opening, it gave Near Acolyte the once over, asking. "What can I do for you?"

"My master orders you, to prepare a feast for everyone who is here in the castle tomorrow and Near Spiritus Frumentus is going to supply the refreshments afterwards."

"Why didn't you say that in the beginning? Then, I wouldn't have had to leave my soufflé, which has probably collapsed by now!" shouted Near Cataearer, angrily. Slamming the curtains shut again.

Near Acolyte stood there, not quite sure what to do. After a short time, it shrugged its shoulders, knowing it was over. It had done everything it was instructed to do and now there was nothing to do, but go back. Leaving, it stirred up the dust on the floor that sparkled, highlighted by the colored dance of light from the window.

On the other side of the curtain it was a different story. A loud shout could be heard.

"Ordering!" could be heard right back into the storage rooms. This one important word caused a sudden increase in the clanging and banging of pots, skillets, and other instruments of culinary science. It had been a while since an order had been taken at the take out window. A shout this loud, meant this was no ordinary lunch.

"Everyone assemble!" Roared Near Catearer, scanning the room to ensure everyone obeyed without hesitation. All the kitchen staff lined up in a row to receive their instructions. The row lined up according to importance, with the Head Sous Chef, the Apprentice Sous Chef next. After them, were the Garn-Mangers, followed by the Entrée Metiers, the Sauciers, and the Baker/Pastry Chef. Last but not the least important, were the rabble of helper Thralls, whose job it was to actually make things run smoothly.

Once in line, hats were being adjusted, clothes buttoned up, and straightened out. Everyone to the right of the first Sous Chef put up its right arm to touch the shoulder of the other, shuffling feet to come into a perfect straight parade formation.

Satisfied they were in formation, everyone put their arms down to their sides, straightened their shoulders, stamped their right and left feet in unison, coming to attention, while keeping their heads looking straight ahead.

Near Catearer removed the wooden spoon from its ear, holding it straight up in its right hand. It proceeded to walk down the line, inspecting each of the staff, giving them the once over. Now, the spoon held two rolls in this ceremonial inspection. First, it served as a symbol of the respectful institution of culinary science. Secondly, if anyone didn't pass inspection, they were sure to receive a smart smack on the bridge of the nose, for their insubordination. Today was their lucky day. Even though there were several "Ahs! Ah Has! and Hums!" No one received corporal punishment, perhaps, since this was such an auspicious order. Near Catearer didn't want to spoil the anticipatory mood everyone was in.

Near Catearer finished going down the row. Spinning around, it marched smartly back to the beginning. It turned to the first Sous Chef, bringing itself to attention, yelling, "Attention! Ready for orders?"

Everyone roared back, "Sir! Yes Sir!"

Near Catearer bellowed out. "Head Sous Chef!"

"Sir! Yes Sir!" it pulled out its wooden spoon that was tucked behind its ear, and held it in front of it.

"Ordering, a Number One!"

"Sir! Yes Sir!" Both of them saluted at the same time, banging each other on the right temple with their spoon, causing both of them to stagger sideways. Near Catearer stepped back, and then stood at attention.

Head Sous Chef stepped forward and turned, moving down the line, facing the Apprentice Sous Chef, before bellowing out the order.

"Ordering, a Number One!" The Apprentice Sous Chef pulled out its spoon, holding it out front.

'Sir! Yes Sir!" Both of them saluted each other with their spoons in a like manner across the temple. The Head Sous Chef stepped back allowing the Apprentice Sous Chef to step forward and move down the line to the Entrée Metier, who reached for its spoon.

"Ordering, a Number One Lachrymosely Soup!" shouted the Apprentice Sous Chef.

"Sir! Yes Sir!" The Apprentice Sous Chef hoped the Garn-Manger wasn't going to be so eager in its saluting, but the subtle hint went unnoticed. A solid blow on its temple caused it to stagger. It recovered, knowing the worst was yet to come. Moving down the line to the Saucier, it stood in front of it yelling. "Ordering, a Number One Melting Mood Sauce!"

"Sir! Yes Sir!" It received yet another overly zealous salute that had the Apprentice Sous Chef swaying. Its brain was showing signs of being pummeled by the salutes. It swayed, stepping over to the Line Cook shouting with a little hesitancy.

"Ordering, ah, a Number One Blubbering Roast!"

"Sir! Yes Sir!" came the reply. This time it closed its eyes waiting for the blow which made it almost miss the Line Cook altogether with its salute. Striking the Line Cook's ear, it showed no sign of pain, even though its ear turned red and swollen.

It was happy to be a lowly Line Cook, understanding what the Apprentice Sous Chef was going through. The Apprentice Sous Chef staggered over to the Pastry Chef, who was giving it a serious sneer of sympathy, knowing what was next. The Apprentice Sous Chef stood in front of the Pastry Cook for a few moments. It got its bearings, then with a heavy sigh, hollered, "Ordering a Number One Bawling Bread!"

"Sir! Yes Sir!" This time the Pastry Cook only tapped the Apprentice Sous Chef on the side of the temple, instead of the normal smack. However, this brought a loud roar from the Head Sous Chef, noticing the kind but undisciplined treatment. Marching right down, it stood behind the Apprentice Sous Chef, giving the Pastry cook a fearsome sneer. The Apprentice Sous Chef was unaware, shaking off the latest effects of the blow. Standing stiff it roared out, "Ordering a Number One Lachrymal Eyes Cream Donut!"

The Pastry Cook swallowed hard, knowing it had no choice, landing a resounding smack on the poor Apprentice Sous Chef's temple. This caused it to stagger back into the awaiting arms of the Head Sous Chef, who having no pity, promptly stood it back up. The Apprentice Sous Chef hardly knew where it was, trying to focus its eyes on the Pastry Cook. Once it knew it had the right person, it weakly shouted.

"Ordering! Ah! Ah! Number One Teardrop Candies!" The last blow from the Pastry Cook was too much. Its eyes rolling back in its head, it fell straight backwards onto the stone floor, with a moaning thud.

The Head Sous Chef looked down at the motionless body, before staring at the Pastry Cook with a sneer of slight approval.

"That's better!" it said. Stepping over the prone body of the Apprentice Sous Chef, it marched back to face Near Catearer shouting, "Ordering done, Sir!" Saluting, it held its spoon in its correct position, hoping it hadn't let Near Catearer down by the Apprentice Sous Chef's poor behavior.

"Dismissed! Roared Near Catearer, causing everyone to scramble to their work stations.

Stepping over the body of the Apprentice Sous Chef, it instructed, "Do something with that!"

Watching Near Catearer turn going into its office, it signaled two helpers to pick the body up and place it on a chair, at the rest table in the corner of the room. It poured a cup of hot tear tea for it to sip on once it became conscious. It remembered what it was like when it was an Apprentice Sous Chef and that happened to it. They just threw it in the corner until it woke up.

Satisfied the Apprentice Sous Chef would be alright, Head Sous Chef went back to Near Catearer's office to go over the details of ingredients and mixing methods for the dishes. Strewn across the large desk, were charts and recipes that needed to be followed to make this feast a success.

"Do we have all the ingredients necessary in sufficient quantities?"

"Sir! Yes Sir! I had the helpers out at the Falls of Affliction gathering ingredients and spices as the tears fell over. Ever since I heard our Lord summoned Near Spiritus Frumentus, I was sure a feast would be ordered. There were sufficient quantities and variety of tears from the Tower of Tears to meet our needs to cook for a dozen feasts."

"Excellent! Your foresight shows you will make a fine Near Catearer when the time is right my friend. Now let's get down to business, shall we?

First comes the tables, I want them set with a full complement of cutlery and china. They should be covered with white tablecloths, embroidered with golden teardrop patterns. Every second setting, should have large lachrymal vases containing the tears of the bereaved, so when they wash their hands there is a distinct sound of sobbing. You know how that spurs them on to eat and drink even more."

"That is most excellent sir!"

"Yes, that's why I am Near Catearer. I must know everything that will please the Lord and the Nears. Now for a start, we will have Lachrymosely Soup. I want a good fresh stock of mournful tears, not those days-old ones, that have had a chance to catch their breath or think about their situation, to see if it isn't as bad as they think. I want the ones coming straight from humans that think they are in the worst predicament of their lives and there is no hope. To that, add the spices, starting with a good portion of Yowl.

I want a long, loud, sad cry coming out, when they put their spoon into the soup to stir it, and plenty of Boo-Hoo to carry the tempo. Use some excellent Sob, to help boost the convulsive catching of breath, and a hint of Weep to lend some lament to it.

We will finish with just a pinch of Whimper, so when they pour the soup off their spoon into the dish, they hear the feeble little cries of fear, continuing almost non-stop. That should set the soup up, so it's not too thin but just the right consistency.

Throughout the feast, we will have an ample supply of Bawling Bread in baskets at each setting, so they don't run out. Have the Baker make more than enough. I'm sure the Nears will use it to wipe the soup bowls clean, so they will need more with their main course.

Tell the Baker to use a good fresh batch of Bawling, which has risen to the proper height. I really want to hear loud crying without restraint, when it is broken apart. We will add lots and lots of Wail, to help give that long drawn out cry of pain when it's broken apart.

Add just a hint of Yamp to give it a raucous cry, then a pinch of Squall, to provide a little loud discordant tearful scream, and a little Bawl so there are loud bawling curses, to really reinforce the overall Bawling. To that, just a smidgen of Outcry to help reinforce the angry expressions, so it doesn't overpower the Bawling, then give just a shake of Blubber, so there are some choking sobs and a hint of Ululation, providing some wail and lament to round out the sounds."

"I am getting goose bumps just thinking about it. So what's for the main course?" Near Catearer started rubbing its hands together excited as well, at the prospects of such a marvelous feast."

"Next we would begin with a Sniveling Salad! Toss together high-pitched Whining, long drawn out Weeping, and weakly mournful Plaintive Sounds. To that add chopped Keen, to compliment the high-pitched wailing, from some mourning of the dead. Add diced Murmur, so when they are chewing it, there is a soft, low, continuous indistinct sound of pain. Add shredded Sorrow to give just the right amount of grief and sadness, covered by a nicely put together Whine dressing. Be sure it brings out the long drawn sounds of the Whining, Weeping and Plaintive Sounds. I'm sure that will be a salad worthy of being munched on by any Near!"

The Head Sous Chef could hardly hold back its enthusiasm, visibly trembling with anticipation.

"The main course will be an ample supply of Blubbering Roast, more than enough to fill them up, even if they want thirds or fourths. We start with a large portion of Blubbering. I want the noisy weeping kind, not that

Blubbering that's been sitting around in the fridge for a week or more, it tends to have more of a mournful lament to it. I want fresh, right off the hip of True Complaint, uttered with gasping, choking sobs while weeping noisily. You know how the Nears love to hear that when they cut into it with their knives."

"Oh yes! They just go nuts wanting more of it. I'll make sure we have enough True Complaint cooked up, so there are no shortages."

"This time I will do something a little different. To it, we will add Melting Mood Sauce made from a wonderful base of soft, dissolving Crying Stock. Mix it with just the right amount of Bewail, Bemoan, and Whimper. It will provide just the right mixture of lamentation and moaning of deep sorrow, with the proper amount of feeble little cries of fear, non-stop. We will put in just enough Moan and Groan, to have the sound trail off in just the right pitch and intensity. We add a hint of Murmur and Sigh to give it that perfect mood."

"Sir you are an absolute genius!"

"Well, I can't take all the credit. Some of this has been a handed down secret, known only to Near Catearers and I will teach you everything when you become one."

"It will be a true honor." Replied the Head Sous Chef, bowing its head.

"We aren't done yet! Now comes dessert. We will make Lachrymal Eyes pastry. A nice light fluffy pastry of dried tears that contains a filling of Flood of Tears mixed with Weeping. I want the tears of the freshest kind, where they have just heard the worst possible news. That way, when the Nears bite into them, there is a gusher of tears that keep them hard pressed licking and sucking on the filling as it comes. Once they have had their fill of everything, we will supply them with Teardrop candies to suck on, made from hardened sweet tears of a human's love's lost cause, that's been thrown to the wind by another who wouldn't give love back."

"Is that all?" queried Head Sous Chef, wiping its sweaty brow with its coat sleeve.

"Yes. We will top it off with Tear Bottles at each setting for them to wash down their tears and I want an equal mix of Crying, Sobbing and Wailing in the bottles to give it the proper tasting blend, just so no one will complain. You are now dismissed to do your duties."

Standing up straight, Head Sous Chef yelled. "Sir! Yes Sir!" It turned stepping smartly out the door to see to the details. It gave Near Catearer a chance to glance over at the table, where the Apprentice Sous Chef could be seen, sitting drinking its tear tea looking a little worse for the wear from its salute training. Near Catearer gave a little 'humph' to itself, knowing it would be a long time before it would promote the Apprentice Sous Chef to anything else, besides dish washing. It looked down at the papers on the table to make sure it hadn't forgotten anything.

Nothing was going to go wrong. Not on its watch.

Lord Misanthropy watched from its throne, making sure nothing was going to go wrong. Not on its watch. The castle took on a new life. Everyone made sure nothing was going to go wrong as scores of Near Thralls moved furniture about and others carried trays of cutlery getting ready for the feast. It had been a long time since the last feast and many Near Thralls, whose lives were one of toil and drudgery, looked forward to some merriment.

Although it would be a cardinal offence to openly smile, punishable by being turned inside out, they kept their lifted spirits to themselves, hopefully deep inside to go undetected by their Lord.

Lord Misanthropy was amused that a feast would make the Nears move, without snarling and hissing at each other, rushing about. Everyone was cooperating and moving as a team.

Its mood was foul with this nagging feeling of apprehension floating somewhere in the back of its mind. Something wasn't right about all this. Something was blocking its knowing everything. It was sure several times it heard far off laughter in the wind, when its attention wasn't on it. It was unsettling. It was Lord Misanthropy, Hater of Man, Destroyer of Will and Subju of the weak-minded. It wasn't going to allow this. It needed a second opinion, announcing to the Near Acolyte closest to it, "If anyone even cracks a smile, I want to know about it! I go commune with my master in the 'The Great Egos', I will not be disturbed!"

"As you command my Lord!" replied the Near Acolyte bowing. Its command was loud enough the closest Nears thought it knew about their uplifted spirits. They quietly informed the others. Everyone was guarded about what they showed about how they felt.

Lord Misanthropy entered the room where its stone rest slab stood, moving and climbed up onto it. Laying down it placed its head on the pillow. A Near Acolyte folded its robe around it, stepping back once satisfied.

Tears started to flow from the Lord's cold white eyes. The Near Acolyte opened its mouth sobbing. This wasn't the sobbing of someone who had just had his or her spirit broken from a tragedy. Instead it was an ancient Song of Sob, used to help its Lord reach the enlightened state required. Lord Misanthropy closed its eyes, emitting a long low sound "Eeeee, Goooo, Ooooo, Sssss" repeating it over and over.

"Eeeeee, Goooo, Ooooo, Ssssss
HEAR US NOW
ANGUISH BOUND
DISCONSOLATE LONELY SOUND
DISPAIRING STATE FOREVER FOUND
Eeeeee, Goooo, Ooooo, Sssss
TEARS OF SADNESS
HARDENED HEAVY HEARTEDNESS
LOST HEART'S MOURNFULNESS
BEATS EMBITTERED FORSAKENNESS
Eeeee, Goooo, Ooooo, Sssss
RUEFUL EXISTENCE FOREVER STRONG
LAMENTUOUS TEARFUL ECHOING SONG
LOST FOREVER SOBBINGLY GONE
LOST, LOST NOW IN THE WOEBEGONE
Eeeee, Goooo, Ooooo, Sssss"

Finally it stopped. Its body slowly turned to a whitish mist, then was gone. The Near Acolyte finished its Song of Sob. The Near, observing its master had gone, stood guard at the door.

No one else saw the Lord go or come back in its private affairs, things a lowly Near wouldn't want to know about. It was better to focus on the feast and these were coming along nicely.

Near Catearer showed up giving the Maitre'd updates on the food preparation. It instructed the near Servitors to assemble at their stations, making sure everything was in order.

Without warning, Near Misanthropy came out followed by its Near Acolytes.

It was dressed in its finest black robe that glistened, caused by thousands of tiny, hardened tears sewn into the fabric. A large, embroidered, golden teardrop was centered on the chest area and back. Small jingling, gold tears, embroidered all the edges.

The gold tears came from the tears of ancient kings and queens who had been seduced by the black lord's whisperings. They once followed the inner promptings of their spirit, allowing the mind to be used only as a tool to manifest material things, and how the world should be around them.

This was long before man's mind was influenced by the Nears. Now, man had forgotten the real truth, living instead in a world of illusion and misery.

It wore a large, bejeweled, gold tear-shaped crown, augmented by two gold earrings with diamond studding. Its golden slippers emitted the worst shrieking and crying of baby's sounds when it walked. The Near Acolytes wore tear embroidered black robes. They were allowed no gold or jewels until they conquered their very own world, in a universe somewhere.

Lord Misanthropy took its place on its throne, looking around. Its own table was set up for the feast. It never ate with the rest. Gazing around, it saw all was in order.

There was silence in the whole castle. Holding a gold teardrop shaped vase, the Near Acolyte spoke in a loud voice.

"BEHOLD THE VASE OF DESPOND

DESOLATE HEARTBROKENNESS
HOME OF THE WOEBEGONE

SORROW'S HEAVY HEARTEDNESS
THE WEIGHT TOO STRONG

HEART STRICKEN WRETCHEDNESS
EVER HELD TIGHTLY UPON

HEARTSICK LONELINESS
LINGERING AND NEVER GONE

THE HEARTBROKENNESS
A LAMENTUOUS SONG

THE SORROW OF DESPOND
WAILING ON AND ON"

Taking off the top of the vase, puffs of dark vapor were emitted, accompanied by a soft wail. Holding the vase in front of itself, it tipped it. The dark contents began to spill out onto the floor.

A high-pitched screaming lamentation erupted from the liquid, as all the stored up heartbroken emotions were released. This was the signal the feast had begun. Billows of dark vapors rose up to the ceiling. The wailing, screeching crying followed it up, increasing in intensity. At the last drop the noise stopped as suddenly as it began.

There was silence, where only a few moments before, existed a sound that would have caused even the strongest of us to break down from a broken heart. Nothing stirred until suddenly a foot stomped the floor, then again and again, rhythmically joined by other feet stomping, until the castle reverberated. All the Nears began to shout from every corner and room in the castle. A procession of Nears filed out of the back hallway, dancing and stomping their feet, moving to positions around the tables, yelling.

"WE ARE THE NEARS
WE ARE THE NEARS
FEAST ON THE TEARS
FEAST ON THE TEARS

THAT'S WHY WE'RE HERE
THAT'S WHY WE'RE HERE
FEAST ON THE TEARS
FEAST ON THE TEARS

HAVE NO FEAR
HAVE NO FEAR
FEAST ON THE TEARS
FEAST ON THE TEARS

WE'RE THE NEAR
THAT'S WHY WE'RE HERE
TO FEAST ON YOUR TEARS
FEAST ON YOUR TEARS"

The Nears filed into the room individually. All Nears were equal in the eyes of their master, or so they thought. However, each did its job to the best of its abilities and was recognized for that. Many Nears were out doing special assignments, so this feast was for the ones available or were able to return without jeopardizing their mission.

Near Immolation, came up from the basement to get away from the Risibility Machine. After it came, Near Dissever arrived, back from a mission to ensure the rain forests were being destroyed as quickly as possible. Near Quietus had just finished stowing away thousands of souls that had perished in manmade or natural calamities, besides its usual drop deads.

Near Disserver pointed to beads of tear sweat on its forehead. Near Quietus replied, "Yes, the humans are disposing of themselves at an incredible rate these days. I left the Shadow of Death in charge until I get back. I deserve a break away."

Near Baet'l sneered visibly, "You can partly thank me for that my friend. The humans are stupid enough to go to war for the slightest reason.

I've just come back to plan my next attacks, which should yield a great deal of casualties for you to stow away."

Near Quietus said gleefully, "Excellent I've got plenty of room for the whole human race if they get foolish enough to destroy themselves in a holocaust. I know as you do, they have already produced the weapons of mass destruction to more than do the job."

Near Credo interjected, "I am doing what I can to keep the sectarian violence escalating within and between the various religions. However, it isn't easy with the odd peacemaker getting in my way."

Near Jingoist added, "I'm stirring up as much nationalistic pride and superiority feelings as I can, causing warfare and hatred between different countries these days. It does keep one busy."

They all nodded in agreement, surrounding the tables, doing a dance that was in rhythm with the stomps on the floor. The dance was kept going until all the Nears stood assembled behind a chair at the tables. The song and sound stopped, leaving only the quiet murmur of sobbing and crying of the tears running down the walls and the fountain.

Near Wassailer stepped forward to the head of the table near Lord Misanthropy, cleared its throat and began.

"OH GREAT LORD
BRINGER OF TEARS
WE GIVE THANKS
FOR BEING HERE

TO ENJOY THIS COMPANY
OF THE NOBLEST NEARS
TO EAT AND DRINK
THE FINEST OF TEARS

THAT THIS WAS THE
GREATEST FEAST OF TEARS
TO BRING US ALL
THE GREATEST OF SNEERS!"

The noises from the tears flowing down the walls and the fountain increased. It was done, to help bring some ambiance to the occasion and encourage the Nears to really enjoy themselves. Before it could go into more toasting, one of the Near Acolytes behind it poked it in the ribs, reminding it no further toasting was necessary. The Nears were happy not having to endure another of its endless toasting tribulations, shouting loudly, "Sneers!"

This was the official ending of toasts and now they all seated themselves. There were no conversations between the Nears. They simply gazed around the table sneering at each other, especially if they hadn't seen each other for a while. The Near Thralls and Servitors scurried around the room, bringing large soup bowls and breadbaskets, placing them in front of them. Some bent down examining the soup, trying to determine what kind it was. Everyone waited until the Lord had been served. When it placed its spoon in its soup bowl for first taste, everyone joined in.

There began a quiet noise of Nears talking and the clatter of silverware, once it was evident they could proceed, looking at what they were about to eat. It was obvious, this wasn't the usual fare, drawn from the lake.

Near Quietus stirred its Lachrymosely Soup allowing some drops of it to splatter back into the bowl intently listening, before speaking loudly, "What's this? I hear a broth of fresh mournful tears, but there is a chorus of yowl to really help boost them."

Near Dissever stirred it's at the same time, "I can hear boo-hooing as well to help bring the other two sounds out!"

"There's just a hint of weeping in there as well. I can hardly believe what I'm hearing!" replied Near Credo.

Near Quietus picked up a spoonful of soup, allowing it to dribble back into the bowl.

"I don't believe this! I hear whimpering as it lands back in the bowl. Near Catearer has outdone itself this time!" It greedily scooped up the soup, pouring it into its mouth. It savored the sounds emitted from the soup, devouring it. The sounds were a mixture of the most horrible mournful weeping of someone, who had just received the worst news of their life, and all hope was gone.

Nears ate like this with all the tear foods they had. They never closed their mouths to chew, to be polite like humans were taught. Rather they totally enjoyed opening and closing their mouths as they chewed, smacked, and slurped.

Smacking their lips, rolling the food around in their open mouth really got the screaming, sobbing, and wailing sounds out of the food, for the whole Land of Afar to hear. The Near that did it the best was considered to be the Near that had the best meal.

Near Naturas Vandalic, hearing the sounds coming from Near Quietus, shouted, "My Lord!" This was the ultimate compliment to their Lord for providing them the best tears for food.

Other shouts of compliments continued. They all tried the soup, slurping and smacking their lips until it almost sounded like pigs eating at a trough. Instead of grunting and squealing, there was a sad, disheartening, wounded, symphony of lamentation floating through the air that would make any of us heartsick forever.

Near Crav, the Near of Lust couldn't wait any longer, seizing a piece of the Bawling Bread. It slowly tore it apart, holding the bread beside its ear, so loud were the sounds coming from the soup being devoured. There were suddenly bawling sounds coming from the bread. Sounds, one would hear from children when something cherished has been torn away from them, never to be given back.

Mixed with the bawling, was the sound of wailing, of someone caught hopelessly in the worst possible circumstances. There was yamp and squall, to give a loud, disagreeable, tearful screaming and some outcry of protest, of an injustice so wrongfully done.

Near Crav stood up, holding the broken bread in its hand, shouting over and over, "My Lord! My Lord!"

Near Pique, resentful at seeing its colleague behaving in this manner, greedily grabbed a piece, ripping it apart. Chunks went flying across the table, sending out even more of the horrible sounds.

Other Nears started doing the same, grabbing and tearing apart the Bawling Bread, sneering with glee at the noises coming from the food. They chewed the bread and soup enthusiastically, between shouts of compliments to their Lord. Just when it seemed it couldn't get any better, out came the main course. There was Sniveling Salad bowls and Blubbering Roast, accompanied by bowls of Melting Mood Sauce.

"What's this?" shouted Near Hebejebe. "I was afraid there wasn't anything more to out do this, but I was wrong. Now I'm afraid, I won't know how to contain myself. If it's anywhere near as good as we've just had."

"Well, live in fear my friend!" announced Near Envi. "I don't believe I will ever be able to leave this table. That suits me just fine!"

Skewering a large piece of the Blubbering Roast, hearing the sounds coming from it, it could hardly stand the excitement listening to the noisy weeping mixed with wailing, bawling and the odd shrieking squall erupting. Poking it with its fork, it exclaimed, "My Lord!"

Holding the piece of Blubbering Roast up in the air skewered on its fork, it shook it to get the full effect of the sounds. It almost reached a state of delirium shouting, "My Lord! My Lord!" One of the Servers had to finally go over to help it sit down, so great was its impassioned arousal.

Other Nears were trying their Sniveling Salads, mixing it all together as the high-pitched whining and weeping came out in a melody with the keen, murmur and sounds of genuine sorrow. Never had such a wonderful salad been presented to the Nears before, making some of them hold it in the air. Stabbing it with their forks, they greedily munched, open mouthed, causing the sounds to become much louder. Sneering approval to their Lord, their mouths were bursting full of salad.

Some wished they didn't have to eat it, preferring just to listen to the sounds. However, their greedy, insatiable desire for tears, made them eat it and everything else in front of them, one helping after another. On and on went the feast, one continuous frenzy, of gluttonous tear regalement. They tried to satisfy their unending hollow hunger.

Time didn't exist. It meant nothing to creatures whose only focus and purpose was to feast on the tears of humans, they had so slyly coaxed into parting with.

The Nears were almost beyond control, consuming the energy of the tears. They devoured everything in a passionate state of frenzied delirium until it was gone.

Some of them resorted to licking out the bowls, gathering up the crumbs of the Bawling Bread, using their fingers to wipe clean the dishes-anything to get more tears! The shouts of 'My Lord' never ceased until it was over. A quiet calm settled over them, until they realized dessert was on trays waiting to be served, once the dishes were cleared away.

The Nears weren't in the mood for polite etiquette. Picking up the dishes that were on the tables, they threw them anywhere, to make room for more. The Servitors stayed back out of the way until it was safe to proceed, bringing out platters of the pastry Lachrymal Eyes and Teardrop candies. Tear bottles would wash down all the tears they had consumed.

Near Irate, angry at having to wait, grabbed one of the pastries as soon as the platter was on the table, and shoved it into its mouth, biting down hard on it. This resulted in a gusher of tears coming from the filling in the pastry, and it gagged as tears poured out of its mouth in a constant stream.

Other Nears watched in disbelief at the amount of tears coming from such an innocent looking pastry. They bit into their own with the same result, having to lick at the pastry continuously while the contents leaked out, accompanied by a weeping sound.

At times, it seemed like the pastry wouldn't stop. When it did, they roared compliments to their Lord. They wiped their lips and beards of the excess tears, licking their hands, not wanting to lose any of it. Some of the Nears drank from their Tear Bottles to wash down the tears. They could plainly hear the sound of crying, sobbing and wailing from the tears in the bottle.

Other Nears tried the Teardrop candies, rolling them around in their mouths, the sweetness of the misery they tasted, satisfied their sweet tooth. Finally, all the desserts were gone, leaving the Nears almost satisfied. Quiet settled over them other than the occasional belch or burp, a mixture of all the sounds settling in their stomachs.

Suddenly, Near Quietus stood holding up its cup, glanced around at everyone, shouting, "My Lord!"

Everyone else stood up in agreement holding up their cups as well, chanting the words in chorus, over and over. Lord Misanthropy had been reveling in its own orgy of feasting and enjoying the many compliments it had received from the Nears. It stood up holding its cup up to acknowledge the toasts given to it. As the cheers stopped it announced in a loud voice, "Bring out the Tear Beer!"

The Nears stared at each other in amazement at the announcement, then in unison started thumping their cups on the table and chanting, "Tear Beer! Tear Beer!"

Not only was there a feast but now there were refreshments. This was totally unexpected. This was a night that wouldn't soon be forgotten in the history of the Land of Afar.

Near Spiritus Frumentus had secretly brought up Tear Beer casks, hiding them in the hallways as well as a fine selection of Sheep dip, Kick-A-Poo Juice, Donkeys Pee, Bathtub Gin and Pig Sweat, bottled just today. Near Rummy, Near Vintner and Near Brewster set up a portable bar, more than happy to serve their finest beverages.

Servitors were busy distributing mugs of beer to all the tables. Near Souse kept up its important responsibility of being tap drip controller, catching any of the spilled beer with its mouth, under the casks.

The Servitors rushed to make sure everyone received their beer, knowing the Nears weren't the most patient being in any world. Thumping their cups on the table in rhythm they chanted.

"WE'RE THE NEARS
WE'RE THE NEARS
WE LOVE TO
DRINK TEAR BEER

NOW WE'RE HERE
NOW WE'RE HERE
BRING OUT THE
TEAR BEER"

Near Virtuoso couldn't bring its piano. Instead it brought along an old fiddle that had been used to knock someone over the head with, more than once. It showed a decided kink in the instrument, normally not part of the fiddle's unique shape.

Its bow had a few hairs roughly woven together, plucked, not cut, from the tail of the shy donkey downstairs. This had interrupted the flow of Donkey's Pee for the foreseeable future. It wasn't the ideal setup for any musician of the caliber of Near Virtuouso, however it would have to do for now. Being a true practitioner of virtuosity, it rose to the occasion, scratching out a tune to the chanting of the Nears, thumping its foot to keep rhythm.

As the feast wore on, the sneers of the Nears became more and more intense, authentic, exposing their true being. A human's sneer is but a shadow of what you would see from a Near.

Sitting at the table, the sneer Near Quietus gave, looked like death itself, coming without conscience, without remorse, and with no discussion for you, whether you wanted it or not.

Near Immolation's sneer was one of total contempt and disgust for any living plant.

Near Venal, responsible for lusting after money at any cost, gave a sneer of someone who had all the wealth in the world, but would not share a penny with a starving person.

Near Naturas Vandalic, produced a sneer that relished the total destruction of any possessions a person had worked a lifetime to acquire, or lives, to be taken away in a few moments of nature's fury.

Near Credo, made sure man developed an excessive zeal for a set of religious rules, believing anyone who didn't follow them was damned. It sneered the worst appearance of a spiritual leader, who catching a transgressor, punished them with expulsion without thought or regret.

Near Baet'l, who made sure man resorted to war and fights for whatever reason, sneered like the commander watching the total absolute annihilation of its enemy, with no hint of mercy.

Near Jingoist, who advocates an aggressive nationalist foreign policy, gave a sneer of destruction, believing they were superior to everyone else.

Near Bane, who looked after any bad luck a person might have, sneered like someone who just played the worst practical joke, producing a cruelty and hurt of the worst kind.

Near Aflik, who brought trouble into a person's life, sneered like someone who had deliberately harmed someone else to bring self-pleasure, watching their torment and tears.

Near Hebejebe, whose job it was to bring fear into a person's life, sneered with a relish at watching the worst fears of a person come true. The kind of fears that you wouldn't want to even think about or even dream could happen to you; this was its sneer.

Near Pique, who caused people to resent others, sneered a sneer of total resentment, the type from someone jealous at a person's good fortune in life, that your life was better than theirs.

Near Irate, responsible for producing anger in a person, sneered with a look of the worst anger, making its face contort into a wicked mask.

Near Envi, who made sure every human became attached to life's illusions, sneered the look of someone who had an attachment to something and under no circumstances, would ever give it up.

Near Hubris, sneered like someone who believed they were the best thing ever invented, believing that the rest of the world was a cheaper copy of them.

Near Crav, who made people lust after things, material or otherwise, sneered like someone who wanted something more than anything else and would not stop until they got it.

Near Acidant, sneered like someone who told you not to do something and when you did, you had an accident.

Now for Nears, drinking wasn't an everyday occurrence. So after more exuberant sneer cheers and drinks snuck in between the toasting and cheering, the sneer cheers became somewhat louder and slurred, as did the conversations. It wasn't very long before every Near was milling around the room. They weren't used to sitting and doing nothing. A few drinks later, some were dancing around the fountain, boo-hooing like they were upset by the baby cries.

Slurring their speech was just fine for Near Spiritus Frumentus. Now it could finally have a decent conversation with whomever it wanted to, saying, "Shober speech sheemed to hav' shome kinda of accent tha' wash difficult for me to underHic!stand." Several Nears agreed with it, crying in their beer, saying it really brought out the beer's flavor.

Near Naturas Vandalic had a bottle of Kick-A-Poo juice it kept trying to pass gas into it, or as it said. "It puts flavor into the bottle."

However, as one Near quipped, "This was a true natural disaster waiting to happen."

Near Immolation kept standing up on a chair trying to stab itself, with the wrong end of a knife yelling, "I sacrifice myself for the betterment of you all!" It would swallow a large gulp of beer then pushed Near Acidant off a chair, hoping it would have a sacrificial accident.

Near Wassailer, was standing on a chair staring at everyone cross-eyed, shouting out a whole list of cheers and toasts. Near Jingoist helped whenever it came around to politics and patriotism. Both of them had to keep Near Baet'l back with a chair since it wanted to fight, thinking they were insulting it as they toasted.

Near Souse, under a dripping tap, was joined by Near Hebejebe, afraid it would get a drip in its eye and drown, even though it tried to catch every drip. Near Souse gargled words of encouragement, at the right technique for tap dripping controlling.

Near Irate was mad at everyone for getting drunker than it was or so it thought. Near Pique was resentful that Near Irate had the ability to get mad at everyone, so it sulked in the corner. Near Envi held onto Near Hubris, wrapping its arms tightly around its leg. It was totally attached to the idea that Near Hubris kept telling it how good it was, compared to everyone else.

Near Bacchus, a true Baachanalian, descendent of the drinking Gods of old, sat in the fountain with Near Credo baptizing each other with beer, arguing over who baptized the best.

Near Inebrious dead drunk in a corner, was joined by Near Quietus shouting, "Bring out your dead drunk!" Taking turns pouring beer into their mouths.

Near Fuddle, drunk as a fiddler by now, joined Near Virtuoso in a vain attempt at producing something resembling music. They had few strings left on their bows and they were attempting two different songs at the same time.

The drunken revelry went on for as long as the beverages lasted or the Nears collapsed. Lord Misanthropy watched in its usual malevolent manner. Tapping its foot now and then, when the fiddle tunes resembled music. It returned compliments by raising its cup, content knowing the Nears would continue with their concerted efforts after such an excellent feast and drunken revelry.

They existed for one reason and one reason only; not because it liked them, but because they would gather it even more tears.

Lurky and Slinks heard the shouting upstairs accompanied by the dreadful noises of the feast and drunken revelry. The human sounds of wailing, screaming and crying in their unlimited variations assaulted their sensitive ears. They crowded together as close as the bars would allow. Memories of the first feast they had to endure came flooding back. They had seen the true nature of the Nears when too much tear beer motivated them. Luckily for them that time, the cell keys couldn't be found.

The problem now, was Lurky was outside at their mercy, which usually meant no mercy, so he wasn't doing well, visibly shaking, whimpering, "Don'ts leaves me's Slinks. They's goin' to hurts me!"

Slinks stared him in the eyes, "Let's pretend they's isn't heres. We's will plays a games."

"A games?" queried Lurky.

"Yes let's plays chase old spid'y!" reaching behind the table bringing out the spider.

"Looks Lurky old buddy. I's gots spid'y and he wants to plays with us!" The spider skittered around on him nudged by his finger.

"Lurky it's seems like he's limbered ups now." Placing the spider on the floor, he gave it a push towards Lurky and freedom. Lurky's curiosity was aroused, now focusing on the spider quickly crawling his way.

Slinks yelled, "Get's him Lurky! Don't lets him gets away!" Still hesitant Lurky let the spider crawl by, headed for the hallway. Slinks kept teasing him. Watch him Lurky! He's a slipperys spid'y. He's leavin'! Get's him!"

Instincts took over, suddenly crouching and making whimpering sounds. He couldn't take it anymore. Just as the spider reached safety he pounced, cupping his hand over it. Slinks jumped around pretending he was excited. Lurky smiled saying, "I's gots him." Making sure it was fine, he pushed it towards Slinks who was squatted, pretending he was ready to pounce any moment, whispering, "I gots him! He's not getting' aways!"

Holding his hand up to show Lurky the spider was fine, Lurky clapped his hands, getting excited.

"Yous really pounced on him that times Slinks. He's didn't stands a chance!" Motioning for Slinks to send the spider his way, he crept back several meters, crouching low to pretend he was hiding. His ears slowly flapped in anticipation, allowing the hapless spider the opportunity to crawl for safety back to its web. After crawling a meter, Lurky jumped high in the air, screaming a blood-curdling growl like he was going to eat the spider on the spot. Slinks jumped around in the cell, encouraging Lurky. "That's it Lurky gets him!"

Lurky landed, covering the spider with his hands, making sure he didn't hurt the spider. He held his trophy triumphantly to Slinks, making Slinks jump around in the cell showing his pleasure.

"That's was a mighty pounce's Lurky! You's really goods at that!"

Lurky was so pleased with himself, he smiled excitedly. This was what Slinks wanted. Without telling Lurky, he had one ear on the stairs for any hint of the Nears coming down. So far none were coming, so he kept the game going.

They continued doing stunts, some spectacular, some not. Time went by without them even noticing the noises from upstairs. Eventually, it seemed the noises weren't as loud or violent as in the beginning.

Finally spider had enough. It wasn't going to be played with them anymore. Several of its legs were sore from being squeezed. When placed on the floor, no matter how much prodding with fingers happened, it just sat there, legs curled in a ball refusing to crawl.

"Looks like spidy had enoughs. I'll puts him aways to sleeps. Maybes he'll plays later." Slinks placed the spider under the dark corner of the table. The spider crawled behind the table leg. It turned around, hiding so it could look out to at least see the Sneakeeze coming, if they changed their minds. Slinks left it alone, going over to the bars, sitting down on the floor across from Lurky.

"I's a little tireds too, Slinks" Lurky said giving out a long drawn yawn.

"Me's too Lurky, maybe a naps in order. It's getting quieter upstairs. I's don't thinks they's coming down."

Lurky looked back towards the hallway nodding in agreement, grateful they weren't going to be tormented this time, or worse. It meant perhaps they would have a decent sleep. Snuggling together, they closed their eyes, content to have had some playtime together. Lurky placed his hand next to Slinks leg for security. There was no knowing how long they might be together or worse, how long they might be apart, as he drifted off.

He was dreaming of a wonderful place, a large field of beautiful flowers and bugs, large and juicy, the good tasting ones. He and Slinks romped around catching and eating all they could. They were so happy, feeling a complete sense of freedom.

Even better, the bugs wanted them to eat them deliberately, crawling and flying over to them to be plucked up. He was reaching for a particularly large one, when he heard footsteps off in the distance, making him look up to see the Lord's Acolytes standing behind some bushes, beckoning him to come with him. Lurky dropped the bug as fear and surprise welled up. Turning to run, he glanced at Slinks who hadn't seen the Near.

Just as he started to shout a warning he jolted awake, staring wide-eyed at the bars and surrounding cell. His heart was racing, gasping for breath. After a moment he realized he had been dreaming. Closing his eyes, he hoped to slip back into the dream and forget about the present horrible reality of life.

Suddenly, he heard a noise, jerking him awake coming from upstairs. He heard footsteps and they were coming down. His heart pounded, reaching for Slinks to wake him, "Slinks theys comin'!" Slinks almost jumped hearing the urgency in Lurky's voice.

"I's only hears one!" Spoke Slinks. Lurky wanted in the cell right now but he couldn't, so he did the only thing he could, face the terror. Slinks kept his hand on his shoulder, facing the dark hallway with him. Imagining the worst, they were relieved to see only one Near Acolyte who commanded loudly, "My Lord wishes to see you, worm!" Lurky stared at Slinks for guidance.

Slinks leaned into his ear, "The only ways to gets me outs is if you's do's what old Lordie Misphtpht wants. I's knows you's cans do whatever its is."

"I's afraid!" said Lurky feeling sad and lonely.

"I's afraid too but you's cans do this! For us! Do it and come back to me." Staring into his eyes, "Go's! It will's be alrights. They needs us. I promises!"

Slinks never broke a promise so that was enough for Lurky to get up letting go of his hand. With his head hanging, he moved over to the impatient Near. Slinks watched silently as they disappeared into the dark hall. Neither knew what future lie down that dark hallway. The darkness just added to Lurky's gloom, he was never without Slinks, not to mention he had no idea what was expected from him now. He just had to do it and get back.

In the Great hall, he could smell the disgusting odors from the feast. Looking around, he was startled hearing the thump of the staff with the announcement, "Hail to the Great Lord Misanthropy!"

Out sauntered the Lord, not too steady on its feet and looking not well. Its slippers made an audible squishing noise, leaving a foot prints on the floor. The Lord's eyes splashed tears down constantly, resulting from too much beer. Plunking down on its throne, sighing it mumbled, "Let's get this over with." It pointed to Lurky, "You worm! Take these three noble Nears to the sounds you found."

Lurky jumped, realizing he hadn't seen or heard them, appearing out of nowhere. The Nears also looked worse for the wear from last night, showing they were still intoxicated.

"I go to lie down. Be gone with you!"

One Near swatted Lurky across the back of the head, making him wince, heading for the side door. He heard a noise behind, turning he watched several Near Thralls on hands and knees, licking the foot print stains, appreciative of the fact they got to taste their Lord's tears. He turned disgusted, in front of him a Near Thrall handed two flasks to each of them. Lurky took his silently, following them out into the brighter light outside.

Travelling a short ways, Near Bane had to relieve itself, saying it couldn't hold its beer like it used to. That brought sanctimonious sneers from the other two, who had no such problems. Lurky could hear the slight sound of crying coming from the urine hitting the ground. Suddenly, he was sure he heard his name called from Slinks back at the castle.

Staring hard at the castle listening, he was interrupted by Near Hebejebe commanding, "Come on worm or you'll wish you had!"

Near Aflik quipped, "Don't be so hard on the worm! He just left his best friend back there and he's homesick already. Isn't that right worm?"

"Oh boo-hoo!" replied Near Bane, causing a chorus of jeering and mocking. Lurky ignored them by trying to daydream about good things. Approaching the Tower of Tears, he was suddenly interrupted by Near Bane hissing, "Hide here!" pointing to go behind a boulder.

The three Nears suddenly disappeared, allowing a man and boy to pass by. Lurky was shocked to see this. However, the man and boy saw nothing as he screamed out about not knowing where their car and his wife were. It was obvious they had been in an accident. Seeing the tower, he took the boy there to see if there was help.

The Nears reappeared saying, "That should add something to the stream!" causing a torrent of sneers. They moved to the bridge partly hidden in the fog, crossing over quickly, in case new souls showed up to relinquish their share of tears. Near Bane ordered, "Let's go!"

Slinks had pulled his chair up to the window, watching Lurky climbing the trail. Happy yet sad, Lurky had to do this, Slinks yelled, "You's can do's this Lurky!"

Once they were gone, he turned to his lonely cell, alone for the first time he could remember. Tears slowly fell down his cheeks, hitting the table one desolating splotch after another. Quietly he said, "You's cans do this!"

Lurky crossed the bridge, as they took a seldom used trail, but it didn't matter knowing quietly he could do this. Alone for the first time that he could remember. That didn't matter, no matter where they went, Lurky would lead them to the sound. He walked slightly behind them, content to have them leave him alone. They kept away from any humans who had the unfortunate privilege of having an appointment in the Land of Afar. Descending downward, the fog lifted, showing increasing vegetation. Seeing it, he knew he would soon be drinking water and eating bugs making his overall mental state better. Lurky was determined to do what had to be done so they could roam free, free from the Land of Afar.

The Nears left him alone, feeling under the weather like they were, stumbling every now and then, breathing heavily at their pace. At the bottom of the mountains, they entered a lush forest, giving Lurky the chance to devour real food, moving or not.

After several hours, the Nears decided to rest which was fine with Lurky, after not really sleeping last night. Lurky could hear a stream off in the distance. Nears wouldn't go near water. They were quite superstitious about it. The Nears each took a good swig from their flasks before settling in for a sleep. "You better be here when we wake or your worm friend will suffer. Understand?" Lurky wasn't going anywhere, turning his back on them, pretending he was settling in. It wasn't long before the Nears were snoring. Near Bane snored the word mischief in a long murmur, Near Aflik quietly snored the word trouble like a horses snort and Near Hebejebe snored high pitched squeals of the word fear.

Lurky left without a sound, ears pointed backwards listening for any change. At the stream, he watched the bubbling water cascading down a small falls, reminding him of the Land of Afar and Slinks. He got melancholic thinking about him, drinking his fill of the cool refreshing liquid. He poured out his tear flasks away from the water this time, still turning the ground black, killing all living things the tears touched. Now with fresh water with him, he started foraging, which is a license to eat anything he wanted, still listening intently. Returning undetected, he settled in to sleep but accidently let out a loud burp waking Near Bane who stared suspiciously.

"Sorry's the teary soups does that sometimes." looking innocently. Near Bane stared at him for a moment before plunking back down, and rolling over.

Lurky didn't close his eyes right away, watching a butterfly floating around some flowers. Without realizing it he slipped off to sleep. He had dreams with Slinks, good dreams until they were interrupted by a shout, "Come on worm! Get up!" followed by a swift kick in the leg.

"Which way worm?" demanded Near Bane sipping on its flask. Lurky sipped from his flask wanting to appear normal, pointing across the stream. The Nears fidgeted, not wanting to cross even with just a hop.

"We have to take a different route, follow the stream until we can safely cross on a bridge." They all had to relieve themselves before starting but as Lurky moved in the opposite direction Near Aflik queried, "Where are you going?"

"I's not goin' bathroom with you's," causing them to mimic him but he didn't listen, getting out of sight and having a snack at the same time. Both ends would be happy. He ate what he could until they yelled. The Nears were in a better mood, sleeping off the effects of the beer.

Lurky didn't care as long as they left him alone. Listening to the birds chirping lifted his spirits. He started mimicking their sounds, doing them precise enough the Nears couldn't tell the difference or cared, moving along.

After a while the Nears perked right up, doing a sort of dancing walk. Near Bane spoke,

"I'M NEAR BANE
REMEMBER MY NAME
I'LL TORMENT YOU INSANE
WITH NON-STOP MISCHIEF
BUT NO ONE TO BLAME"

The other Nears emitted quiet huffs and puffs rhythmically dancing along, Near Aflik spoke,

"I'M NEAR AFLIK
THAT NAME WILL STICK
DREAD COMES SO QUICK
FROM TROUBLE'S HARSH STICK
UNTIL ALL YOU FEEL IS SICK"

They all continued as Near Hebejebe said,

"I'M NEAR HEBEJEBE
YOU'LL NEVER FORGET ME
ALTHOUGH YOU WON'T SEE
I'LL FILL YOU WITH FEAR
UNTIL SCREAMING YOU'LL FLEE"

They kept this up until it was like a mantra, their bodies flowing, reciting their mission in life. The Nears were oblivious of Lurky giving him the opportunity to scavenge. Taking a long swig of his flask, he decided to do his own dance, singing,

"I'S A SNEAKEEZE
QUIET'S AS CANS BE'S
I'S HEARS ALL WITH MY EARS
FARTHER THAN'S YOU'S CAN SEE'S

LURKY AND SLINKS
SNEAKEEZE IS WE'S
WE'S GOTS LISTENING EARS
AND THE QUIETEST FEETS

WE'S SNEAKEEZE
SNEAKEEZE IS WE'S
LISTENING TO THE BREEZES
HEARING THINGS YOU'S CANT'S SEE'S

I'M A SNEAKEEZE
YUP THAT'S ME'S
SNEAKING AND LISTENING'S
QUIETS AS CANS BE'S"

Any nearby wildlife left from the noise, making the kilometers go by uneventfully. The dancing finally turned into a walk and the singing into humming. Eventually, the sun started to set when they came to the seldom used highway on the edge of the forest. It was an opportunity to have a rest.

Lurky was stuffed but when the Nears pulled out their flasks, he went along with it taking sips. The Nears toasted,

"NECTAR OF TEARS
SUSTENANCE OF NEARS
SHED HUMAN TEARS

BELIEVED SO DEAR
SUSTAIN US HERE
TORMENTUOUS TEARS"

Lurky watched the Nears take a long swallow, sneers growing on their faces from the tears. He thought it better to fit in, taking a drink imitating his best sneer, although pasting a sneer on his face was something new. The Nears left him alone, talking amongst themselves, resting until it was dark. Near Bane queried, "Which way worm?" The voice startled Lurky snoozing against a log, he just pointed down the highway.

The Nears walked three abreast while Lurky stayed back slightly, listening to their best stories of how they hurt humans, Lurky tuned out, not wanting to hear of their despicable escapades.

Instead, he thought good thoughts, feeling better about everything. His thinking was interrupted by the distant sound of a truck coming closer from behind them. Instinctively he snuck down into the ditch. He considered how he might get back at the Nears for what they did, so this seemed like as good a time to see what could happen. The Nears continued boasting, ignoring the truck, walking down the wrong side of the road, three abreast.

This was a long lonely stretch of highway, for any trucker to have to drive especially at night. It was rare to meet another vehicle out here, but it was a handy shortcut when you hauled like Bob the Slob. Those were the words painted across the hood of his customized rig. Its bright colored lights cutting through the blackness, leaving a dusty wake of diesel exhaust behind.

Now Bob was a good old boy, a big barrel of a man everyone liked at the truck stops. Even though he bought coffees for his buddies no one sat close or downwind of him. He wasn't into the latest fashion trends, dressing like he had come straight out of the fifties, even down to his diesel stained cowboy boots. A silver chain held his wallet to his pants, attached to his belt which had a large buckle of a scantily clad representation of a woman, he called Thelma.

His checkered shirt sleeves rolled up, revealed a heart tattooed with the word 'Mother' on his arm. His slicked back hair, desperately tried to cover the balding spot, where less patriotic follicles deserted his youthful cause over the years. He wore three day old fuzz, hoping it would cover the younger crevices on his face that kept making him appear older. Bob was happy-go-lucky, always showing an almost toothless grin for the world to see.

Being a company man and all, when policy came down from head office of no more smoking in the trucks, he complied, looking logically at it. Tobacco was tobacco, so he took up chewing it which wasn't smoking.

Changing tobacco habits helped his fingers from being brown stained, but it made it worse for his one sleeve. He used it to wipe excess drool off his mouth whenever he spit into his 'extra chaw receptacle'. He used to spit out the window, until a cross wind flung a gob back into the cab, striking him in the eye, and almost causing him to wreck. So he spit into his can, after that.

Tonight, he almost missed hitting the can not paying attention, humming along to a CW station. He was daydreaming about doing something he'd never get to do. He swerved all over the road, trying to clean up the mess. He touched his lucky charm, a half a dozen raccoon tails hanging off the mirror. They were trophies of the unfortunate victims of his general prejudice against lower life forms. He loved road coons as he called them, turning a dull dark night into the highlight of his day, when they had the audacity to step out into the path of his rig. With the focus and skill of a fighter pilot, he made sure they didn't do it twice.

Just finishing wiping his cheek on his sleeve, he saw the three dark shapes on the road ahead in his headlights. "Tonight's my lucky night! Look at them coons! A triple header at that!" he couldn't believe his luck. He started to sing his coon hunting song,

"COONS ON THE ROAD
MAKE ME HAPPY
COONS ON THE ROAD
MAKE ME FLY
COONS ON THE ROAD
MAKE ME SAPPY
WHEN COONS ARE ABOUT TO DIE

COONS ON THE ROAD
MAKE ME FEEL COZY
COONS ON THE ROAD
MAKE ME SIGH
COONS ON THE ROAD
TURN THE ROAD SO ROSY
WHEN COON INNARDS START TO FLY"

He didn't change the sound of the truck not wanting to alert the coons until it was too late. He started laughing out loud; causing drool to escape down is chin. He could wipe it off later. Right now he was focused on wiping three coons off the face of the earth. He yelled out, "Yee-haw! Hello coons!"

Flicking on all his lights to catch their attention they were about to die, he bore down on them. In that moment, there was a contradictory thought crossing his mind, noticing they were awfully large for coons. He slammed into them just the same.

Two of the Nears disappeared under the wheels immediately. Near Bane stuck to the grill for a short ways, before peeling off and rolling under the truck. Bob tooted his horn but kept going. He was late hauling the load of vegetables to the grocery stores. He could pick up his trophies later on the way back.

Lurky feinting surprise, leapt out of the ditch to see the consequences of his inactions at not alerting the Nears to the truck. He ran over to see if he could be of assistance. The thing he didn't realize was, you can't kill a Near like this. He watched to his dismay as they picked themselves up, brushing off the dirt and straightening up various kinks in their indestructible bodies. Near Hebejebe glanced around with a worried expression on its face. "Where's Near Bane?"

"Over here," came the reply from Near Bane, shaking and brushing off debris from its tumble into the ditch.

"Fine! We've got something we need to do." Was all it said, staring at Lurky.

"You keep walking down the road. We'll be right back."

The others nodded in agreement; facing in the direction the truck had disappeared. In a flash they disappeared right in front of Lurky. He gasped at their sudden vanishing act. However, he did what they said, moving down the road, not wanting them to question about what led to this situation.

The local paper later that week featured a story about a truck driver found staggering down the side of the road by a police patrol car. His clothing shredded and missing one boot, he hysterically screamed about being attacked by large coons that had somehow climbed up on to the truck, assaulting him. The truck was found abandoned on the side of the road thirty kilometers away, with the motor still running, but the truck had sustained severe vandalism. Further investigation produced no new leads. Bob the Slob would give no further comments.

Lurky didn't mind being alone, giving him a chance to go the bathroom. He did enjoy watching the stars at night, especially the bright streaking ones that seemed to fall from the night sky. Watching the stars, he almost ran into the Nears, as they reappeared in front of him.

"Which way worm?" queried Near Bane without any explanation.

Near Aflik stepped forward. "If your ears are so good why didn't you hear that truck?"

Lurky knew he was in glue, however he replied, "I's was daydreamin' and didn't notice's"

"Sure you were," retorted Near Hebejebe. Lurky became afraid.

Near Bane interceded, "We don't have time for this right now, which way?"

Lurky threw up his hand pointing down the road, volunteering, "Until's we's crosses the next bridge."

Near Bane turned putting its arm around Near Hebejebe, leading it down the road. "Did you see the look on his face when we showed up in his truck cab?"

"Ya. He sure sprayed his windshield with tobacco juice when he yelled. Besides what got spilled all over the dash from that can be had in his hand!" Replied Near Aflik as they all laughed. For hours they went over every detail of the revenge on Bob the Slob and how he might think twice about running over anything else in the future.

Lurky stayed well back, not wanting to be the center of attention anymore, deciding he would be on his best behavior. Personal revenge wasn't his forte, especially with Nears.

Travelling for hours without another vehicle interrupting the journey, they came to a bridge with a large fast flowing stream running beneath. After crossing, Near Bane turned to Lurky who pointed in the direction to go. They entered the lightly wooded area that grew along the roadside, deciding to rest and take another drink of tears. This time the Nears stood in a circle, held up their flasks saying together.

"HUMAN TEARS
LIFE ESSENCE OF NEARS
INCONSOLABLE TEARS
GREVIOUS MISERY CLEAR
STRENGTHEN US HERE
OMNIPOTENT TEARS"

Lurky did the same by himself over in the corner, trying to make it look good, hoping there would be no problems over the truck. They left him alone, lying down for a rest. The light of day started to show distinct forms off in the distance. Birds started singing praises of a new day.

He dozed, dreaming about what it would be like to be a bird and fly, to go anywhere he wanted with Slinks, of course. He dreamt they were flapping their big ears, laughing, talking. They cruised over the landscape having a wonderful time. He looked over at Slinks, but instead of Slinks, it was Near Bane staring back at him with its usual sneer. It startled Lurky so bad he woke up to find Near Bane standing over him, causing him to scramble out of the way gasping.

Near Bane chuckled. "Dreams are for fools. This is the true dream. Don't dream your life away worm."

It turned to the others who were standing waiting. "Let's go!" They followed it out of the clearing. Lurky jumped to his feet still groggy from being awoken so suddenly. He followed behind at a distance, upset and thinking about how the Near was able to get into his dreams.

They walked several hours as Lurky filled up again on whatever was available, almost getting caught by Near Bane, who heard him slurping on a caterpillar. Lurky still had his hand up near his face, when the Near looked back. He started scratching his face, pretending he was enjoying it, making little 'ahs' and 'ohs' trying not to spit out the squirming caterpillar in the process. His act stood its ground as Near Bane turned back, saying nothing. Lurky was careful now not to be seen again.

Soon they were out of the woods and walked across a large field with a wooden fence stretching a long ways, so the Nears decided the convenient thing to do was hop over and keep going. Lurky had stopped for a bathroom break when he saw the Nears climb up and yelled. "Don't" However, it was too late.

Lurky and Slinks did the same thing one day long ago when they were exploring the area and that was when they met 'Fang'.

Now, Fang it turns out, happened to be the meanest, fiercest guard dog this side of anywhere, who apparently didn't like company at any time. Luckily for Lurky and Slinks they were on the lookout for trouble the day they met Fang. When all they saw was a set of very large, snarling teeth coming their way, they bounced back over the fence with the help of their flapping ears.

Today, he listened to the silence behind the fence for several moments, until one of the Nears said.

"What's that?" The reply was a very distinct ferocious snarl, as Fang woke up from a nap, at the intrusion. Lurky followed the snarling noise, rapidly moving toward the Nears. The snarling noises were suddenly accompanied by screeching and yelling from the Nears, as Fang had his way with them.

Apparently you can't kill a Near, but a lot of fur flies from any creature, when Fang decides this is the best thing to do to pass his time of day. Lurky watched small clumps flying through the air. Small individual hairs gently floated down, after getting blown over the fence by the breeze, from the lopsided skirmish proceeding on the other side. It wasn't long before the Nears were back over the fence with all their appendages intact. However, they did look a little worse for wear, evidence by many bald patches that were going to take some time to re-grow.

Near Bane gave Lurky a hard glaring stare. Lurky immediately stammered, "I's tried to's warns you's!"

Near Aflik picked up the sign that lay face down on the ground. The words 'Beware of Dog' were plainly seen on the other side, as it held it up.

Lurky shouted, "I's can'ts reads! Ands I'd didn't puts that there's!"

Near Hebejebe whispered to Near Bane it had heard Lurky shout as they went over. Luckily he was let off the hook; however the ice under Lurky was much thinner. Lurky was prepared to fight this one, but the Nears decided they had better things to do.

They left, walking along the fence to go around Fang, who walked along with them on the other side quietly snarling, hoping the Nears would jump back over, and play tear up the rag doll some more. They veered off into the woods, leaving Fang with only fond memories to fill in the rest of his day.

Once in the shade of the woods, Near Bane called a halt to assess the fur damage on each other. Lurky showed which direction they should go, through the pines.

It was unusual for them to walk along in the pine trees, without making noise on the soft carpet of needles. The only noise was the gentle moaning of the wind in the trees, gently swaying around at the whim of the breeze. Not even bird songs could be heard. Everyone remained silent, immersed in the unusual sound of nature. Each of them were totally alone with just the trees, each lost in their own thoughts.

Lurky thought the trees almost talked to him, like they were telling each other about the intruders who now walked amongst them. When he passed by a tree that was close enough, he would reach out, giving it a gentle rub like a sign of affection, thanking them for the quiet music being produced.

Suddenly Near Bane stopped, sniffing the air, "I smell Kick-A-Poo juice!" The others came up beside it, sniffing the air. There was an odor similar in nature, making them excited.

"Let's find out, I could use a drop or two to quench my thirst!" exclaimed Near Aflik.

"We will not get drunk. Agreed!" replied Near Bane giving the other two a stern look. Sniffing the air to track the origin of the odor, they followed the breeze, coming to a chain link fence. Out in front of them, several large ponds emitted the smell they were seeking.

"This must be where the human's Spiritus Frumentus make their own!" shouted Near Hebejebe.

"They sure make a lot. I've never seen vats this large!"

They moved along the fence looking for a way in, missing the signs 'Sewage Effluent Holding Station' and 'Do Not Enter'. Going around the corner, they found the gate wasn't locked, rushing over to the first pond. They were hit by the overpowering smells as the sewage bubbled, releasing gas.

They didn't hesitate, although the smells were stronger than they were used to. They figured it was because the liquid wasn't in a bottle, that's what made it stronger. Getting down on all fours, they greedily lapped and slurped the brownish green effluent up, hardly coming up for a breath of air.

After several minutes Near Hebejebe sucked in a large piece of brown matter, chewing on it, trying to get a sense of the flavor, humans put in their vat. Rolling it around in its mouth, the flavor reminded it of an experience it had long ago and had forgotten about. It was when it scared a human so bad they soiled themselves, leaving behind a specimen. Once the human left running for their life, it checked out the specimen, being the inquisitive Near that it was and realized what it was.

The memory made it connect with the flavor of what was presently in its mouth. Instantaneously its eyes flew open, yelling, "I'm afraid I know what this is!" Both the other Nears looked surprised, with the liquid dripping from their beards.

"This isn't Kick-A-Poo juice! This is poop juice! human poop juice!"

Gagging and spitting, they tried to get rid of the offensive leftover liquid and taste from their mouths. They backed away from the pond faster than they approached it.

Lurky had been watching from the trees knowing what was in the ponds. He and Slinks had been around the humans enough to know. He was roaring with laughter at the antics of the Nears, once they had realized their mistake.

Once the Nears reached the lush grass around the edge of the ponds, they threw themselves down, rolling around and rubbing their bodies like they were trying to get some offensive odor off. They started licking and dragging their tongues on the surface of the grass, alternating with rubbing their faces right down into the grass for the longest time. Finally they each stood, shaking themselves off.

Near Bane turned to the other two, "Let's just keep this between ourselves, if the others were to find out about it we would never live it down." The others nodded quickly. They came back over to the flasks with Lurky, each taking a generous gulp without the usual benediction. They rinsed the tears around in their mouths for several minutes, before swallowing.

Near Aflik quietly spoke, "The tears definitely taste better."

Near Hebejebe replied, before burping. "Ya. Much better."

Lurky looked away from them for fear of bursting out laughing. The look of enjoyment at their plight made Near Bane stare at him. Lurky just pointed at the unobserved signs on the fence saying, "I's tolds yous I's can'ts reads!"

Near Aflik looked at the sign mouthing the word 'Sewage' before saying, "We'll have to remember that sign so we don't make the same mistake again." Causing the other two to look at it and agree.

Near Bane looked at Lurky, who pointed away from the Sewage Effluent Holding Station without saying a word.

They began moving away from the odors and the embarrassing situation quickly. The Nears took the lead, while Lurky followed, doing the odd dance step and pirouette, like he was celebrating a silent victory.

The rest of the trip was interrupted often by a Near quickly rushing off by themselves behind a bush, until they finally got the foreign liquid out of their system. They walked until dusk that started announcing night's encroachment. Coming out from the woods to a field where a small house sat, Near Bane turned to Lurky.

"Is this it?" Lurky nodded his nodded slowly. Sad that he had to bring them here, he had no choice if he were to ever see Slinks again. Near Bane turned to the others, "Let the fun begin boys!"

Wading through the tall grass in the field, darkness slowly made them indiscernible in the half moon. They appeared more like moving shadows as they approached. Near Bane pointed to a tree outside the children's bedroom.

"Let's climb the tree. I sense they are in there." Scrambling up, it was followed closely by the others. Lurky stayed at the bottom since Sneakeeze weren't into climbing trees. Once up in the crotch of the branches, Near Bane spoke to Near Hebejebe without looking at it. "Do your stuff."

Near Hebejebe started sending out thoughts of fear, the kind of fear that makes one afraid of the dark. The kind of fear that makes you afraid even when you keep telling yourself all is well. But it wasn't.

DIANNE WASN'T MUCH OF A dreamer, even though she had the occasional one. The one now was making her afraid, with thoughts of fear that makes you afraid of the dark. The kind when you know all wasn't well. It was Dave who was the dreamer of the family. She had a strong intuition and with the help of visualizations they were doing, it was being brought out more. She was beginning to have stronger feelings and premonitions. She had been feeling very uneasy lately, but she couldn't quite get a grasp on why. It wasn't because of her mother leaving or her uncle being there. It was something else.

The eyes, slowly formed in the dreamless dark zone Dianne was experiencing, not quite asleep and yet not awake. The eyes brought with them an insidious energy of fear, creeping into every corner of her being. Endless thoughts of fearful events and scenarios, invaded her otherwise tranquil state.

So powerful and pervasive was the energy of fear, she started moaning and thrashing around in her bed. Suddenly she burst out of bed, tumbling onto the floor with a thud. Wide awake and breathing heavily, she lay for a few moments gathering her thoughts. The image of the eyes still lingered. She rose, scratching her head wondering what had just happened. The feeling of fear still was there, although not as strong. She looked over at the window, feeling the fear was coming from somewhere outside.

Thinking herself silly, she wandered over to the window pulling the curtain partly open, staring out into the semi-darkness. Once her eyes adjusted to the moonlight, she became scared silly, gasping in disbelief. There, staring back at her were three sets of the same eyes that had invaded her dreams. She jumped back letting go of the curtain. Sure of what she had seen ran across the hall to Dave's room.

Racing to the edge of his bed, she tapped his blanket, whispering. "Dave! Dave! Wake up! There's something out there!" No one living out here wakes anyone else up in the middle of the night unless it's serious, so Dave didn't complain, he just wanted to know, asking, "What's up sis?" Something's wrong with the animals?"

"No! It's something else. I don't know what it is. They're up the tree outside my window! They must be some kind of Boogie Men!" Dave suddenly became impatient, thinking she saw coons or something. However, anything outside at night could spell trouble for the barn animals. He reluctantly got out of bed. Dianne grabbed his hand immediately. He felt the trembling knowing this was serious. Saying nothing more, he went with her to her bedroom window. Pointing she said, "See if they are still there." He complied slightly opening the curtain to look out.

"What are they?" demanded Dave staring at the figures perched in the tree. "Look Di! What are they?" They both stared incredulously at creatures they had never seen before. Being in the country at one time at another you see everything from chipmunks to bobcats to bears, but nothing like this.

"Look at their eyes. They almost shine!"

"I'm so afraid Dave! Let's get Uncle Hugh!"

Almost pushing each other through the door, they ran out of the room and burst through the door of Hugh's room, waking him up from a sound sleep.

"Hugh! Hugh! Get up! Something's outside Dianne's room in the tree!"

Realizing from the tone of their voices something was very wrong. He immediately jumped out of bed and went with them to Dianne's room, saying, "What did you see?"

"Boogie Men! There's three of them sitting in the tree outside Dianne's window."

"Boogie Men?" He suddenly got a terrible gut feeling that almost made him sick.

"Yes take a look! Don't turn on the light!" Dave whispered, shoving Hugh to the window.

Hugh pulled back the curtain and saw the three sets of eyes staring back. He noticed a movement at the base of the tree as two large ears moved about, recognizing it as the creature he had seen.

"Nears! They're here!" A cold unnerving chill rose from the small of his back, travelled up to his neck giving him goose bumps. He let go of the curtain, blocking out what he was looking at.

He stood a moment staring into space as the memories of his accident and his brother's death flooded back like a torrent. Feelings of grief, loss and hopelessness flooded through his being, reliving that night in all its agony and despair, until Dave said, "Uncle! What do we do?"

Hugh looked at the fear-filled eyes staring at him. He resolved not to allow this to happen to these two innocents, not here, not now.

"What do we do uncle?" Dianne implored.

"Come on! Let's go downstairs" replied Hugh saying nothing more, collecting his thoughts.

"Come on, let's climb down," snickered Near Bane, followed by the others.

"This should be fun," replied Near Aflik.

"Ya, could you feel the fear? This shouldn't take too long before our job is done!" Answered Near Hebejebe.

Lurky backed away from the tree, not wanting to be anywhere near these three despicable creatures if he could help it. They all walked over to the barn to plan their strategy. Lurky followed.

"This won't take long worm. Don't be too far away, when it's time to go."

Lurky nodded and moved a short distance away. The Nears made a loose circle and began to dance around as each in turn spoke these words.

"LAUGHTER, SWEET LAUGHTER
WE HAVE FOUND
IN THESE CHILDREN'S VOICES
SOUL'S SWEET SOUND

TEARS AND CRYING
THE ONLY SOUND
WHEN WE ARE FINISHED
AND SORROW IS FOUND

ANGUISH, FEAR AND TORMENT
THESE FEELINGS ABOUND
WHEN WE THREE NEARS
COME AROUND"

Once they had completed the saying, they stood still, followed by a sudden flash of bright light that turned them into pure energy. They would be able to connect with the thoughts of everyone in the house, or move anywhere, unseen and undetected, as they had done to so many countless humans, time and time again, bringing them misery. They were able to do so by travelling on the negative thoughts and feelings that humans were so easy at manifesting.

Lurky gasped at the flash of light coinciding with the Nears disappearing, scampering behind the corner of the barn for protection. Peering out, he saw nothing where the Nears had just stood. After looking around, he decided it was better to move out into the field, laying down hoping the Nears didn't have any plans for him to participate in.

Hugh and the children reached the kitchen and suddenly saw a flash of light outside.

"What was that?" They whispered, concerned.

"I want you both to calm down. This is very important." Hugh said, placing a hand on each of their shoulders, trying hard not show any fear himself.

"What you just saw was them disappearing from the physical world, so they can go into the mental world of thought. Out here they can't physically touch you; however, once they are in the realm of thoughts, they can bring to you negative situations that will harm you. They pick up on your fears, phobias and other negative thoughts, and will bring to you what can hurt you the most. At the very least, they do whatever they can to make you cry.

"Why would they want to make us cry Uncle Hugh?" asked Dave bewildered.

"I listened to your laughter outside and realized you still have the element of love still in it. Laughter does many wonderful things when used properly. Like I said before, laughter like other things is a form of energy. The energy of laughter is one of the true gifts we have, to change the energy surrounding a person, at any given moment. With the energy of true laughter, you can bring a person who is in the darkest of negative emotions, out of that mood in an instant. This is something that can't be done even with hours and hours of conversation or verbal persuasion.

Laughter can be used to make them come out into the daylight from the darkness in their soul, to see the world and situation in a better way. Laughter makes you experience pure positive emotions. It has the miraculous ability to cause fears, worries, and doubts to disappear in an instant. It washes you clean of the anxieties you have in that moment. It has been proven; laughter has the miraculous power to actually heal a person of disease, and should be used more as a therapy.

Laughter is the music of soul. True laughter is free and foolish. It is gay, cheerful and unbridled passion of joy, which only brings good into your life and makes others happy. This is the laughter that Lord Misanthropy hates, and that's why it has sent the Nears to rob us of it.

The night your father and I were in the accident, we were having a good laugh about things that had gone on with us when we were children. Suddenly, our lives were changed forever and the laughter was gone. This Lord Misanthropy doesn't want anyone to enjoy true laughter, it only wants tears.

It will allow its laughter which is false laughter. It is laughter that so many have. You see there are two kinds of laughter. The true laughter is when you laugh with someone. You share it freely, in a non-judgmental atmosphere.

The other is the laughter of ridicule. The one that causes someone to hurt another's feelings because they think they are better than them. It is the laughter originating in the dark corner of the mind. It will bring another's state of being down below where they should be. It is the laughter that makes another feel worthless, insignificant and makes them lose self-worth. It makes good energy shrink and retreat, so that all that's left is dark negativity, thoughts and tears.

It is cruel laughter that is taken in and does more damage than you can imagine, causing more problems as the hurtful energy lives inside the person. It is a hard dark stain that quite often is never softened. This is the laughter Lord Misanthropy wants to hear. It is music to its ears, because it knows those who suffer from the destruction from this laughter will cry a river of tears. It uses those minds it has already enslaved to do its dirty work. It does this through their egos.

After hearing you two laugh, I knew where you got it from. Your father used to laugh like that. It is one of the true gifts your father gave you, without you ever realizing it."

"How do we keep what father gave us, without those Nears taking it away?"

"We will not speak of this right now, until we know they are gone."

"How will we know they are gone?"

"There are two things to watch for. Number one, when they enter into energy form, they will leave behind a mark in the physical world, in the form of a shadow that can only be seen just as the sun is rising or setting. The second thing that happens is you will see out of the corner of your eyes now and then, a small dark flash, like something moving incredibly fast. It will be a darting kind of movement that will make your eyes move to see if there was actually something there, however you will see nothing. When this happens, watch what you are thinking because it means they are moving with the thought energy. If it is something negative you are thinking they can cause problems. Do you understand?"

Both children nodded.

"We will continue our morning visualizations, using the 'Awh" word. We will do another one in the evening that gives us a grateful attitude for all we have. Each of us can be far more than we are today, if we try. These exercises will keep our mental attitude strong and positive, no matter what happens. We will not fall into any old negative patterns that we carry with us, as a form of what I call baggage. These exercises have many valuable benefits that will suit each individual's needs, strengths, and weaknesses. They affect the whole person and bring out the best in them.

The other thing is that if something bad happens to one of us, the others will pretend to laugh at them. We will make fun of them in the manner that is acceptable to Lord Misanthropy. This will hopefully persuade it to leave us alone. In our hearts we must do this to survive whatever they try to do to us, not because we really want to."

Holding out his right hand, palm up, he said, "Place your hand with mine."

They placed their hand on his and then he placed his other hand on top of theirs.

"I vow with all my heart I love you both and will give you my life, if need be to show it. Though we must become actors in our lives, we act this way out of love, not because it is the way of the world."

Dianne broke down, seeking a hug from Hugh who wrapped her in his arms giving her the security that she needed. No man had ever told her he loved her. If her father did, it was a buried memory. Even Dave couldn't hold back the tears. However, he was embarrassed to get a hug.

Hugh placed a free hand on his shoulder. Dave placed his hand on his arm, seeking his own form of support. Hugh's tears came down quietly staining his cheeks.

Now, here he was facing the Nears with his brother's children. This time he wasn't going to fail them. Part of him always felt he had failed his brother, but not this time. After a few minutes, he let go of them, wiping the last of the tears out of his eyes.

"At least they've made the mistake of giving away their element of surprise. We know what we are up against. For now let's go back to bed, we should try to rest. Tomorrow we will get up like nothing is different and carry on as usual. Try not to think negatively, even though your mind will do just that."

He walked them back upstairs, giving them words of encouragement, explaining it wasn't as bad as their minds would want them to believe. They weren't going to be devoured or anything like that, making jokes about it, trying to show them a lighter side of it. Reaching their rooms he turned to them, "Everything will be fine. Just remember to stay positive, no matter what."

"Is this where the stories of the Boogie Man came from?" Dave asked.

"It very well could be. There is an element of truth to all legends," replied Hugh smiling.

Morning finally came. It seemed like eternity lying in bed, afraid to shut their eyes. All they could see when they did was the eyes staring back at them.

The rooster was crowing and the birds were singing, making Dianne get out of bed and go to her window, cautiously to peer out. Seeing only empty limbs where earlier sat the worst reality that could be thrust on any child, made her question whether it had all been a bad dream. Hearing her brother, she dressed going out to greet him. The apprehension on his face brought back the fact this was no dream.

"Did you sleep?" she asked.

"No, did you?" She shook her head no.

They heard a clanging of dishes in the kitchen, making them go down to make sure it was their uncle. Reaching the bottom of the stairs, they couldn't believe what they saw, staring incredulously. Their uncle stood wearing their mother's apron, his hair askew like some mad professor, flour smeared all over his face. He turned quickly once he heard the children. Holding a spatula in one hand and a wooden spoon in the other, he said in a weird loud voice.

"Ah, my Changees! I hadn't expected you so soon. Breakfast isn't quite ready yet!" Giving the spoon a slight flick, it caused some flour to fly into the air in a cloud. He moved his head to the side like he was getting his picture taken by some imaginary camera.

"Well, do I pass for your mother or not?"

Both children stared in disbelief. Hugh burst out laughing.

"I don't think so uncle, she doesn't need to shave." Dave said pointing to the flour coated stubble on his chin.

"Minor details my boy, but I guess you're right. She didn't speak with such a deep voice either. Oh well, my cooking will just have to do." He pulled out a stack of pancakes from the oven. They were cooked to perfection, something their mother hadn't quite mastered when it came to pancakes. Hers tended to be on the dark side, actually more on the black side.

"Come sit, we have much to do today." Hugh kept the conversation light and stayed away from the topic of the Nears.

After breakfast, everyone filed outside onto the porch, sitting in their chairs, ready to do their morning exercise. Hugh looked over the fields, suddenly noticing three barely discernable shadows hovering off in the corner of the field.

He took a deep breath saying, "Isn't the morning air lovely, so full of oxygen, just what we need. Now today we will do a slightly different 'Awh'. We will visualize in our mind's eye, a beautiful blue, white and golden light coming to us here as we sit. The light can be whatever color you want or all three. It doesn't matter. The light will surround you like a protective bubble so we each are in one large bubble. You will see the color or colors flowing all around the bubble constantly moving pushing away any harm that may want to affect us.

"You mean from the 'you know who's?" queried Dianne searching for the Nears.

"Precisely."

They began singing the word, like they had in the past, keeping their eyes closed, but Dave thought of the Nears. Suddenly, three shadows materialized into almost solid forms of hideous creatures and attacked the bubble viciously, trying to get in.

The problem was he hadn't visualized them; he just had to think about them. It was like he was a millimeter away from them on the inside of the bubble, and they were on the outside smashing repeatedly against it, screaming insane curses. He panicked at the outburst and without warning, one of the creatures managed to force its hand through the preventative barrier trying to grab him. He leapt back from the edge of the bubble before being grabbed and yelled: "Uncle!" He almost fell off the chair onto the floor. He startled Hugh and his sister. Hugh grabbed him by the arm to help him up.

"What happened?"

Dave explained in detail what had happened, except for thinking about the Nears, since after all it was just a passing thought.

Hugh knew what he had probably done but it was too late; the Nears were in. He said nothing to build more fear in their hearts, so he started the exercises over. This time he talked them through it, emphasizing the Nears were not able to get through the barrier. He could tell from Dave's breathing the damage was already done. There was a part of the boy that couldn't believe he was safe.

Once done, Hugh stood up giving a stretch saying, "It's going to be warm today. The temperature has gone up since we've been sitting here. Come let's get started, there are latches and hinges to fix and some boards to be replaced on the barn. We'll do that today first. Retrieve your caps my Changees, it's time for change!"

Then, placing his hand on Dave's shoulder he spoke, "Don't worry. We are protected. Just watch your thinking, that's all you have to do." Dave nodded, still unsure.

The goats and chickens greeted them before they even opened the door.

"It sounds like they are spoiled from getting that freedom yesterday." Hugh observed laughing.

"Yes I haven't heard the goaties this excited, since we used to feed them carrots," replied Dianne.

"Dianne, you tend to the animals and Dave and I will scrounge up some boards and nails and start patching up things."

After leaving Dianne, Hugh turned to Dave and said, "The reason they attacked you this morning was they attack the strongest first, hoping to put fear into everyone else, if the strongest becomes weak."

"I'm not strong," replied Dave.

"That's because you haven't had the chance to see it. You have the same strength your father had that I often envied when we were young. You are stronger than you think. Other people would have gone screaming through the woods yelling for their momma, if they had the experience you did this morning.

Dave brightened up hearing this causing him to stand a little straighter.

"My momma's not here and I've got nowhere to run."

"That's right! We don't run! No retreat! No surrender!" placing his hand on the boy's shoulder getting him a friendly shake.

"Now let's start. You measure for the holes and I'll limber up the old single grip, arm strong powered, reciprocating, forest product, dimensional alternation device here." Hugh said, picking up the rusty handsaw giving it a shake in the air.

Snickering, Dave added, "Watch you don't cut yourself uncle. I hear those things can be sharp and in the wrong hands you can lose an arm at the shoulder."

Hugh stared at the boy feinting total surprise.

"Don't you worry son, this here saw is duller than that there chicken's brain over there!" causing them both to laugh.

"Come on, I'll show you how I need the spaces measured so we can cut the boards to fit." taking Dave over to the first hole in the wall.

Dave did his first measurement, having everything ready when Hugh came back. So they started one board at a time, filling in the holes in the barn that needed to be done. Dianne had finished the animals by the time they had put up the second board.

Hugh showed Dianne how to nail the boards in place. The problem they did have, was when they put down hammers or nails, even the tape, they weren't in the same place they had left them, when they wanted to use them again. If they turned away from it or left for a moment it wasn't where they had left it. Once, the hammer was under a board on the floor when Dianne came back from getting more nails, even though she was sure she had left it on top. Another time she left the nails in a neat pile, only to come back to find them scattered all over.

After several hours they were finished, standing back admiring their handy work, as Hugh spoke. "This job we just finished was important. It symbolizes our filling the gaps in our lives that for so long has made us feel incomplete. It shows we will continue to make changes that over time will make us become whole. Just as nothing is instantaneous, it will take time, but you will see changes occur in yourself over time."

They were all thirsty, so Hugh asked Dave to get water from the house. Returning, carrying the pitcher of water and glasses, he had one simple thought about the Nears. Suddenly, he saw a small dark blur out of the corner of his eye like a bird flying by, causing him to flinch. His feet tangled, making him fall forward tripping. He tried to save the tray but as he did, he landed hard on the ground with his elbow scraping severely on the ground. Hugh heard the thud as Dave emitted a loud "Ow!"

Dianne ran to the door yelling, "Are you alright?"

Dave held his elbow crying with pain when they approached him.

"What happened?" queried Dianne seeing her brother was in pain.

"I don't know. I thought a bird was going to run into me and I flinched making me trip."

Hugh knew the Nears had been able to break through the protective barrier somehow, however he said nothing. Instead he helped the boy up saying, "Come on lad, let's get you into the kitchen and see about that elbow. Does anything feel broken?" Dave shook his head no, pulling his hand away to reveal several deep scrapes oozing blood.

"It looks worse than it is, but we'll fix it. Would you get the tray and the rest Di? Just watch the glass from the broken pitcher. Oh yes, I want you to laugh at your brother."

"What!" Dianne exclaimed, looking at her uncle like he just lost his mind.

Hugh winked. "You know what we talked about."

Then she realized what was going on. She put her hand on Dave to make him realize she didn't mean it, she pretended to laugh. She told him how stupid he was to trip over his own feet, and what kind of a restaurant server he would make, going on and on. Finally Dave leaned over whispering, "I get the point Dot."

Taking Dave over to the tap, Hugh let the water flow over the elbow, making Dave wince. He got Dianne to bring over a towel and the first aid kit from the bathroom. He cleaned the wounds.

"We will leave it open to the air to allow it to heal over. It's clean and you should be right as rain in no time. Let's have a sandwich and then I think a nap will do us all a lot of good. We did a splendid job on the barn making the changes we did. My cap salutes you Lady Di and Brave Dave." Lifting his cap, he twirled it in the air.

Lunch was nothing special, since Hugh knew they all needed a nap. They had all been awake for a long time, since they were up long before their usual time. Once they were done, he ushered them upstairs after going over what was next on the agenda.

Lying down was the best thing for the children. Since it was daylight, they weren't afraid to drift off to sleep even with the Nears somewhere around. He lay down, grateful nothing serious had happened, wondering what else the Nears had planned for them.

Drifting off to sleep he had no idea what was going to happen next, not wanting to dwell on the worst. The world of the positive was somehow going to overcome the world of the negative.

Lurky moved into the field afraid of the Nears. Seeing them disappear like that, he had no idea what was going to happen next, not wanting to dwell on the worst. He had become complacent forgetting what they were capable of doing. Walking along, he heard a creek tumbling over some rocks into a large pool. He bent down slurping until he had enough. Standing back up he saw the small footprints of humans. After looking around and sniffing the air, he assumed they had to be from the children in the house.

He felt sorry for them, knowing the Nears were here to punish them for laughing. It didn't make sense to him, laughing made him feel good. He and Slinks were always laughing at things in nature around them, and with each other when they acted foolishly together. He suddenly got melancholy thinking about Slinks, missing him terribly, hoping he was all right back in the cell, alone. He thought perhaps Slinks was being abused by the Nears or worse. He had no idea what was happening to his friend.

Sitting by the water, a tear in his eye blurred his vision, which was quickly followed by others as he broke down. He rested his head on his arm sobbing, his ears wrapped around his face and arms shielding him from the cruel harsh world run by Lord Misanthropy.

He felt so alone and wished he and Slinks could just fly away, or at least get away from Lord Misanthropy and the Nears. Sitting there, Slinks words came back to him telling him he could do this mission. Loneliness came over him. After crying out the emotions he felt, he looked at the water, seeing his reflection. He took his finger, putting it into the water slowly twirling at his reflected image, thinking about everything. He was certainly going to do whatever it took to get back to Slinks, even if it meant sacrificing the rest of the world to do it. He was prepared to be on his best behavior around the Nears.

Without realizing it, his finger swirling in the water attracted a large trout that slowly swam over to investigate, thinking it was food. Lurky forgot what was making him sad for a moment, seeing the fish. He had an idea, going over to a rotting log, flipping it over, and seizing a worm.

He would eat worms if he had to, but with all the insects around, he had better things to eat, so he didn't mind sharing. He knew that trout liked worms, after a trout stole a worm he was washing off in the water to eat once.

Now, this worm wasn't keen on being disturbed from its slumber in the warm darkness under the log, and to add to that, it wasn't in the mood for a bath. Once submerged in the water, it was writhing excitedly wanting to get away. Nothing attracts a trout more than a worm writhing for dear life in water. Rising swiftly, it grabbed the poor worm. Lurky let go, smiling as the trout really showed the worm why taking a bath in its creek wasn't a good idea. Laughing, Lurky quietly spoke to the fish. "Stays there Mr. Fishes! I's be right back." going back to the log.

He managed to find a relative of the first worm, plunging it into the water for the trout, so it could show this worm where its relative had gone. The trout did this with the speed and expertise of a well-practiced executioner.

Lurky laughed, happy to have found a friend, even if it was a trout. He went back to the log. There were no more relatives of the first worm there, or they had gotten the word and crawled away to parts unknown. He gave up, going back to the trout explaining he couldn't find any more food. He walked away as the trout finned waiting patiently, waiting for more.

Lurky went back out into the field realizing he was hungry. The trout moved back down into the deeper water of the creek so it wouldn't become something else's meal. Lurky was in a much better mood after making friends with the trout, deciding he was going to play with something, especially after finding a grasshopper to eat. He crouched down springing on it when it moved, then let it go to fly and hop away before doing the same thing over. Finally he was too aggressive injuring it, so he promptly ate it to put it out of its misery. He found others, doing the same, laughing and pretending he was teasing each of them until he had his fill.

Sitting down to rest, crunching on a particularly big brown one, he pulled one leg out of his mouth, examining it with curiosity. He noticed the rough serrated edge of the leg near the foot. Feeling it with his finger, he realized this could be what scratched on the way down his throat sometimes, when he didn't crunch them up enough. What he did notice was the chunk of meat still on the leg. Sticking it in his mouth he slurped off the meat, leaving just the spur. He flicked it away, not wishing to have it scratch his throat.

Looking around, he noticed he was quite close to the barn, deciding he should investigate when he couldn't hear any humans outside. The goats took a keen interest in him, coming up to the edge of their corral, staring at him wondering what he was. He quietly snuck around the back without disturbing them, hoping his large ears wouldn't scare them away. He made sure no one was around before entering the barn. The strong odors of the barn disgusted him, waving his hand in the air to dissipate the smells, however it did no good. "Stupid animals smells bad!"

Seeing the chickens outside made him look around for one thing he did love. Eggs from birds: any birds. Sure enough, after feeling around in the lay box, he discovered one. Grasping it with his hand, he brought it out into the light, rolled it over in his hands. Smelling the freshness and goodness, he chuckled to himself.

Now a good thief knows you don't stick around the crime scene enjoying your stolen prize. He decided to leave going by the grain containers, he smelled the grain. He held the egg in one hand, and lifting the plastic lid. He helped himself to a mouthful of the feed, grabbing another handful for a snack later.

Heading out over the field to enjoy his ill gotten gains, he now knew a good spot for a treat, waiting for the Nears to accomplish whatever they had to do. He hadn't seen them after disappearing, which suited him just fine.

After sitting down under a tree, he decided it was time for a snooze since he had time to wait. Wait for whatever was ahead and beyond his control. Closing his eyes, he thought of Slinks and all the good times they had and hopefully would have again, even if the future was uncertain.

HUGH WOKE TO THE SOUND of the rooster crowing indicating it was morning, wondering what was ahead and beyond his control, even if the future was uncertain. They had all slept right through, rolling out of bed to get dressed. He barely got his door open when both children were standing in the hallway, yawning and scratching itchy spots from being in bed so long.

"What happened Uncle Hugh? I didn't get out of bed until I woke up a few minutes ago and realized it was morning," yawned Dianne. Dave said he had done the same thing.

"We must have needed it after yesterday. How's your arm Dave?"

"It's much better. It only hurts when I think about it," chuckled Dave.

"I wonder how the critters are doing since we didn't put them away last night." Hugh said. Dianne's eyes flew wide open remembering, running out the back door, then coming back in a few moments later saying.

"They're fine lying down in their paddock. I think they enjoyed a night out camping, and the chickens are fine too."

"Good, the chickens will by habit go back into their coop at night to roost. Our only problem is when the door is open something can get them, but we were fortunate. Today I think we will stain the barn. I think it will really spruce it up."

"Mom will be so shocked when she comes home. When she calls we won't tell her anything. Next time she comes home we'll just let her drive in and get surprised." Dave said.

They all agreed. The thought of it gave the children enthusiasm to do more. After the breakfast they moved out to the porch.

"What do we do today uncle? Do we do a different exercise?" Dianne asked.

"No, we do the same one every day for now, until we know they are no longer here." The mention of the Nears brought a slight change in their light mood.

Dianne couldn't seem to settle her mind down. Bringing up her mother had her feeling a little lonely. She really missed her, and wished she could come home. However, she knew this wouldn't happen, since the school had put her on an accelerated course. She was proud of her mom for doing what she was doing, for them.

Dianne kept trying to visualize the bubble, but her thoughts wouldn't leave her alone. The time was over before she had a chance to finish visualizing what needed to be done. She didn't think it was going to make a difference. Saying nothing, she got up with the others when it was over, and followed Hugh while he explained what they were going to do.

Hugh observed the three shadows still out in the field, when he opened his eyes. He knew somehow there was more to come. He made sure the children weren't put in harm's way by doing the ladder part of the staining. Dianne fed the birds and goats while they got out the stain and brushes.

When they were ready, Hugh showed them how to do it. They reached up as high as they could, while he followed behind with the ladder, finishing the rest. They stained one board at a time, patiently making sure it was all covered the way he showed them. Before they realized it, time had moved along as well. They started having hunger pangs in their stomachs. Hugh recommended they have a drink of water, and then continue. Once in the house seeing the clock, Hugh said to Dianne, "Why don't you make us lunch, while we finish off the corner we are working on?'

Dianne readily agreed, since she had enough of staining, and decided she would make soup and sandwiches. Dave laughingly said, "Don't burn the soup!"

"I'll burn your lip, if you don't get out of here!" Dianne replied, grabbing a spoon pretending she was going to use it as a weapon.

Following Hugh outside, Dave noticed the goat's water was low, so he suggested he should fill it up. Letting Dave do it, Hugh went around the corner to see what needed to be done with the next wall. He came across a board lying on the ground with nails sticking out of it. This was unusual, because he had shown Dianne how to nail it in, remembering this was the one.

Dianne was content to get lunch, humming, preparing everything, putting the soup on and getting out some cheese, sandwich meats and onions. She decided to slice the onions, carelessly thinking about the Nears, trying to figure out what it was all about. Out of the corner of her eye, she thought she saw a swift movement like a dark shadow, just as she sliced down.

The sharp pain of her finger, made her suddenly aware it wasn't the onion she had just cut. Screaming in agony, she flung the knife, as the end of her finger turned bright red from the wound. Holding her hand, she headed for the door, afraid. The blood dripped on the counter and floor in a steady pattern. Tears started flooding down her cheeks, luckily faster than the drops of blood. She started feeling woozy at the sight of the blood going into shock, but she made it out the door, screaming for Hugh.

Hugh had just finished nailing the board back in place when he heard Dianne's screams. Flinging the hammer down, he raced across the yard, followed by Dave yelling, "What's wrong sis?"

Reaching her, it was obvious what the problem was, seeing the red stain on her hand and floor. Hugh gently grabbed her hand saying, "It's not as bad as it looks. It's a long one but not really deep. That's why it's bleeding but we can remedy that. Come on, we'll wash it under the tap and fix you up." Looking straight at her to make her understand he was telling the truth. She nodded her head agreeing, willingly going with him as he put his arm around her for comfort.

'You're a brave girl, and you'll be fine," Hugh said giving her a kiss on the head and a gentle hug.

"But I cried uncle."

"It happens to us all, even me. There are times when the Nears get their way no matter how we try not to cry, but when the pain is too great, tears will flow. This is actually a good thing, because it can release the negative emotion of the pain in whatever form it comes in. This is something that should be done, because while you are shedding tears, you are also eliminating the negative thinking that is associated with the pain you are feeling. It is good to rid yourself of these emotions and thinking at that time, and then there is less to keep dwelling on later, going back over it again and again.

By emptying yourself of these emotions and thoughts, you make space for better emotions and thoughts. Ones that will heal the pain and scars left behind, while you shed the tears here in the physical world. You shed soul tears at the same time from your soul body. You are soul. Feeling and experiencing everything you do out here, including the pain.

This is where Lord Misanthropy and the Nears benefit. When soul has to shed an enormous amount of tears from pain, it ends up going to the Land of Afar. There, it sheds tears alone in the Tower of Tears, hoping to shed itself of the sudden burden of life.

Take, for example, when your father died. There was a great void in me from his death because he was all I had, all I loved. I collapsed in on myself afterwards. I saw no reason for going on, life had lost all its allure, there was only darkness. I had no idea what to do next.

While walking the halls getting my mobility back, I went down to the cancer ward where so many people went to die. I suddenly felt sorry for them, seeing that they were worse off than I was. There was one little boy there who had leukemia. According to the nurses, he didn't have long to live. To make matters worse, he had no parents and no one to care for him. They all tried their best to be with him as much as possible, but they were extremely busy. So I decided that since I was alone, I would do what I could.

That's when I realized love comes in many forms, and when one love is taken from you, you have the freedom to give love again in another way.

You see you never lose the ability to love, you just have to learn how to adjust to who you give it to, and how you give it out. I shared and cared for him as if he were my brother lying there. We became friends and when he would become afraid, I would hold his hand to let him know it was all right. Before he died, he told me he loved me, and I said the same thing back to him, because I did. Love is an emotion that can be felt over and over, at the right time and right circumstances. It is a precious emotion, something that must be freely given in order to receive.

You must remember even emotions are energy. You have the freedom to choose the emotion or energy that you feel no matter what that emotion is, good or negative, for as long as you want to feel it. You don't need to be a victim, reliving the emotion over and over without any control of it. When Bobby died, I had the same feelings I did when my brother died, I realized that these feelings aren't limited to just one person or two, but would be felt whenever I freely expressed them from my heart.

I understood when love is lost in your life. You can either shut down for the rest of your life or move on to give it again like I did Bobby. Now here I am with you two. The scar will always remain, but you can choose to see it as a sad reminder of some tragedy in your life, or a signpost of how your life changed for the better, in whatever form that it will take."

Surveying his handy work, he said to Dianne. "There you are, all bandaged up. I bet this happened because you were distracted just for a second by something?'

"Yes, I thought I saw a dark flash or something moving out of the corner of my eye, so I wasn't paying attention."

"Yes many accidents are caused by a distraction just for a second at exactly the wrong moment. Other things like daydreaming, not paying attention, thinking too hard, gapping out, carelessness, forgetting, foolishness, these are some of the techniques that the Nears use with great effect and precision. Their distractions come in unlimited forms, just as there is no limit to the variety of accidents that can happen."

"I thought these things just happened to people. You know bad luck," replied Dave.

"That's what everyone thinks. Remember, the Nears use your thoughts, you must be careful of what you think." answered Hugh.

"Now let's eat, but don't forget Dave, it's your turn to laugh at your sister."

Dave rubbed his hands together, thinking of what to say. Dave tormented his sister about her stupidity in trying to add extra protein to their lunches.

They finally sat down, Hugh suggesting to Dianne that she not do any more staining that day because it might aggravate the cut. He said

Dave and he would finish up, while she could prepare supper. She readily agreed.

"We go now to resume our task of beautifying the barn. We leave this in your capable hands." Dianne giggled and curtsied back. Getting to the barn, they found their brushes lying on the ground instead of where they had left them.

"We didn't throw these on the ground did we?" asked Dave looking around.

"No, the Nears did this, they never give up. They never sleep. They don't stop."

"You mean they are causing all these things that are happening to us?"

"Yes, it's an unfortunate fact of life, they are responsible for more than you could possibly imagine. Only through our negative thinking, do we allow them into our lives to wreak havoc on us, in whatever form it comes. Over time, if you could stop thinking negatively, their hold and influence on us would fade away. Then, we could live our lives relatively free from their bringing us unremitting pain and sorrow."

"How do you know all this? Who told you?" Dave asked.

"Ah!" said Hugh holding a forefinger in the air.

"Let me tell you a story. First, not all crazy people are crazy. Because of influences such as drugs or alcohol, they are opened up to see beyond the physical reality we know as life. I saw the Nears the night of your father's death when I lay half conscious after hitting my head. It was the trauma that allowed me to see them.

I learned more about them from meeting an alcoholic named 'Leaning Larry'. I met him one night outside the shelter where I was working as a volunteer. I happened to be going home when I turned the corner to go down an alley to the bus stop. I saw him leaning against a wall, having an animated talk to someone who wasn't there. Once I came up to him he stopped talking, or rather whoever was talking to him stopped. I heard him say, "Hey, wherez you thinksh you're goin?" motioning for this invisible person to come back.

I saw the smashed bottle in a small puddle on the pavement beside him. I knew he was well on his way to finding some peace in his intoxication. I startled him when I said hello while he continued to watch his friend. When he turned to look at me I was shocked to see such deep blue eyes. Eyes, that had seen too much misery, too much pain. Eyes that showed a man who had unfortunately given up because he couldn't deal with his life, a life destroyed around him over the years.

"Oh is you! Itz told me you'sh knew it, but it didn' wanna talk to you."

"Who?" I asked, looking at the empty space where he continued to stare.

He leaned over as if to whisper. "Near Quietus, the one whoz takes our loved ones like me Emma, to the Land of Afar. Itz real busy tonight but I asked how's Emma, so it stopped to chat for a min...hic...ute. Itz a hell of a nice whatever, but 'as an awful job. Don't tellsh anyone, I'll getsh in trouble." Putting his finger up to his mouth, indicating it was secret between us, chuckling. Probably he figured I thought he was crazy like everyone else did, until I told him I had seen them too. His smile was instantly transformed into a stare of surprise and shock. "Yoz 'ave?"

"Yes I have. I saw it and two others one night in a terrible car accident. They're real, so you aren't imagining them."

"He stood there for what seemed an eternity staring at me to be sure I wasn't lying, and then he started to cry. He said he also deserved it. He got drunk and killed some guy's brother. He said he looked a lot like me. No one's ever believed him before and he thanked me.

All the years of torment he had endured came out in great uncontrollable sobs. I saw a man shaken to the core but a new man, no longer under the control of the Nears. There was a look in his eyes that wasn't there before, a glimmer of hope.

He had lived on the streets keeping to himself, but I convinced him to come home with me to talk. I suddenly realized he was the one who killed Pat. At first I was stunned and shocked, but later as the hours went by I forgave him, realizing it was not his fault. It was the Nears. We talked about our meetings with the Nears and he started giving me important information about Nears and the Land of Afar.

When his wife had died of cancer, the light in his life had gone out. He was lost without her and having no children, there was nothing left for him to find comfort in, except the bottle.

He began to drink himself to death so he could find and be with Emma. His only problem was, he kept passing out so he never did die. However, when he passed out he was able to visit the Land of Afar many times. He told me how at first he went to the Tower of Tears, where you were tricked into giving them your tears, whenever the Nears were able to hurt you in some way. Most people went there in the soul state during their sleep or at the precise moment a bad event happened, being unaware of going there. The ones who did remember, just thought it to be a bazaar dream they had.

Larry ended up there many times as the Nears did their dirty work on him. His life was nothing more than a hopeless existence on the streets. With nothing but memories, fading with time, he didn't even have a picture of his wife to remind him of the life he once had. He cried when he told me he couldn't remember what she looked like or her voice at times, but I let him know it was normal. There were and are times when I had the same problem with my brother.

Eventually, he stopped going to the Tower of Tears because he had no more tears to shed, reaching a state of emotional and mental numbness. He had no past and no future, and by sheer chance realized that was why he was able to continue visiting the Land of Afar. Anyone who lives in the present and doesn't think of the past or future can go there and freely move about. In fact, he noticed the Nears didn't even detect his presence there, walking by them without them even seeing him.

He met Lord Misanthropy who saw him one day at the Falls of Affliction when it walked by. After scanning him, realizing he was a lost soul, it talked to him. It told him all about how it loved to come and sit by the falls to listen to the many sounds of crying, weeping, and lachrymose sorrow spilling over the falls. Apparently it gave the great lord solace and comfort.

It boasted about how Lake Lamentation was the crucible for all the tears man has shed since the beginning of time. It described how it built its castle from the golden tears of great kings and queens of old, by picking the golden tears from the lake bottom like we would pick nuggets of gold from a stream. It told Larry how the lake was the centre of negative power that went out to the whole world to make people think negatively. That way the Nears could do their jobs, bringing people to tears, and continue the constant flow of tears that they drank to sustain themselves.

Larry and I talked many times. He stopped drinking as the healing took place from his understanding of what happened. Eventually he was able to get a job, start new and now he is married to a wonderful woman he met. We have coffees together and sometimes dinner out. We are all good friends."

Dave could hardly believe what he heard, a fairy tale of horrible content. Dianne interrupted his thoughts. "What's up sis?"

She was so proud making dinner especially for Hugh." Nothing. Dinner's cooking. Mind if I watch?"

"Not at all girly. Just watch!" Painting the boards with a flair. Hugh smiled from the ladder. Dave showed Dianne the finer points he had learned, until a noise from the house could be heard.

"No! The fire alarm!" screeched Dianne in disbelief.

"Come on!" yelled Hugh, ignoring his sore body from being up the ladder, running for the house. Getting there, they flung the door open to be greeted by the smoke cloud of what once was a descent dinner, now blackened and inedible. All the elements were on high. "I didn't do this!" Seeing her efforts ruined brought tears streamed down her cheeks. She ran out of the kitchen yelling, "Nothing's going right!"

They watched her leave, "Should we go after her?" Dave asked.

"No. We clean this up and remake dinner. We'll talk when she comes back."

Dianne needed time to be alone. Life was no longer happy, it was getting serious without her permission. She resented this bizarre intrusion into her happiness. What little happiness she had gleaned from an imperfect life. The barn was her favorite place to be alone, her sanctuary. As she entered, the goats greeted her but she said: "Not now goaties."

Reaching the ladder, she heard a clunk in the corner behind bales of hay. Glancing over, she saw what appeared to be a corner of a large ear, slowly waving back and forth.

"Who's there?" she asked sternly but wondering what it was. It didn't move, so she asked again. This time it answered, "Me's!"

"Come out where I can see you!" She replied, actually quite terrified, thinking it was a Near.

When Lurky shuffled out, she realized it was one of the creatures she had seen the first night. His red eyes were a dead giveaway. "What are you?"

"I's a Sneakeeze. My's names is Lurky."

"What's a Sneakeeze and why do you have big ears?" She queried.

"I's got's really bigs ears to hears anything fars, fars away for your laughters so's the Nearies cans finds you's."

Dianne was shocked, "Why would you do that! They bring only tears and pain."

Lurky knew he had said the wrong thing, but he didn't know what else to do, so he started crying and blurted out, "Old Lordie Misphtpht holds my friends Slinks in prisons and if's I's don't do's this, he's there forevers without me's!"

Dianne suddenly knew they weren't being singled out. This was what this Lord did to anything, obviously. She saw he was genuinely upset and telling the truth.

"There was nothing else you could do. I would do the same unfortunately. "

Lurky stared at her through his misty eyes, "You's woulds?"

"To protect the ones you love, you must do things at times which are against your nature. You aren't here to harm us?"

He instantly shook his head no saying, "Lurky never hurts anyones."

"Where are the Nears now?"

"Don'ts knows. They suddenly nots here." waving his hands around.

"Well Lurky, it appears we are friends against a common enemy." The word friend, surprised Lurky, believing Slinks was going to be his only friend forever.

"You's be's Lurky's friends?"

"Yes. I would like that," she replied,."My name is Dianne." She giggled.

Lurky got down on all fours, crawling towards her, holding his hand out palm down, making quiet mewing sounds, showing he meant no harm. Dianne touched his hand, feeling the warmth and softness of it, as his ear gently touched hers, surprising her. After a few moments, he crawled back before standing up, almost shouting, "Lurky's made friends! Friends has begun! Friends! Friends to the end!"

Dianne started to laugh at his antics, making him even more excited, jumping up on a bale yelling," Lurky must fly!" Flapping his ears, he jumped off landing face down on the floor. Dianne hurried over to him saying, "Can Sneakeeze fly?" Staring up at her he chuckled, "No's! But I"s so's happy's I's could's!"

Helping him out she asked, "What were you do doing in here?"

Pointing over to the grain bin he said, "Getting's a birdy eggs and grainy."

"I don't want the others to find you, so why don't I leave a dish out behind the barn everyday for you. That way you don't have to come inside.

Lurky looked worried for a moment. "Will the others hurts me?"

"I was more worried about you and Slinks. If the Nears see you with me, they might hurt all of us and tell Lordie Misphtpht. My friends won't hurt you." Lurky understood exactly what she said.

"If you's does this for me's I's will leaves you a gift on the porches every mornings until the Nears are's done and we's goes back to Afar."

"Why thank you Lurky, it would help me to know when this is all over. We have all cried because of the Nears, as I'm sure you have too."

"Yes the Nears makes everyone cries sooner or laters." He said sadly.

"I'd better go Lurky. I'm so glad I met you. Maybe when this is all over you and Slinks could come to visit with us sometime," Dianne said, thinking she heard something.

"Yes, I's and Slinks woulds like that's," replied Lurky putting his hand out to her. She held his hand while his ear stroked her arm, so she stroked his head. Lurky quietly started mewing and humming, sharing this moment with her.

Finally she pulled away saying, "I'd better go. Goodbye Lurky Sneakeeze, my friend. Hopefully we'll meet again."

Lurky was in rapture so all he could say was, "Alrighty Dianneeze. Goodbye's for nows." Swooning he watched her leave. He finally recovered enough to go. He needed a nap to settle his excitement. His only nagging thought was whether his new human friend would be all right from the abuse of the Nears. He worried he would somehow possibly lose her, if they were able to cause her death.

Dianne slipped outside, looking around, seeing only the goats and chickens in the yard. Perhaps this was what she had heard, walking quickly back. She decided to go along with the situation, while she thought about how it might be possible to do something.

Food aromas greeted her as she opened the back door. Breathing deep the delicious smells she said: "Ah, that smells so good uncle!" acting like nothing had happened.

Dave was the first to speak up, "You're feeling better, that's not the usual you after a disaster happening."

"Well it wasn't me. I didn't turn everything on high on the stove. I had everything under control, until they interfered," sweeping her hand in the air.

"You're just in time. Everything is just about ready," spoke Hugh watching Dianne closely. Something was different but he couldn't put his finger on it.

"Thank you boys for cleaning up the mess and doing this," pointing to the food.

Putting her hand on Hugh's shoulder, Hugh pointed to Dave saying, "He helped too. It wasn't all my doing."

Dave blushed slightly. Dianne wrapped both her arms around his neck and gave him a big kiss on his neck. It had been a long time since she had done that. They use to hug each other when they were younger, causing Dave to blurt out: "Yuck, dog germs!" making everyone laugh.

"Come sit and we'll eat." Hugh said.

They didn't say much at first, especially Dianne, thinking about her new-found, unusual friend. She almost giggled, thinking about Lurky's ears and how he wanted to fly. She thought it was better to just keep this her secret for now.

After they ate, they went out onto the porch. Dianne's finger still gave her painful reminders of how the day wasn't the best she ever had. It was a small price compared to meeting Lurky. Sitting looking around at nature she asked: "Is there anything we can do to stop the Nears from hurting us?"

Hugh stared at her intently, and said, "The crickets are unusually loud tonight." drawing their attention to the sound.

"Why don't we listen to them with our eyes closed and see what they have to say."

"The crickets?" Both children stared at each other.

They had never really listened to crickets before; they thought it would be fun to give it a try. After all, what could a cricket say except chirp, chirp?

Settling in their chairs they folded their hands on their laps. They closed their eyes staring at the blank screens of their mind's eye.

They listened to the methodical raspy chirps coming from the crickets close to them. Listening, they noticed all the other ones in the surrounding area as well. The noise started to blend into one continuous sound, rising and falling ever so gently in tempo like waves, penetrating their inner being. It seemed like they were riding the sweeping rhythm of an ocean wave coming into shore.

Hugh, staring into his mind's eye, watched as the sound took over, turning everything surreal.

A pulsing golden glow emanated from each chirping cricket, fainter then stronger like it produced the chirping, separately but in harmony. The crickets he saw were the manifestation of sound he heard, but he knew it was the light behind the sound that made the crickets do what they did.

Observing this symphony of colored sound, he noticed a fog creeping into the surrounding landscape. Unnoticed at first, he was now aware of an ominous presence in the fog he didn't like. He desperately tried to keep the fog at bay pushing it back with his thoughts until the struggle made him open his eyes coming out of the experience. He found himself sitting in his chair sweating profusely.

Dianne was intently listening to the melody of the crickets slightly smiling when she thought about Lurky out of nowhere. Suddenly, she was floating above a barren landscape looking down where she saw Lurky with someone else. Curiosity got the better of her. Flying lower, her attention was diverted, seeing her brother lying on some rocks sleeping. A fog crept towards him like it had a mind of its own. Dave started screaming and writhing around as the fog moved closer, like he was having a terrible nightmare. She screamed for him to wake up but the effort brought her out of her experience almost sliding off her chair. Staring at Dave, he was still, his eyes closed, deep in his experience like he was in a trance. She shook his arm to bring him around.

Dave had begun his experience listening to the methodical chirping, all blending into one loud sound. He was floating but through a thick fog. He realized it was silent, too silent, a silence that wasn't good. Somewhere in the silence, he heard a noise quietly at first but gaining in intensity. It was obvious to him if this noise came to him it was his doom. He frantically tried to escape, flailing and trying to float away. He heard Dianne's voice through the fog begging him to wake up. So demanding were her pleas he woke from his experience looking around, wild eyed. He realized where he was and not trapped in a fog somewhere.

"I must have fallen asleep," he said staring at his sister. Before either of them could say anything Hugh said, "Come let's go to bed. We have a long day ahead tomorrow." Neither complained still feeling the effects of their experiences, individually trying to understand what had just taken place. Now conversation wasn't needed, retrospective thought was. Perhaps while sleeping tonight answers would come.

DAWN CAME WITH THE USUAL early bird serenade but it seemed no one wanted to get out of bed, lying and thinking if any answers had come during their sleep. Dave got up, yawning and stretching out the kinks in his body, staring out the window to see what the weather was like. He woke the others as the wood squeaked and creaked beneath his feet.

He made his way down stairs, and sat on a chair staring off, trying to process the unusual dreams he had during the night. It seemed like one continuous dream, linked together. He didn't like these kinds of dreams, they were hard to interpret, and seemed to fade away quickly once he was awake.

Dianne and Hugh stumbled down to the kitchen.

"Morning," Dave quietly said.

"Ya, you've got that right. I didn't want to get up," replied Dianne.

Hugh stared out the window. "This is a good day for doing the outside of the house."

Dianne nodded eagerly hoping to see her new found friend. She opened the door when something caught her eye on the floor, seeing a daisy flower beside a small brightly colored white quartz stone. This was obviously a gift from Lurky. She grabbed both gifts, hoping no one saw her.

Skipping over to the barn, she hoped Lurky would be inside. She sniffed the faint aroma of the flower after putting the stone in her pocket. Reaching the door she called Lurky, but only the 'Nahhhs' of the goats and clucking of chickens could be heard. A sense of sadness overcame her when he did not answer, yet she knew he was better to stay hidden. She knew Dave and Hugh would not hurt him, but she just wanted to keep this secret to herself. Something exciting; just for her.

After she let the animals out, she quietly called several more times for Lurky only to be greeted by silence. She filled a small dish with grain and an egg, taking it behind the barn where no one else would see it except Lurky. She picked up her flower taking it with her to the house, glancing back every now and then hoping to catch a glimpse of him. Once in the house, she placed the flower in a vase in the center of the table. Her actions caught Dave's attention.

"What's up Dot? You're getting horticultural on us, or something?"

Nonchalantly she replied. "No, I was struck by its beauty, that's all," pretending it was no big deal.

"A gift is a beautiful thing Dave, especially when it's a flower. Thank you Di."

Dianne smiled, and then went upstairs putting the stone in her dresser, a treasured reminder of Lurky. Back downstairs she was greeted by delicious smelling pancakes, eggs, bacon and toast. She found it peculiar that she hadn't noticed this when she came in, however the flower on the table made her realize why.

"Well are we ready to make changes to the house today?' asked Hugh.

"Oh yes! Mom will be so shocked at the different appearance of the farm since we started this. Especially, since we haven't said a word to her whenever she calls to see how things are," replied Dave.

After breakfast they went to the porch as usual. Hugh took a deep breath, nonchalantly looking out across the field for the three shadows, hovering ghostly in the distance. Dianne looked around trying to find any sign of Lurky. Dave scratched his head giving out a long yawn sitting down, uninterested in looking at anything.

"This morning instead of doing the "Awh', I think maybe we should listen to the sound of the trees, which is different than listening to the wind blowing through the trees. See if you can notice the difference." They closed their eyes taking deep breaths before settling down. They intently listened for the sound of the trees, whatever that was.

The breeze blew gently so there was no sound to it, however as they listened there was a slight rustling, a low 'Ssss' noise coming from the trees, from the acoustics of the leaves jostling against each other. This was something new to them, listening to trees actually making a noise. It would come and go, according to the whim of the wind doing its will. Without realizing it, their bodies started moving slightly back and forth with the rhythm of the sound, feeling lighter and lighter as if floating.

Suddenly Dianne saw, in her mind's eye, herself rising above the chair going gently higher and higher until she was up around the top of the trees being blown about by the force of the wind. She listened to the sound of the trees blending into one loud noise like she was listening to static on the radio. The noise didn't bother her, having a soothing quality to it. It was almost like the sound helped carry her along over the treetops, knowing how a bird felt, being free to fly.

Being up so high she was able to see off in the distance, where she saw mountains that looked vaguely familiar even though she had never been there. Without warning, the noise stopped, causing her to free-fall towards the ground. She almost screamed, seeing the ground rushing to meet her, resulting in her almost falling off her chair, opening her eyes wide.

Dave picked up the noise right away, and it made him feel like he was leaving his chair right away. In his mind's eye he immediately rose out of the chair, almost shooting straight up like a rocket, higher and higher. The sensation in his body was something like he had never experienced before. He was smiling as the experience continued until he seemed to reach the top of whatever it was. There was only empty space. He started slowly descending like a leaf would as it falls from a tree spiraling gently down, tumbling over now and then.

Turning in a slow spin, he observed off in the distance, mountains brown and barren. A dreadful feeling crept over him, where a moment before he had been thoroughly enjoying his experience. Suddenly the accompanying noise stopped, causing him to free-fall tumbling uncontrollably, clawing at the empty air, and thrashing about. He slid off his chair, hitting the floor with a thud, giving out a loud. "What?"

Hugh had settled in listening to the trees which he was used to, feeling the unfamiliar floating as the noise took him over, even though there was an uncontrollable nagging about still seeing the Nears in the field. When the children shouted almost in unison like they did, he slammed back into his body with the speed of a bullet. This caused him to topple off his chair, staring wide-eyed at Dave sitting on the floor. Dianne gripped both arms of her chair like she was about to take off somewhere else.

"What happened Uncle Hugh? Does this always happen when you do this?"

Hugh continued looking at them both. "Why no. Never before this. It has always been a very pleasant experience."

"It was fun, until the end when I saw the mountains," replied both of them.

"Hugh what does it mean?"

"I'm not sure. However it could have something to do with the Nears and their influence on us." Both children didn't need to be reminded of the influence of the Nears, after Dave hit his bruised leg in the exact same spot landing on the floor, and Dianne's cut was sore again from her grabbing the chair so tightly. They were both fussing with their sore spots.

Hugh saw them, saying, "Unfortunately there's a problem, thanks to the Nears. When they hurt us physically through our negative thinking, we will repeatedly hurt the exact same spot over and over and each time the pain will seem just as intense as the first time. It is a reminder that they were able to do this to us. A 'thank you' calling card, if you want to call it that. Since they were able to hurt us the first time, the hope is it will become a repeated source of tears."

Both children stared down at their wounds, making up their minds they weren't going to allow the Nears a victory, trying to ignore the throbbing feeling, focusing their thoughts away from it.

"Come on. Let's go do some changes. It will help overcome what we are thinking. Dave bring our hats. Di and I will get the ladder, paint and tools we need."

Dianne became a little nervous, hoping Lurky hadn't foolishly gone back into the barn for a snack, after she warned him not to. Reaching the door, she brushed past Hugh. Once inside she gave the interior a fast glance around and to her relief nothing looked out of the ordinary. She moved to the storage room. "I think what we need is here, Hugh."

They picked up brushes and cans of paint and a ladder. Travelling out and across the yard, Dianne nervously looking around said, "What a wonderful day you picked for painting the house Uncle Hugh."

"You're right Lady Di, it is a wonderful day to paint." He said as he started to sing.

"LET'S PAINT OUR CANVAS OF LIFE
WE'LL PAINT IT SO MANY COLORS
THEY'LL ALL MIX IN A BEAUTIFUL HUE

WE'LL PAINT IT ALL JUST RIGHT
LIKE ALL OF NATURE'S FLOWERS
ONLY THE PERFECT COLORS WILL DO

WITH PAINT IT WILL BE A SIGHT
THE CANVAS PAINTED WILL BE OURS
PERFECTLY PAINTED BY ME AND YOU"

Grabbing a brush from her hand, Hugh laughed, "Maybe I'll just paint you!"

To her surprise she saw him waving the brush, making her race ahead of him, careful not to drop anything. Dave heard her, thinking for a second, something was wrong.

Racing out of the house with the caps in his hand and seeing what was going on, he yelled.

"Hey! No fooling around! Put those caps on. We got some serious changes to make today. There's no time for horseplay!"

Looking at each other, both stopped what they were doing. Removing the smiles from their faces they yelled, "Yes Captain Dave! We are reporting for Changee duties sir!" saluting him in unison, putting their caps on.

Hugh kept dabbing her with his dry brush, quietly saying: "Paint. Paint. This brush is meant to paint," making her giggle.

"Stay away from me, it's got dog germs on it from you-know-who," Dave said, pointing to his sister.

"Maybe it's time to paint a dog! Hugh said, waving the brush in the air and going toward Dave. "Grab a brush, Lady Di! Let's paint the dog!"

Dianne picked up a large brush. "Here's a good one. I can paint a thick coat on him with this!"

Dave ran behind the tree nearby as they chased him yelling: "Come back, we want to paint changes on you to turn you into a Davey Dog.!"

Dave ran behind a tree. "Stay away from me you two!"

"Fine. Come on Di. Let's get started and we'll leave Davey Dog sitting under the tree scratching his fleas."

Hugh set up the ladder saying, "I'll fix this shutter first and the rain gutter, once I've cleaned out the leaves. You can paint the lower part and once I'm done I will continue up here."

They left each other alone, once they started. They wanted to see some serious changes to the outside of the house that had symbolized the state of their lives with its worn, faded appearance. Over time it showed the world what misery could look like, once it was firmly in place.

Their brushes worked earnestly transforming the appearance of the walls, bringing new energy to replace the faded old illusion of life; they had grown accustomed to one negative thought at a time.

Moving along, Hugh started humming quietly at first, and then louder as they progressed. Finally Dianne asked, "What song are you humming uncle?"

"Oh it's a song whenever I'm painting. Would you like me to sing it?

"Sure."

Clearing his throat, he began.

"BRUSH STROKES
OF CHANGE
MAKE THINGS ANEW

SOME PATIENCE
SOME MOVEMENT
WILL USUALLY DO

TRANSFORMING
OLD NEGATIVITY
INTO BRAND NEW

ENDLESS WORRY
AND LOST HOPE
WILL NEVER DO"

He sang it several times accompanied by the children singing it themselves. It seemed to make the task of painting the wall so much faster. Every stroke was a deliberate act of renewal, covering over what wasn't right in their lives, into a brighter future.

They worked through lunch and by mid afternoon they were over three quarters way done. There was just part of a wall and some higher trim left to do. Everyone's energy was failing, indicated by more frequent breaks and less zeal in the brush strokes.

Dianne decided to take a break, excusing herself to go to the bathroom. She also used this as an excuse to see if Lurky had been around to eat the bowl of food she left for him outside the barn. She walked to the back, peering around the corner at the dish, which was empty. Just as she was about to refill the dish, she heard a noise inside the barn. It wasn't the animals, since they were all outside.

Excitement rose in her, thinking she would get to see him. After picking up the dish, she crept inside quietly closing the door behind her. She whispered. "Lurky are you there?" She was answered by a squeak on the floor of the loft as something moved. Slowly climbing the wooden ladder up to the loft, she asked again, "Lurky you shouldn't be in here, you know that."

Reaching the top, she peered over the edge for Lurky, but suddenly a black flash out of the corner of her eye caused her to snap her head sideways. Her sudden movement made the ladder move out of place, causing her to topple off, free falling to the unforgiving floor below. As she was falling, she realized she had been tricked by the Nears. Now she was paying whatever price was about to be exacted when she hit the floor.

There was nothing she could do, except watch the blur of her movement. Even though she was in a state of fear of what the outcome would be, there was a part of her that accepted the present moment. She instinctively knew the Nears were just doing their job and it was her thinking that put her in this situation.

If she had of acted out of love and shared Lurky with the others instead of being selfish by keeping him to herself, perhaps she wouldn't be in this situation. Just before hitting the floor, she had a passing thought that perhaps love plays a role in everything. Not just the love that she had for family, but a different kind of love, an all encompassing love.

Hitting the floor, the shock was like something she had never experienced before, paralyzing her instantly as she passed out, making only one quiet sound. "Huuuuugh!

Hugh had watched Dianne cross the yard towards the barn. It was getting late and he knew her enthusiasm for painting was waning. He stopped painting, and went down to talk to Dave, giving him praise on how well he was doing. He realized he had to use the bathroom, so he walked around to the door, looking for Dianne. She was nowhere to be seen. Assuming she had gone to the barn for a moment, he thought nothing more about it.

Dave decided to help Hugh, so he climbed the ladder, even though he had a fear of heights. He almost spilled his pail of paint once getting near the top. The ladder did it's best to make his heart race. Once at the top, he settled down and concentrated on what he was doing. He thought about how things had come to where they were, glad Hugh was there. He really needed a male figure to be around. He wondered if his father had lived, what it would have been like. He suddenly became sad and melancholy. There was an empty space in his heart unfilled by the non -presence of his father.

Daydreaming made him distracted. Suddenly, there was a black flash out of the corner of his eye like a bird was about to hit him. He jerked back, twisting his foot off the rung of the ladder, making him slip slightly. He came out of the daydream gasping, trying to compensate. He over reacted, spilling some paint, and as he tried to avoid it, the ladder came away from the wall, sliding sideways taking him with it. He yelled for Hugh, not knowing what else to do as he fell towards the ground.

Hitting the ground, he felt instant pain. Tears started to flow and along with the pain were hidden emotions that he didn't know he had inside. Lying flat in shock, he felt pain coursing through his whole body, especially his leg that he had already hurt. There was nothing he could do except cry, sobbing uncontrollably.

Hugh heard the noise of the ladder and sharp cry. He shouted, "Oh no! I'm coming!"

A black flash out of the corner of his eye distracted him, enough to misplace his foot on the first step of the stairs. He slid down the first couple of steps before tumbling the rest of the way, feeling each step as he lay in a heap at the bottom of the stairs, unable to move.

Every bone he had broken in the accident throbbed like they were all freshly broken again. He let out a sob, something he hadn't done since the accident. His tears fell to the floor and reminders of all the hurt and anguish he had held inside came to the surface. They fell as liquid coins of sorrow, shelled out for a labor of lament that he never wanted to toil at.

Suddenly he realized he hadn't seen Dianne. His body still hurting, he stumbled outside where he saw Dave picking himself up, sobbing. "Lad, are you okay?"

"Where's Di?" He queried through his tear stained eyes, wiping them with his hand. Suddenly seeing Hugh had been crying too, he asked, "What happened to you Uncle Hugh?"

"I fell down the stairs. Thanks to the Nears," replied Hugh rubbing his aching spots.

"Me too! It was the Nears that caused me to fall off the ladder. I was only trying to help you out uncle."

"I appreciate what you did. If it weren't for the Nears you would have done a splendid job," giving Dave a reassuring pat.

Hugh told Dave he was concerned about Dianne, so they headed across the yard to the barn. Reaching the door they flung it open, seeing Dianne lying on the floor motionless with the ladder on top of her.

"Dianne! Dianne! Are you alright! They both yelled. Dave picked the ladder up and tossed it off her while Hugh knelt beside her.

"Honey, are you hurt?" Seeing her eyes flutter and finally open, he moved some of the hair out of her face. She was breathing heavily. "I just got the wind knocked out of me." She said as tears flowed down her face.

"Just lie still until you feel like getting up"

She started sobbing. "It was the Nears. They tricked me into going up the ladder."

"Don't feel bad, they just tricked us. I fell off the ladder and Uncle Hugh fell down the stairs." Dave said.

Dave and Hugh helped Dianne get up off the floor.

"Isn't there anything we can do to stop this?' Dianne asked, wiping the tears from her face,

"Right now, let's rest until the pain subsides."

The Nears had achieved their goal, there hadn't been as many tears shed in one day since their dad had died.

Dave handed Dianne her cap. "Here, I picked this up for you, put it on."

"Thanks, I am more determined than ever to make whatever changes are necessary. Let's finish painting the house today uncle, even though we are all hurt. I know it's important not to let the Nears defeat us by preventing us from doing what needs to be done, and making us happy."

"That's right Di, no matter what obstacle seems to appear, you must persevere to finish your goal or the Nears will have won."

There wasn't much left to do. They didn't speak as they finished the area. Instead each of them went into their own world of thinking to apply what changes were necessary, as they applied one brush stroke after another of fresh paint on the old faded wood. They used each brush stoke as a symbol of how they could brush aside the illusion of negativity they had built up over time. The negativism turned into a chromatic mantle of divine absolute truth. Once they were finished Hugh turned to them.

"Well done, my Changees. Mere mortals would have faded into the obscurity of defeatism a long time ago, faced with such daunting obstacles and hindrances, displayed this day on the battlefield of almost unattainable aspirations. Tomorrow we go fishing! That's enough of this."

Lurky settled in, finding the right comfort spot under the tree's shade, finding he had enough of this for now. Feeling a sense of contentment, he hoped he would dream about Slinks, missing him the way he did. At least a dream was better than nothing.

A fly made the mistake of deciding his ear was an ideal spot to land for an afternoon snooze. It wasn't a problem, until it began wandering around tickling him. His hand shot up without any other movement of his body, grabbing the fly, popping it in his mouth, before the fly could even begin to protest.

Lurky started making little noises and wheezes drifting off into dreamland. Images started taking fuzzy shape in his inner vision. Suddenly three dark forms appeared out of nowhere. One of them pointed a finger at him, saying, "Get up worm!"

He couldn't move in his dream staring at the Nears. One of them kicked him hard in the foot, causing him to actually wake up.

"Get up worm! It's time to go. Now!" Lurky jumped, seeing the three creatures hovering over him.

"Wha.. Whats yous wants?" Lurky asked nervously.

"We're done with the human fools. That's the last laugh coming out of their mouths" replied Near Hebejebe.

"There is a nice little stream of tears coming from their eyes now." The other two said, mimicking someone crying.

"You's didn't kills anyones, did you's?"

"No! These three were a push over, but we had thought about it," added Near Bane imitating someone being pushed off a ladder. The other two demonstrated a person being pushed down a flight of stairs, all the while pretending they were crying.

"We had them crying, wanting their mommas in no time," laughed Near Aflik.

"Come on, let's get going. We have things to do before we get back home. Let's go!"

The word home brightened Lurky up, because this meant he would soon see Slinks, even if it meant spending a lifetime in a cell. At least they would be together, yet another part of him was sad to leave Dianne without knowing if she was all right. He reached behind the tree bringing out his flask after seeing the Nears had theirs. He wanted them to think he had been drinking tears all this time.

Starting off, the Nears took the lead. Lurky kept stealing glimpses back at the farm, until they entered the trees, hoping at least to see Dianne off in the distance. It never happened, so he decided although brief, their meeting was suppose to be that way.

Quietly to himself, he said. "Bye Dianneeze." As he walked along, he wondered if all humans were as nice as her.

After awhile, he noticed they were moving towards a village nearby, instead of going directly towards the Land of Afar. They stopped when they could see the outline of the village, taking a rest in a clump of bushes until dark. Lurky decided to have a sleep, and again started dreaming of Slinks. This time Slinks was waving to him, showing him a golden key that unlocked the window of the cage still holding him. When he inserted the key, the cage became a cave that felt like home as Slinks beckoned him to come in. Lurky was about to enter it, when the dream suddenly stopped.

"Worm! Get up, we have work to do.!" Lurky awoke to darkness. He had slept longer than he thought and now he was hungry. Most of the insects would be gone until morning, so he would have to find what he could. Excusing himself for a bathroom break, he moved off finding what he could to satisfy his hunger.

When he returned, the Nears said: "You sure go for a lot of bathroom breaks for someone who drinks tears" handing Lurky his flask suspiciously.

Lurky didn't know what to say, hoping nothing was sticking out of the corner of his mouth. "I guess I's justs fulls of it."

The Nears chuckled moving away, much to Lurky's relief. After coming out to a road, they watched a car driven by a woman, trying to apply makeup, heading towards them.

"Here's an accident waiting to happen." Commented Near Bane, closing its eyes.

"NEAR ACIDANT
NEAR ACIDANT
COME HERE NEAR
COME HERE NEAR"

Near Acidant appeared suddenly. Near Bane said nothing, pointing to the car. It just nodded as they disappeared in a flash of light. Suddenly the woman appeared to look up, dropping her makeup kit. As she bent over to get it, she pulled the steering wheel, making the car veer off at a sharp bend in the road. There was a scream, screech of tires and a loud smashing noise as the car hit a telephone pole.

Near Bane reappeared with the rest. Near Acidant was gone. It was too busy to socialize.

"How's that boys!" I told you humans were too stupid to do three things at once," giving each other high fives. Lurky watched the steaming car, wondering if the human was alright.

"Don't worry worm, someone will call for help. Or maybe she will, if her arms and fingers aren't broken," imitating the woman trying to use the phone in a state of severe injury. It scratched its head saying, "Now what was that number to save myself? Oh yes 911."

Lurky didn't see the humor in the situation wondering if somehow, somewhere even these Nears would have to answer for being like they were. Although part of him couldn't even begin to see how, considering whom their boss was.

The Nears didn't look back. Instead, they each staggered along pretending they were injured, joking and laughing about the severity of the woman's injuries. Lurky on the other hand, kept looking back, realizing how horrible the Nears were to humans.

It was dark as they made their way into an alleyway behind a few businesses at the end of the village. Lurky was nervous being in close proximity to humans, however the Nears seemed quite at home. The only thing that stirred was a stray cat that was preoccupied trying to catch a mouse.

Near Bane growled: "A cat to bat!" taking a swipe with its clenched fist at the scruffy feline. It almost hit it, but it sped out of harm's way. The other Nears took up blocking positions to have their turn at the streaking blur of fur, each taking a similar swing at the cat. Finally, Near Hebejebe made contact with an upper cut-like swoop, sending the screeching cat over the wooden fence tumbling out of control. Giving a victory dance it howled: "Near Hebejebe one, cats nothin'!" cheered on by the others.

"Whosh hurtin my puddy cat!" a voice around the corner half moaned out.

The Nears became silent until Near Aflik said: "Luck is on our side tonight. It's Wino Wallace." giving a motion to follow it.

Going around the corner, a figure lay slouched against the wall. One hand hung down, while the other cradled a half empty bottle of cheap wine.

Peering at the Nears through thoroughly intoxicated eyesight, he desperately tried to focus.

"Oh, Ish you my good friend, Nearly Alfi' Lickion," waving his hand clumsily before flopping it back down to the bottle. He put the bottle to his lips and took a long drink, before sort of wiping his chin for the missed drops with his grimy shirtsleeve.

"Whosh your friends Nearly?"

"This is Near Bane and Near Hebejebe. Boys, this is Wino Wallace or Whining Wallace, when he really gets going."

"I shee you, hic! brought your doggy tonight. I hope he didn' hurt me feline friend, Alley Oops."

"No, the cat wasn't in a friendly mood." shrugged Near Aflik.

"Here's boy. Come see Uncle Wallace. I'z won't bite you. I already ish eating." He said looking at Lurky, holding his bottle up. He gave a slurry whistle.

"Do it. Get down on all fours," Near Aflik said to Lurky.

Lurky did as he was told, moving closer to the man, not sure what was going to happen. Wino Wallace clumsily placed his hand on his forehead, smacking him gently then scratching his fur.

"Good doggy, good boy, nice fella." He stopped scratching for a moment staring at the huge ears.

"Thish must be one of thehm big floppin' eared hound dawgs, Ish heard about. You want to watch goin' through doors boyo. Yoush might get one pinched in th'a door," giving one final thump on Lurky's head before turning to Near Aflik.

"Whaz up? Ish we goin' have a convershation or what?

"My pleasure Wallace. Would you like to get ready?"

"Say, have you seen Leanin Larry anywheres, have you? I haven' seen 'im in a long time."

Near Aflik said it hadn't.

"No problem. Bottoms up when th'a tops down!" He turned the bottle upside down slowly draining the contents one serious chug after another. By the time he was finished the bottle, the effects overwhelmed him. He closed his eyes moaning and babbling incoherently, swimming in the hallucinate world that was only his to experience. Near Aflik turned to the others: "I'll be right back," and disappeared with a flash. Wallace suddenly started screaming "Oh no, not again."

Lurky watched in horror as the man cried and moaned. Tears flowed down his cheeks. He writhed in emotional pain, being inflicted with the worst possible thoughts and nightmares. Lurky couldn't watch the spectacle, realizing the Near had entered into the mind of this poor helpless addicted shadow of a man, wreaking havoc on what sanity it still had left. The sobbing and moaning continued, for what seemed to be an eternity until finally there was silence. When Near Aflik reappeared, it wiped its hands together like it had just completed an important job, saying: "Well that's enough for now."

Near Bane went over to the motionless man, picked up his hand holding it in the air, before unceremoniously letting it flop back down. "Yup, he's out for the count!" waving its hand over the man like a referee at a fighter's knockout, much to the laughter of the other Nears. "Come on let's get going."

Lurky walked past the sprawled out man snoring loudly. He wondered what terrible troubles the man had experienced to put him in such a vulnerable state, helpless to stop the merciless assault by the Nears. As they wandered through the alleyway, they would test each back door to see if it was locked. Finally, they came across one that was open.

"Opportunity always opens the door when you knock or in this case turn the handle," commented Near Bane, winking before disappearing into the store. Out of nowhere, there was a commotion and sounds of smashing, breaking destruction from inside.

Near Aflik turned to Near Hebejebe. "It's such a bull in a china shop. I just can't take it anywhere!"

After a few minutes, there was silence except for the click of the door being locked on the inside and a flash. Near Bane suddenly stood outside with them. "That will really get them. How can any place be broken into when it's all locked up safe and sound!"

"That's a good one Near Bane. You slay me!" roared Near Hebejebe holding its sides in laughter.

Reaching the end of the alley, they left behind the buildings until they came to the cemetery, causing Near Bane to stop in its tracks. "Listen!"

Lurky heard the three girls long before Near Bane did. He paid no attention, since humans did go to where stone monuments were set up in rows. He had watched them from a distance, as they laid flowers in front of one of the monuments. Thinking about it, he realized they usually always cried while they stood or knelt by the stones. Innocently asking Near Bane, he wanted to know whether the Nears made the stone monuments there to cry to.

"No, they do that themselves when one of them dies with the help of Near Quietus. I think they are afraid of forgetting who they knew or perhaps they think others will think badly of them unless they put up as big a monument as possible. Whatever is the reason, its good business for us, we just sit back and collect the tears. One of the other Nears turned to Near Hebejebe and said. "Go do your stuff!"

The three girls had snuggled in blankets, after deciding to spend the night in the cemetery. They giggled, telling each other ghost stories, munching on goodies, and waving the small flashlight around at any small noise they heard.

"What's wrong with this thing?" queried one of the girls, giving the flashlight a shake as it flickered on and off.

"Shhh! Did you hear that noise?" asked one of the other girls with a tone of caution. At that moment, the flashlight went on strong and pointed right at the noise, revealing an indistinguishable figure, lying on the grass in front of one of the graves. It sat up giving a good stretch and loud yawn saying.

"THE NIGHT AIR'S WARM AND REFESHING
IT'S SO COLD AND DAMP DOWN THERE
MY BONES HAVE FED THE WORMS
NOW IT'S TIME FOR SOME FRESH AIR

MY GRAVE'S CASKET IS SO BORING
AT MY CASKET WALLS DO I STARE
IT'S TIME TO COME OUT FOR A STRETCH
TO FIND SOMEONE TO TAKE BACK THERE"

Three shrieks blended into one sobbing, hysterical symphony of horrification, staring at this ghoulish apparition that had apparently risen from its ossuarium home. They left everything behind, stumbling and fumbling together, headed for the gate. Tears from sheer fright were flowing down their faces. In the morning as evidence would prove, there was more liquid left on the trail than what could possibly be attributed to tears.

Near Hebejebe reappeared holding a blanket with one hand beside its head for comfort, sucking on its thumb saying, "I is so scared out here with my blankee!"

The others were rolling on the ground with laughter, except for Lurky. He couldn't see the fun scaring anyone, who was holding a midnight vigil beside someone's stone they cared about. The cruelty of that seemed so terrible.

Walking all night, light from the approaching morning started to show on the horizon. A tall wooden fence came into view, indicating this is where Fang lived. Without a spoken word Near Bane disappeared, only to reappear with a bees nest. There were no bees flying around, because they were still inside. The Near had stuffed a wad of leaves up the opening of the hole before they could fly out. From the muted noise coming from inside, the bees were definitely awake now and not in a good mood.

"This should do the job," stated Near Bane giving the hive a good shake. Fang was obviously sleeping unaware they were outside his domain. Suddenly, Near Aflik disappeared, going into the compound. Near Hebejebe got down on all fours serving as a step stool, while Near Bane, with the hive in hand stood on him, handing the hive to Near Aflik over the fence.

There was a whoosh, followed immediately by a growl of surprise. The early morning gift broke open on the corner of the entrance to the kennel, spilling its contents over the head of Fang. This was immediately followed by the recognition from Fang that his early morning guests weren't in the mood for polite social interfacing. The first stings registered on the soft part of his nose. He gave out the first of many vocal protests at the pain that was being inflicted upon him. His only recourse was full evacuation and retreat from his comfortable bed. Yelping and squealing, partly out of indignation and pain, he made the kennel rattle as his whole body tried to get outside all at once through the small opening.

The Nears roared with laughter, and then started on their way, never looking back or caring what happened to the dog, whose only crime had been to defend his territory.

"He sounds busy as a bee!" they chuckled, and then heard a human voice calling the dog. Then there was a scream of pain as the bees found a new source of social interfacing.

They moved through the brush, and reached a game trail, making their movement faster. There almost seemed urgency to their steps. It was when they took a break Lurky realized why. They were almost out of tears. Little did Lurky know that when a Near left the Land of Afar in the physical body, it required tears to stay in the negative consciousness. Should it run out, it would be forced to consume physical things for food and water. This would slowly make it become more positive. Something Lord Misanthropy forbid, with extreme consequences for those Nears that tested its theory.

Lurky on the other hand was such a little piggy, knowing they were going back. He munched, and crunched, gobbled, nibbled, gulped, gorged, devoured and snacked on every plant or hapless insect that came near him.

By the end of the day they reached the foot of the mountains, where the trail led up to the gates of the Land of Afar. They stopped, taking a break and consumed the last of their tears before going on. It got bleaker the farther up they climbed until nothing grew amongst the rocks. The fog enveloped them gradually making everything they looked at indiscernible. This didn't bother Lurky since his whole being was on reuniting with Slinks as he walked along quietly singing to himself.

"LURKY IS SO HAPPY
HAPPY AS CAN BE'S
IT WON'T BE'SLONG NOW
UNTIL SLINKS HE WILL SEE

LURKY AND SLINKS
TOGETHER WE'S WILL BE
HAPPY TOGETHER
SLINKS AND ME'S"

Finally coming around a corner, the Nears stopped for a moment. Lining up abreast they took a deep breath before saying.

"LAND OF AFAR
WE'RE ALMOST HERE
SOLACE AND COMFORT
TO A WAYWARD NEAR
LACHRYMOSE BEAUTY
TEARFULLY CLEAR
HOME DARK HOME
WE HOLD SO DEAR"

Out of the thick fog appeared a wavering apparition, slowly solidifying into the bridge so many had crossed seeking imagined solace, unwittingly placing their precious tears on the altar of deception. They all bowed deeply before making a mad dash for the bridge, trying to be the first to cross, pushing and shoving each other like a game until they were all across.

Stopping to regain their usual solemn composure, they moved along the Road of Anguish in single file. There was no fanfare, no cheering crowds with waving banners and balloons. There was just the wind making quiet gusts of dust, as a form of acknowledgement that the victorious had returned home. Except for a quick movement from the Lord's balcony, barely seen.

They entered through the back door into the Great Hall. Lurky became nervous, hearing lamenting sounds coming from the tears flowing down the walls. Now, he understood in his brief exposure how the tears got there. He wondered what experience had occurred to some humans to make the individual wails and sobs he heard. He realized that these sounds were made only from the most horrible of incidents that can happen to human lives.

A Near Acolyte announced in a loud voice. "Behold our Lord! Ruler of all! It who is all!"

Lord Misanthropy gazed at them with its usual arrogant malevolence. "You have done as asked?"

"We have my Lord. We made them pay for their arrogant laughter that insulted my Lord's ears."

It glanced over to Near Immolation summoned from the basement. "Have there been any more sounds from the Risibility machine?"

"None, my Lord!"

"Excellent! You have served me well" The three Nears showed sneers of superior haughtiness, puffing out their chests, giving each other slaps and pokes of approval. "That is all."

The Near Acolyte interjected. "Sire, what about this thing?" pointing to Lurky cowering in the back.

"I have no further use for this worm, release him with the other."

That one word was all he needed to hear, releasing waves of happiness, knowing Slinks was still alive. Daring not to express a smile or any other indications of his inner feelings, he headed for the stairs after bowing. He didn't want to stay one more moment, in case the Lord changed its mind. All of a sudden the Lord's voice roared: "Stop worm!" Terrified, Lurky thought this had all been a cruel joke planned from the beginning.

"You and your worm friend have freedom to roam Afar without leaving its borders. I may have further use of you. Is that understood?"

"Yes Siree!" he replied. Turning, he almost flew down the stairs crying, so happy was he that now he would be with Slinks and free at that. Coming to the last corner before the cell, he slowed becoming as quiet as possible, peeking around the corner. He saw the most wonderful sight he could ever want to see. There was Slinks bent over playing with something in his cell. Lurky decided to play a joke on him, ducking behind the wall and whispering Slinks name. Suddenly Slinks jumped to the bars of the cell whispering, "Lurky is that's you's? If it is, you's better comes out or I'll box with your ears the wholes live long day!"

Lurky couldn't stand it anymore sticking his head around the corner. Slinks jumped and danced in joy at seeing Lurky.

"You's dids it! I knews you's would!" Tears of joy streamed down his face, trembling with excitement turning around exclaiming.

"Look Spidy, it's Lurky, he's back!"

Lurky stared at the fat bottomed spider he had given Slinks.

"He's gottens so bigs!"

"Yes, he's a goods fly catcher. He's been feedings us both's," looking behind Lurky, Slinks asked. "Isn'ts they's goin' to lets you's in with me's?"

"No! We's free!" Before Slinks could say anything, the door made a loud click opening on its own. Lurky didn't hesitate flinging the door open, dragging the shocked Slinks out before the door changed its mind.

Slinks embraced Lurky with the tightest hug and kiss on the cheek, while wrapping his ears around him. "I's so prouds of you's Lurks. I's knew you's could do this!"

Lurky was in tears, realizing it was more than worth it all.

Letting go of each other they started scampering around in the hall, happy to be finally free together.

Lurky stopped, remembering he had brought the flask down, grateful no one noticed it when he was upstairs.

"Here's I's brought you's some more watey with's energy's plants in it."

"Oh, thanks Lurkys. Spidy and I's was runnin' out." Taking a good long drink from the flask saying, "Mmmm, that's goods, thanks you's."

"Let's goes outsides."

"Waits I can't leaves Spidy. He's deserves a breath's of fresh air too. "Slinks went back in, retrieving the spider. With the spider on the palm of his hand he said, "Spidy say hello's to Lurky."

The spider seemed to know what he said, raising one of its front legs as if in recognition before Slinks placed it on his shoulder. It scampered around behind his neck, peering out at Lurky.

Grabbing his flask from the table in the cell, Slinks joined Lurky and they headed down the hall away from the prison. Slinks didn't even ask any questions about what had happened in order for Lurky to get their release. Reaching the outside door, they quietly opened it without stopping, hoping they wouldn't be stopped at the last second. Their worst fears never materialized as they moved out into the almost sunshine. Slinks drew a deep breath of fresh air, smiling up at the light. They were happy for the first time since they were captured so long ago. Spidy was clinging tightly to his shoulder enjoying the freedom too.

"Come on let's goes over to those rocks. We's stays away from the road." Lurky couldn't agree more scampering off towards the rocks and their freedom that was so righteously deserved.

Dave lay in bed thinking about scampering over some rocks, having the freedom to go fishing, before he flung his blankets off, realizing it was daylight. He hadn't really slept well. He was too excited to have a proper sleep.

Dianne didn't have any trouble waking up either and upon hearing her brother she got up, yawing and stretching. She felt pretty limber considering the events of yesterday.

They went downstairs where Hugh had already prepared breakfast. Dave expressed concern that maybe the Nears would ruin their day.

"Don't worry, they're gone." Hugh said.

"They aren't here anymore?" Dianne said in disbelief.

"No, they've left, I'm guessing last night sometime."

"How do you know?" Dave said, taking a bite of his toast.

"I didn't want to make things worse for you than they really were, but when they were around, they left three shadows out in the far corner of the field every morning. The shadows were the residue from their physical bodies, once they turned themselves into pure energy bodies to do their dirty work. That's what you watch for to see if they're around. I didn't want you to know this, because it would have just added to your fear in the morning. Remember, they are attracted to your thinking which allows them to attack you, especially if you are full of fear. They would have had free reign to wreck havoc all they wanted.

Most people fear something; usually things that haven't happened. Others fear many imaginary events or circumstances that they believe would devastate them if they occurred. This fear, if strong enough will attract the Nears. Fear is a healthy defense mechanism in the face of immediate danger, but imaginary mental fear can cause a person to draw to themselves negativity that otherwise wouldn't need to happen.

"Thank you Hugh for helping us. It means a lot." Dianne said, touching him on the shoulder. Dave nodded his head in agreement.

"Come on Changees, it's time to catch some fish," taking his cap off the rack and placing it cock-eyed on his head.

"Why are you wearing your Changee cap?' Dave asked.

"The trout told me they were overcrowded and needed a change. They asked me to remove some of their cousins, leaving more room for the rest to swim in.

"Whatever uncle!" Dianne replied laughingly.

Breakfast disappeared without the usual polite conversation. There was only fishing on their minds. When they were finished, they practically pushed each other out the back door onto the porch.

"Where were the shadows, uncle?" Hugh pointed to where he saw them.

Dianne said, "I thought I saw what looked like shadows over there, but they kept fading in and out when you looked at them. You couldn't really say you saw something."

"Exactly," Hugh said.

"Are we going to do our exercises this morning?' Dave asked pointing to the chairs.

"No, today we'll do something different, even though it's important to do them the same time of the day every day. You don't want it to become a routine. Once it becomes a routine, you will lose the excitement of wanting to do them each day.

The reason you do them the same time everyday is the energy that you stimulate will surge in you each day at the same time like a rhythm. You slowly build strength at that time. After a while when you've done them enough, you will be able to stimulate the energy at will whenever there is a need. Even if the timing is off, you will be able to do them anywhere. So today, let's just get going and catch some fish!"

There wasn't a well defined trail to walk to the rapids of the gorge. It was more like a natural spacing of vegetation around areas of exposed rock. They climbed upwards ever so gently, although moving along you would barely notice it.

It was so nice getting away from the farm even if it was home. Familiarity can breed boredom especially in the mind, resulting in the same thought patterns over and over. Now in unfamiliar territory there were new things to look at, adventure in its truest form; new thoughts.

They came to a large stone that had been plunked right on top of a flat area of rock by unseen forces of nature long ago. It was just the right height and size to allow the three of them to sit for a rest.

"Isn't there anything we can do about the Nears? Or at least prevent them from having such powerful influences on us," Dianne asked.

Hugh remained silent for a few minutes before answering. "I don't think you can ever actually stop the Nears as long as we use our minds the way we do. After all, negative thinking is engrained in us; it's the way we have been taught to think. Remember when I said there was two types of laughter? Well thought is the same. There is thinking that we use to accomplish tasks, to move through life setting goals and achieving the results we would like to have happen. This is the primary way thought should be. Then there is the other way of thinking which is ruled by the ego. In the vast majority of people, the ego runs their mind, instead of keeping it in its place.

The problem with ego is it collects all the information from the negative events that occur to the person, and makes that person believe this is who they are. In fact, this isn't who they are at all. The ego sets up a false self. Now the problem with the false self is it is usually full of doubts, inadequacies, and wrong thinking and self-abuse. Events keep recurring that allows the ego to whisper in your ear that you will have awful things happen to you, or that you will never have what you want, or be able to accomplish what you truly desire. You begin to feel down on yourself without knowing it. You begin looking around for people who are worse off than you to make you feel better. It is the thing that makes negativity in the world seemingly so important to people. They think negative thoughts all day about other people, themselves, the world, and believe this the correct way to think.

This is the trap door the Nears use to get to us, through our ego. Through our negative thinking they are able to inflict pain and suffering. The true you, the inner you, doesn't work like that at all. It doesn't care about past hurts, disappointments; its chief goal is to support, uplift you, and help you through life's experiences in a positive way, even emotionally.

"Let me ask you both, were you thinking negatively about something when the Nears attacked each time?" Both children's eyes opened thinking about it, nodding yes.

"You see the Nears were able to do what they do best."

Standing up he pointed to the creek.

"Come on let's go. Think about it."

Travelling along in silence, the creek tumbling over the small falls could be heard a long way off. It wavered in intensity at first as the breeze had an effect on the noise, until they got closer where it became a steady rumble. They made their way through the last of the abundant brush lining the creek, coming out to a beautiful panorama of jumbled rocks with water cascading down, splashing, tumbling, sending droplets and spray in all directions. It appeared like the water was competing to make it to the large foam covered pool at the bottom. The water gave off a distinct smell.

"Smell the fish uncle? asked Dave, taking a deep breath.

It was a wonderful morning, with all three catching fish with little effort. By lunchtime they decided to cook up the fish they had caught. Hugh taught them how to arrange rocks as a firebox to allow the pan to sit where it could use the heat to the best advantage. He explained to them how to light a fire even in wet conditions using materials at hand if they were ever in an emergency situation or lost. It wasn't long before the fire had a bed of coals, making the fish sizzle, sending an unmistakable aroma wafting through the air.

They all sat silently watching the meal cook until Dave asked, "So what can we do about the Nears?"

"Well, once when Leaning Larry and I were talking, he mentioned when he passed out from the booze, he visited the Land of Afar to go to the Tower of Tears to cry. After coming out he decided to have a walk around. Knowing he had nothing to return to except the drunken stupor of his life, he wandered along looking at this as a sort of holiday. He went to the Falls of Affliction where Nears were collecting jars of tears, specific sounds from certain tears tumbling over the rocks. They told him the tears gave them the sustenance and power to do the commands of their Lord, the great Lord Misanthropy.

He innocently asked if there was a way the power could ever be diminished or stopped causing the Nears to erupt in hideous contemptuous sneers for his silly question. One of them leaned over to him as if telling him a secret. There is only one way to come close to doing this, and that there was a saying.

LORDLY EGOS
ARROGANT AND STARK
FROM THE LAND OF AFAR
LACHRYMOSE AND DARK

BROUGHT DOWN BY A CHILD
WITH A GOLDEN HEART
WHO LIVING IN THE NOW
MAKES THE POWER DEPART

Turning back to what he was doing, the Near said no more. Taking the hint, Larry left, returning to his slumbering body."

"What does that mean Uncle?" Dianne asked.

"That I don't know. I've asked Larry if that's exactly what the Near told him, and he swears it was. Since he was able to rhyme it off by heart, I knew he hadn't made it up. Now let's eat."

There was no argument from them digging into the pack to get out bread, beans, condiments, dishes and utensils. It didn't take long for the fish to disappear and everyone went back to fishing again. After catching some more, Hugh told the children to stop, because if they kept catching more and more, it might hurt this area. They agreed with reluctant nods and with melancholy because the adventure was ending.

"Besides, there's something else we can do while we're here" he said. "Come on let's sit by the falls."

As they took their places, he instructed. "Watch the water tumbling down. Watch it as a whole, while listening to the noise it makes. As your eyes get heavy from the motion of the water, close them but still see the water in your inner eye and listen to the sound but just breathe normally.

They did as they were instructed, listening to the dull roar that seemed to make the ground almost vibrate with the noise as the power was released. Before long their heads were almost nodding as the rhythm of the steadily falling water affected them. The sound of the water started to drown out all other noises. Their eyes closed without effort, however they could see the sparkling water falling in their mind's eye. A distinct feeling of falling came over them like they were on a fast falling elevator.

Both children felt like they were in the water sliding down, down almost like a boat on the current moving, swaying like they were guided by unseen rocks, moving onward. This downward motion changed to a feeling of being propelled outwards and forwards, on a shiny, diamond sparkling roller coaster. The sound became louder and louder pulsating to the rhythm of their breathing, almost a roar.

They realized they were sitting together just as they were on the log at the beginning of the visualization. The three of them rode together in the same invisible boat, surrounded by this shimmering sea of sparkles.

They smiled at each other from the exhilaration of the ride. Looking over at Hugh they saw he was laughing, totally enjoying himself. The noise of his laughter became louder and louder, breaking through the sound surrounding them. His laughter actually brought them out of the experience; where they found themselves again sitting on the log facing the falls. He had tears running down his cheeks from laughing in the inner so much.

"Wasn't that awesome? Every time I do that one I totally have a ball! The movement that you feel is the movement that goes on in your life nonstop. You are in a state of constant motion whether you are aware of it or not. You are always moving towards your destiny. Even in the physical body, you may be very still, but your body functions are still moving, and your very atoms never stop moving. Your energies are constantly in a flux moving about by the will of the great force, moving the entire cosmos from the smallest particle to universes. The sound is one manifestation of this audible life current, always expressing itself in the form of sound. So from now on when you hear any sound, let it be a reminder of the force that moves all forward.

The sparkling was the other aspect of this great force, the light emanating from it. Whether we realize it or not, even night when it is cloudy there is still light to some degree, we are never without it, and we cannot live without sound. These are the two manifestations of the force, the light and the sound."

He remained silent for a few minutes and then got up starting to gather everything. As they headed back they were listening to every sound surrounding them. These were sounds that mimicked the one true sound that pervades everything. They would never just hear a sound or noise again with old ears, and would now see with new eyes.

Everyone was quiet walking back, and Hugh was glad about that, since he was preoccupied with the discussion he had with the children at the campfire. He knew there was something that Leaning Larry had said to him that night, but he couldn't quite place his finger on it. Thinking about it made the trip go by in a flash and soon they were at the farm.

Dianne went racing across the field in response to the goats calling out to her.

"I guess that leaves you and I to put things away lad," commented Hugh.

"Funny it didn't seem that long coming back, and the birds, they seemed to be singing at the top of their lungs; so loud," Dave remarked.

Hugh just smiled knowing the effects of the contemplation were still happening to them.

Once in the house, he was standing at the window watching Dianne talking to the goats, and as he stared, something came over him. It was the remembrance of a dream, the dream with his brother.

Dave had gone to his room so Hugh went outside, encountering Dianne, and telling her to get something out for dinner. He focused on the barn, with part of him thinking this was absurd to even be doing this. But he went inside, curious. Entering the tool room, he had a cursory glance around. He slowly moved along the dusty stacks of boxes, bins and storage containers, not knowing what he was looking for.

Thinking this was silly, he turned to go when something fell off the shelf behind him. Turning, he looked to see what had fallen. Pulling aside grain bags lying in a heap, he saw an old metal toolbox under them. Picking it up, he found it to be quite heavy, requiring both hands, and placed it on the bench for a closer examination. There was a flimsy lock on it, which yielded to a pair of bolt cutters allowing him access to the box. Not understanding why his brother would lock such an innocent looking toolbox, he gasped when he opened it.

The box was full of gold bars, still shiny even though they had been in storage all those years. With them were the certificates of authenticity, meaning they could still be cashed in. There were many large bars and numerous smaller ones.

He picked one up turning it slowly in his hand, examining it in the light saying quietly, "Brother, brother you have no idea what this means." However the dream details he had with his brother that night started to flood though making him say: "Maybe you do after all."

Realizing there was a larger wooden box lying where the other one was, he tried to move it finding there was no way he could, so he found a crow bar and pried open the top which was crammed full of large gold bars as well.

He remembered his brother saying he was going to do this, years before he was even married. He had no idea how much he had invested in the bars; now at the prices of today there was a considerable amount of money. Standing back up, he went over to the smaller box, and picked up one of the small bars, turning it over in his hand. As he did so, a slow realization of what this meant started coming to him, and tears began to flow down his cheeks.

The tears meant many things to him. First, this would mean a financial boost for Susan and the kids, as a gift from their father and husband. He cried for his brother who would never see the good things that would come from all he had done and he felt almost overwhelmed by it all. He put the gold bar down on the table.

However as he did a tear splashed on the gold bar. He stared wiping his eyes, and looked down as the tear slowly ran off the bar. Then a realization came to him, an idea of what some of the gold could be used for, even though he wasn't sure how or what to do with it yet. For now he put the lid back on both boxes, after slipping a small bar in his pocket. He left the barn before the kids came looking for him.

He made sure he was tear free, not wanting the children to see him like this. He kept one hand on the gold bar, turning it over and over as a plan slowly started to form. Reaching the house he found Dave and Dianne talking at the table while some hamburger cooked on the stove.

"We hate to keep bringing this up uncle, but we really want to know if there is any way of stopping the Nears. We can't stand the thought of them coming back, and what if they attack mom when she returns?" Dave asked.

"I believe your mom is fine. With her being away they're only concern was to attack you two for laughing."

"I thought about what you said about Leaning Larry telling you about the Near saying how to diminish the power, but it doesn't make sense."

Hugh looked serious and then replied. "I believe I know how it can be done. If Larry got it right, and I believe he did, he said that a child must enter the Land of Afar and place a golden heart in the lake of tears, Lake Lamentation, to cause the power to depart."

"So?" Dianne said nonchalantly,

Hugh's face became more serious as he pulled out the gold bar, placing it on the table.

"There's the gold." There was dead silence.

"Where did you get that?"

"You're father came to me in a dream, showing me where to find it."

"Our dad? Did he say anything?"

"No, but in the dream he led me out to the barn showing me where it was located, without saying a word. I believe this bar is to be made into the shape of a heart."

"Okay, but who's going to take it to the Land of Afar?"

"I believe it is to be one of you, or I wouldn't have been shown this by your dad. Somehow he knows you will do it, or at least one of you will."

The look of shock was unbelievable as it sank in. "I can't go to the Land of Afar, especially by myself!" Dianne exclaimed.

"Would you go if your brother went with you?"

Dave almost fell off his chair. "Count me out! I'm getting weak just thinking of it." He looked ashen.

"I know this is a lot to deal with but hear me out. First let me say the golden heart means several things, first the golden heart is a term used when someone's heart is so full of love that they will do anything to help another at anytime, anywhere. It means total selfless service to the world. Your father must have had a golden heart, because whether he knew it or not, perhaps he was supposed to die. The gold wasn't to be discovered until now, for you to do what you were obviously destined to do.

In order for this heart to be made into a heart of gold, it must be made with love, unlimited, unconditional love so that the power of that love is in the golden heart when it's placed in the lake, otherwise it won't work. Whether you know it or not you have that love in both of you. Otherwise the love in your laughter wouldn't have drawn the attention of Lord Misanthropy or the Nears.

I wonder now, if it is the love in the two of you that makes it so nervous. It specifically sent its worst Nears here, hoping to scare you off. I also wonder how many others out there in the world have the golden heart and don't know it. Perhaps that's why they end up going through such awful things at the hands of the Nears as well. Unfortunately, they stop fulfilling their true destiny, if they don't change."

"I am afraid," Dianne said, looking at her brother who was shaking his head as well.

"You have every right to be. However, there is more to tell you, but first let's eat."

It was a quiet supper, which didn't last long, since everyone was lost in their thoughts. Hugh brought out some cookies and made some tea. "Drink this tea. I put some herbal calming tea bags in to help your nerves."

'I think I need a sack full of herbs," Dianne said, with Dave agreeing.

"There is an old saying that a person doesn't make his destiny; they were, in fact, born with that destiny, good or bad. I now know you two have this destiny, as incredible as it seems, but I have more to explain. For example, how do you get to the lake without being seen?"

"Ya, that's a good question," Dave nervously chuckled.

"Larry told me the Near said that even though they could make them cry in the physical world, they couldn't see people who had the golden heart if it was shining when they entered the Land of Afar to visit the Tower of Tears.

What I propose is to make three golden hearts for us to wear as pendants over our hearts when we make the large one. That way the love will shine from our heart centers into the pendants, which should beam like a beacon of love to blind the Nears while you are there. As well, we will take three tee shirts and paint golden hearts on the front to show we have the golden heart in us. From now on the hearts and the tee shirts will be a physical symbol for the whole world to know, we have a golden heart."

Dianne registered a strange look on her face. "I just had déjà' vu again. This definitely must be something that has to be done, but I am so scared almost out of my mind."

"Yes, I had a dream about the golden heart that I forgot about until you just mentioned it," added Dave.

"But how do we get there without being detected?"

"It's the golden heart and the tee shirts; they will make us invisible so they won't see you there as long as you wear it. The only thing is you cannot under any circumstances speak out loud or they will know something is wrong."

"Well that shouldn't be too difficult. We're invisible and just don't speak out loud. The cat's in the bag. The rat's on the run. Give us a few minutes and who thing's done!" boasted Dave smirking.

"Not quite, Brave Dave," Hugh said.

"One more thing, part of the saying mentioned that the child must be living in the now."

"Well, we are. We aren't dead and we are here and now, ready to go."

"That's not quite what they meant. By living in the now, it means having no conscious thought about the past or future while you are there; living completely in the now. Tomorrow I will teach you how to live in the now, but for now let's go to bed. Think about what I have said and in the morning we'll talk about whether you want to go ahead or not."

Both children rose, giving him a hug and went upstairs. Dave didn't even ask if he could go into his sister's bedroom, he just walked in and sat down.

"Why us, Dotty? I don't want to have to do this."

His sister ran her fingers through her hair. "It's not a matter of not wanting to do it. I'm beginning to see life isn't always what we want. It seems to me it is doing what has to be done. I believe what uncle is saying. This might be the chance for us to slow or stop the Nears from harming us, our family, as well as others in the world. Even though it scares me to death, I will go but only if you go with me."

"You're right, I don't want to do this, but look at what they did to us, and I get the feeling it was nothing compared to what they could do if they wanted to."

"After all, look what they did to our father; they really did hurt us in the worst way possible. Dave, I couldn't live without you being around, if they ever came back and attacked us again and done something worse. Besides you're my favorite brother."

"Hey, I'm your only brother!"

"All kidding aside, Dave, I can't see us doing anything else. It's like Uncle said about our future being ours to decide what it should be. I believe what he said about us being protected, so we can go in and out of the Land of Afar without being detected. I'm willing to do this if you come too."

They gave each other a hug, agreeing they would tell their uncle in the morning their decision. Now the challenge was to get some sleep, knowing their thoughts would keep them awake; after all, they were being asked to save the world.

Lord Misanthropy listened contently to the sounds drifting from the Falls of Affliction, the sounds of woe, knowing nothing could save the human's world now. It often listened to the sounds, like a person would listen to the birds singing in the trees. It enjoyed the different notes and melodies coming from every conceivable tragedy that could befall a human.

Picking up some of them, it haphazardly imitated some of them chuckling to itself at the pathetic nature of the noises. Doing so, a creeping doubt ever so faint, crossed its mind that there was a problem coming. When it tried to focus on it, the energy dissipated as quickly as it came.

This sort of thing hadn't happened since it wrestled the golden tears from the great kings and queens of old, so long ago even he almost had forgotten about it. A movement diverted its attention, seeing the two Sneakeeze scampering around the rocks playing stupid games.

"Worms!" the only word escaped its tightly pursed lips. It should have just let them go. However, perhaps they would come in useful later somehow. From what it was seeing, it was obvious they weren't trying to escape. It didn't like the nagging inside it was feeling, even though nothing could be seen wrong in the Land of Afar. As a precaution, it turned to the ever present Near Acolyte: "Send two Near Protektors to the bridge to watch the humans coming across."

The Near paused just for a second. It had been so long since a Near Protektor had been requested, it wasn't sure it had heard him right. However, a Near never asked twice about a command from the Lord. That was a fate worse than death, it meant being turned inside out, and it meant becoming a Ways Away.

The Near Acolyte turned obeying without question, uncertain what to do. It found another Near cleaning the chamber and went over and whispered in its ear. The other Near stood up staring incredulously at the first Near, and then motioned it to follow. The Near in the chamber had heard of them, but had never seen one, although it thought it knew where to look in the basement.

They made their way downstairs, until they finally came to a hallway that at first glance appeared to end. However, there was a setback in the hallway, barely noticeable, fully covered by cobwebs, obviously not used in a long time. Lighting a torch, they proceeded down the pitch black hallway until they finally came to a door. They could hear barely perceivable noises behind it.

Inspecting the door they could see various weapons of protection hung on it, spears, knives, riot clubs, brass knuckles, almost anything one would need to protect themselves. After listening intently they realized what the noises were. They were sounds of snoring, actually a chorus of snoring from several Nears.

Obeying its orders, Near Acolyte knocked loudly on the door. Suddenly a siren went off and a red light started pulsing off and on. Immediately there were roars and shouts coming from behind the door and sounds of intense scuffling around inside, but no one answered the door.

Near Acolyte glanced at the other Near giving a shrug and proceeded inside. There in the light of the torch were two Nears back to back with raised fists, almost twirling around, both shouting: "I will protect you!"

Seeing the two Near Acolytes brought even more aggressive shouts. "We'll protect them!" The Near Acolytes froze as the Near Protektors rushed over, taking a defensive posture against an imaginary enemy near them.

"Don't worry Sir, you are in good hands now. We'll protect you," whispering as if expecting an attack at any moment.

"We don't need protection. We are here to give you an order from our master."

"Nonsense! Everyone needs protection. Scan the room for threats!" The Near Protektors shuffled around in a circle cloistering the two Near Acolytes in the middle.

"All clear!" resulted in a relaxation of their defensive stance while their serious looking eyes continued scanning.

"Now, what was that you had to say?"

"Our master......" was all Near Acolyte could get out before Near Protektor shouted.

"Our master needs protection!" causing the other to shout.

"I'll protect it!"

Both Near Acolytes stared at each other for a second shaking their heads.

"Listen, our master wants you two guarding the bridge to the entrance of the Land of Afar."

"We don't guard! We protect," Near Protektor answered incredulously.

"Alright, alright, it needs you to protect the bridge," Near Acolyte said, realizing it was going to take precise wording.

"We've never protected an object before. It's always been a Near we protected. Is this difficult?"

"No, it's the same as protecting a Near, just don't let any humans you see cross the bridge unless they are going to the Tower of Tears to shed tears. You are protecting the Land of Afar from intruders. Is that understood?"

Glancing nervously at each other, they decided to check their manual of conduct and procedures to be sure they weren't breaking any rules.

"We must be sure we aren't deviating from the parameters set down, governing the scope of operations, procedures and conduct, related to the guidelines established for our responsibilities as Protektors."

Finding a copy of the book on a dusty old table, they opened it and Near Protektor read. "A Near Protektor is to protect in any manner necessary and at all personal cost if required, any Near or Master, unless otherwise ordered. "

"Well, I can't see that you are breaking any rules since the master has ordered you to do this," replied the Near Acolyte.

The Near Protektor turned the page, making sure it hadn't missed anything before placing the manual back on the table.

"As far as I can see, we aren't breaking any rules. So a bridge it is. This isn't complicated is it?'

Shaking its head in disgust, Near Acolyte with forced politeness answered: "I think you will get the hang of it fairly quickly. It's a bridge. Crying humans cross it. If they aren't crying don't let them cross. Got it?"

"We will need weapons. We have a fine selection of weapons for protection. Come see!"

It motioned them to follow it to the back of the room, where it touched the torch to another one on the wall, resulting in an eruption of flames showing a vast warehouse full of racks, shelves, boxes and large crates. Displayed, sometimes in heaps were every conceivable weapon ever made or used, right from a rock to the latest modern killing device.

Proudly going over to a stained round stone sitting on a shelf, Near Protektor picked it up, tossed it up and down saying: "This was the first stone thrown in anger by a human against another. It was given to me by Near Quietus as a gift. But this is without doubt my favorite." Putting it down and rushing over to a pile of instruments of destruction, it picked up a large scythe.

"This was used by someone to slice and dice anyone he didn't consider a friend."

The other Near Protektor shook its head in disgust.

"Aw, that's nothing. Now this is the weapon for protection," it said, going over to a tarp and pulling it off displaying a mini style military gun. It pressed the trigger, spraying bullets all over a wall as fast as it could fire. It sneered, looking back at the Near Acolytes, hoping to impress them. All it saw was them covering their ears, expressing sneers of total disgust so

Near Protektor stopped firing. However, the rotary barrels kept spinning at a high rate of speed.

"I hate it when it does that!" It said, grabbing it and forcing it to stop spinning.

"I told you to read the manual on that before using it. Now you've shot the wall full of holes. You're going to clean that up when we get back. Besides, we need to make room for man's latest masterpiece of protection when we get our hands on it. What was it called? Oh yes; the total death and destruction proton thermo nuclear device. It's the perfect thing to use when nothing is going your way! Just stuff it down the front of someone's pants and let it off. Since we don't have one just yet, maybe we'd better pick out some of these," pointing to grenades, rocket launchers, and machine guns. "It really was good of Near Baet'l to get man to invent these. They're so much fun!"

"Not this time. I think just our hands will be enough," the other Near Protektor said, shadow punching at nothing.

"Fine, can we go now?" Near Acolyte said, pointing to the door.

"Whoa! Not until I check it out." Replied Near Protektor clicking its fingers.

The other Near ran to the door with a torch, stuck its head out into the hall looking both ways. "Looks clear out here boss."

"Good. Let's proceed with caution. You stay in front with the torch. I'll bring up the rear. Shout if you need assistance."

"Say nothing, I want to hear the enemy's movement before they strike." Whispered Near Protektor moving cautiously along the hall.

Finally they reached the Great Hall and the Near Acolytes were never so glad to be there. At the back door, they opened it and gave a forced sneer.

"You will protect the bridge until ordered otherwise. Do you understand?"

"No problem!" they both said in unison.

Near Acolyte turned walking away but could hear them saying, "Ever protect a bridge before?"

"No, I hope it's not complicated. You know how complicated thoughts give me a headache."

Sleep came mercifully quelling unceasing complicated thoughts that can be a headache. Some noble, some the great unknown fears, the what about's and why me's. The mind is a marvelous entertainer except when you want to sleep and it doesn't.

Dianne used a technique Hugh taught her to sleep. She said out loud, "Dianne you will go to sleep now" three times, got into her comfortable position and recalled a pleasant experience, movie or book. She allowed the thoughts of this to float through her mind. Every time the mind tried to interfere by bringing unwanted thoughts she would say to her mind, she didn't want to think about that right now and forced herself to see the fantasy she had been watching.

Dave used this technique as well; it was the only way to sleep. With sleep came dreams, some vague, but one she remembered.

She found herself wandering through a darkness seeking something but she couldn't remember what. She knew she would recognize it when she found it. All that lit her way for a few meters was a shining golden light located on her chest. Frustrated at the darkness, she heard Lurky say, "There's someone!" and turning, she saw Dave but as a golden light. Rushing to him, she was suddenly prevented from reaching him by a glass like wall but saw him talking. Out of frustration, she leaned her forehead against the glass suddenly hearing him, "I'm so glad you found me Di! I was afraid I was alone forever."

"I would never leave you, now let's go find it."

"Find what?"

"I don't know but with our lights together we'll find whatever it is we don't know."

She suddenly woke up with this echoing in her mind, and realized morning was here already, as she squinted at the light. Yawning and scratching, she heard noises downstairs and the smell of food cooking.

"Good morning sleepy head, "greeted Dave merrily.

"You're up early today buddy," She replied.

"We were both up early and made a decision. We are going to cut and shape the gold into hearts, if you want to go through with this."

She got a vivid flash from the dream, blurting out, "I'll do this! I'll go."

"This has to be both your decisions to go into the Land of Afar. I cannot go, being too old, and the prophecy said a child would do this. I can go right up to the bridge. By wearing my golden heart and tee shirt I won't be seen. I will find some high ground to observe and help if need be. By living in the Now, my thoughts about you being in there won't be detected. Come sit. We have things to talk about."

Hugh began," There is only one reality here and that is what happens in each moment as you experience it now. Whatever happens now one instant later becomes the past, never to be changed. The future is always coming to you. It's only what you do now, that will make the past good or bad. It's known as memories. Memories have insidious ways of keeping us unhappy hindering us from working with the future properly. If you couldn't remember the past, you would actually be happy unless something life threatening was happening to you right now. The future would be this great wonderful thing coming to you that you would gladly embrace. The past quite often interferes with our perception of the future.

Living in the Now means being totally aware of the world around you. Most people don't do this. They get up in the morning and are not aware if birds are singing, what the air feels like on their skin, what smells are in the air, and so on. What they don't realize is they are held captive by their mind, living in thoughts of the past or future.

When there is a life-threatening situation, a real imminent threat, the past and future is gone and the person is instantly, intensely, in the Now. Nothing else matters, your whole being is focused strictly in the present and what you need to do in that moment.

When you enter the Land of Afar this is how you need to operate. Stay in the Now, as much as possible or they will pick up your thinking. You will be invisible wearing the golden heart and tee shirt, but there is danger of your mind getting out of control."

"What will happen if they find us?" Dianne asked.

"Nothing will happen in the Land of Afar. They will report to Lord Misanthropy, but once you are out, it will use all its skills to track you down and have no mercy on you or anyone around you. Because you are invisible they will not see you, only pick up on your thinking. You will see other humans there in the soul body that have come to the Tower of Tears under the illusion they are going to be helped somehow by the Nears.

Do not go near them, they won't see you. No matter what you see or hear from them, stay away. Have compassion in your heart for them, for they have experienced some of the worst things that can happen to a human being. But do not entertain thoughts of what they may have gone through. Do you still think you can do this?"

Both children silently nodded their heads.

"Let's go outside then. I'll show you what I mean by living in the Now."

Instead of sitting in the chairs, as was the usual routine, Hugh walked out onto the grass and stared intently down. Pausing at a spot, he motioned the children to come and see. Looking down they noticed nothing until he pointed to the small mound of an ant's nest.

"Watch their activity." Small brown ants came up out of the hole, searching for food.

"These ants have a responsibility of finding food for the rest of the colony, so every day, all day they do their duty for the greater good. Now watch." Hugh placed a breadcrumb near the empty hole.

One of the ants almost walked by the morsel, but suddenly it picked up the scent of the bread and scurried over to it. Feeling the bread with its antenna, it went right back down the hole, realizing the food was too big to handle alone. In a few seconds, out came a half a dozen ants with it, moving over to the crumb. They communicated with each other, and then decided to pull the crumb into the nest with team effort. The first ant went back down in the hole for more help, and emerged with even more ants. Some started tearing the crumb into manageable pieces, disappearing down the hole. Finally the entire crumb was gone.

"See how they worked together achieving a goal. When one found the task too big to handle alone, it went and got help. Through team effort they did what had to be done. Isn't that fascinating?"

Both children agreed.

"Guess what? Did you think about your personal problems or anything about your life while you were watching the ants?'

Suddenly the children realized he was right, saying they hadn't, because the ants were so fascinating.

"Did you know it has taken one hour and twenty minutes for them to do that?"

Dave and Dianne couldn't believe that much time had passed by.

"That's living in the Now. It's a subtle difference in how you use your mind. One way people do live in the Now without knowing it, is when they watch a movie, or read a good book. Once engrossed by the fantasy, time has no meaning and their personal problems disappear. All you have to do is transfer that type of focus into the world around you. Now let's go see if we can shape some gold."

Dianne let the chicken and goats out for food, and then made her way into the workroom where she found Hugh and Dave with a piece of the gold on the table. Hugh made a pencil outline on the gold bar he had.

"Now it's important before we do this that we agree it is our purpose to make golden hearts for our protection with love, especially the large one that will be thrown into Lake Lamentation. You both must think only of times when love was in your heart, times when you gave and shared without hesitation to someone who needed it. Think of special times when someone gave you a gift of love. Feel the love and as you think of these things, silently say over and over what I say.

I GIVE MY UNLIMITED LOVE
ALL MY LOVE, ONLY MY LOVE
TO ALL THE WORLD WITH LOVE
MY WORLD AND THEIR WORLD ONLY LOVE
ALL OF LIFE IS LOVE
I GIVE ONLY MY LOVE

I will repeat this until we are done. While I do this you will put a hand on my back in the area where my heart is. Are you ready?'

He began cutting out the shapes with a hacksaw, gently sawing along the scribed lines. This brought out the one universal shape that represented so many different ideas and concepts in such diverse understanding to the world. It was recognized by anyone who saw it, regardless of their background. This one shape held unlimited feelings in an infinite variation of focus by every human being that had ever lived; the love of another person, the love of an animal, a situation, a place, an idea, a dream, and even perhaps themselves.

He never stopped repeating the verse until all the shapes were completed. Three small ones and one large one that was about to bring change to the whole world in ways even Hugh couldn't comprehend.

"There." He completed drilling small holes, making necklaces, and rounding off the sharp edges. Picking two up, he placed one in the palm of each of the children.

"Here is your symbol of one of the greatest emotions a person can experience. It is the only feeling that comes from the core of a person, from their soul, the higher inner being that dwells in all of us asleep or awakened. All other emotions or feelings are derived from the mind. Only love comes from somewhere other than there. That is why when it happens it can't be explained, only felt.

Keep this next to your heart so that it may guide, help and protect you every moment. Let your love shine, so others will want the same, prompting them to search within themselves for that which is so natural. Once stirred, they will become who they truly are."

Using pieces of leather strips hanging on the wall, he fashioned necklaces to wear them. They each held the crudely made object in their hand staring at it with reverence, understanding the meaning of its significance, in all its myriad concepts.

"Oh! My heart did a little flip flop when I put it on my heart area," Dianne gasped.

"You two have done a wonderful job, helping to place love into them. These will most certainly protect you from the Nears."

Turning to Dave he said. "You probably won't feel what she did. Males are different. They aren't as sensitive as women are to the emotional energy subtleties."

"No, but I do feel better, happier, for lack of a better word." Dave replied.

"Excellent! That's enough to show the energy is working in you as well. Let me try mine on." Hugh said as he placed his heart over his own heart area.

"I do believe there is enough love coming from this heart and both yours for the whole world."

Then, picking up the large heart he turned it over and over.

"Look at how it almost glistens with the power of love flowing from it. Place your right hand on it with me and repeat after me. "I declare we will do with love, what it takes with love, accomplished only with love, we three from the Order of Humanes. I now declare us Changees of Divine Love. This I declare!"

They spoke loudly. "I declare!"

"Now we need something to carry it in" Hugh said.

"I have a leather bag I keep my marbles in, I don't really need," replied Dave.

"Excellent, that will do the job just fine. Let's find some tee shirts to paint golden hearts on."

They all filed out of the barn, beginning to take their first steps on a new adventure, taking them into the unknown, somewhere they had never been, and, if under different conditions, definitely wouldn't want to.

It was non-stop to their bedrooms in the search for a tee shirt that would do the job and it didn't take long, knowing where to search.

Hugh found he had packed a white tee shirt, much to his amazement. He hadn't really remembered packing it. Holding it in his hands made him realize there are times when you are guided without even knowing it, for a purpose that couldn't be revealed at the time.

Going downstairs, he saw Dianne with her paint set, painting a heart on hers and Dave's shirt. Each shirt would have a heart situated strategically on the front over the heart area. Dianne decided a few flowers arranged around the heart would brighten it up. Dave decided a muscle man in the corner of his shirt would do just fine. Hugh painted the words, 'LOVE A GOLDEN HEART' across the shirts under the heart.

"By the way, we have to leave tomorrow morning."

Both children were in complete shock.

"Why so soon, can't we wait a few days?" asked Dave giving his sister a hard stare, desperately wanting some backup.

"Unfortunately, as you know the Nears can still read our thoughts even though we have made the hearts. We cannot lose any time or they will catch on, and we will lose the element of surprise. Everything hinges on you getting into the Land of Afar undetected without them being warned in any way." He saw the fear rising up in their minds,

Promptly he continued. "Let me talk about fear. As you know the mind loves to run in its familiar routines and grooves. When faced with something unknown, especially something it thinks is a threat to its existence, it will try to avoid that situation at all costs. It's the feeling of fear. This feeling evolved from back when mankind was faced with natural disasters or predators. It is a natural defense response that helped in countless situations for our ancestors. When faced with the threat of the unknown it will cause you to imagine the worst possible future possible, making you move away from it. So many people miss out on something new and better in their lives, simply because they aren't able to overcome the thoughts and the fear. Not because the situation would be negative but because the imaginary feelings of dread took over.

When you feel fear tomorrow going into the Land of Afar, you will pause just for a second and face the fear and feel it. Know in that moment you do have what it takes to accomplish your goal, or you wouldn't even be there. Remember, nothing is by chance. Your life has been mapped out, but it hinges on whether you are willing to move ahead in it. When you feel the fear, replace it with a feeling of love. Believing in that love will allow you to take the next step, to move ahead when you need it the most.

Don't forget you won't be alone out there. I will find a high spot on the border so I can see out, watching you for as long as possible with my eyes. After that, I will see you in my mind's eye. Should things get bad and you find yourself trapped, then visualize my face as best you can in your mind's eye, while staying in the Now. This will comfort you and help you connect with your mind so you can find a way out of the situation. Should the worst thing happen, I will come physically to get you.

Remember they won't see you under any circumstances, or hopefully smell you even if they are right beside you, unless you take off your heart. You can whisper, but that's all."

Dave and Dianne stared at each other for a moment. Knowing that they wouldn't be seen or that their thoughts couldn't be felt, even if they were experiencing fear, went a long ways in their decision.

They believed and trusted in their uncle, knowing that for reasons unknown to them, they were about to embark on a mission that a short time ago, would have sounded so farfetched, it could have only been the wild imagination of someone writing a book.

"We leave first thing in the morning."

Part of them wished they would never have to get up to embark on this mission, which could be so farfetched, even their wildest imagination couldn't conceive it before. Morning came faster than any of them secretly wanted it to. There was a part of them that wanted life to just continue the way it was, even if it was mediocre.

The three of them rose, even though it was still dark. Their minds were connected somehow on a level they didn't understand nor even realized was occurring.

Meeting in the kitchen, Hugh laid out the plan. "It will take three days to do this, one full day to get there, one day inside, and then one back. We will leave the animals inside the barn with plenty of food and water. We will pack enough food for four days. I know where all the good springs are, so water won't be an issue. It will mean we can travel light and fast. I know the way there. Wearing our tee shirts will mean we will get there undetected, even if we encounter a Near coming or going to the Land of Afar."

"We might see one before we get there." Dianne said.

"Yes the vast majority of the time they move about in the energy body, allowing them to reach more humans at the same time, who are thinking the same thoughts. However, there are times for some unknown reason, they like to experience the physical world."

They spoke little unless it was necessary as they were packing. After they had breakfast Hugh turned to both of them and said, "Are you ready?"

"Everything will be fine. I haven't had any prompting not to do this, although I do not know what the final outcome will be. I know you will be safe as long as you do what I have said."

"Yes, I haven't had any bad premonitions or warnings about this either. How about you Dave?" Dianne asked.

"I've had some strange dreams about this, however nothing's been bad that I can recall. I'm sure I would have remembered if it was going to turn out wrong."

"Alright, let's go. Remember practice living in the Now as we move along. It will do two things: first, give you practice staying in the present and second, stop you from thinking about future events. Besides we are going through an area that is quite beautiful and you should enjoy the countryside."

They began their journey and finally entered the trail at the corner of the field which led them into the beautiful countryside. They listened to the birds, saw the beauty of the wild flowers, listened to the sound of running water, and took in nature all around them.

Hugh stopped for a moment when they had reached the campfire they had set up while they were fishing.

"From here we will continue upstream, however we must climb higher since the walking is easier. There are a lot of blow downs from severe weather that must have come through in the past. I encountered it on my journey to your place," pointing to the broken expanse of rock making up the hills surrounding them. They headed upstream leaving behind the campfire without looking back.

They weren't reminiscing about past good adventures, they were living in the Now. Climbing higher, they saw countryside they never knew was over the highest hills surrounding their home, and felt a new energy coming from all around them.

"Can you feel it?" queried Hugh. It was the quiet nurturing feeling of nature growing, moving, making sounds. It seemed to enhance their living in the Now, their senses alert to everything. They heard the stream until they encountered a lake.

"Will we walk around?" They asked.

"No! We are going fishing with our boat," revealing it to them under some brush. The feeling of being in a boat fishing was certainly different but the fish were the same, catching all they needed. There was much boasting about who had the best skill but they all agreed luck had a lot to do with it, especially the one that fell into the boat off the hook. Reaching the shore they cleaned the fish.

"We walk beside this stream until we come to the base of the mountains, then up the trail Larry told me about to get to the bridge. We will stop at the bottom and rest overnight then begin in the morning." They continued not wanting to rest; however, by the time they got there they were exhausted. They weren't paying attention until a movement caught Hugh's eye. Plants would go flying up into the air behind some bushes before a creature stood up thirty meters away.

"A Near!" Hugh hissed quietly, turning to the kids who almost ran into him. Gasping they stared past him ready to run but Hugh stood his ground giving them courage. They were certainly living in the Now watching it.

"If it sees us or smells us, this is all for nothing. Let's see what happens. Say absolutely nothing!"

The Near had no sense of smell which made its hatred of plants, especially flowers even more vicious. They watched in fascination as it pulled out one brightly colored weed after another, tearing them to shreds before inhaling their essence and throwing the ashes to the ground. Occasionally, it would stomp on as many as it could with high leaps.

It came right over to the trail going to the bridge, stopping twenty meters in front of them, pulling out a pretty blue flowered plant. Holding it up in the air, it stared right at them saying,

"AT PRETTY FLOWERS
DO I STARE
UGLY PLANTS GROWING
EVERYWHERE

USELESS TREES
TOWERING THERE
OUT OF REACH
FOR ME TO TEAR

BURN, WASTE, DESTROY
WHAT DO I CARE
THE ONLY TRUE BEAUTY
IS GROUND MADE BARE"

Sneering, it ripped apart the plant, flicking pieces into the air, kicking at the odd one floating down. Rolling the blue flowers into a ball, it inhaled a bluish green mist from the flowers.

After taking its life essence it poured the ashes out of its hand into the mercy of the uncaring breeze scattering them to the wind. It stood there almost intoxicated with its sardonic sneer. It reached for its flask taking a large swallow before saying, "Nothing like a good swig of tears to make you sneer." Turning it headed up the mountain trail.

Breathing a collective sigh of relief watching it go, they waiting until it was gone before Hugh whispered," Well, I guess our hearts and tee shirts made us invisible."

"You mean you weren't sure?" asked Dianne wide-eyed.

"It is all theoretical. It's never been done." Now I have confidence about you two going in alone. Up until now, I wasn't sure. We need to backtrack away from any more Nears," pointing up the trail. "Wasn't that amazing seeing what that Near did to those poor plants?"

"I know, I couldn't believe how it recited that saying with such zeal and then just killed it without any remorse. What kind of a Near was that?"

"Larry said that one called itself Near Dissever, which means a Near that tears things to pieces; in this case living plants. Apparently, it claimed to have the ability to whisper into people's ears, thoughts that make them destroy plants, even entire forests. When it does this it actually is able to use the energy essence of the plant it consumes, as a form of energy food."

"Did you see the sneer on its face? It was the worst evil, for lack of a better word, I have ever seen. Do you think it saw us?"

"No, I know it didn't, otherwise it would have disappeared instantly, like that small black flash you saw out of the corner of your eye when you were attacked. I don't know of anyone who has seen them, unless they were in an altered state like when one uses drugs, alcohol, or are semi-conscious."

"Well this is good uncle, we know they can't see us, even when it looked directly at us," added Dave.

"I have more confidence going into the Land of Afar now, but if you hadn't been here today uncle, I would have run screaming for my momma."

"If you two hadn't been here, I would have too!" Hugh said sheepishly.

They decided it was time to eat and while they did, they listened to the sounds of nature, as the darkness of the wilderness was slowly surrounding them. They were glad none of those sounds were the sounds of approaching Nears.

THERE WERE NO SOUNDS OF approaching Nears, but one hoot from an owl was enough to jolt everyone awake from their light sleep. The first light was showing in the sky.

Of all the trees here, the owl just had to pick this one!" exclaimed Hugh, bringing quiet chuckles from the others.

Hugh knew that the owl was brought by spirit to wake them up so that they would be on schedule. He acknowledged with a quiet thanks.

He didn't mind climbing out of the sleeping bag after lying on the unforgiving ground all night. Both children expressed the same discomfort giving him solace in their common suffering. The fire lit their immediate surroundings, giving them an opportunity to relieve their body's nagging urges, without stumbling over any unknown objects. It didn't take long to cook the pre-packaged oatmeal and have breakfast.

After they were finished, they went down to the creek and washed their faces which helped take away the last remnants of sleep, and then packed up and started off again.

"Now that we've seen a Near, we know what to expect, which really helps. It won't be such a shock next time." Dave said.

"Yes, but be totally on your guard. Remember to live in the Now the whole time, so they don't pick up our thoughts. That's the only edge they have on you."

Heading up the trail into the mountains seemed to take on an exertion they weren't used to. Some of it was the steep incline, but some of it was perhaps from the impending knowledge of what lie ahead. Moving along they noticed it became increasingly quieter and there was no breeze. The plants thinned out until there wasn't even lichen clinging to rocks.

They noticed thick fog beginning to develop. Walking through it actually caused swirls. They were breathing heavier now from the change in air density. Hugh stopped to take a breather. The fog was getting denser, making it hard to distinguish any notable landmarks. To put it quite frankly, if it weren't for the well-marked trail they were following they would have been lost.

It became very still, almost deathly quiet, except for the sound of their breathing. Hugh whispered, "We must be getting close. I had better say the words Larry told me about."

"IN THE FOG
HIDING FROM SIGHT
HEARTLESS LAND
BLACK AS NIGHT

SEE IT NOW
THE LAND THAT'S HERE
THAT SEEMS AFAR
YET SO NEAR"

The fog thinned out. Hearing voices far off made them stop. Staring, they watched as people seemed to materialize out of nowhere on a trail off to the side, some adults, young people, and children. It was obvious from the crying, weeping and sobbing they were all in the throes of some horrible experience. They could see the two Near Protektors standing on either side of the bridge, greeting the souls.

"These are energy bodies or souls if you want to use common terms, come to shed tears for the Lord Misanthropy. Tears caused by the efficient work of the Nears. The trouble they had experienced, causes tears which makes the inner energy body want to get rid of them. The energy body is the part of them where only good and positive exists, and so to have sorrowful energy thrust on it is something it can't live with. So without the person being aware of it, their energy body mistakenly comes here in the belief it is shedding the energy and ridding itself of the negativity through soul tears.

The people are actually where they live, crying real tears because of some misfortune, feeling emptiness inside that comes with the shedding of tears. The great emptiness is what makes soul leave the physical body so it can come here to rid the heavy burden placed on the light body."

"So these aren't actual physical people, only their inner light bodies or souls as we call them?"

"Exactly, and I am sure they won't see you either because the veil of tears has them blind. Because you have the golden heart, you are not experiencing the same sadness energy as them, so they can't see you."

"What should we do? Dave asked, as more souls were appearing and forming a loose row of souls waiting to cross over the bridge.

"Considering there are so many, just mingle with them crossing the bridge. Remember not to say a word, no matter what happens. I will find a high spot to watch. Go in fast, place the heart and come out. Stay in the Now. Are you ready?"

Both of them nodded reluctantly. He gave them each a hug and said. "You are brave for doing this, something good will come out of this even if we can't see it yet. Remember, I will be with you. Just visualize my face like I told you, if you have to."

They walked over to the edge of the border of Afar, watching the poor wretched souls filing by until there was a gap, then motioned for them to move into line. They instinctively held hands stepping in behind an old man who looked like he had seen too much pain and suffering. They paused a second, looking over their shoulder for Hugh who was standing there motioning to them it was alright, so without saying anything they nodded, focusing on the Now, and started crossing over the bridge.

"Don't you fret. Don't you worry. You have come to the right place to remove your burden. See beyond the Land of Afar, enter at once sick of heart you are, if you live in fear please enter here. Shed your tears because peace and happiness you will find here." Spoke a Near Protektor.

All the children could see was a sneering Near carefully scanning each soul to be sure everything was the way it should be. They obviously appeared differently to these souls, having the veil of tears pulled over them. The children could only surmise these Nears appeared to them in whatever form they wanted them to, so that they would make the journey across. Their hearts were pounding so loud they were sure the Nears could at least hear them. When they got right up to the Nears they never even looked at them. They crossed through, visualizing Hugh's face even stronger inside, drawing on the strength and feeling of security they received from his face.

Hugh was right: they couldn't be seen. They moved quickly past however in their haste, Dianne accidentally brushed against one of the souls moving with them. She almost fainted as the energy of sorrow the woman carried rushed into her. The soul didn't even notice so great was her suffering. Dianne had to stop herself from losing control, biting hard on her hand with her mouth, almost falling to the ground.

Dave grabbed her dragging her out of the way, feeling his sister shake from the emotions she was feeling from the woman. Seeing a jumble of large rocks, he pulled her behind them getting her to sit. He decided to take a chance, whispering in her ear, asking if she was alright, since she was sobbing. She cupped her hands over his ear, telling him she had picked up on the entire energy of the sad situation the woman had experienced, all the memories, thoughts and agony. It felt like she was actually going through it.

She told him she needed rest, so without arguing he stayed with her. She laid her head on his shoulder sobbing until the energy that wasn't hers, slowly rained away. There was no way to tell time in the Land of Afar. It seemed like eternity until she quieted down, finally rid of all the energy. He let her rest until he looked straight at her and mouthed the words.

"Are you all right Sis?" She nodded, although she seemed exhausted and whispered. "We have to do this! We must!"

They rose from their hiding spot, thankful that the whispering hadn't attracted the attention of the Nears. Moving back to the road they noticed the sign at the bridge.

BRIDGE OF DESOLATION

Beyond the edge of the bridge, nothing could be seen so thick was the fog. They knew now they were there to finish the task placed on their shoulders. This was more for the sake of the unfortunate souls going there than for themselves. Stepping back on the road they noticed it was almost sticky, covered in a film of tears left by the countless souls.

Looking down at the end of the road, Dave noticed the small sign.

ROAD OF ANGUISH
MADE FROM THE BLOOD
BUILT BY THE SWEAT
PAVED WITH THE TEARS.

He pointed the sign out to Dianne who was totally disgusted. There were small flashes of light on the road accompanied by rolling thunder, as if to signal it was too late to turn back. Knowing they had no choice, they moved down the road, seeing the Tower of Tears ahead of them, glowing yellow in the sunless light.

Dave now understood the name of the road, following the souls moving ahead of them. The sounds of sorrow, mourning and utter despair pouring out of their mouths, almost deafened them. Like background music, echoes of the past sounds of grief of countless souls came who had passed that way before. This happened with precise results, as the souls' wailing increased with intensity as they approached the door. Noticing the road branched off at the tower, Dave motioned to take the branch.

They needed somehow to get away from the constant lamentation they were immersed in. There was a drain on their energies from the sound, especially for Dianne. Moving a short ways along the path he had to help prevent her from stumbling several times whispering, "Come on Dot, we have to get off this trail and rest." She nodded, sweating profusely.

He looked up after whispering to her, seeing two Acolytes coming around a corner in the trail about thirty meters away.

"No! Nears!" was all he could whisper to her, forcefully pushing her over off the trail behind a large boulder. Dianne almost fell down, slumping on the ground. Dave kept a lookout as they tried to continue to see

Hugh's face. The Near Acolytes were going to help the others at the Tower of Tears with the large influx of souls.

Dave couldn't understand what they were saying until they reached opposite to where they were hiding. One Near suddenly came to a complete stop.

"I smell humans." It snarled loudly, producing a fearsome loathing sneer, sniffing the air. "I know that smell anywhere!"

"You've been downstairs helping Near Spiritus Frumentus again, haven't you?" the other Near stared at it incredulously.

"No, I tell you I smell humans!"

"There hasn't been a human here since we built the bridge and put up the Fog of Duprey."

The Near who smelt them, moved over closer to where they were hiding, searching for any sign of what made the smell. They saw nothing even though they were looking straight at Dave and Dianne.

Dave and Dianne were holding onto each other trembling, trying not to allow their thoughts to get out of control, living in the Now, which wasn't hard to do with this terrible threat standing a few meters away. It was only the fact that they knew the Nears couldn't see them that kept them from screaming and fleeing. The reassuring comfort of Hugh's face as they looked down at the ground, seemed to give them strength and courage to endure the momentary crisis.

The Near that hadn't smelt them became impatient.

"Come on you lout! If the others report us late we'll be drinking the worst of the tears for a while and you're not doing that to me. I'm leaving!"

"Fine, but I thought I smelled something."

"That's your trouble, you try to think."

"Shut up! Drink some tears or something."

"I'd rather drink some of yours, seeing you are getting such unusual side effects.

"Shut up."

They were gone. Dave and Dianne sat there trying to get their emotions under control, holding onto each other until Dave whispered in her ear. "They thought we smelled!" waving his hand in the air like he was trying to dissipate some of the Nears odor. "Peeuu!"

Dianne smiled. "They smelled like your socks after a couple of weeks."

"More like your bad breath," replied Dave swatting at his sister's arm. "Come on. We have to get off this trail before we get caught. Let's go this way; the lake must be down in the small valley ahead."

Hugh watched the children go towards the bridge full of mixed feelings, wishing desperately he could go with them. He looked around to find the highest point of land where he could get a good view of the Land of

Afar, and headed towards it as quickly as he could. When he reached the top, he scanned the area below, seeing the valley with the lake, the Tower of Tears and off in the far distance the castle shimmering. He could see the Road of Anguish winding towards the tower, until it disappeared around a rise of rock somewhere behind the tower. He couldn't see the children since they were mingled in with the others, but he knew he could help in one way without actually seeing them. He sat down with his back against a rock getting comfortable, which suited his complaining body after the climb.

He settled down taking a good drink of water and then relaxed. Closing his eyes he focused on the land below him in his mind's eye, imagining he could see the children's golden hearts, wherever they went. He had a great deal of practice over the years and so it wasn't long before he began to see two glows, faint but perceivable. He just watched.

Dave and Dianne picked their way through the jumble of rocks and large boulders. There was nothing else, no vegetation, no birds, no nature, nothing. It seemed like the creative force had forgot this land. It was like it had been passed over, lost for all time. There wasn't even the sun shining to give a sense of time or comfort. Yet there was a feeling that this land was somehow alive, containing a strength that couldn't be seen or touched but you knew it was there waiting.

Moving down, they couldn't see the lake; a fog covered the bottom of the valley. Before long they could hear noises, human noises, but not the kind you would eagerly rush up to greet if you were lost in a lonely land like this for companionship. It was the sound of moaning and wailing again, sounds no one wants to hear, sounds of unremitting grief, tears falling unbridled.

Peering over the ledge they saw the cause of the sounds, watching the tears tumble over the Falls of Affliction, splashing on the rocks. There were two Near Thralls doing something at the falls, however it was unclear what it was. The problem was, there was no other way down, except by moving pass them to get to the lake.

Dave looked questioningly at Dianne who only shrugged, indicating they had no choice, since there was no other way to go. Continuing down, they had to turn around facing the steep wall of rock to climb down, making it harder to see where to put their hands and feet.

Suddenly without warning Dave's foot slipped on a stone, loosening it. Tumbling down it clattered against the other rock making sounds that seemed like thunder. One of the Nears stopped, standing up scanning the rocks to see what was going on. The other Near didn't bother to pay attention, so it went back to helping.

Dave and Dianne froze on the wall for what seemed an eternity. Seeing the Nears didn't really care, they continued down, anxious to reach the bottom before anything else went wrong.

They stood only ten meters from where the Nears were crouched over, watching the tears fall in a glistening stream. The air felt like a sea breeze, salty, and damp.

The air was also filled with sounds, many sounds, as countless tears poured over the rocks, making one final tearful expression of mankind's verbal grievous insults inflicted on them by an unseen, unknown, uncaring enemy. The Nears were enjoying it, mimicking some of the more unusual sounds of lament they heard.

Surrounding them were teardrop shaped containers, arranged in rows and in cases. As one Near listened to the sounds coming over the edge, it would point so the other Near would reach out with a teardrop shaped golden handled tear catcher, scooping the particular sounding tear the other Near picked.

There would be a flash of golden light, as the tear catcher would draw the one sound out of the glistening flow of tears. The tear catcher had been in the possession of the Nears since the beginning of time stolen from the kings and queens of old, and it came in quite handy for what they were doing.

Pulling the tear catcher back, they listened to the sound reverberating from the teardrop they had captured.

"Near Catearer should have a good use for this sound in one of its many delicious culinary creations," the Near said, pouring the tear gently into one of the small flasks, careful not to lose a single portion of the drop. The tear made a last hollow wailing sound before plopping unceremoniously into the container.

The sound put both of the children into a trance. They weren't used to these sounds since they had never experienced the kind of tragedy that some unfortunate soul had. There was an energy coming from the sounds as the Nears funneled each one from the falls. The energy flowed into the children deeper, into the core of their emotional world, bringing such sadness and sorrow that without even realizing it, they started crying, losing their focus on the Now.

Suddenly without realizing it, Dianne let out a slight whimper, lost in her grief from the last sound she heard, loud enough for one Near to turn its head to see what made the sound. There, standing a few meters away were the almost visible images of two human children watching them, causing it to shriek. "Look, humans!"

Its speaking brought Dave out of his trance, realizing they had slipped out of the Now and could be seen. He instinctively grabbed Dianne by the arm shocking her back from the world of sorrow she was deeply entrenched in.

They both focused on the Now, causing them to disappear from the Near's sight, moving at the same time from where they were standing. The Near stood staring incredulously at the empty space where it had seen them. The other Near stood up to see what its friend was talking about. There was nothing there when it looked, saying, "You haven't been sipping these tears again have you? You know how they make you hallucinate."

"I tell you there were two humans standing right there," pointing where it had seen the children. The other Near looked around.

"In full view? I don't see them. Where are they now?"

"They weren't in full view, it was more like a spirit appearance. You know where you see them but you don't.'

The Near gave its friend a long hard sneer of contempt.

"I'm counting the drops when we get back and if any are missing, I'm reporting it to Near Catearer. You're sampling the goods again." Packing up the containers and getting ready to leave, it let it know it didn't want to hear any more nonsense. "Look, I told you I saw them!

"We don't have time for this. Near Catearer is waiting for these ingredients. I won't be late and take another flogging because of your foolishness." It then hoisted the containers over its shoulder, not trusting its friend, should it decide to sample any more tears on the way back to the castle.

Moving past its arguing friend, it stepped on a tear, the only visible evidence the children were there, causing the Near to give up. It walked a few steps before turning to look back where it had seen the children, then seeing nothing it shrugged, deciding not to mention it when it got back to the castle.

Dave and Dianne stumbled away from the falls; careful not to step on any stones. They concentrated on Hugh's face and focused on the Now. They didn't look back until they had gone quite a ways down towards the fog, where they knew the lake was. The sound of the tears became quiet as the tears stopped flowing over any rocks, becoming a slow meandering stream reaching the elevation of the lake. They were both in shock from the experience and they were totally exhausted from the energy they had taken in.

Flopping down against two large boulders, Dave sat slightly ahead and down from Dianne, reaching into his pack. He pulled out the bottle of water, giving it to his sister before taking a long swallow.

"That was close. I hope they didn't really see us. I guess we'll know if the army shows up! Dave whispered. "I am so tired Dotty, I need to rest before going any further."

"Yes bro' I could use one too, perhaps just a short one."

It was what Dave wanted to hear, so he made himself comfortable and started to relax focusing on the Now, as tired as he was. Dianne did the same thing, and before either realized it they were asleep.

You've heard the expression 'Hounds of Hell'? Well Rabid was the 'Mutt of Mad'. It had been bred in the world Lord Misanthropy came from, a gift given by its great master.

Its job and only job was to tear the sanity from anything it happened to come across, anything alive and thinking. It didn't differentiate. It just attacked, except for its master, the one holding the power over it.

It had been quite bored floating around above the lake after being placed there by Lord Misanthropy. That was until it had the opportunity to use the full expression of its talents on hapless Nears who came to get some tears from the lake, without knowing Rabid was playing there.

To drive a Near insane was nothing to Rabid, they were a dime a dozen. Its training since it was a young Mania was Nears. Mind you, they never volunteered for the job of being a victim in training. It was kind of thrust upon them so to speak, when they made a mistake or their master was in a rather disagreeable mood. Rabid had been given lots of practice, so it was at the top of its class when it graduated from the Academy of Beastial Dementia.

It had learned that the mind of any Near was basically a big sarcastic nothingness, full of empty space. Lacking any true thoughts, it could be shredded bare and rearranged into a maniacal antithesis. It didn't take long once in the mind of a Near as it swam about. It savagely derailed what little train of thought might be speeding along on the one track of consciousness, turning it into a wreck. This is what it had done to the Near Thrall who had come for a container of tears. Once it was done with its attack, the Near was found swimming around in Lake Lamentation, quite insane, singing a song it called 'Swimming in the Rain."

Rabid, floating around looking for something to use it talents on, was becoming tedious. That was until it picked up a thought, then another and another, perceiving two streams of thought coming from the far shore. These weren't the usual simpleminded shortcomings of feigning intellect it was accustomed to.

No, these were full-blown uninterrupted cascading surges of thoughts, one after another, almost crowding each other to be expressed. Here was something worth the challenge, something deserving of its finely honed skills, something worth driving insane. It started moving cautiously, deliberately towards the prey, until the intensity of the thoughts turned it into an insane frenzy. Wanting so much to have its way in the minds of whatever was by the shore, it threw all abandon aside, streaking headlong towards the unsuspecting prey.

Dave and Dianne had slipped into a light sleep, victim of the heavy negative energy. Unaware of the consequences of allowing their inner thoughts to be expressed without their control, they floated out around them at first, and then further and further away. The tear energy had put Dave into almost a comatose state, however Dianne was lucid. Seeing images from her past that she had forgotten were there, expressing long forgotten hurts and sadness.

While she dreamed, she could see a fog with the face of a hideous creature moving toward her and Dave, slowly at first, then with tremendous speed. She called out to Dave in her dreams. He didn't respond making her become frantic, being unable to make her body move to protect him.

She kept having flashes of him driven insane if this creature reached him, so the only things she could think of was to continue calling him as loudly in her sleep as she could, helplessly watching the beast, unable to protect him.

Hugh had noticed the two small golden specks in his inner vision had stopped, watching as one seemed to grow faint, like it was somewhere else, the other was there but pulsating slightly. This was when he noticed a black speck materializing out over the lake, a speck that he got the immediate impression was horrible beyond anything he could imagine heading towards the children.

Suddenly he could hear Dave's name being called by Dianne in a frantic manner, realizing this was danger of the worst kind. The only thing he could do was focus all his thought and energy on making his golden light move towards them, surrounding them in protection, pushing the light out away from them towards the impending danger, like a wall.

Focusing, sweat poured down his face, so great was the resistance of the black speck getting closer and closer to harm the children. In his mind he was imploring the children to move, however it seemed like they couldn't pick up his mental impressions, as if they were asleep.

Dianne could hear Hugh calling their names off in the distance of her dream imploring them to move, watching in horrid fascination as the creature was almost to them. Looking down she noticed hers and Dave's golden hearts were shining brighter than anything she had ever seen, to the point of almost blinding her. Somehow, she realized in that moment she was dreaming, managing to come out of the sleep.

Opening her eyes she stared, the beast was indeed coming over to them in the fog. Moving towards them, the image of this insanely ferocious face sneering and snarling could be seen in the middle of the fog. It rose up ready to devour its prey, cascading down towards her brother. Dianne instinctively reached for her brother to try to pull him to safety. She whispered his name as loud as she dared. Every fiber of her being wanted to scream his name out loud, warning him of the danger falling towards him.

It woke him up, opening his eyes to see the fog face leering at him as it attacked, prompting him to do only one thing. He stared at Hugh's face as hard as he dared, while Dianne did the same thing. Without warning their hearts became so bright, the face of the creature became golden in color from the glow that appeared like a covering of protection.

The creature fell onto the shield of golden protection with the force of universes colliding. A bolt of lightning struck Rabid full force. It screamed at the first injury it had ever received, as the love produced by the bolt shocked it into recoiling back.

It couldn't withstand the force of love that had struck it. The fog retreated back over the lake as far away from them as possible. The children jumped up, understanding they had fallen asleep, but not knowing what this creature was, only knowing it was from Lord Misanthropy and they had better act and quickly. Dianne noticed they were closer to the lake than she thought they were, so she whispered anxiously for Dave to get out the golden heart. He fumbled with the bag, his hands still shaking from the experience they just had.

"What was that Di?"

"I don't know, but let's do this while we have the chance, in case it comes back," motioning towards the fog swirling over at the far side of the lake like a pacing caged animal.

Dave retrieved the gold heart from his pack, holding it up for his sister to see, then with her nodding approval half trotted down the rocks to the edge of the lake.

The rocks were slippery causing him to almost trip several times much to her worry, as she whispered over and over. "Do it Dave! Do it Dave!" Dianne whispered as Dave raised his arm to throw the heart out as far as he could into the lake, but he tripped lunging head first towards the lake of tears.

"No!" Dianne almost shouted out loud, as she watched Dave stumble. His forward motion made him pitch the heart by accident only about three meters out into the tears with an unceremonious plunk. He stared in amazement at his fumbling attempt to make it a world record gold heart toss, than looked back at his sister for guidance, who only shrugged.

He looked back at the lake seeing the only sign the heart was there were the waves radiating out from where it had landed. Looking back at his sister he shrugged as well. After all, the heart was in the lake; that was that. He had expected some great cataclysmic flashing of light and thunderbolts or something but there was no evidence it was in the lake once the ripples dissipated. Walking back to Dianne, he whispered, "Well, I guess it's done.'

Then, looking back at the fog at the far end Dave said, "Let's go Dotty. I don't trust that thing whatever it was to stay over there forever."

"By the way, that was quite the pitch. Did you learn that at baseball this year?'

"Shut up Dot, besides my recovery was almost flawless." Dave replied, pretending not to be offended by his botched throw.

They decided to get away from the lake before crossing the stream of tears, knowing they shouldn't go back the way they came in case Nears knew they were around. They would cross the stream to go out around the Tower of Tears before crossing the bridge, even though the terrain looked rougher than they had come down through.

Moving back up the trail, they kept a constant vigil not wanting to be surprised by any more Nears or anything else that might be lurking out here. When the sound of the falls became louder they decided it was time to cross, not wanting to become mesmerized by the sounds again.

"We better try to get across here," whispered Dave, pointing to a gap in the large boulders. Dianne nodded in agreement, moving over to the edge of the stream of tears looking down, trying hard to block out all the sad sounds emanating from it.

Out of the tears there came images of the terrible tragedies that had caused such tears, as her psychic nature opened up. Horrible events flashed through her mind, reliving other people's awful moments, in full surround sound and high definition, like she was watching the horrific ordeals through their eyes and ears.

A sick feeling flooded her stomach making her lurch across, turning to motion Dave to follow. The look of anguish on her face made him think a Near was coming.

He scrambled across, losing his balance just as he reached her, making him place a foot backwards right into the stream of tears. There was an unbelievable surge of energy flashing through his whole body. The feelings from the tears poured through him, causing him to give out a quiet tormented moan of agony. Dianne reached out grabbing him, feeling some of the same energy he was experiencing. They collapsed into a heap. Dave sobbed uncontrollably experiencing the rush of energy from the tears. His sister comforted him knowing what it was like.

Now Lurky and Slinks were out scrounging for anything to eat, since they had been let go by Lord Misanthropy. Their water was getting in short supply, meaning they would soon be reduced to drinking tears. This meant they would become their old melancholy selves again, including Spidy.

"Slinks I's will starves to deaths instead of drinkin's those old tears." Lurky said, spitting on the ground to emphasis his point.

"Me's too Lurks, let's keeps looking." Lurky stood there feeling hopeless when he heard a noise. Perking his ears into the listening position, he scanned where he heard the noise, then it came again faint but noticeable.

"I's hears something Slinks. I's hears humans!"

"Are you's sure?" Slinks asked. A human had never set foot in the Land of Afar. He was sure Lurky's hunger was getting to him.

"Yes, I's sures" replied Lurky knowing his ears never let him down.

"Come on let's goes see's. Lurky said moving off in the direction he heard the sounds.

His ears picked up the whispered conversation, which was strangely familiar. Sneakeeze have strong sound memories. Once they hear a sound or voice they never forget it, however Lurky didn't believe what his sounds memory was telling him, until he heard the words of the only human friend he had ever met. Poking his head out from behind a large boulder he was shocked to see her.

"Dianneeze?" She almost jumped, startled at his voice.

"Lurky?"

Dave could barely see though the flood of tears still pouring down his face, reaching for a rock to protect them. He desperately wiped at the tears so he could see the threat.

"What is it Di?"

Dianne, so happy to see Lurky, she whispered. "Lurky what are you doing here?"

"Slinks! Its Dianneeze! The one's I's told you's about!"

Lurky jumped around and then slapped Slinks on the back. If it had been any other time there would have been a wrestling match over the severity of the slap. However, manners seemed to be in order right now. Slinks let it go. Suddenly Lurky stopped.

"Why is you's whispering Dianneeze?"

"Because Lord Misanthropy and the Nears won't hear us."

Dave stared incredulously at his sister talking to this creature like they were old friends. Especially after going through what they had to get there and seeing the Nears up close and personal.

"I's so happy to see's you Dianneeze, I could flies!" Dancing around flapping his ears, he imitated a bird before remembering to whisper. Lurky looked at Dianne for a moment then asked, "Can's we do friends touch Dianneeze?" holding out his hand palm down.

"Why, yes Lurky, I missed not having friends touch with you. " This caused Lurky to giggle in anticipation until he reached her hand holding it gently. His ear came down to caress her arm, making little mewing noises. He glanced curiously at Dave as he remained where he was.

"Is this you's brodder, Dianneeze?"

"Oh! I'm sorry; yes, this is my brother Dave."

"Will Daveeze do's friend touch?" Asked Lurky, staring at Dave.

"Sure he will, won't you?" answered Dianne giving her brother a glance. Dave stared at the two creatures that apparently were friends with his sister, who never kept secrets from him.

"Sure, sure, I'll do friends touch." Giving his sister a look, not knowing what to do. Not wanting to appear out of the loop, he held out his hand while Lurky crawled over to do the same thing. He was surprised how soft and gentle Lurky actually felt, becoming relaxed, realizing they were no threat. Slinks stayed back watching in amazement as Lurky did the friend's touch with both of them. Not quite believing the story told him until now.

Lurky turned to Slinks.

"Can Slinks do the friends touch?" Both Dianne and Dave nodded it was fine, allowing Slinks to do the same. Once he was done, he moved back beside Lurky after poking and feeling both of them.

"They's smells much better than a Near's does; kind of nicey, cutsy." Then pointing to Dave's back, Slinks asked, "Is that's thing stuck to your back?"

Dave chuckled, removing it, replying.

"No, we use it to carry things."

"Does this means you's comes to's stays with us? You's could lives with us heres in the rocks."

Dianne shook her head no.

"Good, cause if you's stays here there isn't much to eats and once your waters gone you's will have to drinks teary soup, which makes you's feel sad." Slinks showed them the flasks of theirs with what little water they had left.

"Besides you's will gets caught by old Lordie Misphtpht."

"No, we can't be seen by Lord Misanthropy or the Nears because we wear these shirts with a golden heart on them and these necklaces. We crossed over the bridge to get here and they didn't see us. That's how we know they can't see us."

"But we's can see you's." replied Slinks not understanding.

Only their Lord and the Nears can't," causing both Sneakeeze to ponder on it for a few moments, before pointing to Dave who started to cry again.

"He accidentally fell into the stream, and is feeling the effects of the tears. " Slinks went right over to Dave stroking his arm gently.

"Is okay Daveeze. I did the same once and I's cried for a whole week. Didn't I's Lurky? "

"Yes, it wills goes away eventually."

"If you's not staying, are you's going back homes?"

Dianne nodded yes, causing Lurky to fall prostrate on the ground.

"Please, please, please take us with you's, if Lurky's you's friend, you's can take us with's you's. Please, please!"

Dianne didn't know what to say except. "Lurky I don't know?"

Lurky started to sob uncontrollably at the words. They had been so long captives in the Land of Afar without hope, except for his brief release to aid the Nears. Now here was the only chance for an escape, but it appeared hopeless. He didn't know how much longer he and Slinks could survive on bugs and teary soup before they were driven crazy, or just gave up and died. His hand slowly crept across the ground, like it had a mind of its own and touched Dianne's shoe. Dianne almost burst into tears seeing Lurky groveling at her feet. Dave was bawling his eyes out, partly from what he was seeing and the rest the continued after effects of the tear dunking.

Staring at her brother she said, "What do we do?'

"Is it possible if they wore our tee shirts they might be protected from the Nears like we are? We still have our hearts and I packed two other tee shirts in my pack, just in case we might have needed them on our trip. That way we could wear them with our heart necklaces on the outside." Dave said chokingly.

"We have nothing to lose. We have to try and if it doesn't work, they will have to stay until we find another way."

Dianne bent down to Lurky who was still sobbing, she grabbed his arm, pulling him up, and told him what they proposed to do, making him cheer up. He wiped the tears from his eyes, as did Slinks who had been crying too. Dave brought out the tee shirts for themselves, removing the painted ones and putting them on the Sneakeeze, although it was a struggle to get their ears through the neck hole.

'Now listen Lurky, if this doesn't work, and the Nears do see you, are you willing to go back without us? We have to leave no matter what. Do you understand?"

Reluctantly, he agreed, having no choice knowing that this might not work.

"Now, what we have to do is cross back over the bridge when some souls cross over to come in. Most important, none of us can make a noise or even whisper or they will know we are here. Do you understand? More important, if they see you, you must pretend you don't know we are there so we can get across. Agreed?" Dianne asked.

"For's good lucks, we's won't say nothings more until we's across. Right's Slinks?" Slinks agreed hoping this was going to give them good luck.

Moving out, they walked quickly. Finally they approached the bridge, keeping focused on the Now, even though their hearts were racing, not knowing whether this was going to work or not. They were coming up quite close to the two Near Protektors standing guard. Lurky and Slinks kept looking at the ground, not wanting to stare at the Nears. Dianne and Dave stared at the Nears to see if there was any sign this wasn't going to work. Several times the Nears looked in their direction without seeing them, giving both the children confidence this was really going to happen liked they hoped.

It wasn't very long before another group of unfortunate souls appeared to cross over into the Land of Afar preoccupying the Near Protektor, giving them the opportunity to start to cross.

Finally they were across, but all of them still expected to hear the Nears shout out an alarm, but none came as the fog slowly enveloped them making the bridge disappear like it was never there.

They kept moving, remaining silent until they were startled by a dim figure standing on the path. All of them stopped, hearts pounding, until they heard. "Dianne! Dave! Who or what do you have with you?"

"Uncle we are so glad to see you. We thought you were Lord Misanthropy or something else!' Dianne and Dave ran over hugging Hugh, then Dianne turned pointing to Lurky and Slinks.

"These are Sneakeeze, I met Lurky on the farm one day in the barn and this is his friend Slinks. Give my uncle a friend's touch. It's all right."

Lurky obeyed going over in his usual manner, much to the surprise of Hugh who accepted the friend's touch, then repeated the ritual with Slinks after being introduced.

"I think I saw you, or one of you on the tail on my way to the farm originally. I remember your ears."

"Yes Hugheeze. My ears is hard's to miss."

"We found them in the Land of Afar and just had to bring them with us. The tee shirts worked the same for them as they did for us. Please can they come and stay with us?"

"Well, it's only a matter of time before the Nears find out we were in the Land of Afar, so I can't see this bringing any more harm. Although I have no idea what your mother is going to say about them or us doing what we've just done."

"Leave that to us uncle, we know her soft spot." replied Dave almost sobbing.

Seeing him break, Hugh asked concerned, "What's wrong with him?" Dianne answered for her brother who was taken over by another wave of sadness, which he had been able to suppress up until now.

"It's a long story, but he fell into the stream of tears."

"Are you alright son?"

"Yes, let's just get going, please," Dave replied between sobs.

"Yes, let's get some distance between us and this awful place, before we're caught," turning to lead the way back home.

Lurky turned to Dianne saying.

"Is we going to lives with you's Dianneeze?"

Dianne turned replying, "Yes, you two are and you can have whatever you want."

After a few minutes of silence Lurky replied, "Can's I have a squeaky ball?" flapping his ears excitedly. Spidy stayed out of the way of his ears, happy to be out of the Land of Afar and into bug country finally.

Slinks sighed saying nothing. Instead he shook his head, knowing what this meant.

Lord Misanthropy felt uncertain, shaking its head, not knowing what this meant. Things just didn't seem right even though the flow of tears had significantly increased. It was obvious the Nears were doing their jobs, but there was something unsettling that kept Lord Misanthropy from truly relishing its life. Perhaps it was time for another feast to take its mind off this nagging uncertainty that kept creeping into its malevolent mind.

Moving out onto the balcony for some time alone to daydream, it remembered back through time when it was sent by its great master to enslave the human race which, at that time knew nothing could be made of tears before its coming.

Through its guile, cunning deceit, it made mankind produce the sea of tears that became its ever since, flowing in a never-ending stream. However as it daydreamed, a single thought passed, bringing up a long forgotten feeling similar to the one it was experiencing lately, when it almost lost control of mankind.

It quickly shook it off; not believing it could happen again, so enslaved was mankind now. To change the subject, it ordered the Near Acolyte to make ready preparation for the welcoming back feast.

Coordinating with Near Spiritus Frumentus, Near Catearer and the staff, they would celebrate the success of Near Aflik, Bane and Hebejebe. That would help alleviate its boring nagging doubts. Yes, a feast was in order, and it would oversee everything itself.

Plopping itself down on its throne, it barked out orders to the Near Thralls who scurried around the castle making preparations. Near Acolyte kept coming back to it reporting the progress, as the various departments were contacted to make ready for the feast. It watched as everything was brought out, dishes, silverware, place settings, all arranged meticulously in order.

The volume of the fountain and tears on the wall was turned up to bring some ambiance to the impending celebration, making Lord Misanthropy hum and sing its favorite parts of the wailing sobs of sad sorrow, floating through every corner of the castle. It watched partly in fascination as the Nears did their jobs. At one point there were so many scurrying around even it was amazed there were so many Near Thralls. No wonder it needed such a volume of tears just to feed them.

It took time; however time seemed to move so quickly when so many were busy around it. The three Nears were in the basement getting ready in their finest dress, to receive their toast of honor on a job well done. Bringing down these upstart humans, who dared to laugh.

It gave one final order to have fresh tears drawn from the lake for the toast, as a tribute to the Nears for being so successful in their task, which was done.

When the barrel arrived, a thoroughly frightened Near Thrall reported Rabid had seized two other Near Thralls dragging them into the lake, tormenting them until they killed each other in their insanity. Lord Misanthropy sneered deliciously. After all, shouldn't it's pet have its fun in this time of celebration? This was more like it. Thanking the Near for the report, the Near scurried away, fearing for its life that it wouldn't be sent back for more tears.

The time had come. Everything was prepared as the Great Hall was filled to capacity with all the Nears, including the Near Thralls. Even the two Near Protektors had been relieved of their duties at the bridge to join in the celebration. They now stood on each side of the throne surveying the room for threats.

Not in a millennium had such a gathering of Nears been seen together in one castle. It was a grand occasion, worthy of inscription in the Great Book of Boasts, which rested open on the writing table in the corner. Near Scorer was at the ready, holding its golden pen in hand, dabbing it in the container of ink made from the blackest tears, hoping to record in its finest depiction, the glorious events about to unfold.

The room became silent as everything came to a final climax, except for two thumps of Near Acolyte's staff, announcing the procession of the three Nears of honor. The volume of tears had been turned right up, lending an eerie quality to the grand spectacle unfolding. The three Nears dressed in their finest, strode to the front in single file, accompanied by Near Thralls on either side dressed in their own regal dress.

The three Nears aligned themselves in a row in front of their master, showing their best self-righteous sneers. It was obvious they were lording it over all the other Nears present, that they, of all Nears were to be honored this day; something that hadn't been seen in a thousand years.

A Near Acolyte spoke in a loud voice,

"ALL HAIL OUR LORD
THE HOST OF ALL LACHRYMOSE
PROVIDER OF ALL OUR TEARS
TO THIS WE TOAST

ALL HAIL OUR LORD
GREVIOUS HEARTGRIEF HOST
GIVER OF ALL WOEFULNESS
TO THIS WE BOAST"

Lord Misanthropy looked like a peacock, its chest puffed out, dressed in its finest robe, smiling malevolently at its three faithful servants. Everyone was served a golden goblet of fresh tears for the toast, which began with special words from their Lord.

"It gives me great pleasure on this grandest day to show a small gesture of gratitude and respect for the job well done by these, my obedient Nears, who through great sacrifice and perseverance, rid the world of the last laughter. To you!" It picked up its tear goblet, holding it in the air signaling the toast, followed by all the Nears, except the Near Thralls who unfortunately remained on duty. The Nears reveled in their honor and glory. They all sneered their worst hideous masks. The other Nears noses were visibly out of joint, each askew in its own personal position on their faces.

There was a moment of silence as they all drained their goblets of tears. Some even licked the inside of their goblets to get the last drop. Then one Near looked surprised, staring at the appearance of the Near across from it.

Without warning, it laughed, pointing at the ridiculousness of the Near across from it who suddenly started to laugh as well. Like a chain reaction they all started laughing until it became a great laughing roar; each making fun of the other's appearance, much to the absolute shock of Lord Misanthropy who stood up, mouth open, not believing its eyes.

By now the Nears had started throwing food at the other Nears in a sign of playfulness. Lord Misanthropy became so angry, smoke actually started to float in the air above its head.

It trembled violently as rage rose inside, replacing the usual malevolent demeanor it showed. The three Nears that hadn't joined the toast, turned not believing what they were witnessing, as bedlam took over in the room.

Lord Misanthropy stared at its goblet. Tradition dictated the Nears drink first before it, then saluting it at which time it drank. It was the only thing that saved it from drinking the tears. It threw its goblet on the floor violently, wanting nothing to do with an obviously poisoned drink. Looking over at Near Scorer who had drank its toast with the others, it was now pouring black ink all over the sacred book and itself and laughing ridiculously, while doing so.

The great lord could take no more, screaming at the top of its lungs, a scream from all the accumulated sorrow heard throughout time. The sound was heard all over the Land of Afar, reverberating in the mountains far away.

The room went dead silent except for the occasional tittering from the Nears most out of control. Pointing its gnarly finger at the three Nears it shouted, "You did this! You lied to me! After all I've done for you! There is only one punishment fit for this! I hereby declare you turned inside out!"

A gasp came from everyone hearing the words all Nears dreaded. Lightning from a black cloud that instantly appeared above its head, travelled down its arm. It caused a blinding flash of light, accompanied by a thunderclap sound and smoke where the Nears had stood. When the smoke cleared, the three naked humans writhed on the floor in obvious agony, surrounded by the fluids left from the transition.

Pointing to what had been Near Bane it said, "You will suffer at the hands of mischief until you are driven helplessly insane!"

Staring at Near Aflik, "You will always have trouble. You will always be in trouble. You will have trouble follow you for all time!"

To Near Hebejebe it sneered the worst. "You will live in fear through all eternity! You will always be afraid of the dark! You will be afraid of your own shadow! You will always be filled with fear!"

The Near Thralls shrank back when it commanded, "Take them to the bridge and toss them over to the cruel world partly of their making! Good riddance! Let them taste the true salt of bitter tears from now on!"

Suddenly it heard a thumping noise coming from the basement stairs revealing Near Immolation panting, "Sire! Sire! The machine has spoken again..." It stopped short of a detailed account, when it saw the three humans that shouldn't be there on the floor.

Lord Misanthropy screamed again, causing all the Nears to fall to the floor in case they were next on the inside out list. Some of them tried to crawl under each other.

Lord Misanthropy now needed some time alone to figure this out.

The only real question now was.

What was Lord Misanthropy going to do?

What will Lord Misanthropy do?
Will everyone else live happily ever after?
Find out in the next upcoming book.

www.ingramcontent.com/pod-product-compliance
Lightning Source LLC
Chambersburg PA
CBHW030817310726
48980CB00006B/527/J

* 9 7 8 1 4 2 6 9 2 6 6 9 3 *